SILENDA

KELSIE STOKER

Silenda

By Kelsie Stoker

© Kelsie Stoker

ISBN: 978-1-912092-34-5

First published in 2024

Published by Palavro, an imprint of
the Arkbound Foundation (Publishers)

Arkbound is a social enterprise that aims to promote social inclusion, community development and artistic talent. It sponsors publications by disadvantaged authors and covers issues that engage wider social concerns. Arkbound fully embraces sustainability and environmental protection. It endeavours to use material that is renewable, recyclable or sourced from sustainable forest.

Arkbound
Rogart Street Campus
4 Rogart Street
Glasgow, G40 2AA

www.arkbound.com

SILENDA

KELSIE STOKER

palavro
PUBLISHING

SUPPORTERS

The publication of this book was enabled through a dedicated crowdfunding campaign on Crowdbound.org. Among the many supporters, we are particularly grateful to:-

Gordon Calderwood
Evelyn Stoker
Cheryl Stoker
Mitchell Stoker
Drew Paton
Sean Munro
Jessica Ho
Elizabeth Gebbie
Diane Niven
Elizabeth Campbell
Kelsey Banks
Arlyn Paton

'There are more things in heaven and earth, Horatio, than are dreamt of in your philosophy.'

- William Shakespeare, *Hamlet*.

CHAPTER 1

THE FEARED THING

Horatio

I used to believe in the light like a vampire believes in the dark.

I suppose it became about survival. That was when I was a Lux – when my faith lay beyond black leather and dangly earrings. Before my earphones and a deafening saxophone solo became my only refuge when the world got too loud.

I used to believe. *In next.*

In a better place; a place beyond the dirt and the grime and the sickness. Beyond Randy Redding's sallow grey skin and yellowed fingers. A place where I wouldn't have to feel *everything*. Where Zeb's smile doesn't make my chest feel tight.

When I roll over in cotton mornings, there is blood on my pillowcase. I have a recurring dream that I've been stabbed in the throat. My faith in the light used to ooze from me and it was fear that drove the knife in deeper. No matter, I'll always be left with a scab that will never truly heal.

It's too dark behind my eyelids at night. It's not even black – it's just nothing. There's no light to thread my flesh with an orange glow. It's just *nothing*. That's when my wound reopens. When the dark becomes too frightening to bear.

SILENDA

Zebediah has traces of purple in his hair, weaving through the black like the glow of a harvest moon in a darkening sky. His skin, smooth like deep brown moonstone reflects the yellow tones in his hazel eyes. I watch him as he paces the roof, letting the blue wind sift through his jean jacket. It blows in his hair, too.

The sunset bleeds behind him. A purple sun.

I wish I could be like him.

I wish I could let go like he can. Feel the sky and know that I live beneath it.

Breathe, Horatio.

I have to remind myself to breathe. I'll just die if I don't.

I trace the blue veins on my transparent skin. I always stare at my wrists when Zeb jumps onto the wall on the rooftop of the Grand Library. We're at least 20 storeys high. I wonder how many times I've seen his indigo Dr Martens perched precariously on the ledge of golden stone, and yet still I imagine myself in a little log boat travelling down a cobalt stream under a fleshy sky.

Zeb says I can't see the world beyond myself. Even my greatest adventures lie beneath my own skin. He says I was designed for the world to colour me in, that my pale blue eyes and deathly white skin were made to be decorated in ink or exposed to the world's most beautiful sights. He says my piercings don't count, that it's like cutting holes in paper.

Only colour can make a canvas art.

Zebediah has lots of colour behind his eyes. It's hard to imagine that he believes in the dark. I may look like Dracula, but he is the real vampire. His flesh doesn't burn in the heat of the sun, but it rots there. Ageing and decaying into the abyss of darkness. The sun doesn't burn me either, but the darkness bursts and blisters with the same ferocity.

Zeb is an Umbra. He believes it's dark when we die, but that doesn't mean he's not afraid.

I think he is.

Sometimes I think he's afraid to be wrong, too. It's eternity that scares him more than anything.

His hand stretches through the wind, gesturing for me to join him, cream pearls on his muscular arms. He's steady on his feet. He trusts himself. I take his hand. He eases me onto the stone wall and we watch the stream of traffic far below us. Neon lights glow on the blue pavements as traffic lights orchestrate the flow of vehicles. Shades of scarlet lace the sky. When he drops my hand, I turn away from the Urb below us and face back to the library, my feet still firmly on the ledge. I imagine I'm falling backwards through a violet sky, the wind weaving through my black hair. I wouldn't plummet, I'd just float. Slowly and steadily falling through the air. The clouds would catch me like a plane in turbulence.

I close my eyes.

The sunset understands me. It swells in my heart. It doesn't know about itself, you see. It melts and weakens and it's not one thing until it fades to black. It's undecided. It weeps in colour and lets the night take it with grace.

'Don't jump!' Zeb cries, hopping off the ledge and back to the safety of the rooftop. He lights a cigarette and puffs smoke at the air.

'Why not?' I always say. He knows I won't jump and that I just want to hear what he'll say to stop me.

'Only a stake through the heart can kill a vampire, Harry.' Zeb calls me Harry. 'You'll just be a bloodsucker in a wheelchair.' I laugh as I jump from the wall and steal the burning thing from between his lips. I choke when I take a draw, crushing it under my foot soon after.

He frowns. Supposedly, most Umbras have a talent for numbing their feelings. There's not a corner in West Town absent of a liquor store or a neighbourhood without a drug dealer. Zebediah smokes a lot. Cannabis, tobacco – it doesn't really matter. It gives him something to blow back at the wind when the wind only cares to blow in his face. It's not easy to believe in the temporary, to believe that everything you work for, everything you are and everyone you love, will one day perish.

It's not easy for me to admit that the light in my heart has been fading. My home in East Town is pretty in the sun with my mother's dahlias flowering on the front porch. Angelo's tan skin is the picture of youth when he skateboards in Centrum Park. It's impossible to imagine the park outliving him or autumn leaves falling without him. It's hard to imagine anything existing without them – *without us*.

We are too alive.

It would hurt my uncle the most if I moved away; if I moved to West Town or the Urb. If I became an Umbra, I wouldn't just be telling my family that I don't believe in a god or an afterlife, it would be like telling them I'm going to die, that one day I'm going to depart this life and I will never be seen again. I can't extinguish everything they have dreamed I will be.

I can't.

Uncle Basilio would rot with embarrassment. The East Town mayor with an Umbra nephew? It just can't happen.

It's easy for Angelo. He makes our parents so proud. He has so much faith. It emanates from him and cures him from the toxicities of the world. It is his antidote. It makes him untouchable. His preppy polo shirts and straight white teeth are like a shield – and maybe something to do with our parents' dentistry. Either way, my black leather and leopard print silk makes my parents cringe in a way he never could.

I spend most of my time in the Urb. The city accommodates me. It doesn't matter who I am in the city – a Lux or an Umbra. Maybe people make assumptions about me because of the way that I dress. Either way, I'd belong there. Either way, Caleb Hayes would ruffle my hair and call me 'son' when I got to work at his record store.

Working for Zebediah's father means getting to see Zeb sprawled across the checkout counter on quiet days, complaining about his failed romantic conquests. It also means getting to talk about music all day with Umbras who would never assume I'm a Lux in my dark attire.

I wander around the Urb on my lunch breaks, watching how the people of the city live. I like to people-watch. I like to remind myself that there are people who can be content grabbing coffee from the same café every day or crossing at the same traffic lights, that it's irrational that such mundanity should drive me crazy.

One fundamental problem with losing my faith is that every moment feels like a wasted one. I'm never doing enough, never appreciating enough. I have constant anxiety. It makes me want to ask Zeb to run away with me, to see the world. To watch the stars on the other side of the globe. To watch the sunset at the time when it rises over the Grand Library.

We could ask Randy to come with us.

I've always hated the guy, but deep down I know he has always hated himself. He was my high school bully back in East Town. My dark clothes and scepticism didn't flatter the Lux lifestyle. It pissed off my parents, but it pissed off Randy the most. His red hair was always neatly combed, his school shirts always bleached white and steam-ironed. He hated me. But when I see him now, smoking on Rennie Street, I see the real him. When someone shows you their true colours, or lack thereof, you should believe them. Randy Redding is as scared as I've always been. A Lux boy that the world extinguished the light in. He can't believe in heaven – some people just can't. But he's scared of the alternative. And just like Zeb, he has developed an art for numbing it.

I think Randy should listen to Zeb. Most people are phonies – properly crazy. But Zeb is real. He says that heaven isn't a destination, it's a pursuit. Every moment my smile falters, he reminds me that heaven is something I should try to find in the mundanity of daily life, regardless of where my faith lies. You know, *just in case*. I think that moments on the rooftop with him are pretty close. Everything that clouds my mind dispenses into the wind and the sun and the moon; when they are out together, they remind me how small the world is. There's a reassurance in being insignificant.

Zeb lights another cigarette, cupping it from the wind and watching the one beneath my black boot fizzle out to ash. He heads for the exit and I follow him, fleeing the roof from the metal stairs that crawl down the side of the building. I always think that, if there were a zombie apocalypse, we could pace to the top of the library and unscrew the stairs from their holding. They're very unstable. They might even crush a few zombies on the way down.

'Come on,' Zeb says as we cross the street into an abandoned multi-storey car park with yellowing walls. 'You promised!'

I did. I promised.

It's hard to trust Zeb sometimes. He never lets me down and his intentions are so obviously pure, but he makes very questionable decisions. I've seen him with blood dripping from his nose, his t-shirt half-torn and his neck bruised with boysenberry bite marks. There are never any explanations with him. He walks into the car park with a reckless strut, shaking his blue denim jacket from his back. His white tank exposes the tattoos on his muscular arms, the black ink only a few shades darker than his skin. Zeb has had tattoos since we met in the Urb at 16. He has a wolf on his back, howling at the sun.

The sun.

The back of the car park hides a small room with several out-of-order ticket dispensers. Vines crawl up the walls of the damp space and a large man with black ink that covers almost his entire body sits in the corner with an electric needle in hand. His black tongue lisps as he welcomes us.

'Hey, Stig,' Zeb says, gleaming and patting the large man on the back. 'This is my friend, Horatio. He's here to get tatted.'

'Horatio,' Stig states, stretching out a gigantic hand to greet me. I shake it cautiously. *He's so big.* I'm so skinny that I think he could snap me in half like a twig. 'What can I do for you?'

He stares down his needle like he's examining the gleam of a freshly sharpened knife. Zeb whispers something in his ear. 'Got a lot of trust in your friend here, boy, lettin' him decide what yer getting!' he says.

'Yeah,' I say, chuckling. 'I promised him I'd go through with it, but I'm terrible at making decisions. Especially irreversible ones.'

'Let me guess,' Stig says, pointing his needle in my face like a finger, 'you're a Libra.' I laugh before I assess if it's the safest option. I choke on my hesitation soon after.

'Stig is primarily a master of body art, but he's very into astrology and horoscopes. He performs tarot card readings at the weekends,' Zeb says.

'Really? You don't believe in that stuff. *Right?*' I ask Zeb and he shrugs.

'I live in the Rowleys,' Stig says. 'I'm not a Lux. Couldn't be, son. Look at me!'

'So, you don't believe in any god?'

'I dunno. Do you?' Stig quips.

'I dunno. But you believe that stars can determine our characteristics?'

'Why not? Gotta have faith in something.'

The whirring needle pierces the upper layer of skin on my left arm without warning. I wince, clenching my fist and grabbing my inner thigh in short intervals.

Zeb had told me about the Rowleys when we met four years ago. It's where the undecided go, he says. It's not a ceremonious thing, but it's a deprived part of the city that nobody bothers with. It doesn't matter what you believe, who you are or what you look like. Nobody comes around except other people like you.

'Is that why you set up shop here?' I grimace after a moment of letting the needle work. 'Nothing going in the Rowleys?'

'Aye, son,' Stig says. 'They won't give me a permit in the city and there's no jobs in the Rowleys, not even at the tattoo parlour.

It's all poverty, son. Jobs are like pixie shit down there. I've been here for years, no bother.'

'Why won't they give you a permit in the city?'

'A dinnae look how they think a should for the things a sell, do a? Guy like me practising spirituality lookin' like this? Doesnae fit their status quo, bud.'

I nod. It's shit. But he's right.

I can only imagine the look on my uncle's face if he saw Stig in Lux territory.

I try not to tell people that my uncle is the mayor of East Town; of the Luxies. Especially since his conversation with my dad over dinner last Sunday. Maybe if he had kept his sandy brown hair long and his white shirts unbuttoned like he did when I was little, I would like him better. He used to walk around the garden in his bare feet. Now his hair is slicked back, his top button done and he makes me call him *sir*.

He says that the West Town mayor is out to get the Lux community.

'Tyson Turrow wants to take over. He's nothing but a power hungry bastard!' My mother shot him a disapproving look with an obvious glance at Angelo, who she doesn't know has probably used the curse more frequently than his uncle.

My father had spent the whole night nodding and humming in agreement. 'He insisted I meet with him for coffee the other day. I, of course, agreed. I wasn't going to conform to any sort of petty behaviour, you know?' My father nodded. I held in a snort.

'He wants us to have mixed schools. He thinks the two communities are too *segregated*, that we should try to get along better. Not that I have anything against that.' He does. 'But I know, up in here,' my uncle dug his index finger into his left temple, 'that's not what he really wants. He wants to reach out to our community, to have some sort of control so he can teach our kids his ways and wipe us out. If he gets his way, the whole city will be crawling with Shadows. There won't be a single Lux left.'

My uncle had leaned in closer, grasping onto my father's attention more so than he had previously. 'Since our meeting the other day, he's been dead quiet. Not a word. Not to me, not to my men. He's planning something over there in his big fancy mansion in West Town. He's planning something terrible, Damien. I know it.'

Such accusations could result in full-blown war. But I try not to think about it. I try not to think about a lot of things, actually.

That's the difference between Randy and me. *I don't think*. For me, it's denial. For Randy, self-loathing. Because he is a lost one, a nobody, an outcast who tried so hard to believe in something he couldn't.

Maybe that's why he hated me so much. Because I wasn't trying too.

I think I can feel the needle vibrating agonisingly against my bone. Or like there's a bee trapped under my skin. It's hard to tell how long it's been when Stig pulls away to evaluate his work. My entire left arm burns.

'There ya go,' Stig says, wheeling away in his rusty chair.

I stand and cross to the cracked vertical mirror on the opposite wall with Zeb gazing over me. My left arm is decorated with an enormous lightning bolt that cracks and breaks across my flesh in black ink. It's like nothing I've ever seen before. Unlike a cartoon lightning bolt, it breaks off from itself in long branches of black, crawling up towards my collarbone, up my neck and down my arm.

It's beautiful.

'I love it,' I say. Zeb rubs my back with a cheesy grin.

'Why a lightning bolt?' I ask him as we emerge into the purple city streets.

'Because I think that's what you would be if you went to the sky. I know you're not sure what to believe, Harry, but I think that you'll be bright and beautiful and fill the sky with light if you become an angel. When you get scared, just look at your arm and remind yourself that no matter what happens, you are all the light you will ever need. Right here, right now.'

We stop in our tracks. I look at him. He shines in the dark. He always has. He wraps his moonstone arm around my porcelain neck and tackles me into a playful headlock.

I don't know if I'll ever be an angel.

But I know that he will, if a life beyond this one awaits him.

I don't know how to deal with the pain. Zeb can't cure me. Neither can the sunset or the stars or the catharsis of a crack of lightning brightening the sky. Maybe if I had fangs protruding from my gums I would feel okay – if I wanted to pierce Zeb's throat and suck him dry.

I wouldn't have to worry about it. *About death.*

Because I'd live forever. I could be the feared thing. Instead of the thing that fears everything.

CHAPTER 2

THE MISSING

Carson

The brilliant black sky weeps over the isolated streets of the city. The traffic lights decorating the roads switch frantically, disturbing the clarity of the tears from above. The roads are empty. Nothing but puddles lie.

Quiet.

Red. Amber. Green.

The streets are vacant of people, but not of life. The city buzzes softly into the distance like any other night. Lights glow on the skyscrapers, engulfing the bridge, winding through every twist and turn. The firmament is dotted with flickering balls of fire. Even the alleyways benefit from the surrounding life.

Nothing is ever dark in the Urb. Except the beliefs of half its residents.

He sees me.

I see him, by the lamppost in the square where he sometimes stands. Many months ago, we made an unspoken agreement to pretend that the streets are as unoccupied as ever at such a time of morning.

I am a believer in the dark, but my mind screams in colour. It cries to escape normality and to live a life separate from what follows it; a life that is not *dependent* on it.

I think he does too. I like to think so, anyway. It helps me sleep.

The bench is wet. Not cold. It had been icy the previous night, but a strange humidity seems to have swept through the atmosphere somehow in mid-November. The rain is warm, perhaps not for the drops of a domestic shower, but certainly for an autumn trickle. I do not sit for long, I never do.

I run to the beat of the wind, to the beat of my heart. The silent wheels of long, low cars follow suit. The light grabs the vehicles too, dragging them silently across the smooth, silky roads of the Urb and across the bridge at a soothing speed. I spot a scarlet red vehicle and I chase it. I only see two or three cars a night. The people of the Urb don't tend to stay out late anywhere but the chain. I never go near the chain. Well, I haven't since the Awakening.

This is how I forget; how I forget to have forgotten. Exhaustion shuts down anything I have to think about, so I run all night and sleep all day.

You'd think it would become repetitive, tedious, but I feel alive. I challenge myself. I stand surely on the tallest buildings in the city as a dark figure and a proud shadow. The Grand Library is the greatest with the exception of Centrum Tower, where I simply can't seem to get past security, which might have something to do with the fact that it's the largest Lux building in the city, blocked with corporate offices.

I'd love to feel the atmosphere that far up.

The Awakening may be an ostentatious title for a moment so absurd. I can't start the story with any context like, 'It was a gloomy Sunday afternoon...' because I simply do not remember what the weather was like, what day it was, or anything before it happened.

I woke last year in a flat the size of a cardboard box in an Umbra apartment building. I rolled over on a cold mattress, arms reaching across the bed, grasping nothing. I shot up, my mind searching, *grasping nothing*.

Initially, there had been insane confusion, the inability to process anything. My head was a bizarre concoction of common sense and a lack of personal information: memories, my name. I felt like a cliché, that perhaps I was about to live out my own *Total Recall* style adventure – but nothing.

Nothing exhilarating happened at all.

I was left with only one connection to my past. A letter paperclipped to the sleeve of my navy sweatshirt. My name: Carson Whitmoore. My age: 19. My story? Nothing.

The apartment could have been bigger, yes, but each narrow closet and petite drawer was filled with clothes of all colours and plenty of cash. Notes stuffed in jean pockets and in randomly placed envelopes, behind units and under the metal-framed bed. By the end of my scavenger hunt, I had enough money to last me a few stable jobless years. Whoever had left me the letter, certainly had money to throw away.

Screaming followed.

Crying.

Showering under an unfamiliar head; an unfamiliar anything. What is most peculiar is how much I can remember. Firstly, I know what a shower *is*. I know that my city is divided by Umbras and Luxies. I know that I'm an Umbra, regardless of how dedicated I am to the idea. It's like I remember everything about the world and nothing about *my* world. Nothing about my upbringing, my story, my family.

My memories have been stolen; extracted.

Most days, I read the letter that had been left with me. It is the only connection I have to my life before the Awakening. It was addressed to me and signed by no one. It was vague and harrowing, and I keep hoping that the more I read it, the quicker the mess will unravel.

SILENDA

It's been just over a year now.

It stated: *Carson, There is no way to justify your situation. There is no way to explain to you why we had to take your past without destroying our every intention. You couldn't live with what you knew. You are Carson Whitmoore, you are eighteen years old. You were born on October 25th.*

Start again.

Find any happiness the confusion can allow. The rent for your apartment is being paid for and you will find a steady supply of money and clothes in your bedroom.

Everything you need, I'll supply you with.

I've got you.

No signature and so vague it's almost laughable. Imagine being born into the world and instead of the steady aid of your parents, you're given this letter. That's it.

It's really quite ludicrous. Perhaps I should be terrified that someone is watching me, observing me from a distance; someone responsible for the extraction of my personal life.

But I'm not.

I feel a sort of reassurance. Like I have a friend out there somewhere. Someone that cares about me and doesn't make me feel so alone. Perhaps any sort of friend is better than no friend at all.

Some early mornings when I return from a run, I find new items of clothing, money, food in the fridge. Someone out there has a key to my apartment. I could be sleeping in my uncomfortable bed and a stranger could creep into my apartment and shoot me in the head.

Yet somehow, that doesn't scare me so much.

I've got you.

That's the snippet that really plays on my mind.

I've got you.

I imagine my empty head feeling as light as a grey balloon, daring to float off my shoulders and leaving me ultimately empty, but before it can, the firm hand of a stranger grasps my string and yanks me back down to earth. It feels good to have someone looking out for me, it does, only I can't help but feel I'd prefer, *you've got me.* I want to truly have them.

I don't want them to hide.

I'm still chasing the car when I see him. I don't know much about cars, only that the one I've been chasing tonight is red, low to the ground and blessed with tyres that spill across the road like flooding river water.

The lights are bright and the smooth red paint captures the colours of surrounding life. Vehicles in the Urb are often high-tech and silent, failing to disrupt the quiet of black early morning. This car, however, shamelessly booms some hip-hop in a language I don't understand. It's not long before I debate coming to a stop. When someone decides to race your car it's not usually in one's interest to let them. Every other night, each car I've challenged has raced ahead. After all, it's a little uncomfortable riding the roads side by side with a self-confessed maniac who runs all night and sleeps all day – *but this car?* It just lets me chase it.

The mysterious vehicle rolls over the neon rainbow of the Urb bridge. I follow it. My lungs are on fire, my breath is paced from experienced long-distance running, but the wind rushing towards me gets caught in my throat when I meet his eyes. Perhaps it's his piercing stare or maybe the shock of making eye contact with anyone at all, but my green eyes are well and truly stolen by the man reflected in the rear-view mirror.

The first thing I process about his appearance is that his hair is pink: candy-floss pink. However, this is often what one first notices about a person with striking and unnaturally coloured hair. I think if his hair had been a more subdued colour, his eyes would have gathered my attention first. Deep brown, small and hooded by their lids, but so striking that they give the illusion of being large.

The reason I know all of this is because the car seems to have considerably decreased in speed, the way it might when being pulled over by the city police.

He's careful as his hand grazes the steering wheel, caressing it like the cheek of his lover. He has a gentle look in his eyes, and I'm suddenly very aware of my existence. Usually, I chase cars like they steer themselves, like there are no eyes present to disapprove of my unusualness, but now, all at once, I realise that this man can *see me*.

I'm self-conscious, slowing to a walk. I zip my hoodie up to my neck as the cold starts to bite.

People that exist feel the cold.

I'm walking, but the momentum I had gathered when running takes a while to die down and I can't help but walk vigorously in the direction I was headed in. My breathing levels out to the pace of my walking until I manage to stop, my hands on my knees, my red hair engulfing my face in an autumn forest. I'm blinking hard, trying to allow my body to catch up with my head.

I hardly process the halting and screeching sound of his car as it stops in the middle of the bridge.

The air is icier on the bridge. It shadows the Urb river, and my breaths, although shallow, feel like icicles jabbing the back of my throat. I bring my head up slowly, squinting my eyes until I see a pair of black-laced boots moving towards me before stopping a few yards away.

I wait for a voice before regaining myself entirely, but the wind whistles on unaccompanied. I compose myself and look up.

He's tall and more of a man than I had first thought. His face is young, but his body is strong in stance. I stare for a moment, realising that I'm not overly interactive with other human beings. After all, the only conversation I've had in the last month was with Tam, the local grocery store cashier.

The man doesn't say anything for a while and it's terribly

uncomfortable. All I know is that I focus on looking anywhere but his eyes and instead watch the dauntingly black river ripple in the wind. I feel a blush crawling up my neck and dread it reaching my cheeks.

'What are you doing at this time in the dark morning?' he says. I don't know what I had expected him to say, but the statement about the time catches me off guard. He makes it sound like it would be acceptable to chase his car in daylight.

'Running. What are you doing?'

He looks at me like I've insulted him, until the look fades. 'Driving,' he replies.

'Um, cool.' There's a pause. 'See you later then?' I hug my hoodie tight to my body and turn on my heel to walk away from the stranger.

'Hey!' he yells, stopping me. I turn back, reluctantly. 'Don't you need a lift home?'

'Uh, my apartment is just down the road,' I say, gesturing with my thumb over my shoulder and backing away. He looks unconvinced and awkward like he really doesn't know why he got out of his car in the first place, but there's something else behind his eyes. Something similar to a deer caught in headlights. 'I'll drive you,' he insists. I go to shake my head but there's something about his expression that tells me he wants desperately for me to let him, and there is something in my gut that can't say no.

'What's your name, then? I'm not getting in a stranger's car.' I would get in a stranger's car. I have very little to lose and little tolerance for regret.

'Bennet Lee, and you?' he replies, plainly, like he doesn't really care what my name is or like it's his line in a play he'd rather not participate in.

'Carson Whitmoore. Or Cara.'

I'm not sure what happens after this. If he were to walk to his car, I'd follow him, except he doesn't for a very long and unsettling 30 seconds. What is different from before, is that I stare back, trying desperately to unravel what is going on. When I can't, I further study his appearance.

His skin is a smooth beige. His eyes are harsh in shape but soft in intent. His lips are full and pink. I wonder if he's studying me too.

He walks to his car so suddenly I almost forget to follow him.

Bennet opens the driver's door and I get in the passenger seat. With the push of a button, he starts the ignition and his radio booms full blast. I jump a little and try to conceal it. The car rolls gently over the bridge before turning around at the bottom and crossing back over.

'My apartment is the first turn off down St. Vincent Street,' I say, realising he probably needs to know. He nods before turning his music up even louder. I think my eardrums are going to explode. I've got no clue what the singers are saying. I look over at Bennet to see him mouthing the words silently.

The journey is awkward to say the least. The music is loud, and we stay quiet. I'm focusing so hard on looking out the window it's a miracle I haven't dislocated my neck. Bennet taps his fingers on the steering wheel.

I feel like I should ask him about his life, maybe get to know him a little, but I'm unsure what to ask or whether he'd want me to ask. 'So, where do you live?' I settle for.

He lowers the music and looks over at me. 'West Town. I study at the university there. I'm big on music. I study music technology.'

'You don't say,' I snort as he hums again, only this time more audibly above the music. 'I think I prefer the Urb. Although I can't really say, I've never been to West Town.'

'I could keep driving. You could crash at my apartment and I could show you around.' Bennet's eyes go almost fearfully wide as if he's struck the greatest idea in the history of ideas, but they soften at what I'm sure is an uncomfortable expression on my face. 'Yeah, terrible idea. I'm sorry. You don't even know me,' he says, and it crosses my mind for a split moment that maybe this guy is crazy. I mean, we are strangers and he so quickly invited me into his car and now his home. What's worse is that I've gone along with it until now.

If there's a handbook on what not to do in life, this is definitely in it.

Yet there's a small part of me that's desperately fighting to spare his feelings. 'No, it's not a terrible idea,' I start, 'maybe one day, but I'm really quite tired. I don't usually go out in daylight. I'm more of a night-owl.'

'Really?' He looks surprised, almost too surprised. 'Why is that, exactly?' he says, head flipping from the road to my face.

'I'm a red-head, I burn easily,' I tease and he chuckles. 'I don't know, I guess I like how the city looks at night. I like how the empty streets make me feel like I own them.' I look through the rear-view mirror to see my city rushing behind me. 'Although it does get kind of cold this time of year.'

I don't know if I imagine it or if Bennet looks completely taken aback by me. 'I bet,' is all he replies with as his voice goes quiet. He turns his radio off and slows down the car, turning finally down St. Vincent Street.

'This is me,' I say, unbuckling my seatbelt and exiting the car. Before closing the door, I poke my head in. 'Thanks again for the lift.'

Bennet nods, graciously. His car remains as he watches me enter my apartment building.

It's only when I'm readying myself for slumber that I realise how much the events of the night have unnerved me.

• • •

When I rise, I feel awful.

I didn't stay out as late last night as I usually would. I'm sure it was only around three o'clock in the morning when I decided to sleep while my usual time is around eight. I suppose I was just exhausted by the adrenaline of the night; the cold air chilling me to the bone and the interaction with a stranger.

The light of the sun creeps in the window, bringing shadows with it. When I check my alarm clock, it's only noon. My sleep pattern has been turned on its head, but as my eyelids refuse to close again, I am forced to get up.

My stomach growls.

The blazing pre-winter sun disrupts my vision as I emerge into the city. I bring my hand over my eyes to see hundreds of busy citizens rushing back and forth on their Tuesday afternoon activities. It must be reaching the end of lunch hour as people dressed in black and blue suits flood out of cafes and drug stores, calling for taxis or walking purposefully towards their workplaces.

I see teenagers kicking cans and laughing. Children ride their bikes and chase floods of pigeons. There's a small boy in a bright yellow t-shirt that catches my eye. He crouches beside another boy in a dark green jumper who is attempting to reattach the chain of his bike. Soon, the mother of the boy in yellow takes him by the arm and yanks him up harshly, dragging him down the street away from the Umbra boy and the broken bicycle. I realise I'm rarely around other people enough to see this division in practice. It's always easier to hear of these things than to witness them first-hand.

Car alarms sound the atmosphere. I hear the opening and closing of shop doors, the scuttling of busy footsteps and the chorus of numerous conversations. I'm so aware of it all as I am so unused to being among it. It fascinates me. A few yards later and I've reached the grocery store. When I enter, the owner gazes over from the till. He's a grumpy old man and he's always looking over at the roof of the Grand Library muttering something about 'lingering scoundrels'.

Touring around the aisles, I grab a carton of milk, a loaf of bread, sliced ham, a packet of frozen chicken nuggets, a bag of apples and a box of sugar puffs.

I dump my items at the checkout and prepare to hand the old man his pay in cash. He frowns at me. I tap my nails on the counter as he scans the items slowly. I'm pretty sure he's doing it intentionally to piss me off.

Beep...beep...beep.

That's when I hear the bang. So excruciatingly loud that I'm sure I've gone deaf. The ground of the store shakes tumultuously and, before I know it, I've crawled behind the counter, crouching into the smallest ball my petite form will allow. The old cashier has his wrinkled hands gripped firmly over his ears, his wide eyes piercing into mine as if screaming a thousand questions I don't know the answers to.

It's a short eternity before the trembling ends, but what follows is not any better. The glass windows of the store have shattered and everyone outside is running in the direction I came in. I pull the old man to his feet as a long crack begins to appear in the ceiling of his shop.

There is an intense sound of crumbling buildings. I'm almost positive the plates of the earth's surface are rubbing against each other. I dart out of the grocery store with the old man on my tail, only to be caught in such fear that I'm nearly swept off my feet by passers-by.

The old cashier runs off in the direction of the others, leaving me to my own devices. I'm sure my heart would sink if I weren't so high on adrenaline. As I look over at the source of commotion, Centrum Tower is on fire, burning to the ground and taking its neighbouring buildings with it like a line of cascading dominos.

I should hit a sprint. Really, I should. If I were a character in a movie, I'd be screaming at myself to run. But I don't, because the Umbra boy in the green jumper stares weakly at his demolished bike under a café building that is seconds away from crushing him.

I want to cry. I'm not typically heroic, but my experienced feet are carrying me towards him before I can change my mind. Just as I'm about to scoop him out of the way, a middle-aged man in a suit beats me to it and I've done no good but take the younger boy's place.

The sudden extraction of my target catches me off guard and I don't have the reflexes to turn around so smoothly. I find myself in a whole lot of danger. I expect my life to flash before my eyes, for everything I've been missing to come flooding back to me in a wave of lost memories, but nothing does.

I guess that's bullshit then.

Just as I'm readying myself for the end, my feet leave the ground.

The Luxies are right, I think, *I'm going to the sky.*

Except, instead of going up, I'm going sideways, with firm hands gripping my waist.

Someone saved me, I think.

I grip my hands onto their shoulders as I watch the café crumbling to the ground and pink candy-floss coloured hair bobbing up and down beneath my vision.

I can't help but think I'm missing a lot more than I thought I was.

CHAPTER 3

THE ROWLEYS

Horatio

God didn't make me strong.

You know, if he made me at all.

He didn't make me resilient or brave. He didn't make me bold or especially curious, or even steady on my feet. If God made me, why did he make me question him?

Are you reading this, God? Are you there?

Do you know all the evil of the world, do you know the pain you cause?

Do you know of cancerous cells and fucked up brains? Do you know that sometimes I think I resent you?

I was born with paper-thin skin. The world rolls me up like a joint, lights me on fire and smokes my ashes. With every exhalation, a part of my soul is surrendered to the sky. Sometimes I like to imagine the particles of myself drifting through the wind, nothing expected of me when I'm not held together as a rushing tree of veins and arteries.

Morning comes too soon.

When my body makes rough contact with the carpeted floor, it hurts. I think I knew it would. I startle awake with a groan and a shake of my hair. The harsh morning sun spills through the crack in the blinds and my eyes crinkle in an attempt to adjust.

'Horatio! It's nine o'clock!' My mother's high voice wafts upstairs from the kitchen, as does the tempting smell of crispy bacon sizzling under the grill. My stomach cries and I think it's the only thing that gets me to my feet. I stumble into the kitchen like a zombie, *a vampire zombie*. My mother takes in my appearance and sighs. 'It's four minutes past nine, Harry.' She shakes her head before turning her attention to a pancake that she sends flying into the air before it plummets back onto the pan with a flop.

'I'm very aware of the time, mum.'

She raises her eyebrows and hums, her blonde bob swishing around while she cooks. 'Well then, you will know you're going to be late for work. You can't expect your father and I to chase after you, Harry. You're 20 years old.'

She's right. I am going to be late for work. I have approximately 20 minutes to shower, change and get a train into the Urb. As far as my mother and father are concerned, I work in a Lux-only café in the city. I don't. I wouldn't dare set foot in a segregated café. 'I know you usually take the train, Harry, but drive your brother into the city on your way, he's going skateboarding in Centrum Park with his friends,' she says cheerfully, almost like she finds joy in inconveniencing me.

Angelo saunters into the kitchen. 'Harry, I'm going skateboarding in the park, what are *you* doing today?' He picks up a pancake and takes a large bite. I feel a knot forming in my stomach at the extension of the word *you*.

'Working. You know that.'

The thing about my little brother is that he's agonisingly smart. He may hang around in oversized hoodies with perfectly swept hair, but he's no dude. He's insightful, perceptive and without a doubt, on my case.

•••

I much prefer taking the rocket train into the Urb to driving my mother's bumblebee-yellow convertible. The rocket train is bullet-fast and has carriages dotted with balls of white light that I think look beautifully high-tech on a purple evening and impressively industrial on a grey morning.

Angelo, however, loves the car. He thinks it makes him look cool as he waves to passers-by, his music booming from his phone into the Bluetooth stereo. I really have no idea what he's listening to but it's bouncing so loud that I can feel it in my chest. It's a 40-minute drive to get to the city.

I snatch the phone from Angelo at a red light.

'Hey! You can't drive and use a phone at the same time! It's literally illegal,' Angelo whines as I scroll through his music library. I'm sure I can feel my eye twitching at my brother's excessive use of the word literally.

'Chill out,' I say, eyes glued to the device. 'We're literally at a red light, so I'm literally not driving.' I mock him before *Rebel Rebel* by David Bowie blasts through the speakers and I thoroughly feel like driving. I like to walk to this song, like John Travolta in *Saturday Night Fever*. It makes me feel empowered. I grip the steering wheel when the green light appears, racing over the Urb bridge, wind blowing curls into my hair. I'm thankful for the open-top as the wind rushes towards us and grants me the release I always crave.

Refreshed is one way to describe how I feel when we slow down at Centrum Park.

The park is disguised in an abundance of crisp leaves: red, orange, yellow. Sunset colours. It takes all my might not to follow Angelo out of the car and jump around in them, listening to the crackling and crunching beneath me. It's not until my brother has closed the door of the vehicle that he turns to give me a knowing look. He leans into the car and gestures to a plastic bag tucked under my leather seat. 'So, I assume that's got the rest of your Umbra clothes in it, then?' Angelo doesn't look half as sinister as usual, more amused. I'm already late for work and I don't have the time to argue with my little brother or explain myself to him so I just nod, shifting uncomfortably in my black leather jacket that covers my bright orange t-shirt. 'Have a good day at work,' Angelo says before disappearing. I can already see his friends enjoying the skateboard ramps behind the tall trees.

'Have fun! Text me!' I shout after him as his brown mop disappears.

I do worry about Angelo. I want to keep him safe. I know his friends think I'm strange, and it's perfectly okay if he pretends to hate me more than he actually does when they're around the house. I wouldn't wish him the teasing I received at his age from Randy Redding.

I'm walking. I expect to see the redheaded druggie when I approach Rennie Street but he's not there, not huddling in his usual corner by the bins in the alley outside the record store.

It's another block before I reach work and am met with a large CLOSED sign. I try the handle and I'm not sure why because the lights inside are very obviously off. I'm confused for a second because I'm almost positive nobody told me the store would be closed for the day.

That's when I hear him coming towards me. Zeb is the kind of person you hear before you see. 'Horatio, your life would be so much simpler if you would just read your texts.' Zeb is now standing right in front of me, perceptible in the blinding November sun, his eyebrows knitted together.

My eyes flicker to my phone. Text from Zeb Hayes at 08:20:

Store is closed today. Dad's got other plans. Want to do something else? I'll think of something :)

'So, did you think of anything?'

Zeb ruffles my hair, the same way his dad does, before bursting into laughter. I notice he's cut large holes in his denim jacket and stitched purple fishnets to fill the gaps. His swept-up hair has tints of vibrant violet.

Zebediah stops laughing and it feels like he's looking straight into my soul. 'I did think of something, but I don't know if you're gonna like it.'

I'm never one to say no. Especially not to Zeb, and I feel it's mainly because what could've been scares me. I tend to dwell on lost opportunities, so even though my legs are exhausted and my mismatched wardrobe choice gets me a few baffled looks, I continue to follow Zeb through the city. It's early afternoon when the busy streets evolve into dark alleyways.

'I don't see what the big deal is,' I groan as I shoulder a cold grey wall and stumble over a decaying can of some sort of soft drink.

'It's the only place I can get them, okay?' Zeb looks me up and down. 'Trust me, you'll fit in just fine.' He's serious, but I think he's taking joy in how much stress this whole trip is causing me.

This is all totally irrational, to stumble openly into the sleaziest part of the city all for a birthday present. 'Super Sounder headphones!' Zeb had sung. 'They're technically not even out yet!'

The sun is piercing, but it barely sheds any light on the dark pathways and decaying buildings around us, it lights the way as much as the straw slit in a carton of juice.

'Who's this birthday present for, anyway? They must be pretty important to you.' I hate that a surge of jealousy rushes through me. Zeb is always the best at gift giving, but I wonder if he's ever entered the Rowleys for me. 'His name is Bennet Lee.' He glances back to make sure I'm keeping up with him. 'He's big into music, studies it at university. You know his sister.' I shake my head. 'Yeah, you do!' he says. 'Gia Lee? I told my parents I was taking her to prom when I was really going with Gregory Walters?'

'Oh, yeah...' I say, remembering her in her turquoise dress sliding gracefully into the back of the black limo when Zeb hadn't come out to his parents yet. 'Bennet is a great guy and he's had a tough time recently, so I'm making it my responsibility to make this birthday a great one. It's his twenty-first.' I nearly ask him about Bennet's 'tough time' but decide it's none of my business.

I don't like it when Zeb talks about his other friends. I know his Umbra friends probably wouldn't like me if they knew me, what with me technically being a Lux and all. I let Zeb talk, though. 'His name isn't really Bennet,' he confesses, and it sounds like he regrets telling me this towards the end of his sentence. I don't say anything. 'His name is really Hawk. Hawk Lee, but he had it changed because I kept calling him Birdboy.' Zeb walks ahead as he speaks, and I feel like an idiot stumbling behind him.

'Oh, would you imagine that?' I snort.

It's my worryingly bad reflexes that causes Zeb's assertiveness to dissolve much faster than mine when the tremendous rattle shakes the ground. The shock knocks him off his feet and I've only half processed it when I'm backing up against the grey building beside me, my palms pressed flat against the bricks as if trying to find cover from an airborne threat. The resonance of the rumble could be from above, but it could also be from the centre of the earth – or even from inside my own head.

Wherever its origin, it's sounding everywhere now.

After a few eternal minutes, the sound becomes distant. I rush over to Zeb. He is still on the ground, but he is pushed up on his elbows and his eyes are impossibly wider. He looks at me like I should be dead, like I'm someone he knew long ago and my presence has provoked a thousand lost memories. I offer my hand and he accepts it, reluctantly, as if the shock has disorientated him so much he isn't sure I'm not a danger to him. When he's back to his feet, a couple inches beneath me, he regains his senses.

'What the hell was that?' he says. Zeb refers to the fiery afterlife an awful lot for someone so certain of its fantasy.

'I don't know,' I say, trembling. 'An earthquake I'm guessing?'

Zeb and I stay as much pressed up against the wall of the granite building as we do to each other, shoulder to shoulder. We stay there for a half-hour before the reverberation ends. Sirens can be heard in the direction of the city centre.

We don't say anything. Soon, Zebediah is rising, brushing off any dirt from his skinny jeans and pulling me to my feet. 'Right,' he says, running his fingers through his well-groomed hair 'Let's get heading!'

'What?' I say. 'There could've just been an earthquake!' I search Zeb's face for any signs of a rational thought. 'Like, the crust of the earth may have just actually moved, causing great destruction and possibly death, and you want to continue gift shopping in the mother-fucking black market?'

Zeb raises his eyebrows, his arms folded smartly over his front, a reckless glint in his eye that always makes me feel like I don't know him as much as I'd like to think I do. 'Horatio, we're almost there! I'll be quick, I swear. Then we can head straight back into whatever shitstorm awaits us in the centre.' He is so insistent, which confuses me because my parents, living in East Town, are far more likely to be safe than his parents who actually live in the Urb. I mean, there's my Uncle Basil, who's always doing business in the city, but I hate that I can't force my heart to feel any dread at the thought.

That's when I remember.

His sandy brown hair shifting in the breeze, his tan hands tucked into his jean pockets and his perfect white smile forcing me to mirror his youthful excitement as he disappeared into the park. *Angelo!*

I don't make any attempt to verbally communicate my panic to Zeb, I'm just fishing hungrily for my phone in my pocket and dialling my brother's number with shaky hands. I hold the cold screen to my ear, already feeling guilty for dropping him at the park.

Beep...beep...beep.

A few rings feel like 50 before someone answers. Muffled voices, shaky breaths and nearby sirens sound. 'Harry?' he says and I almost cry.

'Angelo!' I can see Zeb looking pitiful in my peripheral vision. 'Are you alright? Where are you? I'm on the outskirts of the city. What damage has it done? The earthquake?'

'I'm fine. The boys and I ran. Earthquake? What do you mean earthquake?' Angelo says as I'm yelling something about tectonic plates down the line. I stop talking to listen. 'Horatio, there was no earthquake. It's the bank. Centrum Tower, it's been bombed!' he says, hurriedly. 'It took half the street with it.' Angelo begins to cry. 'I'm with Uncle Basil. He was supposed to be in the building, but he had to leave for lunch. Mum and dad are on their way to get me now. I'm okay,' he says before pausing. His next words shake me. 'There are bodies, Harry...' I'm about to reply but there's some rustling on the other end before my uncle's voice is in my ear.

'Where are you, Horatio?' he says quickly. I'm hardly going to tell the mayor that I'm in the Rowleys where only the misfit undecided live and drugs are more accessible than food.

'Work let me off,' I decide to say. 'I went for a walk with a friend. I'm not too near the centre.' Luckily, my uncle doesn't take much interest. 'When you're heading home, take the rocket train at the nearest stop. I don't want you seeing anything you can be spared from.' Then I hear him talking to someone else. He's a busy man. 'Okay, son, take care of yourself. I'll be at your house later to see you're safe. I'll let your parents know you're okay.'

Then Uncle Basil is gone. I lower my phone and glance at Zeb who seems to be far more concerned than he was before. His eyes pose a question. 'It's Centrum Tower,' I say, 'it's been bombed.'

After some discussion, I decide I'd much rather follow Zeb on his quest in the Rowleys than face a dark reality at home right now, so we edge further into an almost post-apocalyptic stretch of smashed glass, dull buildings and loose telephone wires. I further explain the situation to Zeb and he reacts with a long-winded rant about terrorism and ultimate division in beliefs. As it turns out, his parents are visiting his grandparents in West Town and he had texted them to let them know he's safe.

I'm pretty exhausted when we're officially in the centre of the Rowleys. I know we've made it when we reach a red sandstone wall covered in graffiti. There is a recurring phrase articulated in various colours and bubble-like shapes:

We can show our own, but we will never know, she's made of glass but we never tiptoe.

And another word, over and over again: Silenda, Silenda, Silenda. 'Who is *she*?' I ask Zeb, referring to the woman who's 'made of glass'. He pauses but he doesn't say anything, looking me straight in the eye. He shrugs, eyelashes fluttering. 'How often do you come here?' I decide to ask instead.

'Rarely. I only come here when I really need something.'

The place is such a dump that I struggle to imagine it selling high-tech devices and the latest labels.

'Where do they get the stuff they sell here, anyway?' I ask him, utterly confused by the whole concept, especially considering we've been in the Rowleys for 10 minutes already and the only person I've seen is a heavily inked, although oddly friendly looking biker guy in a *No Doubt* t-shirt.

Zeb points at two muddied black vans parked outside a large industrial building that looks like an enlarged tin can. 'All the factories in the Urb are robot run, there's basically no manual labour these days. Guys from the Rowleys just break in the back, steal the products before they can be released into mainstream stores and take them here in the vans so people like me pay them good money to get the latest stuff.'

'Sounds so simple.' I'm genuinely shocked by the city's lack of security.

'Nah, they're not ninjas,' Zeb says. 'The city police know for sure, they just let it happen. They don't want to create any publicity around it. Don't want us to know these misfits exist,' he continues, matter-of-factly. 'The people here have got to make a living, no one is going to employ a misfit, and the misfits aren't going to fake faith. The people who live here are honest with themselves.'

When Zeb says this, I feel a surge of guilt. I have no idea what I believe, what's worse is that I'm not sure I have the strength of mind to settle in a place like this just to be honest with myself.

We're at the front door of the industrial warehouse. Zeb is just about to brush his knuckles on it, when a surge of fear runs through me. I'm unsure what kind of guy is going to open the door and supply Zeb with the Super Sounders. Everything about this place is disgusting. It smells like tobacco, and I feel like I'm inhaling it every time I breathe and, for some reason that may just be in my head, the sky is an eerie grey compared to the crisp blue in the Urb.

Once Zeb has knocked, it's seconds before a middle-aged man peeks his head around the door. He has messy blonde hair and brown eyes. He reminds me of Shaggy from *Scooby Doo*. 'Zeb! Buddy! Hey, how you doin'?' Zeb's face lights up immediately and he embraces the man. 'Who's your boyfriend?' Shaggy says, looking at my mismatched orange t-shirt and black leather jacket approvingly.

Zeb swings his arm around me. 'This is Horatio,' he says, 'he likes girls.'

'Aw, a shame,' the scruffy guy says, rubbing Zeb's shoulder.

'Truly,' Zeb replies. 'He is a beauty, true Dracula type.' I blush. 'Horatio, this is Jason. He runs this place.'

Jason nods, proudly, before stepping aside to let us in. The building is surprisingly modern on the inside, lit with green tinted lights. Rows of metal shelves are occupied by boxes upon boxes of phones, laptops and even bikes. I'm taken aback. Jason rummages through a large crate in the corner.

'This is our new stock,' he says, before successfully pulling out a small black box labelled *Super Sounders Headphones*. There ya go, son. Got them special for ya,' Jason says, smirking lopsidedly.

Zeb embraces him again. 'Thanks, Jason,' he says. 'Bennet will love them.'

'Hawk's a good lad,' Jason reminds him. 'Will I see you in West Town this weekend?'

'You will!' Zeb exclaims.

I feel detached from the conversation. I've never been to West Town. Anyway, my mind is too occupied by the weight of what happened to Centrum Tower. Zeb must notice my distractedness as he wraps up his conversation with Jason but, before we leave, the older man pulls Zeb away from me, whispering frantically into his ear about the tower before disguising his concern with a smile and a wave directed at me.

We're heading out of the warehouse, Jason affectionately patting Zeb on the back and waving us goodbye until we are dots in the distance. I continue to look back at him, trying to puzzle through his hurried whispers to Zeb.

We pass two police cars on our way out of the Rowleys. Tape surrounds a small blue shed that is rusting to the point of being nearly brown. The sirens are off and the officers look melancholy and like they would rather be anywhere else.

The Rowleys are little cared for.

Zeb has his arm around my shoulder as we walk quickly. He is guiding me out. He knows something is wrong, I know he does.

I can't rip my eyes away from the scene, especially when the officers approach the shed door and wedge it open with a tool that resembles a large metal candy-cane. The force of the instrument has the door swinging open fiercely, and I swear I nearly cough up my lungs when I see him.

SILENDA

It must be all the shock my body has endured today because my legs nearly go from underneath me. If it weren't for Zeb holding me, I would have fallen to the ground.

Behind the rusting door, a pale body hangs. Limp, with a rope tied tight around his neck. His red hair hides his empty eyes.

Randy Redding, my high school bully, hangs lifeless before us.

Dead.

CHAPTER 4

CANDY FLOSS

Carson

His hair, pink as candy floss. His eyes, deep as the darkest chocolate. His skin, a warm sandalwood.

It hasn't taken me all too long to realise that I may have been led into a false sense of security. That for all I know, this man is the evil witch's gingerbread house personified and I await the same fate as Hansel and Gretel – burned alive in a little oven like Centrum Tower burned to the ground.

I'm staring out of the rocket train window, the Urb dwindling away behind us. A tsunami of people have flooded the carriages in mass hysteria, a buzz of screaming and crying following suit. The train is packed tight, but Bennet and I have managed to squeeze into some narrow seats.

With each stop, what once was a chaotic scene turns slowly into a silent collective of tired faces as the last running train to West Town travels rapidly on the tracks.

The monotonous voice of the Urb announcer booms through the air. Tonight the city will be locked down.

My apartment, for sure, has been taken in the wreckage, being only a few buildings away from the grocery store. I wonder what became of that fat little cashier; not my most valued acquaintance, but one of my only. I think of all my clothes and cash, my creaky yet comforting little bed and my travel-sized television where I'd keep up-to-date with the city's events.

I'll miss the city.

I'll miss the moon – I don't hold out that Bennet will conform to my strange sleeping habits. Honestly, any place with a freaking shower and I'll be fine.

Mostly, I'll miss my friend.

The man in the dark who had held onto the string of my balloon for all the time I've known. It appears I've floated away. Somewhere in my mind, I have convinced myself that it was him who wrote me the letter. This is probably nothing but wishful thinking. I wonder if he'll find me, if he'll leave me a trail of everything I need. Perhaps like a baby bird, I must face the reality of life on my own.

It's difficult to explain why I start to cry. I don't know if I'm in shock over the day's events, distressed by the air-piercing screams and the thousands who must have occupied the tower. It could be that I'm finally giving in to how bewildered and anxious I feel with how little I can remember. Or it may be that I'm just a lonely balloon gliding through the atmosphere with no true purpose, absent a hand to keep me down to earth.

What I'm most confused about is that I can't seem to decipher whether Bennet has taken hold of my string or if he has been the one to cut me loose. I do know that he saved me. I also know that he didn't go home that night on the bridge, that he must have been watching me. It is too convenient that he was immediately there to save me the second I needed saving.

I know this is strange. However, I also know that he sits in the leather train seat next to me, his eyebrows knitted together and his hand searching for mine at anxious intervals.

It's one of those days where I can feel the sun almost piercing through me. I don't often experience the sun, but I like the way it feels on the back of my neck through the train window. I try desperately to concern myself with this and not with the abundance of reasons I should be crying, or how it's been 10 minutes and Bennet is no longer looking my way, yet his hand still sits firmly beside mine, our pinkies touching.

There's numerous reasons why I don't want to think about this.

Firstly, I don't know him and a feeling of uncertainty rises at the intimacy of it. Secondly, I'm so mad about everything that I just want to be the only person on earth and his persistent touch is a constant reminder that is not the case – and lastly, his beauty makes me fear that I may start to act irrationally.

The train comes to an uncomfortable halt when we reach West Town. It's so abrupt and sudden for the speed it was going at that I'm surprised it hasn't rebounded and darted its way back into the city. I don't stand up immediately, pulling gingerly at a loose bit of wool hanging off the sleeve of my mustard jumper. I don't notice that Bennet has stood up until I see his hand is no longer beside mine. I look up at him, expectantly.

Perhaps I'm waiting for him to comfort me or take my hand and guide me out the train because I'm really feeling sorry for myself; instead, he glides down the carriage towards the door confidently, following the remainder of the shell-shocked crowd. He must have observed how much of a lost puppy I am because he, without a doubt, expects me to follow him.

In reflection of the resident's beliefs, the sun has disappeared when we step off the train, shadowed by clouds of deep grey, and it's frankly quite hilarious. I'm laughing before I can stop myself. Bennet turns to look at me as though I'm insane and, if he accused me, I'm not sure I would have the facts to argue.

It's raining a little and I like the smell of it; the earthy aroma from the pavements. I'm not even disheartened by the sogginess of my jumper. Everything is so different in West Town than it is in the city. The city is high-tech, bright and practically made of glass. West Town is full of Gothic buildings that look like they have been around for hundreds of years.

A block from the train station is a building that is quite possibly the most beautiful structure I have ever laid eyes on.

The bricks of the castle are a shade of golden-brown and vines crawl up the sides, adorning pillars and semi-oval windows. It's huge, surrounded by endearing little benches and Victorian-style streetlamps. It looks perfect under a grey sky, prettier with rain as if it were designed to be viewed on a day like this.

Bennet edges closer to the castle and I follow him, trailing down the path incoherently like a dog he's just adopted. After a while, he turns on his heel and waits for me to catch up. I'm not sure why we're heading towards the building. For a moment I think Bennet must be a prince.

When we reach the building, we go under a large brick arch and are met with a moderate stretch of grass. I suppose, if royals lived here, we'd call this area 'the grounds'. Bennet heads towards a dark wooden door in the side of the building. I've been quiet for so long that I can't decide when to speak again, but I need to ask, 'What is this place?' I stare up at the spectacular walls around us.

'This is West Town University,' Bennet states, simply. 'The dorms are up there.' He nods to the top of the building where several turrets emerge and continue into the clouds. 'This is where I live.'

Behind the oak door is an abundance of golden steps that lead to the top of the largest turret. After a narrow spiral of stairs, there is another wooden door that Bennet pushes open to reveal a long corridor with grey stone walls lit with hanging orange flames and decorated with a dozen arched doors. I follow him to the first door on the right where a key materialises in his hand and he clicks it open.

I almost have a heart attack. Bounding towards me as quick as a flash of lightning is the tiniest, fluffiest little dog I've ever seen.

With burnt orange curls and marble-like brown eyes, how could I be intimidated? But she stops so abruptly at my feet and stares up at me like I'm some sort of absurdity.

'Don't worry, she doesn't bite,' Bennet calls, as he's already entered the open-plan kitchen. 'She's just very protective.'

'Oh.' I swerve past the little dog and hover in the living room. The kitchen is right beside it, no wall splitting us. It's silent for a few moments. 'What now?' I ask.

Bennet is moving frantically around the kitchen, opening and closing cabinets and then opening and closing them again. He doesn't turn around to answer. 'You can stay here for the time being; as for the city, I'm not sure. The tower was bombed.' He stops being erratic but he still won't face me.

'Bombed?' I mean to shout, but it comes out as a whisper. I don't know what I expected. A regular old fire? A sizzling cigarette butt discarded on the trail of a curtain and left for dead? A chemical leak? I sit down on the wool-covered armchair behind me when my vision is disrupted by dancing black spots.

'Yeah, that's what everyone's saying. They don't know who or why, but it's an act of terrorism nonetheless.' Bennet turns to face me with his pink hair falling onto his forehead. I wonder how he knows this, but I decide such terrifying news must spread as quickly as a fire itself.

I rub my hands over my face. I feel dirty and sweaty and panicked and dizzy.

'Are you alright?' Bennet asks, and I feel like yelling at him, because obviously I'm not alright. I mean he doesn't know I can't remember the most part of my existence, but he does know I was nearly crushed to death by a falling building and *that shit changes you.*

I exhale shakily because I really do not want to snap at him, not after he saved me. Not after he took me home last night and to his apartment today so I wouldn't be homeless in the wake of the bombing. I hate owing people but, nonetheless, I owe him.

Bennet disappears into a room on the other side of the living room from the kitchen, but I barely notice because I'm too busy trying to steady my breathing. After a moment I feel a hand on my shoulder. Bennet has returned with a large white t-shirt and a pair of grey sports shorts. 'Hey, sorry this is all I have for you to wear. We'll sort that out later. You should shower, de-stress a little.' He gestures to the door behind me.

I nod in thanks and head over to the bathroom. When I enter, the walls are a mosaic of cold grey cobblestone, pleasantly brisk under my sweaty palms. There is a small bathtub in the corner with a contemporary steel showerhead that hangs over it like a robotic storm cloud. I pull back the silver-silk shower curtain and my heart pounds in my chest.

A loud gasp sounds from the bathtub. I fall to the ground, my nerves shattered from the frights I've endured today and I find myself face to face with a strange fully-clothed man in Bennet's empty bathtub. His hair is purple – *what is it with the people here?* His eyes are dark and as wide as saucers. I don't move and he gapes at me.

It's a long 30 seconds or so before I can speak. 'Bennet!' I call back into the main room, eyes still trained on the stranger. 'You never mentioned you have a roommate!' I hear Bennet rustling around behind me before I feel his presence at my side.

'That's because I don't,' he says, sternly. 'Zebediah, what are you doing here?'

Zebediah is quiet for a moment and when he speaks it's but a few notches louder than a whisper. 'It's your birthday.' *It's Bennet's birthday?* I think, and it's bizarre that I feel guilty. He throws a small black box Bennet's way, which he catches with ease, then weighs it up in his hands. I think he's going to thank him, but Zebediah rises in the bathtub along with a threatening finger directed at me. It catches me off guard because I forgot I was here, like for a moment I was but a mere moth attracted to the bathroom bulb.

'The real question is,' Zebediah starts, 'what is *she* doing here?' My head aches profoundly.

These people know me.

'Zeb, calm down.' Bennet lowers his arms as if trying to convince the man to drop his weapon. Zebediah lowers his pointing finger. 'I guess you could say she's Hayden's birthday present for me.' *Excuse me?* I think. *Who is Hayden? Birthday present? Have I been tricked into some sort of prostitution?*

Bennet places his hand on my shoulder as if in fear that Zebediah will take me away. He's trembling.

'What in the name of Turrow are you thinking?' Zebediah is yelling now. 'Tyson is going to kill you, do you realise that?'

'We've got it all figured out, Zeb,' Bennet says, calmly, and I'm completely unaware of myself until I feel the stab in the top of my arm, the support of Bennet's body as I drop to the ground and see the shock in Zebediah's eyes as he beholds the needle.

The world spins into a black abyss.

• • •

My eyes twitch in their sockets. I think they're burning until I'm aware of a homely coal fire dancing and crackling in a blur of what I can make of the space around me. I know I've been unconscious, but it's difficult to say whether it's been for a year or a minute. My vision is foggy. I don't open my eyes completely in fear that I'm in danger. In fear that the candy-floss boy will sense my wakening. I have been apprehensive since he offered me a lift home in the early hours of the morning. Although kind, it was sudden. I'm too much of a cynic to accept kindness without suspecting some sort of alternate motive. He saved my life, I can't forget, but has he saved me to slaughter me himself?

SILENDA

He stabbed me – with a needle, which I guess could be worse, *but why on earth would he need me unconscious?* I think of the boy from the bathtub, how he had demanded to know why I was with Bennet, how he had said that Tyson Turrow, the mayor of West Town, would kill him. My head is spinning and I think I'm going to pass out again because I know nothing.

I know nothing.

I want to go back to the way things were before, to before the Awakening, to before I forgot. I'm only just starting to focus on what Bennet had meant by, 'I guess you could say she's Hayden's birthday present for me,' when I stop thinking about anything. The floodgates in my mind must have closed because everything has stopped streaming out to the forefront and all I can think about is the sweet and musky aroma of the coal fire, citrus and pine. I feel a cold breeze and a spritz of rain from what must be an open window, it's harsh but comforting.

Comforting because it means I'm here, because it means I'm alive.

I think I'm intoxicated by the smell of petrichor as I'm obnoxiously relaxed for someone in my situation.

What do I have to lose, really?

I open my eyes fully. I turn my head in a dazed state and I am no longer facing the fire but a pained looking Bennet who gazes into the flames. He looks mesmerising, sitting in a mediocre wooden chair, and it hurts me – it really does. I don't know why I feel a pang in my chest as I see the orange light illuminating his smooth skin, his plump lips, his throat. I'm sure I'm admiring him in his tight black jumper and his *black hair? Wow, how long have I been out?*

My hands scurry to my chest, patting down my body, searching for my mustard jumper. Instead I find a large grey hoodie in its place. My hair rests on my chest, although I'm sure I had tied it up.

I'm too busy watching Bennet and his new liquorice-coloured hair that it's a moment before I process the chorus of bickering at the other end of the cabin; a cabin lit by candlelight, casting shadows of strangers onto the walls; a cabin that I did not pass out in. I am not in Bennet's apartment anymore.

I look over to see Zebediah throwing hands with some scruffy blonde guy. 'Curiosity killed the cat!' I hear him whisper aggressively.

'Yeah, well, did that cat live a fulfilled life?' the other man argues. I have no idea what they're talking about. I've stopped caring, too. My eyes flick back over to Bennet who has his hands clasped and pressed to his forehead like he's praying to the flames. He still hasn't noticed I'm awake.

I have two options.

I could spring up before anyone has any time to react, attack them all with the cushion I'm lying on and run.

Or I trust him.

I trust the man who saved my life and respect the debt I owe him. Neither option sounds appealing. I'm too drawn to Bennet to beat him with a stool, but have too much self-respect to fall at his feet for whatever reason he needs me. It's too late, however, because I'm already making startling eye contact with the blonde man across the cabin. He looks over at Bennet and coughs, my eyes must look like headlights as they skim over to assess Bennet's reaction. He sits up straight in his chair, his hands resting on his knees. He looks at me so intensely I swear I can feel his gaze burning my skin more than the fire that spits beside us.

He looks over at the blonde again, warily, before returning his attention to me. 'Hey,' he whispers and it's the most gentle 'hey' anyone has ever uttered. I let out a breath of relief because even with that I feel more safe. He looks genuinely concerned for me, so I take advantage of it. I turn on the waterworks, and it's easy to start with the trauma of everything that's happened.

Tears streaming, I plead, 'What's happening?' Bennet stands up. 'Where am I?' I continue, tears falling rapidly. In reality, I simply do not have the life in me to be as sad as I'm trying to convince him I am. He crouches down next to my stool like I'm a small child who requires the most sensitive attention. Zebediah and the other man make their way over to us. Zebediah hovers and the blonde sits down at a wooden desk, opening a paper-thin laptop.

I think Bennet is going to cry. 'I'm so sorry...' he trails off, but the blonde kicks him in the back lightly, warningly '...I can't tell you,' he finishes, his hand trailing up to touch my cheek, but I jerk away. My rejection hurts him, I don't know why, but it does; I can see it in the way his soft expression hardens as if suddenly infuriated. His anger seems to be less with me and more with himself. It's silent for a couple of seconds, filled only by the crackling of the fire.

Bennet and the blonde exchange eye contact multiple times and I can feel Zebediah looking down at me with sad eyes, but I don't meet his gaze. 'This is fucking ridiculous,' he groans, running his hands over his face and down the back of his neck. He paces until he reaches the fire, staring at it with a determination that could put it out.

'Oh, shut up, will you?' the blonde snaps at him with an expression of such distaste that he looks as though he is permanently unimpressed.

When Zebediah turns around he resembles more of a lion than a man. 'Don't start with me, Hayden,' he says, edging closer to his desk. *Oh, so this is Hayden.* 'The two of you are out of your minds! When Tyson comes after you, I'm not going to back you up.'

In response, Hayden moves his chair out from behind his desk. It's so confusingly threatening. He walks around it slowly before reclaiming his seat. When Zebediah rolls his eyes and turns to the fire, Hayden snakes his arm around his waist and pulls him onto his lap. Bennet lets out a small sigh and I look on bewildered by the apparent significance of this event. Zebediah stays there for a second looking the most upset I'm sure I've ever seen anyone, before he stands up, straightens his denim jacket and strides into the next room without looking back.

When Zebediah leaves, the room is silent. Even the fire begins to quieten. Hayden has moved his chair back behind his desk and types furiously on his keyboard, occasionally furrowing his brow and tracing his finger over the screen as if it will better increase his understanding of what he's looking at.

Bennet, confusing as ever these last – *how many hours?* – has his head resting against my legs where I remain situated in my stool. I have to resist the urge to run my fingers through his hair as much as I have from kicking him as hard as I can muster.

I'm far too exhausted to leave or to think of anywhere to run, so I stay exactly where I am. My eyes skim around the cabin that is furnished floor-to-ceiling in dark wood. The windows are decorated with blood red curtains and matched with a rug in the centre of the room that is laced with a mud green. I feel as detached from the cabin as I feel detached from the world; I turn my nose up at the decor as a distant critic.

The curtains are shut over all the windows, except for the small window beside me that has been left ajar to allow for a refreshing breeze gifted by the wet, grey outside. I stare out of the window absentmindedly and, with a present mind, do all I can to avoid touching Bennet.

When Zebediah enters, the room noticeably stirs as if he had left us like a pot to simmer and has now returned with a giant wooden spoon. He wears nothing but a pair of blue denim dungarees and it doesn't take a genius to establish that he is extremely toned. His hair, once styled up, now falls over his face, black and wet with traces of purple only creeping through underneath. He must have left to shower – and also to spread whatever news he has that would provoke Tyson Turrow – because a striking blonde girl enters the room behind him.

Hayden shoots up like a scruffy, overwound jack-in-the-box and makes a direct break for the door when he sees her. Zebediah doesn't look ready to stop him and avoids his eyes, but the girl slams her hand against his chest forcefully and pushes him back into the room. 'Right, you sons of bitches. Sit down! Now!' she yells.

Bennet had also risen to his feet at her arrival and now sits on the floor again like a scolded schoolboy.

Hayden is at his desk and Zebediah remains standing by her. I assume she doesn't count him when she is addressing said 'sons of bitches.'

When the room is settled, I look at her properly and my heart feels offbeat and baffled. *I know her.*

Her long hair is white-blonde and messy as if styled to be that way, she is tall and slim with black leather jeans and a cropped white shirt. Her eyes are – well, the right eye is an astonishing blue and the other is a startling brown – both shadowed with a dark shimmer.

The figure paces, and she is a figure. She is as present as a statue, a monument, an ancient fountain. She stops at Bennet and lifts his chin with her chipped blue fingernails. 'Happy Birthday, Hawk. Weren't Zeb's headphones enough for you?' She takes her hand away with a flick, I think to leave a scratch. *Hawk?* 'And you, Hayden? I'd act surprised but your attitude has always known no bounds.'

Hayden stands up. 'Look,' he says, 'I'm not trying to hurt anyone. This wasn't some crazy birthday present for Hawk, okay?' I listen intently. 'It's a rescue mission. Yes, I'm selfish. I'll never be able to argue that.' He glances at Zebediah. 'Yes, the science interests me. I mean, I'm a computer science student. But Hawk is one of my best friends and he's falling apart!' *Is he?* I think. 'Look at him! He's a broken man.'

The girl looks at him sceptically.

'I know it's a long shot,' Hayden continues. 'I know it is. But I can fix this! It doesn't have to be all gone. My uncle – your dad – when things go wrong he's one to burn it all to the ground, but he acted too hastily!'

The girl breathes deeply. She looks at me with her famous eyes, adorning billboards all over the city. Model, actress, socialite, mayor's daughter and a mighty presence, Astrid Turrow approaches me with a small smile. 'Welcome back, Carson Whitmoore.'

CHAPTER 5

THE LIGHTNING

Horatio

For want to think of anything else, I've observed that leather seats really bother me. The way they strain under my thighs and stick to me on hot days. What's worse, is crummy leather seats. The rocket train has crummy leather seats, and I struggle to understand why anyone would want to consume anything sideward gazing through windows that move so fast they give view to nothing but blurs of blue and green.

Zeb had to leave me at the station. He ruffled my hair and embraced me for longer than usual, his lips somewhat grazing my collarbone. I think he was looking for heat; reassuring himself that my somewhat sickly complexion hadn't left me in the same state that the world had left Randy.

Then I was alone.

Even with the bombing of one of the largest buildings in the city, Bennet Lee's birthday could not wait.

It's hard to say how long I stand outside my house.

On the walk home from the train station, I think of absolutely nothing. I am going through the motions. When I approach my front door, I am astounded by the flood of thoughts that come rushing to the forefront all at once.

The last thing I need is to contain them.

However, I'm sure I don't have much choice. My parents will be worried sick, no matter my father's choice to admit it. I cannot turn away now.

I tell myself this. A few times, actually. Yet I'm still outside the limestone building, staring at the lavender and Spanish red roses on the patio. The thing is, I'm sensitive. I know as soon as I close that front door behind me, everything will hurt. The trauma of the tower and of Randy – an incident I do not even know how to start explaining to my family.

I'm about to twist open the copper doorknob when my father emerges in his work attire with a large black sack in his arms. He isn't startled to see me. My father is never startled. He raises his silver eyebrows artificially and spins us both around, giving me a once over with his piercing eyes.

I'm standing on the patio watching him heave the black sack into the backseat of the Jeep once he's satisfied I'm alive. 'Long time, no see,' he says, brushing something non-existent off the front of his grey trousers as he walks back towards me. I don't answer him, hands in my leather pockets, nodding back at the car. 'It's Angelo's old TV, I'm taking it to the dump,' he says. I nod again, trying to act like I'm okay. 'How are you holding up? It's just tragic what's going down in the city.'

There's a rope around my neck.

I don't think my father can see it, but it's there nonetheless. It's tight and I can hardly breathe, never mind reply. My eyes are watering and possibly bulging out of my head. There's a rope around my neck – there's a rope around Randy's neck.

I wonder if Randy loathed himself more than he's ever loathed me. He probably did. I wonder if I loathe myself as much as Randy loathed me. I hope I don't loathe myself as much as Randy loathed Randy.

SILENDA

There is something exhausted in my father's eyes.

There is a rope around my waist. It's squeezing my insides like a firm fist around a toothpaste tube, forcing my contents up into my throat, and I know it's only a matter of time before it egresses as nausea. I'm choking and for a second I'm sure my intestines are in my throat, everything I am, is in my throat; there's no room for anything else – not for oxygen, not for words.

I can feel my father's hands on me, shaking me. I try to tell him he shouldn't handle fragile things with such aggression. He's screaming, I think, but it sounds like he's deep underwater. Perhaps my insides have spread to my ears from my throat. He looks like he's underwater too. I double over. My mother doubles over the toothpaste tube to squeeze out her money's worth.

I throw up on the patio.

• • •

I stay in bed for a day.

I feel like 13-year-old Horatio again. My mother comes rushing in every hour or so to record my temperature, which the last four times has been completely regular. I try to explain to her that 35 degrees is perfectly normal, but she insists if it was 35 degrees outside I would not be leaving the house without my factor 50 suncream, and therefore shall not have a body temperature of 35 degrees without a plentiful serving of vanilla ice cream.

That's a lot of fucking ice cream.

There isn't much to do with my time when I'm not working or wandering. All I can manage to accomplish in the week that passes is obscene amounts of watching television. Really shit television, like *Sally Sleuth's Nightmares in the Kitchen*. I never imagined myself having any kitchen related nightmares until 17 episodes of Sally yelling at the top of her lungs, holding a wooden spoon. I can now recite nearly every advertisement on the Food For You Network.

My favourite is the new Dior perfume advert, purely because I get to see *her*. Astrid Turrow is a scandalous sort of woman. I say woman as I don't mean to offend, but at 21, her larger-than-life eyes and flat chest contribute to a younger aesthetic that isn't quite warm enough to be deemed 'womanly'.

I think about Astrid Turrow a lot. I think a lot of people think about her a lot. It's hard not to, the way she is draped over the city like an icon of the Italian Renaissance. A religious icon, in a way, if making a point of being publicly unreligious, can be considered a religion of its own.

She's hard to avoid. Even harder by the way that her eyes sink deep into my soul and touch a part of me that only the sunset can. I don't mean this in a sickeningly infatuated way, but by the way that they represent to me the things that I repress. The light and the dark, cooperating as one undecided unit. Deep brown and vivid blue; representing the city divide and the helpless, restless unknowing that grips tightly to me.

I suppose it can be argued that I *am* infatuated with her.

But I'm not, not really. The fact that she looks like an ethereal Valkyrie probably makes this hard to believe, but my obsession with her is purely rooted in my obsession with people. I like to watch people – *in a totally normal way.* I think about people and I render them in my mind as characters with backgrounds and traits. It's easier to do with Astrid because her life is often public information, with so many stories about her accomplishments and reckless behaviour. Her extraordinary life is a reassurance to me that human beings are not as static as I sometimes feel.

Zebediah knows a lot about her. He runs in the same 'circles', he says. He talks a lot about her because he knows I like to hear about her, like her adventures in Tokyo where she learned to ride a Solar Glider, the world's fastest motorbike and her ex-relationship with a young prince and the royal ball that she turned on its head.

SILENDA

Violins and champagne flutes became guitars and beer bottles. Mozart was replaced by Debby Harry and carriages with trashy pink limousines. She cut her gold ballgown to above the knee and supposedly had the whole place up in arms. There were those who enjoyed her rebelliousness, and those who were repulsed by it, hence the termination of her association with royalty.

When I imagine her spinning around the dance floor with her heels in her hands and a smirk on her lips, I can't help but think how unbelievable it all sounds. Imagine being the violinist at the ball? Or the poor seamstress who designed her gown? I suppose it's a little inconsiderate. Although, this is probably just something I tell myself so that I don't drool on her if we ever cross paths. I hope one day that we might, but as each day passes it seems more and more unlikely that Zeb will ever invite me to West Town. He's been distant in the week since the bomb – since Randy. I suppose I have been too.

My mother was horrified to hear about Randy. I had to tell someone who knew him. She was very involved at school; she sat in the front row at every play and was head of the parent council. She saw Randy dressed as a tree or slouched over in the assembly hall many times. As a way of avoiding revealing my whereabouts, I told her I had overheard someone at work talking about his passing. She cried and cried and demanded I tell her if I feel anything but content with my life. She had gone on and on about attending his funeral, which of course she did this afternoon; black dress trousers, designer heels and a lacy handkerchief to match.

My mother mourns in style.

I love my mum, I really do. I know for a fact, however, that if I moved to West Town or lived as an Umbra in the Urb, I'd break her heart. It may actually stop carrying oxygen to her tissues and she may actually die. I can't be responsible for that.

• • •

It's Saturday.

Zebediah had called in the morning short of breath on his post-breakfast jog. It probably doesn't help that he takes cigarette breaks which, I've told him before, *is disgusting*. Anyway, he asked if I'd like to head to the Panic Room tonight and I agreed.

The Panic Room is a dance club in the Urb, not a bomb shelter, although you'd think the latter would be more enticing after last week's events. I haven't spoken to Zeb properly since it happened. Just an 'are you okay?' text once in a while, to which I replied 'alright'. There wasn't much else to say. I find in such situations that it's better to say less. When there's too many questions, it's better not to ask any. It's the first time Zebediah has asked me to a club and, frankly, it's the first time I've been to one. I've been to gigs. Really fucking good gigs with beer and sweaty people and music so loud you think your eardrums will pop, but there tends to be less dancing, intentional touching and awkward sexual tension.

I imagine there is awkward sexual tension. I mean, we're animals, it's sort of like a den for mating rituals.

I'm not sure what to wear. I'm not sure if I'll like the music or that I can stomach as much vodka as Zeb can; but I intend to try. I decide that attempting to look good should be the first step. Zeb always looks stunning, and I want to keep up with that so I don't look like a shaggy black dog trailing behind him. I get a haircut in the afternoon, and it's the first time I've not felt the tickle of my hair on my ears. My new look is short at the sides with thick, choppy layers on top. I don't often observe much that I particularly like about my appearance, but my new haircut emphasises a shadowy bone structure that I was not aware of. It verges on sallow, so I decide to eat a burger.

I have to admit, I look pretty hot.

SILENDA

I wear all black: jeans, boots and an open-collar satin shirt that feels heavenly against my skin. Everything emphasises just how pale I am. I think Zeb is about to have a field day with the vampire jokes. My silver jean-chain matches my long dangly earring that kind of makes me look like someone's butch aunt, but somehow that is definitely a good thing. When I'm leaving, my father is reading on the front porch. He looks me up and down.

'Where are you off too, then?' he says, looking surprised or something resembling pride, which is strange regarding my attire. I tell him I'm meeting a friend in the city for drinks, never mentioning Zeb. 'I don't like the way you express yourself, outwardly. You know, as a Lux at heart.' He's surprisingly gentle. 'However, you sure do look as handsome as I did when I was your age.' He laughs and, for a second, it's the most calm I've felt with my dad for a while. He tells me to enjoy myself, and I walk to the train station with a pang of guilt in my chest.

My father is nowhere near as unbearable as he can be with my Uncle Basil around, but nothing stings more than what feels like misplaced pride. I'm a liar. Not directly, I suppose. But living under his roof makes me a liar. *A total fucking liar.*

The sky is purple. The city lights come into view after a half-hour on the late train. It's verging on 11 o'clock. The sky in the Urb is never black; there's too much life in the artificial stars of distant windows, the traffic lights, the lampposts and the neon signs. There is nothing more beautiful than this. Nothing is static in the city. I enjoy the walk to meet Zeb in the centre. The rain is light and I don't mind because it is beautifuly illuminated in the yellow glow of the lampposts. It smells good on the pavements and is the perfect picture for the distant sounds of the bustling life that remains on the streets.

I see Zeb standing under the pink light of the Panic Room sign, smoking what doesn't smell like tobacco. He gasps at me when he sees me approaching. 'Holy Mother of Darkness, Horatio

Young, you're hot! Who knew?' Zeb laughs. He looks amazing in black leather and his wet-look black and purple hair. You have to put in an effort to go out with Zebediah, otherwise you'll spend the whole night feeling like a troll compared to him. He offers me a draw of his joint but I decline, unsure I'm willing to betray my inhibitions so early in the night. Perhaps part of me hopes that Astrid Turrow dances here on a Saturday night.

The club is lit by gold studs of light embedded in the walls. The floor and the bar are a dark chocolate oak and a lot classier than I had expected. Neon lights adorn the walls with names of cocktails, drugs and song lyrics. I have to admit there is something utterly hilarious, although worrying, about the word 'cocaine' being displayed in cursive blue neon. There is a strong smell of red wine. The dancefloor is hot and claustrophobic, the pumping blood of the dancers rushes and pulses around the room like ruby ethanol in a stemware glass. I put my lips to the rim of my drink and follow my friend to the centre of the floor.

Zebediah is a natural dancer. Everything about him screams sex. He's so fit, too. I swear he bathes in baby oil; there's no way anyone can sweat that prettily. I, however, am none of these things. I'm five vodka shots and two glasses of wine down before I can even bring myself to join him in the middle of the floor. There's lots of women and none of them are Astrid. A short girl with dark hair dances around Zeb and I immediately recognise her as Gia Lee, Zeb's fake prom date. She's really beautiful. Her skin has a gorgeously warm tone and she has the most captivating eyes. I think I could kiss her, but I'm not good at committing to the decisions I make and I don't want to lead her on.

She inches closer to me and touches my upper arm. Her hands are petite and make me look a lot more muscular than I truly am. Her hand travels to my wrist and then my fingers before she places my hand on her cheek, forcing me to kiss her, otherwise we'd be in a pretty awkward engagement. I lean in and enclose her lips with mine. Her mouth is hot and she tastes like cola. It happens so quickly, as most things do under the influence of spirits.

I'm surprised when she pulls away to look at Zeb instead of me. Zeb is drunk and laughing. 'I'm impressed, Zebediah,' she says, cackling. 'That's some tasty fresh meat.' This place is like a zoo. I laugh too because I'm suddenly convinced she was just playing around and doesn't expect me to spend any more time with her. I'm too nice to retreat from the situations I get myself into, so it's best not to get myself in them.

I have a lot more fun than I expected to. The vodka acts like WD-40; I'm a rusty old bike and it's loosening my chain. My head feels freer on my neck, my eyeballs feel...*warm*? I've never been this intoxicated before. I like it. I'm good at acting sober when I'm drunk. So, when 4 o'clock comes and Zeb and Gia are danced out, I make a good argument for getting myself home. They're heading back to West Town and I really don't feel like intruding upon anything. Zeb has made it as good as obvious he doesn't want me there. I won't take advantage of his drunk leniency.

The rain is heavier when I leave the club. It feels cold on my skin and, after an encounter with so many sweaty bodies, I'm entirely comfortable with it. The streets are dark and isolated and I am at one with the quiet and the icy air.

Lightning breaks the sky.

I'm staring down St. Vincent Street in the direction the flash originated.

It flashes again.

I've only seen lightning once before, but there's something unnatural about it. It's so low. It's not as high in the sky as I had imagined. I picture it starting a fire in the street.

It flashes again in the same spot.

Lightning never strikes the same place twice.

It's one of those things that I've heard and can't remember where, but I know it to be true.

Three times in the same place.

It's probably the vodka and this new existential need of mine to be anything but static, but I head down the pile of rubble that remains of St. Vincent Street. Sometimes I hate the philosophical torment that I put myself through; it makes me impulsive in order to feel catharsis. It's bound to be my Shakespearean fatal flaw, my downfall, my hubris. I follow the lightning. I find the approximate spot that I'm sure it hit and find nothing – no sign that it was ever touched.

The street is narrow and dark. I look around for witnesses and see nothing. Hear nothing. The lightning strikes again. Right in front of my face. All I see is a flash of bright white light. I think I've gone blind, I think it's struck me.

I feel a sharp pain in my neck. I feel something cradling me. Perhaps I'm dead.

Everything goes black.

CHAPTER 6

BLUE SPHERE

Carson

The sound of the waterfall is almost overshadowed by the pelting of the rain on the pavements in West Town. The cold brick buildings smell fresh and somehow old. Bennet tells me that this particular area with the cobbled village, the student cabins, the waterfall encrusted mountains and the university, is called Bellumside. It's particularly gloomy, although this is supposedly a good thing. The rain offers a strange sort of psychological relief. The cold air allows the oxygen to feel so crisp that I imagine it has been imported from a place where no creature has ever breathed it.

I take it in for a while – Bellumside. Otherwise, I'd be forced to face the claustrophobia of the wooden cabin I woke in and the stares of its inhabitants so piercing I could feel every bone in my body grinding.

After Astrid Turrow had dropped my name from the heavens and straight into the fiery pits of hell where it burns now in my mind, she suggested that everyone get a decent night's sleep after the chaotic events of the day. Zebediah retreated hesitantly to his bedroom and a snarky Hayden rejected Astrid's advice, turning on the television and watching Centrum Tower burn to the ground on repeat on every news channel available. Astrid had simply shrugged him off and padded upstairs.

After a few rounds of the news and emotive rhetoric that did not seem to elicit even a frown from Hayden, Bennet insisted I follow him to the couch where I should sleep for the night. The layout of the cabin and the gaped wooden stairs that stretched to a second floor suggested that there should be more bedrooms, but I was far too mentally drained to challenge him. Bennet fetched me a thick throw blanket and a box of tissues for my remaining tears and plodded upstairs, whispering to Hayden to keep his eye on me and making sure to lock the front door of the cabin securely and check it – *twice*.

It wasn't long before Hayden fell asleep softly in his chair, a large sub-sandwich in his hands and the television still humming quietly about the Urb's 'devastation'. It seems apparent that Bennet and his friends are not entirely distressed by the city bomb, despite the Urb's history of 100 years terrorism-free. Perhaps it's that the Lux tower does not affect their way of life as Umbras, although from watching them last night, it's somehow difficult to imagine that they were even surprised by the attack.

With the humming of the television helpful in covering the creaking of the floorboards, Hayden did not even flinch when I headed towards the open window. No one seemed to notice that it was open and, despite the hospitality of my hosts, I had no intention of continuing to cohabit with a crowd of strangers who had drugged me.

It's times like these that women like the statuesque Astrid Turrow cannot capture my jealousy because there is no way she would have fit through the little window.

But I sure as hell did.

I treaded softly from the couch and placed the thick throw beneath the window. I carried one of the wooden chairs and gently placed it upon the throw so it would not be audible against the creaky oak boards. I placed a pillow atop the chair to avoid the sound of my boots on the wood and, at an appropriate height to proceed, I pushed the window as far open as I could muster, held tightly to the sill and wriggled myself out of the cabin as smoothly and quietly as my core muscles would allow.

I was careful to roll to the ground gently, allowing my weight to transfer to my shoulders and thankful for the soft and silent grass beneath me. I tucked my hand back into the cabin to close the window over so that the wind would not wake Hayden.

It was a cool night, but the rain had come to a quiet halt and allowed my walk into the village to be a somewhat pleasant one. There seemed to be a chorus of wind chimes from shop windows and a small buzz of conversation through the fire-lit windows of pubs and homes alike. The cobbles sounded beneath my feet and the wind blew gently in my hair. I wasn't sure what I was looking for until I came across it – a small bed and breakfast above a rusty old pub.

My heart sank at the sudden notion of my penniless pockets, but I sprang into action at the thought that perhaps I had tucked some cash away in the worn sole of my boot; something I would often do on my runs in case I became hungry or lost. Rightly so, I found a stash of at least 50 pounds worth of notes tucked discreetly between the folds of brown leather.

At my triumph, I expected to walk straight through the black door of the B&B, but instead I found myself sitting outside on the rain-soaked pub stools below, tired and deflated.

I'm not sure why, but I had been particularly conscious of my tongue, like it was a big swelling mass that did nothing but block my airways. I imagined what it would be like to not have a tongue at all, until this thought had me choking on my own breath.

I'm used to running – running not to think. The hazardous and chaotic events of the last couple of days should really have ignited a fire within me, a Hollywood-style opportunity to recover my past and extract knowledge from those who once knew me. I looked up at the windows of the B&B, staring at the warm amber glow from within and imagined myself sprawled on a dusty old bed and hatching a plan, or at least debating my next move. But instead, I was sitting in the rain debating the position of my tongue in my mouth. I took one final and longing glance at the warm and welcoming glow from the window, considering again the paper notes of cash in my hand, until my legs surely, yet regrettably, carried me down the street. Leaving the cabin had been an error, a frightful and impulsive error.

Any information I had hoped to find, could in fact, only be found there. Staring at billboards of Astrid Turrow in the Urb or thinking about the feeling of Bennet's eyes burning my cheeks could never reveal anything I desired to know.

However, I needed to form a plan. It didn't take long to come up with my next move. My options were limited, my mind jumbled and my heart ready to go home to a building that had been scattered across the street it once stood on.

I jogged back to the cabin window and used every ounce of strength I had remaining to pull myself back through it. Feeling like an idiot after a pointless journey, I imagined that my 10 minutes in the rain allowed for some clarity of mind. This is up for debate, however, as I found myself tiptoeing to the kitchen and grabbing the bread knife that Hayden had used to make a sub sandwich.

I snuck upstairs like a silent assassin, pushing open creaky wooden doors as I eased through the narrow corridor. A sleeping Astrid looked unapproachable even when dreaming. Zebediah was missing and Bennet was tucked under his duvet, lying straight and still on his back like a vampire in a coffin.

It's hard to justify my actions through anything but adrenaline and fear, but I held the bread knife to his throat and used my other hand to shake him awake. As his eyes widened in shock,

SILENDA

I snapped my petite hand over his mouth and demanded in a loud whisper that he should follow me downstairs and onto the lawn outside. He managed to keep a somewhat cool exterior. I suppose his eyes had widened to a cartoon size at his first realisation of the knife, but as soon as I grabbed his arm and dragged him through the cabin, he began to accept his fate. I don't think I had imagined him looking bored, either.

I threw him in front of my vision on the front lawn. He had obviously given into this as the height he had against me did not permit for any aggressive strength on my part. I was suddenly taken back to the night on the bridge; the two of us stood a metre or two apart, staring at each other in silence. This time, Bennet looked a lot more tired and I'm sure I looked a lot more crazy.

I couldn't continue to be passive. I couldn't be the one who needed saving or the one who ran away. I needed to make my anger with him known.

Bennet's tired expression evolved eventually into exasperation at my silence and I quickly realised that the bread knife lay casually in my hand. I pointed it upwards again and he did not flinch. Probably because I'd have to be a pretty good throw from this distance to even graze him.

It would have been a real shame to have killed him, too. What, with his abdomen exposed, his bedhead hair and his eyelids slightly swollen from sleep. He sighed.

'Your hair was pink,' I said. 'Yesterday, or this morning – whenever that was.' I wasn't entirely sure how much time had passed since he had drugged me in his bathroom.

'You brought me out here in the middle of the night to ask me about my hair?' he said, deadpan. Bennet is completely punchable.

'Well, no, obviously not...' I began, knife shaking at my attempt to be assertive. 'It's just a little odd, or a little *sociopathic*, actually, to colour your hair while the drugged girl in your sitting room is still out!' Bennet looked tense, like his intestines were tying themselves in knots. 'Do we have to talk about this right here?' he snapped in an urgent whisper.

'Who the hell would even hear us?' I attempted a timid step towards him, using all my courage to look as threatening as possible. It seemed to be somewhat successful as his hands rose up in front of him like a wall of protection as he gingerly stepped back.

'It was just something that Zebediah and I were trying out, alright?' Bennet began. 'Zebediah is the guy with the purple hair.'

'I know,' I say.

He lowered his voice so that it was hardly audible and carefully assessed his surroundings. 'It was a rebellious thing, I suppose. A bit stupid, really,' he continued. 'It's a fucked up system.'

'What is?' I pressed, edging closer and forgetting the horizontality of my blade.

'You know, the Luxies and the Umbras. If you're aware of your own feeble human stupidity and the inevitability of the unknown, you're cast off to the Rowleys and treated like shit.' He couldn't look at me when he said it. I hadn't done much thinking about these things since the Awakening. I suppose I had been too consumed with my own mystery.

It came out before I really understood it myself: 'I don't think it's really about knowing,' I began. 'It's about where to direct your faith. Everybody has faith, it's just about knowing where to put it.' I was shivering in the grey wind as Bennet considered this.

'Do you know where faith comes from, Carson?' My name sounded naturally from his lips. I shook my head. Bennet's eyes were pouring into my being when he spoke. 'Faith is our innate human reaction to fear. Our only purpose here is to survive, repopulate and die. Nature needs us here so we trick ourselves into believing we're important or that we go somewhere after this whole thing so that we stick around until our time expires.'

I tried to keep track of his words, looking at the knife and then to his face, trying to understand if this had anything to do with me.

SILENDA

'So, you're an Umbra? I mean, that's what Umbras believe, right?' I rushed him, eager to ask more personal questions.

'I'm clever enough to know that I'm stupid,' Bennet said, exhaling, and I was becoming impatient. He must have observed this. 'Hear me out!' he continued, backing further away. 'I know that there is no way on earth that I could thoroughly prove that what I just said is correct. We live on a big fucking rock that floats. A blue sphere. Who can really say anything for sure? If you kill me right now and I rock up at some sort of after-world and a god, or 72 gods, are willing to greet me, I'll be happy to see them!' I tried hard not to smile, directing my glare at his forehead, struggling hard to look him steadily in the eye.

'I understand,' I finally say. 'But why did you have pink hair?'

'Right,' Bennet looks lost for a second. 'I'm not an Umbra. I was brought up to be one and I like it here. I'm not a Lux either. I don't know what I am and that's okay, I think. Zebediah feels the same. We thought that if we dyed our hair a vibrant colour and lived in West Town, that we'd be making some sort of statement.' I was met with a sort of weightlessness at the notion of something finally making sense to me. Bennet's confession felt like stumbling across a peaceful and silent river in the chaotic jungle of my mind. There were still plenty of vicious vines and thick thorns to slice through with naught but a bread knife, but untangling anything felt like a decent start.

Bennet had been waiting for me to say something, to pressure him further, and in my right mind I would have held that knife up to him until the early hours of the morning. But soon the peaceful lake had evolved into a tsunami of new information that had my mind violently washing up on the shore of the unknown.

I desperately needed to sit down.

I felt the damp grass beneath me before I had even decided to sit, the knife falling limply at my side. Bennet was quick to rush to pick it up and for a split second I was sure I had orchestrated my own end, until he buried it in a plant pot at the front door and encouraged me to take his hand. With few other options, I accepted.

Bennet snuck back into the cabin and pulled on some old trainers and an oversized hoodie and insisted I walk with him for a while as he talked briefly about the raw benefits of fresh air. He told me about Bellumside and how he was sure the air was the freshest here far outside of the city and, eventually, after some rocky expanses, we were met with the most breath-taking view I have ever encountered.

• • •

The waterfall screams loudly into what feels like an endless chasm of rich green hills and meadows. The water reflects the grey sky and rushes beautifully to encase the rocks below. We sit side by side at the top of a rocky cliff that looks precariously over the flowing water.

Bennet glows so elegantly against the wash of the sky, but I try hard not to think about it. He does not touch me where he sits. He is close enough to hear me, but not so close that he should worry I will push him. We may have exceeded that phase of our encounter, anyway.

I say encounter as to not further complicate the bubbling tension between us that has, in the two or more days we have been acquainted, threatened to spill, spit or explode completely, scalding us both in the process.

It's a somewhat comfortable silence, despite my curiosity as to why he has brought me here in the first place. With so many pressing issues, I decide to start with an especially urgent one. 'None of you seemed to care about the tower,' I say.

There's a pause.

'Centrum Tower?' Bennet asks, matter-of-factly, and his need for specificity feels like the epitome of my concerns. I nod quickly. 'What makes you think we don't care?'

'Well, Hayden was watching the news channel last night and didn't seem to react at all to the devastation. I mean, there were fires, bodies. The whole street was practically wiped out and none of you seemed particularly affected,' I voice my suspicions as carefully as I am able.

'First of all, Hayden has no soul. He's pretty evil,' Bennet says. 'Evil, how?'

'Just really entitled, I suppose. He's the mayor's nephew. His own father is a pretty regular guy, but Hayden grew up like Astrid Turrow's brother because his father didn't want him involved in his dodgy dealings, or his drunkenness. He works in the black market. Doesn't have to, but Jason and Tyson grew up rough, and Jason likes his people. Anyway, Astrid and Hayden have never had to go without. It makes Astrid full-on, but it makes Hayden bitter.' This dynamic is easy to imagine as Bennet voices it above the sound of rushing water.

'What about the rest of you?'

'We tend to be in the know, being so close to the mayor. His mansion is within walking distance and we're best friends with his daughter. We tend to hear about these kinds of threats before they even happen.'

'Then why didn't you stop it?'

'Because we thought it was going to be an Umbra-targeted attack. The mayor had security all over Umbra centres in the Urb. Even the Grand Library which is open to everyone. We were prepared. We were just the wrong people to be prepared.'

'How did you even hear about an attack in the first place?'

'Everyone's got to have an inside man. Tyson and Mayor Young had a meeting a week back that didn't go particularly smoothly. Tyson wants more integration and Young perceived it as a threat. Some kind of overthrow, I think. Anyway, our insider, who I don't even know, heard Young chatting with his superior, Lucian

Fletcher, about a future terrorist attack. After the meeting went so bad, Tyson took precautions and we assumed that the Luxies had it in for us. Turns out, they were concerned about an attack on themselves.'

I nod in understanding, trying hard to retain all the information I can manage. 'So, although it sounds bad, it was a relief I suppose that it wasn't your people that were targeted?'

'Unfortunately, yes.'

'Why do you, a music student, have access to this information?' I demand.

'A good leader has men everywhere.' Bennet leaves his words hanging for a while before he continues. 'Whoever planted the bomb, they have nothing to do with Tyson. But it's safe to say that it's not making any of us in West Town look very good.'

There's a long pause as I chew on this for a while, trying desperately to keep up. I hadn't really thought about the implications of a terrorist attack in the city until now. A Lux-targeted attack could only really mean one thing. Some Umbras have it out for the Lux community and Bennet is right, an attack a week after Turrow's proposal for community integration was rejected by Young, does not look good.

I listen to the rush of the waterfall while Bennet assures me that once we get some sleep, Astrid will take me into the city to answer some more of my questions. I nod slowly until I fill another pause. 'You never told me why you got rid of your pink hair.'

He breathes deeply before he speaks. 'I was hoping you'd remember me this way.'

CHAPTER 7

THE GLASS CITY

Carson

The city has a heart. Astrid supposes this is the centre of it.

The limousine stops and starts, following the sea of steel and rubber that crests like a wave when the green man says GO. The interior is black. Black leather that creases and strains uncomfortably under the denim on my thighs and blacked out windows that make it far less achievable to avoid her eyes. I strain through the dimmed windows and make out the scattering of shadowy figures holding cups of coffee and shouting into the middle of the street, hoping to dive into a taxi and sail turbulently into the tsunami of traffic.

I try not to watch her.

She hasn't said much since she forced me into the long limousine in West Town after Bennet and I had returned from the waterfall. I imagine she is not the sort of figure who catches the train. Her long legs seem endless as she stretches them out in the leather seat opposite me. She sits like a man. I suppose it is not particularly forward thinking to observe that anyone 'sits like a man', but she takes up as much room on the long chair as she can with her thin frame. There's a dominance in it.

She lit a cigarette a few blocks back. She had assured me she would not usually smoke anything that isn't herbal, but she intends to ease her mind rather than get high. Despite her lack of words on the journey, it is easy to suppose that Astrid is a very full-on sort of person. She is intimidating in the way that she over-shares and in the way that she seems to feel obligated to justify herself. It's this sort of discourse that makes it hard for a person to reply. It is unavoidable to make judgements when responding to that sort of thing. I decide to smile instead.

She takes a few more drags, puffing smoke into the air and lazily watching it diffuse around her. She rubs her forehead against the back of her hand and I worry she will set her long locks on fire. Her heavy brow and hooded eyes look puffy like she has been crying or deprived her body of much needed rest. Her baggy shirt is tucked into a pair of vinyl trousers that cling tightly to her shapely thighs. She is the sort of girl that makes a baggy shirt look suitable for the cover of *Vogue*.

I try to feel jealous of her beauty, but it's far easier to fall in love with her than envy her, especially in the way that she doesn't seem overly invested in her own appearance. However, it should also be said that she isn't the sort of woman to deny her good looks.

It's easy to become infatuated with her aura. Already in two hours of her company, I am too distracted by her presence to even question where we are going, why she knows my name and the other peculiar events of last night.

Astrid puts out her cigarette in the discarded cap of her empty coffee cup. She stabs her thumb into the stereo embedded in the canvas roof of the limousine and blasts Diana Ross. She crosses her legs, running her pretty white hands through her blonde hair and mouthing the words to *Upside Down* along to the groove of the guitar riff. She's dancing now, flailing her lanky arms around and laughing her head off. I start to think she may be crazy. She grabs my pink hands and forces me to dance along with her. I can't help but laugh too despite the rising fear in the pit of my stomach. She asks me if I've seen *Dirty Dancing* among other irrelevant questions.

She sings a little more, this time to Carly Simon, before she abruptly stops the stereo. It feels colder now. Her asymmetrical eyes turn towards mine. She squints a little, looks me up and down and tilts her head.

I feel obliged to speak. 'You're a little erratic.' I don't mean to say it. I should have asked where we were going or what was going on – the important questions. The observation just sort of comes out.

She laughs suddenly, her cheeks deflating and her eyebrows sunken. 'You're right,' she says, sighing. 'I'm no good at this sort of thing. Wouldn't you rather dance than talk about, you know, *the situation*?'

'It would be nice to know what the hell is going on,' I snap a little, at my wits end with these strange people from West Town.

'It's a bit of a long story. I fear for the lasting effects on your mental state if I tell you.' She looks suddenly hot and anxious. 'My father would kill me.'

All this talk about Mayor Turrow's concern weighs heavy on my conscience and I wonder what on earth I could have done to be on his.

Astrid turns to make sure the limousine driver is not listening through the tinted glass divide that separates us. She breathes deeply and begins, 'The guys in the cabin are students at West Town University. The cabins are relatively new student accommodation. They're supposed to add to the woodland aesthetic of the school. It's worlds apart from the Urb, right?' She's right about that. 'Well,' Astrid continues, 'let me tell you about my cabin mates. Zebediah majors in law. He can talk the absolute ass off you, and he's manipulative as fuck. Super nice though, super sexy. You'll like him a lot.' *Right*, I think, *bathtub guy*.

She clears her throat and sits on the edge of her seat. 'Then there's Hayden. He's a computer science major. He's kind of mean, but he's my cousin so I've got to love him. Just don't take anything he says to heart. I reckon he has shit he's suppressing.' I try not to take him purchasing me as a 'birthday present', whatever that means, to heart. It seems somewhat impossible.

Astrid rambles on again. She talks quickly. Erratic is right. 'Then there's me. Fashion graduate, but I like to think I have other assets.' *You must,* I think, as we drive past a billboard with her face plastered on it. 'We all share the cabin when I'm not at my place in the city. That's where we're headed right now.'

I wonder why she doesn't mention Bennet. 'Um, what about Bennet?' I ask. She looks confused for a moment.

'*Who?* Oh, Hawk? He's a music tech major. He changed his name recently for stupid reasons. I try to ignore it.' I nod, trying not to show too much interest in him for reasons I can't really explain. She doesn't seem to want to say much more about him, anyway. 'We are a sort of community, you could say. We call it the Nether Cabin. I'm not sure why. I think it was Hayden's idea and we tend not to argue with him.'

Astrid plays with a large ring on her finger, she seems unable to sit still. 'We have a new guy moving in soon, not sure who. Not heard anything about him, but he's registered for arrival tomorrow. The Nether Cabin is a lot bigger than it looks so it should be comfortable.' I wonder why she is telling me all of this.

I hope this is going somewhere. I hope she is setting the scene for the answers I so desire. 'Anyway,' she proceeds, skittishly. 'I suppose you could say the Nether Cabin is somewhat politically active.' I'm too frightened to pressure her for more when she pauses. 'I'd like to elaborate, Carson. I really would. I just don't think that I'm equipped to tell you the next part. But please don't worry, I'm taking you to someone who can.'

SILENDA

•••

The limousine pulls up outside the most fantastic building I have seen in the Urb. I've never been to this part of the city on my runs. I suppose this must be where the elite settle. The glass structure scrapes the sky with gold rimmed windows and all sorts of neon lights emitting into the dusky and darkening afternoon sky.

Astrid slides gracefully out of the backseat, dragging me along behind her. She swings her expensive black leather bag over her shoulder and walks expertly towards the glass doors in her skinny black heels.

'I'm in the penthouse,' she says. 'It's a quick elevator ride, don't worry.'

She's right. The elevator in the core of the building is like an enormous glass chimney and soars up through the floors like it will never halt. When the elevator stops abruptly, we step out into a huge open-plan apartment with an uninterrupted glass window that has an astonishing view of the city. The bridge I love to run across is nothing but a dot in the distance.

Astrid's dining table is of long black glass with contemporary and peculiarly shaped green and purple chairs. Her angular sofa is sunken into a square pit in the floor. She tosses her handbag into it. The ceiling is so high up that the grand chandelier twinkles like the brightest star in the sky.

Everywhere I look there is a bowl of fruit and a bottle of wine. 'Eydis!' Astrid yells loudly as she pours herself a glass of red. She gestures the bottle towards me, raising her eyebrows. I shake my head. She takes a large gulp, grimaces a little and pours the rest down the sink. I think she must see that I look quizzical when she says, 'It's for the nerves. I'm actually not that much of a drinker, but red makes anyone look sophisticated.'

She strides through the kitchen and into the lounge, pushing open a set of large double doors to reveal a large bed chamber with thick golden sheets, cream marble pillars and an astonishingly abundant collection of high heel shoes which are arranged neatly on a tall case of shelves that stretch up the wall.

The room is far too organised to be Astrid's.

I realise that I had been unaware of my own presence. I'm peering over Astrid's shoulder and following her swiftly around the room like her shadow. 'Eydis!' she calls again, only this time into an equally grand bedroom with periwinkle satin sheets sprawled unceremoniously over the bed. Astrid lets out an enormous sigh, runs her hands through her hair in frustration and begins to curse, 'Shit, shit, shit, shit, shit!' her tone is shriller with every profanity. 'She's gone to the safehouse,' she cries, 'the bloody safehouse!'

'The safehouse?' I inquire, becoming increasingly anxious.

'Yes, the safehouse, Cara!' She's yelling at me. 'Oh, right, sorry, I forgot. You don't know me, and you don't know the shit that we're in. *You don't know the shit that we're in!*'

'Then tell me, Astrid!' I yell. 'Tell me what the fuck is going on! Tell me why I'm in a crazy supermodel's apartment, tell me why a purple-haired dude yelling in a bathtub is the last thing I remember before passing out. Tell me why my apartment crumbled to the ground and why I can't remember anything except my own fucking name and tell me why everyone keeps bringing up the freaking mayor of Weird Town!'

Astrid looks startled.

I straighten my jumper and mop my brow with my sleeve, in an attempt to compose myself. 'And who the hell is Eydis?'

'Uh, Eydis is my roommate,' she squeaks. 'Who keeps bringing up my father? Is it Hayden? If it's Hayden, I swear—'

'Astrid!' I'm trying to pressure her into talking but she stands almost a foot taller than me in her heels so I move over to the stools by the kitchen island and hope she follows me.

We settle on the mauve stools and Astrid pours more wine, this time with a glass for me that she does not offer but instead places under my nose with a striking and unreadable look in her ambiguous eyes.

'The guys in the cabin,' she starts, 'they have a theory.'

'A theory?' I lean closer.

'There's this...organisation.' She coughs. 'Silenda they call it. There's been disappearances all over the city. They're taking people off the streets, abducting them, running experiments... '

'What kind of experiments?'

'To find the truth.'

'What truth?'

'The truth of what happens after we, you know...' she begins to visibly sweat, *'die.'*

My heart thumps in my chest so fast and radiates an anxiety so intense that I'm sure Astrid can feel it on her skin.

She continues, 'Rumour has it that they bring their subjects to the brink of death. Well, no, they *actually kill them*. Then they bring them back. All the while running experiments on their brainwaves to try and evaluate what they saw or where they went.'

Fuck.

'Okay, so what does this have to do with the students in the cabin?'

'Well, we're trying to stop them, aren't we? We've been honing our skills, scheming, planning, trying to work out how to fight back. The only problem is that we don't know where they're based and, after the fall of Centrum Tower, we suspect it could have something to do with them.'

I steady my breathing, trying to stay calm. I steady my heart like I'm running across the bridge. 'If you don't know where they are, then how do you know they exist?'

'We didn't know. Jason did. You did.'

Fuck.

'*What?*' I can't even begin to say anything else. I wish I was running. *I wish I was running.* I take a large sip of the wine in front of me.

Astrid rests her hand reassuringly on my thigh. 'Cara, I need you to stay calm when I tell you what I'm about to tell you. I was going to leave it to Eydis to tell you because she is a lot clearer on the issue than I am and she's really much better with her words. But I realise the anticipation is killing you.'

We both breathe.

Astrid squeezes my leg. 'They took you,' she says. 'You went missing. Hawk and Zeb found you stumbling around the Urb dazed and confused the next day, you couldn't remember who you were, where you had been. We tried to bring you back round, but you were so distressed. You wouldn't talk, you wouldn't eat. It was tearing us all apart. A few weeks in, Hayden found your diary. You'd been tracking Silenda for weeks and using the walls of your bathroom to pin locations and people you suspected of being in the know.'

Astrid takes another long swig of wine. She takes a pack of cigarettes from the pocket of her leather skirt and a lighter from her heeled leather boot. It's difficult to explain why I care but I take the lighter from her and lower her cigarette. She smiles, wryly. 'You're right. First cigarette I've had in four years was in the back of that taxi. Wouldn't want to have to get Botox for wrinkles around my mouth.'

'What happened after you found the diary?' I press, eager not to lose her wavering attention.

'We checked all of the pinned locations and we stalked and interrogated every name, but they were all dead ends.'

Another sip of wine.

I consider this for a while, pulling some grapes from the glass fruit bowl on the kitchen island. I hadn't realised how hungry I was. I bite into an apple too. The loud crunch fills the silence between us. Astrid's eyes skit about the room, and before she can finish yelling at her Bluetooth radio to play some ABBA, I stop her. 'Why can't I remember the boys finding me?'

Another sip of wine. She sighs. 'Like I said, we'd been trying to bring you round for weeks. You wouldn't eat. You just cried and yelled out nonsense we couldn't make sense of. It was scary. You nearly gave Hawk a nervous breakdown. He was your best friend.' The mystery of the candy-floss boy is solved. Somehow I don't feel much better. She continues. 'We didn't have a choice. We thought you were going to drive yourself mad! So we called in my father.'

'The mayor?'

'The mayor. Who, believe it or not, is rather fond of you.'

It seems suddenly an urgent matter to ask about my parents, 'Where are my parents, Astrid?'

'They're alright, don't worry. They supported every decision my father made for you. They didn't have a choice. I mean, a lot of dogs get put down by loving owners.' She sips more wine as my liking for her is supported only by the notion that she means well. 'Hayden wiped your memories again. This time, wiping whatever it was you could remember from your abduction, whatever was killing you slowly. My father found you an apartment close to Tam's store because he is a friend of your father's. He kept your parents posted when it was too painful for them to see you. My father would watch you on your runs and leave money in your apartment.'

Astrid reveals this so casually, as if my whole conscious eternity hadn't been solely relying on the man in the square who watched me run. I always suspected him. It was easier on the cold nights to reassure myself that he was my protector rather than my stalker. Never for a second had I supposed he was the mayor of the Umbras.

I was wrong about him in one sense. I thought I had seen the colour in him. The bright ambiguous beauty of uncertainty. I felt it in my pores as the wind hit my skin. I felt it in my hair as it flew back behind me, in the deepest pit of my stomach where I felt the constant ache of fear. Most importantly, I felt it in my mind; the relief of admitting to myself that I knew absolutely nothing and I never would. Perhaps it had been the isolation that had conceived the idea that he could feel it too.

'So, you're telling me that my friends, my parents and the mayor of the Umbras sent me away to be alone and confused so that I didn't compromise the mental health of the people around me?'

I'm yelling again.

It's bubbling. The anger, the pain, the fear – everything I had to run not to feel. Everything has felt numb: the taxi ride, Bennet's apartment, Centrum Tower. I had been going through the motions.

Left, right, breathe. Left, right, breathe.

'You were going to leave me that way forever? Why did Bennet come and find me, Astrid?' I jump out of my seat, which soon proves a mistake as Astrid towers above me like a fair-faced Gothic sculpture.

'Carson, remember that I am your friend. I love you. We didn't have a choice!'

'Why did Bennet come and find me?' I ask again.

'We decided not to tell Hawk where you were placed.'

'*Placed*?' I'm crying now. Fiery fucking icicles. Astrid composes herself, hands in the air in the surrender, as if her admission of regret makes it all okay. 'How could you? How could my parents? The mayor?'

'We didn't feel like we had a choice, Carson. We'd rather you were lost and happy. My dad left you the note so you would know someone had your back. It was better than watching you deteriorate. It was a hard decision, I promise you!'

Astrid is crying too. Icy fucking flames.

'You gave up on me!' I know that I'm burned with tears now. My face is as red as my auburn hair. 'Why didn't you tell Ben – Hawk?' I correct myself.

'He wanted to keep trying with you, he was determined that he could bring you back around, but it had been weeks.' She's panicking now. 'He was out-voted. We knew if we told him where you were that he'd just bring you back. It seems that he had recruited Hayden and persuaded him to tell him your location so he could bring you home.'

'He was the only one who cared!' My voice breaks like weak glass.

'No, Carson. We all cared, we thought we were doing what was best. Hawk just deals with things differently than the rest of us.'

I'm panicking. My eyes dart crazily around the room, searching for a way to abandon this moment, to jump ship and swim to shore where the sand is warm and the hot sun can dry my tears.

Suddenly, I'm wondering about Eydis. Eydis, the safehouse and why Astrid had been so determined for her to break the news. 'What about Eydis?' I try to elaborate but I'm not sure what I'm even asking.

'I haven't seen her since the bombing,' Astrid states. 'She's been seriously paranoid about Silenda. She thinks it was an act of terrorism on their part and she's concerned that it won't be an isolated incident. The safehouse is at the edge of West Town in the woods. Impossible to find unless you're looking for it.'

'Why did you want Eydis to tell me this, Astrid?'

Astrid chews on her thoughts for a minute before she replies. 'She's been in talks with Hayden for a while. She's a neuroscience graduate and she thinks that she can bring your memories back. It was supposed to be a gift to Hawk. That's why Hayden and Zebediah have been arguing in the cabin. Zeb thinks it's too much of a risk to your life. You know in case it, uh, fucks you up.'

'*My life?*' The fire in me is burning out to nothing but a pile of ashes which tickle my lungs and leave me choking for air.

Suddenly I feel far more alone than I had in the four walls of my St. Vincent Street apartment. When those walls crumbled to the ground, it seems that mine did too. The room is moving. I am moving. I chug the remainder of my wine, wipe my mouth with my sleeve and head for the door. I hear Astrid screaming after me, but her words are contorted with the persistent ringing in my ears.

I avoid the elevator and somehow find a majestic flight of marble stairs that I descend in what feels like a lifetime but was likely minutes. I have no idea where I am. The traffic lights gleam in the gloomy darkening sky and I follow the forest of glass wherever my legs take me.

For the first time, I am sure I am running to something and not away from it.

CHAPTER 8

THE RECRUITMENT

Horatio

It seems that nothing ever stands still.

Nothing ever stands still – *except me*. I never change. I pretend things aren't happening because it slows them down. I run away when things get too tough so I can clear my mind in place of addressing my issues.

I have a fear of being static because that's all I ever have been. And I hate it.

Perhaps it's for the best that I've ended up here.

There haven't been many moments in my 20 years on earth that I've felt anything but ordinary, but this moment makes the cut. It must have been a few hours at least that I've been tied to this chair, milky-white wrists strapped down firmly to the steely arms of the metal seat beneath me. My hair falls forward into my eyes. I try desperately to blow the hair from them to no avail. The laces of my black boots have been untied and expertly wrapped around the legs of my chair. The room is dark and smells like iron, gas and coffee. The weak flickering lights in the ceiling above flash a dull, industrial green and allow for my attention to be drawn solely to the small black camera in the corner of the room, pointing down towards me, red light on. I suppose someone is laughing at me trying to fix my hair with no available hands. Most likely whoever smells like coffee.

If I were a murderer, as I'm assuming whoever has abducted me most likely is, I would definitely have duct-taped my mouth by now. I mean, sure, I can't move, but they must be tired of me yelling at them.

My throat aches, my eyes are itchy and I feel like I'm going to throw up with the amount of vodka still swimming around in my system. There is, for sure, only so much yelling a person can do before they begin to feel it pointless. So, taking some time to question my existence, fears and pace of events over the last few days feels like a good enough use of my time.

I think a lot about Gia, too, about the feverish way that she kissed me. I suppose that's part of the reason I didn't go back to West Town with Zeb. I didn't want Gia to make any drunken moves on me that I would be obliged to reject. It's seeming like a beautiful girl making moves on me all night is a far better option than this – *Goddammit, Horatio.*

I'm laughing before I can stop myself. Hysterically terrified and completely and utterly drunk – not exactly a winning combination. 'Hey!' I yell, trying to catch my breath from giggling, 'got any music? I didn't get all dressed up for no music!' My hysteria is met with the industrial buzz of the ceiling lights. I continue, mostly to humour myself. 'And if you're going to kill me, can you at least fix my hair? I'd like to be a pretty corpse!'

Silence.

It's not for another hour or so, and an agonisingly intoxicated rendition of *Believe* by Cher, courtesy of moi, that the reality of my situation begins to kick in. Sobriety sneaks up on me like a hooded figure with a gun: unexpected and completely unwelcome. I sit up straight as my stomach churns, swallowing thickly as a desperate attempt to keep the contents of my guts exactly where they are.

I look around the room. Large steel walls encase me. I try to use my core muscles to turn my chair, but when I almost topple over on my first attempt, I find it to be more advantageous to turn my head as far around as I can. The room is empty and vast like a small, sheltered car park. There are a few pipes running up the sides of the walls and one that appears to be leaking. It's clear that wherever I am, it's been retired from whatever it was built for. It dawns on me for a second that the room appears very similar to the warehouse from which Zebediah picked up the Super Sounder headphones for his friend. The tin-can style of the building makes me wonder if I'm in the Rowleys.

There's a door on the left-hand side of the building. I try again to manoeuvre my chair with all the strength I can muster. With a clatter, I find myself nose to the concrete flooring. I taste blood. I wish that I were cool and calculating, at least fit like a ninja, but it soon sinks in that I may just die on the concrete floor before my kidnapper even returns.

It's a long time before I can find the motivation, or energy, to try again.

I try to wiggle my feet out of my boots, but they've been tied far too tight. I try to waggle my hands from under the tight leather bonds that strap them down, but my skin begins to burn against the fabric. I scream, 'Help!' and other pleadings. As expected, nobody comes to my aid.

Just as I'm about to succumb to my drooping eyelids and heavily falling chest, the door at the left of the room swings open, revealing a smallish looking young man in a dusty blue suit who strides in and looks upon me fondly, as if I had been awaiting his arrival.

'Horatio!' he says, white teeth gleaming. 'Should we get down to business, then? Follow me!' The man chuckles at my inability to get up from the floor, clearly amused with himself. As he comes closer,

I notice he is a lot younger than he had initially appeared, with sandy blonde hair, bright green eyes and a pale, pinkish complexion. When he notices I am not laughing with him, he kneels to untie my shoelaces and release my wrists from their leather bonds. He takes my hand softly and pulls me off the ground.

I evaluate his physique as I decide whether or not he'll be able to catch me when I run. He is really very short. He must see in my eyes that I'm ready to sprint for the door as he grips my upper arm firmly, a chaotic grin twisting his features.

His grip is frighteningly strong despite his stature and despite my advantage of height. I decide I should listen closely to what he has to say. 'Lucian Fletcher.' He releases his grip and stretches out a veiny hand for me to shake. I reluctantly accept, waiting for him to continue. 'I'm the superior aid at the mayor's office. Soon to be running as deputy!' he says, confidently.

'Which mayor?' I ask. My voice comes out deep and hoarse.

'The one and only, Basilio Claudius Young.' He pauses. 'Follow me.' He doesn't give me much of a choice as he resumes his grip on my arm and ushers me strongly out the door of the tin-can building, which from the outside looks like an abandoned warehouse. It is immediately clear, as daylight pours into my vision, that we are indeed in the Rowleys. Outside, waiting for Lucian and me to emerge, are a long line of the mayor's officials, dressed in black battle fatigues, harbouring rifles and blank expressions. Lucian looks up at me, pleased as the assembly of men slap their guns into their opposite hands and hold them firmly by their sides.

My uncle stands beside them. He does not speak.

I fiddle with my dangly earring waiting to be beat up by the overwhelming stench of toxic virility. The assembly of men turn on their heels and walk synchronously forward through the worn-down buildings of the old industrial estate. Lucian gestures for me to follow, so I do, far too confused and far too curious to deny his request. After 10 minutes of marching and my awkward stumbling, we reach an even larger industrial warehouse. This one, however, appears to be in use. The soldiers remain outside. Lucian opens the metal door and we enter behind my uncle.

The room is brightly lit with numerous desks and chairs so that it appears like a pop-up office. It smells like coffee. My uncle stands by a water cooler. He speaks to me for the first time. He doesn't even turn around.

'Harry.' He fills a plastic cup with water. He hasn't called me Harry for a good few years. It's nostalgic hearing him say it.

'Uncle Basil,' I croak.

He turns around. 'What the hell are you wearing?' My uncle looks me up and down. He is wrapped characteristically in a dark blue suit with his dyed black hair combed back neatly.

'You kidnapped me on a night out. I was at a club.'

He pulls out a chair, straddles it backwards with a sigh. He gestures to the seat across from him. I walk towards it cautiously and sit. He takes a sip of water and lets out a delayed chuckle. 'I wouldn't say kidnapped, Horatio, would you?'

'There's an army outside.'

'They're only for our protection, son. This is the Rowleys, you know? The cast-offs are dangerous,' he says.

I sigh, dramatically. 'More dangerous than you? You tied me to a chair!' I'm not afraid to yell at my uncle. Nothing I haven't already tried at Sunday dinner.

'I had to make sure I could get you here swiftly. And keep you here. We had to wipe out the industrial estate of scoundrels and misfits before we could even think about having this conversation. You wouldn't have come to meet me at my request. It all had to be very discreet,' he says. Lucian nods in agreement.

'Wipe out?' I remember the firearms outside and shiver. My uncle shakes his head and refuses to comment. He pauses for a while, so I speak. 'You struck me with lightning.'

He laughs. 'I didn't. We drugged you.'

'I did!' Lucian speaks up, hand in the air with obedient enthusiasm. I look over at him tiredly.

My uncle smiles at Lucian and speaks again. 'Do you remember the lightning storm the year I took you and baby Angelo to the fireworks display in the Urb? We were at the top of Centrum Tower and you loved it up there! We sheltered under the balcony of my penthouse office. You loved the lightning, even more than the fireworks. It excited you.' He smiles at the thought. 'I had to get you down the alley by St. Vincent Street to pick you up discreetly. I knew you would follow the lightning, the idiot that you are!' I don't laugh with him.

'So you can control the weather now?' I ask.

'Lucian here created our very own lightning hologram. Now you can see lightning whenever you'd like.' Lucian laughs violently, hardly able to stay still as pride oozes from him.

How bizarre.

'So you kidnapped me because you wanted to show me some holographic lightning?'

My uncle looks bemused and slightly frustrated. 'Of course not.' He gets up from his chair and strides over to a mini-fridge. He pulls out two bottles of beer, cracks them open on the corner of one of the discarded tables. He sits back down, handing me a bottle. He sighs, and it's a good 30 seconds before he gathers the energy to speak. 'Horatio,' he says eventually, 'war is blooming.'

'What?' I had assumed all the speculations were hollow.

'Centrum Tower was bombed by the Umbras. Tyson Turrow can be held accountable.' He takes a sip.

'Terrorism?' I ask, on the edge of my seat.

He nods slowly.

'They're trying to wipe us out, Harry. Just like I said. Turrow is out to get us. There will be no Luxies left. It'll start with the mixed schools, which I have disagreed to, by the way. Integration will become degradation, invasion, *elimination*.' He leans closer. 'There's security all over the city now. There are rumours that the Grand Library is next.'

Not the library, I think. 'Shit!'

'I'm scared,' he says. 'It's my responsibility to protect us Luxies and I failed. All those lives lost in the tower. How can I know when they will strike again?'

I take a long swig from my bottle of beer, forgetting how sickly I feel from the night before. I think about Angelo in Centrum Park. What if he had decided to buy a bottle of water from the lobby vending machine? What if he had gone to the market down the street? He was so close. Regardless of how I feel about my uncle right now, I search for something to say to help him. 'How can I know?' he asks again.

'You need someone on the inside,' I say, 'to get close to Tyson. Couldn't you send Lucian to intern as Turrow's right-hand man?' Lucian frowns.

Basil pauses for a moment. 'Funny you should say that, Horatio. That's exactly why I brought *you* here.'

'Me? What am I going to do? I've got no political experience, how am I going to work for Tyson? I work in a... coffee shop!' I stop myself before I say record store.

'You don't need to get close to Tyson to get close to the problem, Horatio. We know about your friend. We've had an eye on him for a while now. We think he may have something to do with the bombing,' My heart stops. He can't be talking about Zebediah. *Not Zeb.*

'Uncle, I—'

'It's alright. You can count on me not to tell your parents. But you do owe me your help.' His tone is firm.

'Zebediah is not a terrorist, there's no way...' I think about the day of the bombing. The record store was closed. He took me to the Rowleys for a stupid birthday gift. What if he was trying to get me away because he knew the bombing was going to happen? I recall how relaxed he had been and it feels like I'm going to throw up.

I spring out of my chair and run for a small bin in the corner of the room and vomit out my feelings. My uncle silently sips his beer as I bring up my insides behind him. I compose myself and sit across from him again.

'I know it's a lot of information to take in, Harry. You need to try and stay calm.' My uncle stands and puts his hand on my shoulder.

'What does this have to do with me?' I finally say. 'If you're asking me to hurt Zeb, I won't do it—'

'No one is asking you to hurt anyone, Horatio. It's like you said, we just need an inside man.'

'Why me?' I plead.

'Because you'll be the most convincing,' Basil says simply. 'Look at Lucian.' I do. 'He'd stick out like a sore thumb. He's got Lighty written all over him.' Lucian takes this as a compliment and grins widely. I look at Lucian and his bright pink cheeks and clean-shaven face. He looks like a man who has his shit together. He looks like a man who doesn't believe life is nothing but the beginning of the end.

'The way you dress has always pissed off your father, and you know I'm not a fan, but right now, you're exactly what we need!' My uncle's eyes grow wild at the chance of finding the saviour of the Luxies. Somehow I don't feel qualified to be that person.

'What would you need me to do?' I look at him with what I'm sure are bloodshot eyes and a paler-than-usual face.

'You need to move to West Town. Pretend you're moving in on Umbra territory. You've changed your mind. You're one of them now. Keep close with Zebediah Hayes and his friends. There's a whole bunch of them. The mayor's daughter, too. They're up to something, I know it.'

'How do you know it?' I try to imagine my best friend and the city's most ubiquitous supermodel as a terrorist organisation, but there's a large part of my brain that just won't process it.

Lucian steps closer to us with a cocky grin. It seems he has been programmed by my uncle to smile uncontrollably. 'I stepped in,' he says and my uncle nods. 'I was at Mayor Turrow's mansion a couple of weeks ago passing on a message for your Uncle Basilio, when I saw young Miss Turrow talking feverishly with her cousin, Hayden Turrow, in the hallway. There were whispers about the bombing, and it sounded to me like they were frightened. Why should they be frightened? It was a Lux building that was targeted. Unless they were frightened of being caught.'

I'm in no position to mistrust Lucian, despite his crazy eyes. The horrors my uncle has prophesied are far too immense for me to have the time to speculate.

'So, what's the plan?' I ask and my uncle smiles.

'We tell your parents I've got you a scholarship at East Town University. You should visit them every so often so they don't have the desire to visit you on campus. I've already got you a scholarship at West Town, studying music technology.'

'So that's the part that's in it for me?' I actually smile. Suddenly this situation doesn't seem entirely bad.

'I thought that might persuade you,' he says. 'We have already provided you with student housing and you're scheduled for arrival tomorrow. You'll be staying in the cabin Zebediah has recently moved into.'

'Great.' *You know, apart from the fact that he may be a terrorist.*

'There are others who will be in the same accommodation as you. We're not sure if anyone outside the cabin will be involved, but that's for you to figure out and feed back to us. Hayden Turrow will be there and Miss Turrow, too. The mayor has been seen coming and going from this specific cabin to keep an eye on his daughter, so try to keep track of him too.'

'How will I feed back to you?' I ask.

'Take notes when you can, but of course be discreet. Listen in to conversations, get involved, make them trust you. It shouldn't be too hard when they see how fond Zeb is of you.'

My heart sinks. 'I don't want to betray Zeb.'

'I know, Horatio and he doesn't need to know. But you'd be doing this for the good of our community. You would be keeping your family safe and defending your beliefs.' *At least he's right about the first part,* I think.

'Okay.' I allow my uncle to proceed.

'Have you heard of the unity ball?' I shake my head. 'It happens at West Town University every year. It's sort of like a prom. East Town students are invited to attend a ball at the West Town campus to converse with fellow students of *alternative* beliefs.'

'That sounds nice,' I say.

'Yes, you would think. It's clear to me that it is just another way for Tyson to get close to the enemy.' Uncle Basil squeezes his fist until it turns white. 'Anyway,' he continues, 'I attend every year, as is expected of me. It isn't until the end of term. This is where I expect you to meet with me and pass on your notes. It is up to you how you explain your way out of the cabin at the end of term. I will be providing you with a physical notebook. Anything written on another device these days is far too easy to hack.'

It seems easy enough, I think. Zebediah knows I can't make decisions; I don't think he would suspect a thing should I decide by the end of term to move back to East Town. Plus, he has already proved that my belief status is not a factor that affects our friendship. Zebediah as a terrorist, however, might.

I try to remember that my uncle's theories are not solid. Proving that Zeb and his Umbra friends are innocent is equally as likely as proving them guilty.

'How did you know Zebediah was my friend?' I decide to ask. My uncle does not hesitate in his answer.

'Lucian has been keeping a distant eye on Astrid and Hayden

since he heard them in the hallway.' Lucian nods along as my uncle explains. 'Last night he saw Astrid get in a car and Hayden and another man arguing on the cabin doorstep. He followed the man when he left and a young girl he picked up on the way. Can you guess who he was meeting?' *Me*, I think. My stomach churns again at the thought of being watched. I hadn't a clue that there were any lingering eyes upon us last night, and I suddenly realise that Lucian's height is most likely advantageous if he's going to be my uncle's spy. Although I guess that's me now. *Lanky old me.*

'Oh.' I feel guilty for reasons I can't explain. 'You found his name on the hall listings for the university, then?'

'Very good, Horatio!' Basil beams. 'There should be three of you in the cabin. You, Hayden and Zeb. Astrid comes and goes as she pleases. A young woman named Carson Whitmoore is recorded as having dropped out of her criminology course and moved out of the cabin. If you hear any word about her it would be interesting to learn her reasons for leaving.'

I etch the name *Carson Whitmoore* into the back of my mind, sure not to forget it.

'So, effectively, what you're saying, is that a bunch of 20-year old Umbra students are working as Tyson Turrow's private army to take down the Lux community by literally blowing up our economy? And one of them just so happens to be my best friend and another is a world-famous supermodel?' I'm laughing internally but try extremely hard not to patronise my uncle.

'That is exactly what I am saying.'

'Exactly.' Lucian echoes.

Right.

I take a sip of my beer, absentmindedly, forgetting the aggressive churning in my stomach, but not minding so much if it loosens the tension in my chest and the pounding in my head.

'Can I get some fresh air?' I ask without realising I was going to. My uncle smiles softly and gestures to the door.

I had forgotten about my chauffeurs, so as I'm standing outside with my messy hair, bloodshot cannabis-eyes and a half-buttoned shirt, I have a whole parade of armed men staring at me. I have always tried to limit my smoking, but I decide I'd feel a lot less uncomfortable if I had something to do with my hands. I search my pockets for my phone and realise my uncle had probably taken it to make sure I wouldn't tell anyone about our meeting, or to make sure my father hasn't been tracking me.

At least I won't be static, I think, as I consider my uncle's job for me. It's only when I look again at the army of armed officials that I realise he probably isn't asking.

CHAPTER 9

WEST TOWN UNIVERSITY

Carson

I should have better considered my situation before I started running.

The rain had flooded the streets last night, bouncing so hard off the ground that I stopped to watch the puddles splash. It was almost dark when I left Astrid behind in her apartment and now it is almost morning.

I ran steadily through the city streets until I found the Urb bridge that Bennet's car had slid across only a few nights prior, but what feels like a lifetime ago. I sprinted across it, trying to burn any anger I had built up inside. With an absent mind, I found myself back at my St. Vincent Street apartment, forgetting for a weak moment that all that awaited me was a pile of rubble. I was cold and sweaty and wet with no home to go to.

I sat in the rubble and cried for a while, wondering if Tam from the store had made it out alive.

Eventually, after an exhaustive amount of crying, I moved to the small bench in the square where, who I now know to be Tyson Turrow, would watch over me. The rain soaked through my clothes and the cold air nipped at my skin as I tried to sleep. So, with no energy to run, I strolled around the city streets to keep my body warm and ticking over. It wasn't long before I hopped on a late train to West Town. I didn't dare think about going near the cabin in case Astrid had returned in search of me.

But Bennet doesn't live in the cabin.

Although he is not innocent in abandoning me, *he tried*. That's all anyone can do. It's strange to be told that someone is your friend rather than to know it, but it is the only thing that Astrid had said to me that held anything close to a chance at getting my life back.

The sky is white in West Town. White-grey and abundant with clouds. I wander around the beautiful stone buildings with pointed arches and low sloping roofs. Everything here is beautiful and I decide I like it a lot in West Town, particularly the university and the vast loch that surrounds it. I imagine a past version of myself wandering the university halls with a book under my arm, sitting by the lake and eating lunch and laughing with my friend, Hawk.

Cara and Hawk don't seem to exist anymore. Instead, I know Bennet and he can only know Carson Whitmoore, the name that is nothing but a label for the girl who is broken. The girl who can't even remember him.

Carson Whitmoore is a non-believer. I think about what Bennet had said about us living on a blue sphere. I don't believe that we go anywhere and I don't believe that we go nowhere when we die.

And quite frankly, I don't care.

I make a conscious note to encourage Bennet to dye his hair candy-floss pink again.

I wonder what made Cara an Umbra. I wonder what made that version of myself so sure that I would just be a corpse in the ground or ashes in a jar and nothing more. What sort of ego must I have had to think that I had the ability to know that? We don't know anything. It's not a perfect world.

I listen to the wind blow the leaves in the trees, the rattling of branches and my footsteps on the cobbles as I approach the university grounds. I see him in a far up window, sitting on the sill and reading something intently, earphones in.

He's beautiful. And so sad that I can almost see it emanating from him. Maybe it's not always stormy in West Town.

Maybe Bennet is the storm.

I know it will take me a while to muster up the courage to go up to him. I think it may be the pain in his eyes or the uncertainty of the nature of our past relationship that makes me so unbearably anxious. It took a knife to his throat to get him to open up to me, and yet it is impossible to ignore the inexplicable pounding in my chest every time I see him.

I sit on the soft grass, remove my leather boots and dip my pale feet in the cold loch. I stare at my reflection in the clear water. It's been a while since I've seen my own face. I hated my reflection for a long time after the Awakening.

There is something dark behind my eyes. Something unfamiliar. After all, the person who knows me most, is me, somewhere deep down, somewhere deep in the jungle of my mind. My red hair is tangled. I have dark circles under my eyes, and my tight black jumper, which actually belongs to Astrid, is clinging to my bust so tightly, it looks like a second skin. I much preferred Bennet's hoodie.

I look so pale against the water that I'm almost ghostly. I imagine for a minute that the Cara staring back at me is a ghost. The ghost of the girl I imagine sitting here for lunch.

It's Saturday and West Town University is deserted. The only people I see are Hawk through his porthole window and Hayden sitting under an apple tree. I think about going over to interrogate him for a second before I change my mind. Hayden's aggressive encounter with Zebediah in the cabin was so cold it makes me dislike him intensely.

He's reading. A book about programming that I can only just make out from the distance he sits at. He hasn't noticed me, which I'm thankful for, as the Hayden I have conjured up in my mind would unhesitatingly shove me into the lake.

I hope an apple falls on his head.

I'm so carried away with my own thoughts and observations that I don't notice Zebediah sitting next to me and removing his shoes until his feet are in the water. It could be his thick fluttering lashes or his warm hazel eyes that immediately make him comfortable company, but I smile at him, reassured, as he places his hand over mine on the grass. When he sees that his advances have been a success, he smiles widely, pearly white teeth that make the heart swell. Astrid is right, Zebediah is stunning.

'Someone ran away from the scary blonde lady,' he says with a laugh. 'Did Eydis talk to you?' His eyebrows furrow prettily.

'Astrid told me everything,' I say. 'I suppose I made her.' The peace of the moment diffuses a little when I remember that Zebediah, too, is responsible for sending me away. He must read my expression.

'I'm so sorry, C. There is so much that I regret. So many bad decisions, but there is nothing I regret more than giving up on you. At the time, it seemed like the only way. It was an intense time.' The way he says it and the look on his face makes him a lot easier to forgive than Astrid. It may be Astrid's blunt way of being that makes her harder to like, but perhaps I'm jealous that she can assert herself by simply filling a door frame. I would need stilts, a whole lot of makeup and therapy before I could emanate that sort of confidence.

I sigh, close my eyes and focus on the cool water between my toes when I speak. 'So, tell me about these bad decisions,' I tease

Zebediah laughs. 'Well, I've smoked a few joints, kissed a few frogs, got in a few fights,' he says, mid-laugh. I recall his physique from a couple of nights prior, wearing only dungarees and decide quickly that I wouldn't dare get in a fight with him.

'Fights?'

'Let's just say that there are certain parts of the Urb where being black, gay and an Umbra isn't well-received by some people.' He splashes his feet in the loch, suddenly shy.

I place my hand back over his on the grass and gently squeeze. 'Fuck those guys.'

'Yeah, they wish I would.' We relieve our sad smiles with a small laugh. 'You really don't remember anything?' he asks.

'No. I think I've spent most of my anger though. I just want to work out what to do next.'

He nods. 'You always were ballsy, Cara. Astrid had some real competition in you when it came to leading our pack.' He doesn't stop smiling and I lean in, surprised by this comment. 'When I saw you sitting by the water just five minutes ago, I was not at all surprised to see you. They should have sent Tyson's army if Astrid wanted to keep you around. And she's too lazy to chase you. You've always been fast.' It's nice to hear him speak fondly of me. I feel suddenly guilty for having previously branded him *bathtub guy,* and for thinking only of Hawk in my past.

I'm starting to understand that the others were my friends too. I lost all of them. I look over at Hayden again and try to imagine us as friends. Zebediah sees me looking at him. Perhaps I shouldn't ask, but I do anyway. 'What happened with you and Hayden in the cabin?' I nod over at the oblivious blonde. The dark circles under his eyes are perceptible from across the grounds.

Zeb sighs before he speaks. 'He was ready to bring you home without thinking things through,' he says. 'It's a lot of information for you to take in. I disagreed with the plan without further discussion. You know, to make the transition easier for you.' Zebediah looks sternly at Hayden as he speaks. 'But Hayden dives into everything head first. He doesn't consider how anyone else feels.'

'That may have spared me a night of crying in the rain,' I say.

Zeb doesn't ask. 'Yeah, well, whatever Hayden says, goes. Plus, it would have been less infuriating if I thought he was doing it for you, or even Hawk.' He looks up at 'Hawk's' window.

'But it's all about his own scientific endeavours, it's always about him.' It seems pretty believable.

'Scientific endeavours?' I question.

'Did Astrid tell you about Eydis trying to bring your memories back?' He looks at me, cautiously, like he might break me if he says the wrong thing. I nod. 'Well, Hayden is helping her out with it. There's just something so irritating about Hayden when he gets excited. It makes him cocky and selfish.' Zeb takes a minute to breathe. 'Plus,' he continues, 'I want to know how much of a risk it's going to be for you. This is about more than just science.'

I decide I'm fond of Zeb. He has my best interests at heart, but doesn't make my chest feel tight like Bennet does.

'What he did to you was really shitty,' I say about Hayden, hoping that Zeb will be reassured by my allegiance to him.

'Things are tense at the moment. But honestly, he's always had a problem with me.' He frowns.

'Why?'

'He's just an arsehole.' We sit in mutual agreement on this for a while, Zebediah blinking through his thoughts before he stands and picks up his shoes from beside him. 'I have a study session with my tutor in a half-hour so I better go dry off.' He squelches away in the soft grass. He turns around for a second. 'Can I trust you not to run off? I'd hate to be the last one who saw you and I just walked away,' he teases, knowing fine well that it's unlikely.

I shrug. 'Where would I go?' He smiles as he saunters through the large doors of the castle.

Gathering my thoughts and reassured by Zeb's kindness, I let my feet dry in the soft breeze before I approach the central turret of the university. I push open the arched door at the bottom of the tower and climb the spiral staircase to the top until I am met with a long hallway of dorms. I knock on the door I know to be 'Hawk's' and hear a squeaky bark.

He opens the door.

His hair is black and his t-shirt is too. He looks alarmed.

'Cara?' He removes his earphones and places his book on the table by the door. 'I thought Astrid had taken you to see Eydis?'

'Eydis is in the safehouse,' I state, not really sure what I'm telling him.

He frowns.

There's a pause. 'Can I come in?'

'Yes, of course, sorry!' he says in an attempt to be enthusiastic. The little dog from before comes running up to me. Instead of barking, she nuzzles up to my leg.

'You never told me her name,' I say.

'Her name is Red.' He smiles, sadly, kneeling down beside me where I pet Red's soft curls.

'Did you get her when I went away?'

'What do you mean?' he asks, eyebrows furrowed.

'When they took me. When they sent me away,' I say it calmly and wait for his reaction.

'You know about that?' He's looking at the floor.

'I know about everything, Hawk.' He looks up at me, wide-eyed and soft. 'Why did you change your name?' I stand, hoping to assert some dominance as I question him.

He stands almost a foot above me.

'Zeb tells people it's because he kept calling me Birdboy, which I admit was pretty irritating, but...'

'But what?'

'It's nothing.'

'Oh.'

I swear I've never seen a soul look so deflated.

I think about his hand next to mine on the train, the sweet way that his voice softens when he says my name and the way his head rested against my legs the night I woke up in the cabin. With the memory of his affection, I move closer to him, the points of our shoes meeting. I reach for his hand.

Suddenly, he looks hurt, offended. He pulls his hand away swiftly. He moves to the window, trying not to look at me. I'm about to say that I'm sorry, but I decide that would be too close to admitting I'd made an advance on him. Instead, I stay quiet, wallowing in confusion and trying to pretend that nothing happened.

I look around the room, searching for something to comment on, to say, to erase the tension in the room. Seconds turn to minutes and Hawk is staring out of the window and I'm staring at the back of his head, watching him from the other side of the room. I'm about to head for the door, dejected and disappointed, when he scrambles from the window, swinging on his black coat and moving swiftly out the door yelling, 'It's Zeb and Hayden!'

What is?

I follow his long black coat quickly through the corridor, down the spiral staircase and onto the green grass of the university grounds. I hear them before I see them. Hayden lies on the ground below the apple tree as Zebediah straddles him, barefoot, throwing his fists as Hayden tries to reach up and grab his neck or pull his hair. I immediately wonder what Hayden must have done to ask for a beating.

He's the sort of person you imagine has it coming.

Hayden's nose is bleeding profusely. Hawk runs to the scene, trying to pull Zebediah away, but he isn't strong enough.

Eventually, after a few minutes of laboured breathing and Hayden screaming profanities, Zeb gives up, stands and brushes down his grass-stained jeans. 'You had it coming!' he yells, pointing a finger at Hayden who remains on the ground, propping himself up on his elbows with a disgusted look on his sallow face.

'You need to learn to take a joke!' The blonde wipes his bloody nose on the sleeve of his striped jumper and pulls himself up on a low sloping branch before kicking his scruffy trainers into the ground in frustration.

Zebediah has the same look on his face that he did the night he stormed away from Hayden in the cabin. His eyebrows are furrowed in hurt and his lips are pursed like he's about to yell, but instead he just breathes, turns on his heel and walks away. Hawk looks on, distressed and powerless as Hayden rams into Zeb's back, pushing him to the ground and watching as he rises again without looking back and continues on his way.

Hawk waits for Zeb to be out of earshot before he confronts Hayden in an aggressive whisper. 'What the hell is wrong with you? Will you ever learn to leave him alone?'

Hayden huffs and his bloodshot eyes of a deep black-brown fall to the floor, his dimpled cheeks slowly rippling into a psychotic grin that seems present on only one side of his pale face. He walks away without saying a word, his ripped baggy jumper hanging from his shoulder.

I'm not sure if I say it to Hawk or myself, but I sit on the grass exactly where I'd been standing and sigh, 'I hate that guy.'

Hawk looks like he wants to walk away but instead compels himself to kneel beside me. 'Are you okay?' he asks, softly.

'What about?' I snap. 'The fight, my amnesia, or you pushing me away?'

'I didn't mean to push you away.' He twiddles a thick black ring on his finger. 'This is all happening so quickly. I don't know what's best for you, but I don't think getting too close to me is the right thing to do.'

'Why not?'

'As soon as we're fighting in the front line against Silenda—'

'You mean once we figure out where they are?'

'Right,' he agrees. 'Things are going to get dangerous pretty quickly. I'll risk myself before I risk anyone else and I'll do it to avenge the friend that I lost in you. I want to do this for you. But you have to keep your distance from me.' He looks serious.

There is a dramatic pause.

'That is just stupid,' I say. He looks taken aback.

'How is it stupid?'

'Because,' I say, 'no one is asking you to be the hero. I'm not asking you.' I stand up to walk away. 'Anyway, if anyone is going to find Silenda and put an end to the deaths and disappearances, it should be me. I started the hunt, I should at least play a part in ending it.'

Hawk shakes his head, amused. I raise my eyebrow at his patronising chuckle. 'It's nothing,' he says quickly as he watches my expression sour. 'You just sound a lot like the Cara I used to know.' He's still kneeling when he watches me walk away. 'Where are you going?'

'Keeping my distance,' I say. 'Since that's what you want.' I have my back to him as I walk away. I can feel him frowning.

I feel accomplished by my unwillingness to let him play with my feelings or decide for me what part I should play in taking down the people who took me.

I want revenge more than any of them do.

• • •

I'm walking barefoot across the grass and feeling the soft heat of the cornsilk sun on my skin. It's strange to exist under a bright white sky of cumulus clouds.

I am so used to the dark.

The hill that divides the campus and the student cabins has a beautiful view of the university from its peak. Ahead of me, the student cabins are abundant. The Nether Cabin stands tallest, with the mayor's mansion proud in the distance. Bellumside unfolds behind it, surrounded by thick green forestry.

I hadn't noticed Hawk following me until he speaks. 'Not so big when you see it from here, is it?' The wind blows in his black hair.

Is East Town bigger than this?' I ask.

'I've only been a couple of times to visit a friend, but yeah, I think so.'

'Why is that?'

'It's common knowledge that more Umbras are likely to end up as outcast's in the Rowleys than the Luxies are,' he says, simply. 'Suppose there's not as many people here.'

I chew on this idea for a moment.

'Why do you think that is?' I ask and he shrugs.

'I suppose it's easier to believe in an afterlife than it is to believe in the dark. I think a lot of Umbras get confused, they just can't be sure what to believe and they don't feel right living among the people who do know.' I look up at him as we walk, trying to suss out his personal opinions on these matters.

'I'm not sure I care,' I say. 'That's probably part of the reason I tried to take down Silenda. I think it's better we don't know. It's the only way we can be happy.'

'You've always thought that way. It's interesting to see that hasn't changed.'

'I think these are fundamentals,' I say. 'I don't remember you, but I remember what I believe in and what my favourite cereal is,' I explain.

He looks thoughtful. 'I remember Hayden being very particular about your memory extraction, he tried to keep as much intact as he could.' It doesn't surprise me that it was Hayden who ultimately played a role in taking my memories.

He's the only one sinister enough.

We're walking over to the cabin when a thought occurs to me that should have been one of my first questions to Astrid. 'How did I even know that Silenda existed in the first place?' I ask. 'I get that I was onto them, so they took me, but how did I even find out about them?'

'Well, people were disappearing, turning up dead in the Rowleys,' Hawk says.

'So? What's to say it wasn't aliens? How did I know that those incidents were related to Silenda?'

Hawk sighs, deeply. 'I think the best person to ask that to, is you.' He pauses for a moment. 'We found your diary.'

I tell him Astrid had mentioned that and the maps in my bathroom.

'Hayden and I visited every spot on the map and found nothing. They were all in the woods. There was no sign of anything there or anything that even used to be there. Too many trees.'

I nod along so he knows I'm listening.

'After that, we tracked down and interviewed every name mentioned in your writing. There were a few people who had reported missing relatives, things like that. As far as I know, you found out about Silenda from Jason.'

'Hayden's father?'

We're nearing the cabin now. We stop a few metres from the door so Hawk can finish explaining things without the others overhearing. 'Jason was taken too. He was one of the first disappearances. He remembers everything. He remembers the big, white clinical waiting room he woke up in. He remembers the video he was made to watch before being taken into the lab. He says everyone wore masks, and when it was over he woke up back in the Rowleys.'

'Jason knows what happens when we die?' I say, alarmed. I think about the truth being what drove me so crazy after Silenda dumped me back into the world.

'No,' he replies. 'He remembers who took him, but he can't remember how he got there or back, or what exactly happened to him. He said they were injecting people with some sort of serum that sent them into cardiac arrest. His theory is that it didn't work on him. He doesn't think they could kill him, so they just put him back.' He shrugs and I know I've drained him dry of any answers he has.

It's silent between us until blazing sirens fill the air around the cabin. Two stocky policemen emerge from a haphazardly parked car and break through the Nether Cabin door, demanding its residents put their hands in the air. Hawk becomes immediately alert and rushes over to a third officer, a plump woman in illuminous orange vis who waits by the police vehicle, hand on her holster. 'What's going on?' Hawk demands.

'Step away from the scene please, sir,' she says, firmly, ushering him back with a hand on his chest.

He takes a telling and retreats to my side as we look on anxiously as the scene unfolds.

After a series of inaudible yells, the two police officers reappear from the cabin with a denim-clad young man between them.

Handcuffed and dazed, Zebediah is ushered from the building aggressively and thrown in front of the female officer as she states, 'Zebediah Hayes, we are arresting you on suspicion of the murder of Randy Redding. You do not have to say anything but anything you do say will be relied on in court.'

Zeb looks over at us, wide-eyed. One of the officers forces Zeb's head down and into the backseat of the car. They speed away before I could even begin to process what has happened.

'Who is Randy Redding?' I ask Hawk, panicked.

'I have no idea.'

CHAPTER 10

PAPER SPIRIT

Horatio

People like Lucian kill me, they really do.

He's so set in his ways that he can't see for a second what's beyond his nose. I've been trying to work on my tolerance, so I try to assure myself that Lucian's beliefs are his own and that I should respect and have empathy for what helps him sleep at night.

I try to avoid imagining that all Luxies have fed themselves lies to help them sleep at night. It seems too close to intolerance to think like that.

Lucian needs to work on his tolerance too.

It's almost nightfall again and, after an exhausting day of lectures from my uncle, we're in the backseat of a small van disguised as a window cleaning service that transports me discreetly to West Town.

After the events in the Rowleys, we left my Uncle Basil behind to his business in the city. He shook my hand roughly, kissed my forehead in glee and bid me adieu.

I wish that he had chosen any escort but Lucian.

With no time to don other clothes and a return to my parent's house far too suspicious, I remain in my sweaty satin shirt and skinny jeans from the night prior. I remember a packet of chewing gum Zeb had bought me from the store next to the Panic Room still tucked away in one of my denim pockets. I fish for it and offer a piece to Lucian who quizzes me on where I purchased it. He denies his piece, insisting that he would rather 'burn in the fiery pits of hell' than chew Umbra gum.

Yikes.

I shrug off his absurdity and chew slowly as I look out the darkened window from the back of the van. I've never been to West Town before and the tall, narrow, old stone buildings take me by surprise. The sky is beautifully grey and it's the sort of place that makes you want to have a beer in the rain or believe in witches.

The van rumbles over the cobblestones, jerking a petite Lucian around in his seat. We pull into a village that shadows a picturesque estate of tall wooden cabins.

'You're up, Horatio.' Lucian says, teeth gleaming. 'You're right down there!' He points to the cabins. 'The tallest one, right at the front by the loch. It's a bit of a walk but we wouldn't want your new roommates spotting you emerging from a window cleaner's van. That would be odd.' Lucian rocks back in his seat, hand on his chest in hysterical laughter.

I grin awkwardly.

'When am I expected to visit my parents? Won't they want to visit me at East Town campus?'

'Your Uncle Basilio has assured me that he has things under control on that end. He most likely told them that campus visits are forbidden at such a prestigious school, or perhaps too distracting for you. As for your sudden departure from home, Basilio sat down with your mother and pleaded that her 20-year old son will do better not looking back. You can't work in a café forever, you know!' Lucian punches my shoulder, humorously.

It hurts.

'Right.' I rub my arm and feel slightly saddened by my mother and father's contentment at seeing me suddenly leave home without a goodbye.

'You can visit them anytime you wish, as long as you keep your story straight.' Lucian slides open the van door and steps out, flattening his light grey suit. 'Well, come on then!'

I slide along the chair and out into the cold wind that blows up my shirt. I feel my ankles for the first time after being tied to the chair and the burnt skin from trying to wiggle free from the shoelace bonds.

Lucian throws open the double doors at the back of the white van, revealing two large suitcases and a guitar-shaped black case. 'These are most of your things your uncle had Angelo pack from your room and, of course, since you'll be studying music, we brought your guitar!'

I smile, sincerely, glad for my guitar and some fresh attire. 'Thanks.'

'Now, don't expect me to walk you to the door, we might as well announce to the whole town what we're up to.' Lucian makes a shushing gesture as if my mission isn't to investigate the potentiality of a full-blown Lux-Umbra war. I nod, desperate to escape the man's company, which makes me inexplicably uncomfortable.

I swing my guitar case over my shoulder, take a suitcase in each hand and begin my journey towards the cabin. My suitcases roll haphazardly along the cobbles as Lucian waves me off. Without turning around, I hear the sliding shut of the van door and the rev of the engine as it pulls away.

Suddenly alone, the air turns colder and harsher. I pass a few antique stores and woollen mills until I reach a rustic looking coffee shop with a warm coal fire flickering through the window and windchimes hanging from the door that blow slightly more violently than one would hope.

I push open the wooden door with a jingle and am greeted with a gracious old woman who pours me a steaming cup of cocoa that I chug down in a desperate attempt at warmth before I continue on my way.

The forest of cabins is approaching as I suck on my scalded tongue and try to prevent my luggage tipping over on the uneven ground.

A blonde man clearing tables outside an old tavern smiles at me with a hint of recognition in his eyes. I feel a sudden sting of guilt and keep my head down as paranoia begins to kick in at my imposturous task. It's only as I'm reaching the cabins that I recall his face as Jason, the shaggy guy who I had met briefly in the Rowleys with Zeb. I feel rude for not smiling back.

The cabins are tall with flights of stairs crawling up their sides. Some of the cabins are adorned with vines and others simply shadowed by trees. The tallest cabin of them all stands at the foot of a vast loch, with a beautiful balcony and a large contemporary glass window for a fourth wall on its top floor.

I imagine that from the balcony there is a view of the whole expanse of water and what I imagine to be the towers of the university poking out from behind a large hill that divides it.

Vines crawl up the side of the cabin where the steps to the second floor begin and continue around the ground floor where a small door marks the entrance of the structure. I wheel my luggage clumsily across the slightly squelchy grass and approach it. Before I knock, I notice a small rectangle of bark that appears to have been cut from a tree with the words *The Nether Cabin* carved and hung above the door with rope. I stare at it for a while, heart racing at the thought of my new cabin buddies behind the door.

I pull up my jeans, button my shirt a little more and remove my earring. I throw my hair out of my eyes and knock gingerly.

It's a couple of minutes and some inaudible murmuring before a young man stands in the doorway, looking at me unamused. We stand at the same eye level, but he makes me feel small. A mess of loose blonde curls fall over his black eyes and he scratches his head. I follow his hand and my attention is immediately drawn to his black and blue nose. I wonder if a guy worth beating up is the best person for me to first encounter.

'You must be Horatio Marino,' he says, gesturing me into the cabin and picking up a folder which he skims through lazily.

Must I? I think. It would have been helpful for my uncle to mention the name-change. Though, I suppose having the same surname as the Lux mayor wouldn't be a great start.

'Uh, yes – that's me!' I stumble and end up sounding too enthusiastic.

The man looks up from his files, closes over the folder and sizes me up. 'You don't look sure.' I note the suspicion in his tone. I smile awkwardly and fear sounding defensive if I speak. 'Hayden Turrow,' he says, stretching out a slim arm.

Hayden Turrow, I think, *hence the suspicion.*

'Good to meet you. Uh, who else should I be expecting to meet today?' I look around the cabin at the high ceiling and the tall staircase. I hear nothing but Hayden Turrow's breathing and the isolating sound of a ticking clock. 'I'm a friend of Zebediah.' Hayden looks alarmed.

'Just me as of now,' he says. 'The others are,' he pauses, 'out.' I nod awkwardly as Hayden leans against a desk with a large PC and other high-tech devices I don't recognise. He drinks from a paper cup of coffee. 'Want a sip?' he asks, holding the cup out towards me. I think it odd to ask someone for a sip of coffee instead of just offering them their own cup, until I realise that it's straight whisky. I gag and try to recover my dignity.

'Rough day?' I ask, looking from the paper cup to his visibly broken nose.

'I don't see eye to eye with your friend,' he says.

'Zeb did that to you?' I'm initially taken aback, but as I think it through, I've always known Zeb to have parts of his life that he preferred not to talk about. I'm not naïve enough to believe that people that bubbly aren't suppressing something.

Especially bubbly people who chain-smoke.

'It doesn't matter now,' Hayden says and I'm sure I look quizzical. 'Haven't you heard?'

'Heard what?' I press cautiously.

'Zebediah has been arrested. For murder.'

• • •

The log fire burns and sparks aggressively as the wind outside sends gushes of cold air under the crack of the wooden door. I'm slouched over a glass of vodka-soda that Hayden insisted I accept after I declined more whisky. I had considered it safer to comply, despite my stomach's shock at the volume of alcohol I've consumed over the last couple of days.

After filling his cup, Hayden flops on the corner couch beside me, as far away from me as he can.

'Murder?' I say for the hundredth time since I changed my clothes and took my bags upstairs.

Hayden runs his hands over his face. 'Are you still asking me? Because I'm sure I've answered that question the same way for the last 45 minutes.'

'I just don't understand how this has happened. I mean, he didn't do it! Right?' The alcohol has me tearing up and searching for reassurance.

Hayden huffs. When I had asked him who had been killed, he met me with a short 'I dunno, some guy,' which is exactly where my patience with Hayden began to run thin.

'Don't ask me to question what Zeb is capable of.' He points at his screwed-up nose. 'He has violent tendencies.'

I'm standing up and lunging towards him before I really think about what I'm doing.

I need Hayden to trust me enough to invest information in me and yet I'm holding his scruffy jumper by the neck and threatening to give him a bloody lip to match his nose if he accuses Zebediah of anything so preposterous ever again.

Hayden puts his hands on either side of his face in surrender and laughs suddenly, despite not even cracking a smile during our entire interaction so far. 'Wow, wow, wow!' he says, grinning. 'Firstly, you don't look like the kind of guy who's thrown a punch in his entire life. And secondly, I don't like the guy, but I don't think he's a murderer!'

'You don't?' I back away from him and choose to ignore his implicit comment about my physique.

'No!' he says. 'I didn't always hate him. We grew up together.'

'What changed?' I sit back down on the tawny leather couch and cling to my vodka-soda with shaky hands.

'We used to be best friends. I guess, as we entered adulthood, we became different people with different opinions on how certain things should be.' Hayden sips his whisky, slowly. I don't pressure him for more answers and imagine if I did, I wouldn't get many.

Hayden tries to take my mind from Zebediah's arrest by talking about classes at West Town University, which I talk about casually, remembering the information my uncle had given me about my music course. Hayden launches into a long speech about his computer science class and uses a lot of jargon I don't understand, so I nod along attentively, warming my chest and loosening my mind with drink. She swoops in like the Wicked Witch of West Town as a strong gust of wind carries her and a small tornado of leaves through the door in a sudden and dramatic clatter.

Her black eye makeup is running down her face and her hair is soaking wet. 'Is she here?' Astrid Turrow shouts into the cabin and turns to find only Hayden and me.

'Get caught in the rain, cuz?' Hayden asks, laughing. I sit uncomfortably in my black jumper, pulling at my sleeves, pretending to be busy and eternally grateful for the vodka.

'Gosh!' Astrid slams the door behind her. She continues to speak as she marches upstairs, leaving muddy footprints on the wooden steps as her voice echoes from the top floor. 'I had to get a freaking train!' she continues. 'It was so busy and everyone who'd been in the city was soaking wet. We all just sort of sat there stiff in our own sogginess, making each other wet through osmosis or whatever.'

'I don't think that's how that works!' Hayden yells up to her.

'Anyway,' she huffs as the sound of running water and the bang of discarded boots suggest she is running a bath. 'I got off the train in the village and had to walk all the way here in the storm in my brand-new pair of Versace Labyrinth boots! Ugh, I'm going for a bath!'

I look over at a calm Hayden, wide-eyed at his cousin's franticness. I wipe my clammy hands on my jeans and he seems to notice. 'Models,' he sighs, 'it's all photoshop, am I right?'

I laugh, but even panda-eyed and drenched, I swear I have never seen anyone as strikingly beautiful as Astrid Turrow.

'Who was she looking for?' I ask.

'That's a bit of a long story,' he says. 'I'm sure you'll be filled in eventually. Once we know you're on the same page as us.'

'Same page?'

'You know, morally.' There's a dark look in his black eyes and I make a mental note to keep an eye on Hayden.

There's another gust of wind as a much smaller figure fills the door frame, her face red with tears. I recognise Gia immediately and wish with a sudden anxiety that Zeb had never mentioned my last name.

She sees me as soon as she brushes her windswept hair from her eyes. With the gush of cold air that accompanied her blowing out the log fire, Hayden gets up to retrieve more wood from 'storage'. Gia rushes towards me and collapses on the couch, burying her petite head in my shoulder.

'Oh, Horatio!' she cries. 'Are you here because of the news about Zeb?' She lifts her head and I try not to cringe at the wet feeling of her tears seeping onto my shoulder.

'I've decided to study here,' I say. 'I didn't find out about Zeb until I got here.' This makes her cry uncontrollably and I hold her awkwardly and silently for a half-hour until a fresh-faced Astrid comes plodding down the stairs, wrapped in silk with her blonde hair flowing dry. She looks at me curiously, and I try my hardest not to blush. I look away, pretending to focus on consoling Gia and trying to seem not at all distracted by Astrid's pretty neck.

'You must be the new guy!' she says, a finger pointed at me and looking at Hayden to correct her if she's wrong.

I'm about to answer before Hayden beats me to it. 'Yup!' he says. 'This is Marino. Say hello, Marino.'

'Hello,' I squeak, obediently.

'Marino? That's an interesting name,' she says. 'Is it Italian?' I'm pretty sure I do have Italian roots somewhere, but I shake my head, simply not prepared to pretend to be Italian for a semester.

'My first name is Horatio,' I say, shyly.

'Nice to meet you,' Astrid replies. Even her voice is pretty. And her eyes are even more captivating in real life. I want to ask her about the prince she dated and the ball she hijacked. I want to ask her what celebrities she's met and what music she likes and what it was like to ride the Solar Glider, but the sound of Gia's crying distracts me.

Astrid joins us on the couch, comforting Gia from her opposite side. 'It's alright, G, we'll work things out,' she shushes, her pale arm around Gia and her fingernails brushing my shoulder.

'So, you heard?' Gia wails, lifting her head momentarily from the crook of my neck.

'There isn't anything I don't know, sweetie.' Astrid sounds gentle but at risk of sounding patronising as she presses her cheek against Gia's shoulder. She mumbles against her raincoat, 'I love Zebediah. My father will pay his bail, we will get him out. I promise.' I hope she means it. I watch her silently when she talks.

Astrid looks me dead in the eye as she rises from the couch.

It's hard to read her expression. It must be the suspicion of the Turrows. I suppose if a person is plotting a religious revolution, they may be suspicious of the new guy moving in on their territory. I'm staring back, blue eyes piercing into her ambiguous ones.

She feels like the sunset, the undecided sunset. No matter where her soul goes when she dies, she will never fade into blackness. We are staring for what feels like eternity until the front door swings open again for the third time in the last hour. Astrid turns away as the gust of wind blows through her hair. I really need to stop being so infatuated with this woman. I haven't been this infatuated with anyone since I met Zebediah. I don't know what it is about me, perhaps it's a deep-rooted co-dependency, or the desire to invest my belief in a person if I can't invest it anywhere else.

Maybe I'm just lonely.

When I first met Zebediah, his beauty was confusing. I was 16 and he was the only person on earth who would listen to me rant about how lost I felt – how lost I feel. This reliance climaxed when we were 18.

He had been standing on the rooftop of the Grand Library, black hair blowing in the wind, brown skin so warm when I felt so cold. He had left his phone in the pocket of my leather jacket and when he reached for it, it felt like slow motion. His full lashes had been fluttering and his throat bobbing where he swallowed thickly.

I kissed him.

Full on the mouth, hands in his hair. He kissed me back, too, but when he pulled away, he looked sad. We didn't talk about it for a whole week until Zeb opened up to me, sure I had made a mistake. A friendship as valuable as ours should not be tarnished by any complicated romantic feelings, he had said, particularly on my part, as I've only ever been attracted to women.

I had no choice but to agree with him, but my adoration for him, romantic or not, has never faltered, and thinking about how scared he must feel right now makes my chest so tight that I struggle to breathe.

I follow Astrid's gaze to the door where a tall man and a short woman stand looking red-faced and flustered. They look exhausted, like they've been running. The petite woman looks blankly at Astrid who yells, 'Where the hell have you been, Carson? You can't just run out on people like that!'

The red-head looks down at her muddy boots and doesn't respond. *Carson*, I think. The name I had urged myself to remember.

The man beside Carson encourages her gently into the cabin and closes the door behind him. He's tall with a long black trench coat, numerous rings on his slim fingers and an intimidating aura around him. The pair pause to catch their breath as Astrid approaches them, arms folded. Gia and I turn our heads and Hayden emerges from the storage room he had disappeared to for a suspiciously long time.

'The Rowleys...' Carson wheezes. The man, who I observe by resemblance, to be Gia's older brother, tells 'Cara' to sit down and she does, on the bottom of the stairs across from the door.

He removes his coat and hangs it on a stand before running his hands over his face and speaking. 'There's some dangerous shit going on in the Rowleys. And in the forest,' he begins, taking off from where Carson had breathlessly begun. 'Zeb couldn't have killed that Randy guy, but his DNA was found at the scene, his fingerprints round his neck—'

I stand up immediately, hypnotically, and say, 'Randy, who?'

'Uh, Redding,' the tall man says, looking me up and down, trying to decide whether he should know me.

'Randy Redding killed himself,' I say. 'I was with Zeb, we saw the police taking his body, there was a rope around his neck. A rope!' I cry. 'He was with me!'

Everyone looks at me.

'I'm sorry,' Gia's brother says, 'who are you?'

I go over and shake his hand, eager to hear what he knows. 'Horatio Marino,' I say, set on my new name. 'I'm the new guy. I'm a friend of Zeb's. Music tech student.'

'Me too,' he replies. 'Bennet Lee.' He pauses. 'So, you were there when this guy killed himself?'

'Well, I wasn't there when he did it, but we saw his body being taken away and it was blatant suicide. There was no questioning it! I knew the guy, he hung around outside Caleb Hayes' record store. He never had a home. It didn't come as a surprise when I saw him, as awful as that sounds.'

Bennet nods, understanding.

Carson is sitting with her head in her hands, her eyes darting around the room and settling against a wall as if she can see a ghost that no one else in the room can see. She stands up, situates herself next to Bennet and prepares to speak to the eyes that have been drawn to her.

'*They*,' she glances at me nervously, 'are primarily picking people up from the Rowleys,' she breathes. 'I suppose it's easier to take people who are less likely to be missed. It helps them keep a low profile.'

I look over at Astrid who looks absorbed in Carson's soft yet serious tone.

Carson pauses for a long moment before moving her hair and pulling down her jumper at the shoulder to reveal the crook of her neck. 'This mark,' she begins, 'your father has it.' She's looking at Hayden who moves close to her, paper cup in hand.

'Yeah, he does.' He takes a brief look and turns up his nose, sceptically.

Gia rises and I follow her until we are close enough to observe it too.

Two small holes are visible on Carson's neck. The mark is red and unsettling. She must see the distaste in our faces as the red-head darts her gaze fleetingly to Bennet before pulling her hair back over her shoulder.

'What is that?' Gia asks, looking up at her brother with grave concern. I follow her eyes as he seems to be the most assertive person in the room.

Bennet takes his hands to his face and shakes his head. Carson simply looks timid.

'It's probably where they drugged you,' Astrid says, striding to the front of our collective vision in a pair of leopard print slippers and a nightgown of aquamarine silk. 'Silenda,' she says. 'It's probably where they drugged you,' she repeats, only this time she elicits a chorus of gasps and cries.

Bennet springs forward. 'Don't you dare speak their name here!' he exclaims. 'Especially not in company.' Hayden laughs chaotically at Bennet's sudden outburst and is met with a threatening glare that shuts him up.

'Why not?' Astrid refutes, calmly. 'It's not my secret organisation to keep secret. And I'm not putting anyone in any more danger by talking about them than we're already in.'

The room goes silent except for the sound of Hayden sipping more drink from his paper cup. All eyes turn to him and he takes the opportunity to speak. 'Are we really still on this?' He yawns dramatically. 'It's probably an insect bite. The midges around here are fucking lethal.' Hayden chuckles into his paper cup. 'Also, Jason is an alcoholic.'

Jason? I think. And then I see the resemblance. The shaggy guy that had sold Zebediah the Super Sounder headphones and the guy that had smiled at me in the village on my way here. *Hayden's father.*

'Hayden, stop being in denial! You know what really happened, I know you do!' Bennet snaps. 'You know they are real!'

Soon, another realisation hits me. *Silenda*, that's what Astrid had said. Suddenly I remember the words that had been written on the brick wall entrance to the Rowleys. The words that Zeb had simply shrugged off.

SILENDA

'That word,' I finally say. 'Silenda. It's written all over the Rowleys.'

'Yeah, it is.' Astrid squints at me as if wondering what I'd be doing in the rough outskirts of the city. 'We can show our own but we will never know, she's made of glass but we never tiptoe. Silenda, Silenda, Silenda,' she says.

'Yes, that's it!' I say, remembering the eerie riddle.

Hayden lets out another untimed chuckle. 'Did I say my father was an alcoholic? I meant an alcoholic graffiti artist.'

I look over at Hayden and direct my question at him in the hope he'll know the answer. 'Who is she?' I ask. 'The woman who is made of glass?'

'Earth,' Hayden says, simply. 'The whole tiptoe thing, it's about protecting our planet, you know? My father is big on recycling.'

Astrid scoffs. 'I really don't think it's about recycling.'

'Gee, Astrid. Global warming is a real and serious issue.'

Astrid strops over to the stairs where Carson once sat and runs her fingers through her hair. 'Uncle Jason is talking about our religious habits. We spend our whole lives fighting and debating something we can never know. He means we're not gentle with our world, we don't respect her and we don't respect each other. He thinks Silenda are the epitome of that disrespect. They're exploiting nature.'

Bennet nods feverishly and Hayden collapses onto his chair, spilling a little whisky on his jumper on the way down.

Gia, who has only just become consolable with her tear-stained cheeks, says, 'Cara, Bennet told me you still can't remember being taken, but didn't you notice the mark on your neck while you were living in the Urb?'

'Well I noticed it, but I didn't really think about it. I didn't really think about anything. I'd have gone crazy if I haven't already,' Carson mumbles, her words trailing off. 'The reason I'm saying this now,' she continues, breathlessly 'is because Randy Redding has the exact same mark on his neck.'

The room falls silent.

All that can be heard is the ticking clock and the familiar sound of a soap opera theme song playing quietly on the television in the background.

Astrid rises. Hayden looks suddenly concerned. Bennet puts his hand on Carson's shoulder and Gia cries hysterically once again.

I stand static in a room full of fear-ridden strangers.

CHAPTER 11

ALL THE THINGS WE LIVE FOR

Carson

Hawk and I watch stunned and unmoving as the police car speeds away with Zebediah in its back seat. Hawk begins to run, but he's far too late to have any chance of catching the car. Besides, it would be futile if he somehow could.

He falls to the ground, knees tucked up to his chest, swaying unsteady on the lawn outside the cabin. Hayden stands on the cabin doorstep, staring into the distance where the police car once sped away. He rushes out to comfort Hawk in a moment quite out of character, whispering something inaudible in his ear and grabbing his hand to get him to his feet.

'So, how the fuck are we sorting this out?' Hayden says, looking from Hawk to me. When he looks at me, his eyes graze my entire body as if checking for any signs that I'll dart away, or like he's assessing my levels of familiarity with him.

Hawk lets out a frustrated breath. 'You stay here,' he says to Hayden. 'Astrid says the new guy is moving in today and he'll need someone to greet him and check him in.'

'Why's Astrid not here?' he asks.

'She's in the city. She was supposed to be taking Carson to

meet Eydis and explain the whole situation, but Eydis wasn't around so Astrid took the liberty of breaking the news herself. Which, as you can imagine, didn't go down very well.'

I stand awkwardly.

'Okay, so I'll check in the new guy,' Hayden says. 'What are you doing? I'm assuming you're taking Nemo the fucking clownfish with you?' he says, gesturing to me. *Excuse me?* I think and spend far too long figuring out what he could possibly have meant. An insensitive reference to my memory loss? My red hair? I decide to scowl at him either way.

Hawk looks at me like I'm some sort of misbehaving puppy and frowns. 'Yes, I think it's best that Carson stays with me. She's not safe on her own and I'm not leaving her with you.'

Hayden laughs, his white teeth gleaming in a wealthy yet crooked smile that does not match the fear in his tired black orbs. He shuffles his feet momentarily until he's somewhat kicking the grass with purpose.

Hawk puts his hand on his shoulder. 'We'll get Zebediah out of this.' He reassures the bloody-nosed blonde who immediately feigns confusion, salutes us sarcastically and backs away into the empty cabin, closing the door tight behind him without another word. Hardly even another breath.

'He has issues he's suppressing,' Hawk says to me, still looking at the closed door of the cabin.

'So I keep hearing.'

We're still for a while. It's been a hectic morning and a hectic couple of days. It's nice to be still, before we are forced to process Zebediah's arrest and everything that surrounds it.

'Is Hayden really going to fulfil his birthday gift to you?' I suddenly ask.

'I don't know. He's working on it,' Hawk begins. 'Is that what you want? Your memories back?'

I think so, I think. It has never occurred to me that regaining my memory could ever be a bad thing, but maybe my memories hold a lot of trauma I'm currently free from. 'I don't know,' I say and he nods like he understands.

There's a pause.

There seems to be an eternity of silences between Hawk and me, despite the many things I'm sure we have to say to each other. It becomes awkward so I break the quiet with a shaky breath, 'Why did you want this? Why did you want to bring me here?'

'Because you're my friend. Because I wanted my friend back,' he says.

'Right,' I say and he frowns at me. 'It's hard to imagine us as anything but strangers.' He nods, sadly, until I decide we owe Zebediah every ounce of mental strength we have remaining, even if I can't quite recall our friendship. 'What now?' I ask.

Hawk sighs. 'We need Tyson.'

• • •

I know that I can never know.

But I think it will be black. And I'm entitled to *think*.

The sun never really emerges from behind the grey firmament in West Town, but even with my eyes squeezed tight, my black vision is threaded with orange light. It's as dark as anything seems to ever get, behind my eyelids. I think it will be darker than that. And I think I won't know about it either. You know, when I *die*.

He looks better this way too.

His tawny-beige skin warms against the light. I watch the thick ripple of his throat when he swallows. His broad shoulders hold the black wool of his sweater. Every little thing about him is engraved in my mind. I think he's special – Hawk. I think he's really ethereal and yet incredibly earthy. He makes me conscious of the weight of the organ in my chest. He makes my stomach turn in a way that makes me feel like I'm flying down a vast hill on a bike, letting the wheels take me wherever they ought to. My insides haven't quite caught up yet.

I think believing in the dark, despite my acknowledgement that I can never truly be sure, makes the world more beautiful. Everything is sharpened because I feel that when it's all over, it really is over. There will be no warmth, no heat, no saliva to swallow thickly, no breaths to take, no eyes to pierce the flesh of my being.

Nothing. Hawk is beautiful because he's not. He's not one of a kind. He's not forever, either. But he's here and I'm here, and gosh, I really like how life feels when I'm near him. I don't entirely know what he was to me before, but I know what he is now. He's a beautiful stranger, he's a distant familiarity. He's the feeling of déjà vu, the feeling that my chest has beaten heavy for him before. That my body has felt raw life with him.

Hawk feels like death. Cold, black and static death. *He is to live for.*

I hold onto the feeling of him, too afraid to reach for his hand as we journey to Mayor Turrow's esteemed home. In my mind, I imagine the mayor living in an enormous mansion with crisp gold linings, marble floors and an abundance of pillars. I'm not sure why; it's hard to say why the brain generates such ideas. Perhaps it's where I would live if I were him, but as we journey up the great grassy hill with the estate of cabins far beneath us now, we edge closer to the mayor's mansion in its true form: a thunderous castle-like mosaic of stone.

It's immediately hard to imagine Astrid growing up here, sneaking out of the delicate glass windows in her Versace leather, when she should ideally be fleeing down the front steps in a whimsical lilac ball gown to meet her prince. I am sure she would much sooner hop on a motorbike and head out clubbing instead. It's far easier to imagine Hayden at home in such a place. He fits comfortably into the role of a king's troubled nephew who storms the castle corridors like a pathetic storm cloud, drinking straight brandy from a glass canister and leaving a poor swollen-lipped damsel in every room. But perhaps I'm making harsh judgements.

The fantasy castle has a post-modern heart, with red plush chairs the shape of lounging female silhouettes. Lamps stand tall in ambiguous shapes and the walls are adorned with carefully framed covers of high fashion magazines, featuring Astrid on every one.

The open-plan downstairs space is large, bright and colourful. The corridors are adorned with large oil paintings and the ceilings are fantastic with Gothic murals that depict completely mundane narratives. There is a particular one of a statuesque dog jumping for a stick by a vibrant blue river. There's something almost comical about it.

As we move through the house, Hawk evidently searching for Mr. Turrow, we come across a lengthy dining table adorned with plates upon plates of food. The dining chairs of dark wood and red velvet stand tall and straight and surround a feast of glazed roast chicken, pork and golden tiger bread cut into thick slices. A large glass bowl of trifle, a fluffy Victoria sponge and a rich dark chocolate cake catch my eye. A large fruit bowl centres the table with fragrantly ripe bananas, red and green grapes and the largest strawberries I've ever seen. It becomes apparent rather quickly, that I haven't eaten all day. My stomach growls aggressively and my mouth waters at the scent of the slow roasted pork. I'm in a trance when he enters. 'Hawk,' a wise voice states as the sound of leather shoes on marble flooring follows. I was right about the marble.

'It's actually Bennet now, sir,' he responds to the mayor.

My eyes follow his and land on Tyson Turrow. He stands, a lot younger than I had pictured, with a white button-down shirt open at the collar and a suit jacket hanging from his person unceremoniously. His suit trousers appear a little baggy and his messy brown hair looks at least like he had attempted to comb it, should he not have attempted to shave his greying stubble.

His eyes are a deep brown like Astrid's left eye, and he looks astoundingly like her. Tall and handsome.

'Huh,' Turrow shrugs, 'with a name like Hawk you'd have to be an idiot to change it,' he refutes humorously, although there's something sharp and accusing in his tone. I stand behind Hawk like a shadow.

Tyson peeks round at me. 'Cara,' he says, softly. 'Please, have a seat. You were always too busy to eat properly. I assume, despite your dejectedness, that you're running on an empty stomach.' My shoulder's drop in relief and I realise how stiff with anxiety I had been.

The three of us sit at the dining table, Hawk taking a hefty slice of chicken breast and sandwiching it between two slices of bread with a thick layer of butter. I copy him, very much liking the look of his creation.

Amazingly, Tyson takes a spoon to the gigantic trifle. My body sings with relief as I sink my teeth into my first bite of the feast.

'Are you expecting someone?' Hawk asks, scanning the table of food and observing Tyson's dishevelled, half-ready appearance.

'You,' Tyson says, nodding with a mouth full of cream. 'I knew it would just be a matter of time before one of you came up here to convince me to bail Zebediah out of jail.' He swallows. 'And frankly, I'm quite offended you didn't assume that I'd already be on it. You know news spreads to me quickly. Anyway, I supposed whichever one of you turned up, you'd be hungry, perhaps in need of a little comfort food. I made sure to have enough should all of you turn up. Especially since Carson is back with us.' He winks at me but directs a threatening glance at Hawk, who nods awkwardly and I realise why he hadn't been entirely disturbed by Zebediah's arrest. Distressed and confused, yes. But not defeated. The mayor seems, despite his chaotic appearance, to have things under control.

Mr. Turrow grins maniacally and it suddenly makes sense why Astrid is so intense. She should hardly have any regular old father.

SILENDA

There's something about the man that is oddly comforting and safe, but certainly unconventional. 'What happened to the pink hair? I thought it was some sort of rebellion?' Turrow asks and my heart begins to race. Could it be that the mayor of the Umbras is an ally of the undecided?

He must sense the fear emanating from me. 'Don't look so frightened, Carson. Us Umbras aren't quite as dogmatic as the Luxies. The controlled one's, anyway. I won't chase Hawk off to the Rowleys. I, for one, am not exactly thrilled by the idea of being nothing but a rotten corpse or a pile of scorched flesh being blown away in the wind at some beach I liked when I was breathing. It's not exactly exciting, but I can't help what I believe as much as Hawk can't help not having a clue. Why should he have a clue?'

'You really believe that?' I ask and he looks pleased to hear me voice something.

'Of course, I do. That's why I proposed mixed schools to Basilio. Us Umbras live like there's no tomorrow. Because there might not be. Some Luxies spend their whole lives trying to prescribe meaning to things where there isn't any, hoping it'll all culminate and reach clarity when they get hit by a bus or lose the feeling in their left side.' He's laughing. 'I'm sorry,' he says, 'strokes aren't funny.'

It's hard to believe he means this.

'But wouldn't a heart attack be so much less of a bummer if you'd lived every day before it to the best of your ability?' Turrow goes on, 'If you hadn't wasted your life waiting for the next part? If you hadn't been so run down by how shit the world is that you conjured up a fantasy to numb your innate human fear instead of making the best of what you had?' He searches my face. 'I think so, anyway.'

Hawk lifts his glass of milk to the mayor's words and laughs, 'A world with cake is a good enough world for me!' He takes a great bite of the jam and cream sponge from his plate.

'May we rot in our graves!' Hawk chimes with the mayor. I try to feel fearful at his words but the silly smiles on their faces make it impossible. I can see why Hawk and the others from the cabin like Astrid's father so much. He just doesn't seem to care.

'You aren't even a little frightened?' I ask.

Tyson swallows his wine. 'Not at all. We are natural beings and nature will run its course.'

I pour myself some water from a large glass jug. 'Don't get me wrong, I respect whatever anyone on this earth wishes to believe. In fact, I envy some of them. Those with spirit. Have you met Eydis?' I shake my head. 'Eydis is a Lux, but she's independent in nature. She has her gods. She has her rituals and her prayers. But she does it on her own terms. She doesn't let any old white guy like Young dictate how she should behave all the years she lives. I respect that. It's the organised Luxies that I pity.'

'Organised?'

'Unfortunately, they're a strong majority. They follow the words of a book or an artless human and they create limitations upon their lives. A lot of them reject people like Eydis or Zebediah. Not all of them, but enough.'

'People like Zebediah and Eydis?' I question and Hawk shakes his head.

'A life with so many rules, regulations and limitations, is a life with intolerance, Cara. Zebediah is gay. Many controlled Luxies view his lifestyle as one of sin, as one that shall be rejected by their god.' Tyson stares into his wine glass, sorrowfully. 'Eydis is a beautiful woman. Her skin is almost obsidian black. She has vitiligo and a Lux had told her that her black skin had made God cry and that's what had washed her skin white.'

My stomach churns and a sudden hatred rises in my throat. I spring up from the table. 'That's awful!' I cry. 'Is that why people think you bombed Centrum Tower?'

'Gosh, Cara, I haven't seen you so fiery in a long time. Whatever has been put in your head in terms of the bombing,' Tyson eyes Hawk, 'forget about it. If it was an Umbra bomb it had nothing to do with us. I wish no harm upon anyone. If the controlled Luxies find peace in their order, then I'm pleased for them. But no one should allow their faith in anything to disturb the existence of others. But the bomb was not mine, and not in a million years could it be.'

My mind is like a spinning wheel until my thoughts culminate. 'Before,' I begin, 'when you said it'd been a while since you'd seen me fiery, that's because it's not been a while since you've seen me at all. You were watching me in the Urb, weren't you?' Tyson furrows his brows in a weak attempt to deny any knowledge of what I'm talking about.

I'm standing, leaning into any intimidation my petite stature will allow. There's an awkward silence and Turrow stands.

He turns and I observe him: his square jaw, walnut hair, broad shoulders. Handsome. Familiar. Soon the room is transformed in my mind's eye, the white ceiling is replaced with a starry black sky. Traffic lights switch frantically. Cars speeding. The bench, cold. The rain, heavy. He watches me.

'It was you!' I demand. 'You watched me. The whole time I was at St. Vincent Street, you were there! Astrid said so.' We're all standing now. I point an eager finger at Tyson and Hawk rises with a stern expression.

'You were there?' Hawk accuses. 'That whole time, you told me I couldn't go. I was in pieces and you told me to suck it up for the good of Carson. You said that I'd only confuse her. That I wouldn't be able to stay away!' He's yelling and my heart is swelling in my chest.

Turrow is firm with his hands in the air, defensively. 'I had to make sure you were okay, Cara.' He turns from me. 'But at no point had I approached her, Hawk. I promise you. I only watched from afar.'

'I could have watched from afar! And my name is Bennet!' Hawk yells deeply, the bass of his voice in my feet. Tears build in his black almond eyes.

The mayor looks immediately angered by his rising tone. 'Sit down, Hawk. Sit down, now! I had to look out for her. I should have looked out for her before and maybe Silenda wouldn't have taken her in the first place. I just couldn't listen to my brother. Goddamn alcoholic made me think he was crazy!'

'I hardly slept a single night the whole time she was gone!'

I search Hawk's eyes for feeling as tears pour from mine.

Turrow strides towards him and places his hand on his shoulder. He breathes deeply before he speaks, attempting to calm Hawk the best he can. 'She was my daughter's best friend,' he begins. 'I was the adult and I let her down!' There's a sharp look of pain in his eyes but all I can think is, *Astrid was my best friend?*

'She was *my* friend too,' Hawk mumbles, a violent glare in his eye that rejects anything Turrow could say to soothe him.

'You were pining after her before she even disappeared!' the mayor snaps as he removes his hand from his shoulder. 'Not in a million years would you have stayed away! I was doing my duty as the central adult in Carson's life. You'd simply have been stalking your ex-girlfriend to make yourself feel better. The only thing you cared about was relieving yourself from your own guilt!'

The room fills with shock and hurt.

And then it falls silent.

CHAPTER 12

ALL THE THINGS WE DIE FOR

Carson

'Bennet!' I yell as I run after him down the steep grassy hill so speedily I almost tumble into a forward roll. His long legs stride on without looking back. Hawk had held his heart like he'd been nursing a stab wound when Turrow had called him out.

It's a wonder he's kept his intestines in.

He'd stormed out immediately, and Tyson had returned to ploughing through his trifle with a guilty look on his face.

'Bennet!' I yell once more, the strong wind blowing my hair into my face so violently that it feels like I'm being whipped. The adrenaline that had kept me chasing him begins to fade and I have a tight knot in my stomach that I'm sure some roast pork sandwiches and several slices of cake have to answer for.

My short legs tire in my attempt to keep up with him and my breath begins to thin in a fight against the cold air. I slow to a stop, hands on my knees, hair in my face that for half a second looks like an autumn forest that I'd much rather be in. Black spots dance across my vision. I know from all my running that I'm not unfit and I must just be reaching the end of whatever has kept me going these last few days. At my wits end, I yell, 'Hawk!'

He stops dead in his tracks, his black hair blowing in the wind and his body pivoting slowly to face me. His cheeks are red with tears and his lips swollen. 'Say it again,' he says, flatly.

Far too tired to debate his reasoning, I do. I say his name once more. His real name.

'For a second there it seemed like maybe you'd remembered me,' he says.

'I'm sorry.'

'What for?'

'I'm not sure.' And I'm not. I'm really not sure of anything at all.

'My father's name is Bennet,' he says eventually.

We are silent.

'Why'd you change your name?' I ask, eyes squinting in the wind, trying to suss him out, hoping that this time I'll get a real answer.

'I guess I wanted a fresh start when you left. I didn't want to be me anymore.'.

'Why not?'

'Because I blame myself for what happened to you.' His stained cheeks are reddening deeper as he pulls at a thread on his sweater. My heart thumps in my chest at the sudden fear that my only real figure of reassurance since the Awakening, should be about to turn me away from him.

He shouts over the wind. 'We were on bad terms when they took you.' I look at him expectantly, but I don't want to know. Something in my gut screams at me.

I don't want to know.

I can't bring myself to stop him.

'I used to disappear in the nights,' he continues. 'You started to notice, and I didn't want to tell you where I was going. One night, you followed me into the Rowleys.'

'What were you doing in the Rowleys?' I ask.

'I was meeting Astrid. She was helping me with my music, with lyrics and vocals. She said that if she could get involved in the process that she'd pass on a tape to some big-shot producer in the Urb.'

I consider this for a moment. 'Why didn't you want me to know about that?'

'Because I wanted it to be a surprise. A lot of the songs I had been writing were written for you.'

Immediately, I grieve more than ever for a past when I knew him. A past where Cara and Hawk relied on each other. A past where I was his muse and he wrote songs about me.

He continues. 'Except, the night you followed me, Astrid had a lot to drink. Her and some prince dude were on and off a lot at the time and she was vulnerable.' A nervous heat washes over me.

Please stop.

There's a pause. There's always a pause between us.

'She kissed me,' he breathes. *Please stop.* My heart sinks. *No*, it plummets. I feel somehow guilty that it hurts so much. 'You saw us. You tried to act like you weren't upset but I knew that you were.'

I take a deep breath before I speak, frightened of the answer. 'Was I your girlfriend?'

'No,' he says. I breathe. 'We've never...' he pauses, exasperated in the wind. 'You were my roommate, just my roommate. And my friend. But I kissed Astrid back and I hurt you. I think you thought we'd been hooking up or something. You thought that's what I'd been out doing every night!' He edges closer to me, ducking to catch my eyes with his but I'm too embarrassed by everything he's saying that I can't look at him.

He goes on, nonetheless. 'Things were already stressful between us. I didn't want you pursuing Silenda and you told me I had no right to stop you. You were the only one that believed Jason Turrow. I thought you were both nuts. I think you were frustrated by my protection over you. It ended up just spurring you on.'

He looks at his feet. 'We were yelling at each other in the street outside the old tattoo parlour that night in the Rowleys. I remember your tears looked blue in the neon lights and I tried to reach for you. You told me that you didn't care, that I could fuck Astrid all I wanted because you'd never feel that way about me.' My whole body feels warm with shame at his words.

Hawk's tears are drying but his eyes remain large with sorrow when he goes on. 'We were screaming. I was tired and you hurt me. I guess I had already convinced myself that nothing would ever happen with us, despite how we were with each other. But it hurt to hear you say it.' I try to shake my head, but I'm frozen in place.

How could I possibly reassure him when I have no idea how I felt? Did I love him, loathe him, tolerate him? I desire him, I know that. But maybe I just desire human touch. Maybe I'm tired of feeling lost and lonely. Hawk begins to cry again and it feels like my heart is in the fist of a frustrated man, squeezed tightly in his unforgiving grasp. 'I left you,' he croaks. 'As soon as you'd said it, I went back to Astrid. We got high and we hooked up and I came home. I didn't check to see if you were sleeping, I didn't even check to see if you were in bed. I didn't even look at your side of the room! I left you in the Rowleys. And that's the last time I saw you.' I'm crying again.

'We found you in the Urb the next day, and you couldn't remember who you were. We tried to bring you back, but you were a shell of the person you were. When Hayden wiped your memory and Tyson sent you away, he forbade me from seeing you because of how distraught I had been. I just couldn't forgive myself. I was a terrible friend to you, Cara. If I hadn't left you that night...' his voice breaks. 'This is me trying to fix it, but I can't fucking think what I'm supposed to do now!'

Hawk falls to the floor, his knees buried in the thick wild grass and his head in his hands. 'How could I have messed up so badly? Silenda took you because of me. And now Zebediah is in jail and I bet he became an easy target the second he started strutting around with bright blue denim and purple hair. My stupid rebellious idea!'

I edge towards him, timidly. Afraid of the way he looks at me. Afraid of all of the things he's told me. Afraid that, if I think about it enough, I will blame him too.

I try not to think that he's pretty when he cries, it feels shallow and unfeeling, but his eyelashes are thicker when drenched in tears and his lips are fuller. Saltier. I hate that I desire him. I hate the stirring feeling in my stomach and how quickly my knees have become weak and my heart inflamed for him.

In only a couple of days, it feels like we have never been apart. Perhaps my heart has a memory. My muscles remember how to flex, my legs remember how to walk and my heart remembers how to desire him. I must have wanted him to some degree before, so much that his assumed sexual relations with Astrid had made me so angry. Did I want him? Did I feel that Astrid had tarnished my chance to hop into bed with my handsome roommate? Or, is it possible that I... *loved him?*

I decide I can only act on what I know to be true right now. What Carson Whitmoore knows right now. Not Cara. And what I know is that Hawk's tears have me moving towards him and kneeling down beside him.

'You think Zebediah was framed?' I ask, recalling his words about him being an easy target.

He looks up, bouncing his fist on his knee. Knuckles white. 'Well, he didn't do it. There's no way.'

I think momentarily about Zebediah's violent encounter with Hayden, but decide instead to nod in vigorous agreement with Hawk if it means keeping him from spiralling further.

'I'm sorry.'

'What for?' he asks as we echo our earlier words. Only this time I know why I'm apologising.

'For telling you that I could never feel for you. For hurting you. Mainly because I don't think that could have been true.' I smile softly at him and hope that when I rise and offer my hand that he'll take it, and he does.

'I'm sorry, too,' he says, brushing down his jeans as he rises and wiping his cheeks with the back of his hand.

'What for?'

'For sleeping with Astrid,' he mutters.

'By the sounds of things, you didn't owe me anything.'

'I saw how the kiss hurt you, and I went back to her anyway. I left you in a dark alley, Carson. If you should feel safe with anyone right now, it shouldn't be with me. I'm a bad person.'

'You're not,' I demand, before I realise I was going to. 'You saved me on the day of the bombing. And you were the only one from the cabin who never gave up on me. You were the only one who came back for me, even though you were the only one who had no idea where I was.'

'Maybe I was selfish,' he says. 'You could have gone the rest of your life without knowing about Silenda and I took that away from you because I missed you.'

I think on this for a second. 'I think it's dark when we die.'

'Huh?' he says, taken aback by the sudden turn.

'Hawk,' I say slowly, liking the way his face looks when I say his real name, 'I have nothing to lose in this life. But I have everything to gain.'

• • •

The quiet between us is agonising.

Despite our collaborative attempt to make sense of and move on from Hawk's confession, the air between us has become thick.

With Tyson Turrow focused on freeing Zebediah from his potential murder charge, Hawk has decided we ought to aid the situation in any way we can. Regardless of whether Turrow can release Zeb, there is still the issue of whether or not he actually committed the crime. And if not, who would want to make it look like he did?

After a mumbled debate with himself, Hawk decides that Eydis should be the best person to turn to next.

Still in the safehouse, our quest to Eydis sees us searching through endless trails of red and orange leaves in the Bellumside forest. We must walk about a mile with no particular path. Hawk has pulled out a compass and insists we head north, with it being his only real sense of where to go. It certainly is a safehouse when he struggles to find it and knows it exists.

Eventually, we reach a large pit in the ground. Half buried beneath a pile of leaves is a remarkably contemporary wooden cabin with large blacked out windows and a door that we have to slide down a hill on our butts to get to. Hawk knocks the door three times, pauses, and then knocks twice.

Silence.

Finally, she comes to the door. One of the most beautiful beings I've ever laid eyes on. Her black hair is in luscious spirals that fall down her back. Her skin is almost as black as coal, except for the illustrative splashes of white that travel up her neck and round the sides of her face like symmetrical vines.

She says nothing when she sees us. Eydis has obviously been aware of my return and looks almost tired to see Hawk. She wears a black slip dress and her full lips are pursed and shimmering red. She sighs before turning on her heel, leaving the door open for us to enter. Her tall, slim figure grants her the most beautiful curvature in her back. Her shoulder blades are sharp and elegant and affected also by her vitiligo.

Mesmerisingly, the white skin on her back appears to have been intricately decorated with black ink that depicts the solar system, beautifully lit up by white stars.

She's visibly older than us and the others in the cabin, but it's hard to place how much by.

Hawk takes his shoes and socks off when he enters and I copy him. The wooden floor is cold on my bare feet, but the main room is lit with at least 20 white wax candles that give warmth to the room where the windows are shadowed by forestry. I place my shoes on a rack by the door next to Hawk's Doc Martens, what I'm assuming are Eydis's red open-toe heels and a mystery pair of men's trainers.

Eydis lights a few more candles with a long wooden match and sighs. 'Cara,' she says, 'I'm sorry this happened to you.'

'You mean Silenda?' I mumble, shy under her striking eyes.

'No. I mean that Hawk was an idiot and couldn't just leave you to get on with the rest of your life.'

'Oh.'

Hawk rolls his eyes and wanders into the kitchen. He returns with a glass of water for himself, for me and some red wine for Eydis, probably to soften her up. Eydis accepts the glass without looking at him and stands static in the centre of the room. Hawk brushes her waist as he passes her and I cringe. 'I guess you're here about Zeb,' she begins, 'since you're not exactly Tyson's favourite person at the moment.'

'I think he had to learn that the hard way,' I say, glancing at Hawk.

'Well, you were right to come here. But I think you might want to sit down.'

We do. We situate ourselves on a sofa of soft hazelnut velvet and wait for Eydis to continue. Just as she's about to speak, a scruffy blonde man materialises from the next room, his hair tousled and his clothes half on. Hawk looks amused as the man's eyes widen to almost twice their original size when he sees us.

'Carson?' he exclaims, pulling on the rest of his white t-shirt.

'She doesn't remember you.' Hawk saves me from having to explain the lack of recognition on my face.

'Eydis, did you know about this?' the blonde man says.

She nods and explains the situation to the man, calling Hawk an idiot as many times as she can manage.

Hawk turns his head towards me where we sit shoulder to shoulder on the couch, his breath tickles my ear when he whispers and I try equally as hard not to lean into him as I do to not push him away. 'That's Jason,' he says. *Hayden's father*, I think.

Jason sits beside us on the couch. He gives me a kind smile, but he doesn't pressure me to talk to him, which I greatly appreciate.

Eydis takes centre stage again, making sure we are all seated. Jason puts a hand on my shoulder.

'The body is at the mortuary in Purgatorium Hospital in East Town,' Eydis starts and I assume she is talking about the man that Zebediah has been accused of killing. 'I have friends in East Town. As you know, I am a Lux. I may choose to retire in the Urb and, as of now, West Town, to ensure my safety from Silenda, but I am most connected in East Town.' The three of us on the couch sit quietly as she talks, plainly. 'Luckily for Zebediah, I have a friend who works in the very same hospital, with a key card that grants her access to the mortuary.'

'What are you saying?' Hawk interrupts her and Jason shoots him a disapproving look.

'I'm saying that I'm currently in possession of the photographs taken during Randy Redding's post-mortem. His cause of death has been ruled as strangulation, self-inflicted or otherwise. I personally don't believe this to be true which begs the question of whether Silenda has inside men. But that isn't the most riveting part.' Eydis goes over to a small desk drawer opposite us and pulls out a pile of large photographs before striding over and throwing them down on the coffee table in front of us. The three of us sit shoulder to shoulder like we are under interrogation.

I lean forward to examine the images.

His body, his vehicular matter, that which his soul no longer inhabits, lays sallow and grey on a long metal table. Most of the photographs focus closely on Randy Redding's neck, which is a cool yellowish-white and threaded with horizontal tinges of red and blue and purple. His eyes are closed over and his vibrant red hair is the only true colour that remains.

It's only a matter of seconds before I have to avert my eyes, feeling my roast chicken and pork sandwiches rising in my throat, but Eydis insists I look again, directing a long red fingernail at the side of the corpse's throat.

'*What is that?*' I ask, staring at the double puncture wound in Randy's neck.

'Same thing you have,' she says, 'and you.' Now looking at Jason.

My hand snaps immediately to my neck, feeling the two small holes Eydis is referring to. My hand shakes a little and my body winces at the echo of pain that it elicits. In my time in the Urb, I had always known the mark to be there, but I had never given much thought to it, often feeling dysphoric when I looked in the mirror, or too panicked by my thoughts that I would run to avoid them. I look at Jason, who is also holding his neck.

'Jason and I are certain that this is a mark from Silenda. Something they probed your neck with to induce cardiac arrest. Our current angle is that Randy was taken by Silenda, too. Zeb had nothing to do with this guy's death. I think that Redding was unable to be revived after Silenda experimented with his brain waves.' I shiver. 'But for some reason, Zebediah's fingerprints are around his neck. It's likely that they tried to frame it as a suicide, and when they realised a post-mortem was ordered, they put Zeb at the scene if anything suspicious should turn up.'

'Why?' I ask.

'My bet? Silenda are on to us. Someone's trying to get Zeb out of the way. It's not just about him, but it's certainly personal. They're likely to pick us off one by one.'

A wave of fear fills the room. Goosebumps run up my arms and I can almost feel them on Hawk too.

'We have to warn the others,' Hawk says.

'I'll leave that to you,' Eydis replies. 'Jason and I – we aren't going anywhere. This is deep shit. It's every one for themselves now. I've done my part getting you these.' She gestures to the photographs. 'The gods will welcome me when I'm ready, but I don't want to die yet."

Eydis, is there something you aren't telling us?' Hawk asks. 'I mean, you've been in this safehouse before Zeb was even arrested.'

Hawk has a point, and my heart begins to race as Eydis lowers herself on the opposite couch, allowing her thick curls to topple forward as she buries her head in her hands.

'They found me,' she says. 'In the Urb. Astrid had been in West Town and I was alone in our apartment, sleeping. I woke when I heard the creaking of footsteps on the floorboards and I thought I'd imagined it, but I didn't want to take any risks, so I got my gun—'

'Gun?' Hawk presses.

'Astrid and I have slept with guns under our pillows since that perv broke into our penthouse last May.'

'Oh, right,' Hawk recalls. I don't ask.

'Anyway, I wasn't expecting to find anything, but when I poked my head around my bedroom door, I saw him walking around our apartment, looking through drawers and carrying a tranquiliser gun.'

'How did you know it was a tranquiliser gun?' Jason asks.

'Well, because I shot him and I checked,' she says.

'You killed him?'

'Well, of course I did! What did you expect me to do?' she cries.

'Where's the body, Eydis?' Jason asks.

'In the river.'

There is a grave silence as the weight of her words sink in.

'How could you be sure they were from Silenda?' Hawk asks.

'I don't know,' she says. 'I just knew. He was clad in a black army vest and thick boots and... I just knew,' she repeats.

'That's what they looked like,' Jason says, standing. 'That's what they look like in my dreams – *memories*,' he corrects himself and a feeling of impending doom fills the room.

I put my hand on Hawk's arm. 'We need to tell the others.'

The journey out of the forest is nothing like the quiet that accompanied us on the way. Hawk won't stop talking. He speaks frantically, panicking, telling me that 'we're screwed' a million times over.

I try to reassure him but it's like he can't hear me. The journey out of the forest feels endless as my head thumps with the volume of information that has been dumped on me, both life-threatening and heart-breaking.

Hawk's hands flail around him as he rants and I trail quietly beside him, but we both come to an anxious and abrupt stop when there's a rustling of footsteps in the bushes behind us. Hawk backs up silently behind the closest tree and pauses. His eyes dart to mine and pose the question, *what was that?*

'It's probably just a squirrel,' I whisper.

'Heavier than a squirrel.'

'A bear?'

'There are no bears in West Town.'

A few nervous minutes pass. Eventually, we come to an unspoken agreement to emerge from behind the large tree that had disguised us among its low hanging orange-leafed limbs. Hawk's footsteps are cautious upon the crunch of the ground as he examines the surrounding forest. He turns and nods his head slowly, signalling for me to follow him. That's when we see him.

Black army vest. Gun scanning the trees.

Hawk breathes, 'Run!'

CHAPTER 13

SKILLFUL AND DARING

Horatio

Angelo had packed my suitcase full of my black clothing, band posters and an abundance of my favourite books. As I'm unpacking and decorating my new room of creaky wooden floorboards, a large wooden bed and a single chest of drawers, I decide my brother isn't so bad.

For a moment I'm pleased with myself. I stand back and observe my small bedroom and my humble ensuite bathroom (if an ensuite bathroom can ever be humble). I get a sinking feeling in my chest, the same feeling I get after I wake up from a thrilling dream and realise none of it was true. Suddenly, I'm back in the real world where my house isn't made of chocolate and I didn't just meet Johnny Depp.

Instead, I'm in an empty room, empty of feeling, with nothing but a completely mediocre day ahead. Soon this feeling of discontent bubbles into something far more heart-wrenching. It's probably because I never make the time to think. I have been running on adrenaline since my uncle recruited me and the reality of Zeb's arrest has me dropping my knees to the floor like I'm suddenly made out of lead.

I cry for a while and I think at some point I must have fallen asleep because my distress falls in and out of being. For fear of coming across as frail and stupid should any of my new roommates walk in, I brush down my ripped jeans, stand up and try to compose myself.

I pace the room, hands in my hair. I catch a glimpse of my red face in the mirror of my new bathroom and grimace. I smooth down my posters of Fleetwood Mac, David Bowie and Blondie, although I suppose it's just Debbie Harry. I admire my guitar as it sits on its stand and throw on a record.

There's something utterly pretentious about records in the post-modern age of technology, where pizzas come out of vending machines and the average person can photoshop themselves flawlessly next to Justin Bieber, but I like a little bit of pretentiousness, as long as it's coming from me and not the people around me. I suppose I'm a hypocrite, but I prefer to account everything to irony.

I play some Foreigner. They are completely cheesy and entirely brilliant. There is nothing sexier and yet slightly angsty about a saxophone solo. But I can't really enjoy it because I'm crying again. *Urgent* plays on in the background and, although it's a song about what I am presuming is a need for animalistic sex, something about the chaotic electricity and urgency of the bass and the strings and the hypnotic brass has my head spinning.

'Hey, Marino, you okay? I know Foreigner are a bit shit but you don't have to cry about it.' Hayden hovers in the doorway.

I dry my eyes with the back of my sleeve, hoping I can make it look like I was never crying at all. I decide to ignore his comment about my taste in music. 'It's just Zebediah.' I'm thinking as I speak. 'And all the confusing things you guys were saying about... Silenda?' Hayden ignores me as he goes through the books I have propped up on a shelf in the corner of my room.

'Vampires?' he inquires, picking up my copy of *Fast and Fanged*.

'I don't know,' I shrug with a croak in my voice, 'I just like them.'

He picks up another book. This time it's not mine, it's a book that Zebediah once gave me to educate me on why it was so hard for him to come out as gay. I forgot to give it back to him and Angelo must have shoved it in my suitcase beside the other books he packed for me. The book is titled, *Heteronormativity: Old Ideas in the New Age.*

'Is this a gay book?' Hayden asks.

'Well, it's a book about not being afraid of it. You can borrow it, if you like. It's Zeb's.'

'No, thanks,' he scoffs. 'Zeb wouldn't want me borrowing his books. Plus, I like tits.'

'You don't need to be gay to read it. I'm not gay.'

'Whatever.'

Hayden hangs around for a while, sitting on my bed and demanding conversation from me when really I would much prefer to hide under my new duvet and cry. He puts on a new record, this time by Blink 182. He tells me how much he is loving the new wave of pop punk but how he misses the old misogynistic lyrics that used to annoy Astrid so much that she would become physically violent.

He's laughing, so I decide that it's alright to laugh too. He tells me about his computer science course and that it's his last year so he should soon expect an internship at one of the largest technology organisations in the Urb.

He runs downstairs and brings back his super thin laptop that it's hard to imagine anything can be stored on. 'I've been working on something really cool,' he says. 'In the wrong hands it could go to shit, but in the right hands, the world could be a far better place.' He types quickly and I like the sound that it makes as his fingers dance rapidly across the keys. Ultimately, he brings up a picture of a mic which moves every time it picks up a noise.

He watches me to see my reaction.

'I programmed this,' he says.

'What is it?'

'Speak into it. Try and say enough sentences that you suppose you've used every letter that you possibly could in the English alphabet.'

Confused, I speak a few sentences, making sure to use the words fox, zebra and xylophone to ensure that I'm getting my x and z sounds in. My rambling must sound absurd, but Hayden looks reasonably pleased with my efforts.

Immediately, Hayden is typing a completely new sentence. He types, *Centrum Tower burned to the ground*, and the mic feeds him back the same sentence, but in my voice.

I look on astounded. 'Oh my God, how is that even possible?'

'It would be futile to explain it to you, Horatio, when you wouldn't be familiar with any of my computer jargon. But effectively, this mic here can recognise and adapt the sound system of your dialect and regurgitate its qualities in any sentence I desire. Like I said, in the wrong hands this software would be extremely dangerous. I call it Maudify.'

'Why are you showing me this?'

'If I could do something to impress you I thought you'd be more interested in becoming my friend. The rest of the guys in the cabin tolerate me at best. I thought with some fresh meat in the cabin, I could find someone who is actually good company.' Hayden looks at his hands in his first moment of vulnerability. I decide I don't mind Hayden too much. It bothers me that he has a problem with Zebediah and it worries me that Zeb wouldn't be pleased to see me acquainted with him. Especially as I am unaware of the events that led up to their distaste for one another.

It is safe to say that Hayden has an energy that can be interpreted as rude or obnoxious. But I don't mind him so much, and it doesn't matter anyway. He is the perfect person to get close to when it comes to feeding back information about the Umbra government to my uncle.

He is the nephew of Mayor Turrow and he may not be as easy on the eye as Astrid, but he is interested in investing information in me. When he leaves my room, I take notes in the notepad my uncle had packed for me and hide it under my bed in a folded pillow case so that no one will find it.

When I write about Maudify, I'm not sure whether I will pass on the information to my uncle or whether I will rip it out of the notepad before the unity ball. I had no choice but to agree to the task I've been set, but in no way do I trust my uncle with such dangerous technology, let alone trust him at all.

I stay in my room for most of my first day in the Nether Cabin. When it's time to eat, Gia's brother Bennet shouts up the stairs for me to come down. I thought that in student accommodation it would be a fend for yourself situation, but I venture downstairs to find a long table adorned with five plates of food. It becomes apparent that the people of the cabin are a friendly group.

Bennet has been on dinner duty this evening and serves us fried chicken with a side of creamy pasta. In the centre of the table are slices of garlic bread that look buttery and delicious in the warm light of the dining room. My stomach growls instantly at the sight. The only thing I have consumed for the last day is alcohol. My liver is pretty angry with me.

Sitting at the table is the striking red-head known as Carson Whitmore, Bennet Lee, Hayden Turrow and his beautiful socialite cousin, Astrid Turrow. I sit down quickly so as not to stare at them all too long because there seems to be something quite surreal about having dinner with these people. There's something intimate about it and uncomfortable in the way that they all know each other, and I am the new and unfamiliar stranger.

To fulfil my uncle's task, and in the fear of what may be at expense if I do not, I decide that I will need to befriend these people pretty soon and gain their trust so they will confide in me before the ball. Maybe then I'll find out more information about Silenda and the mark on Carson's neck. There had been a disturbed expression on Bennet's face and sweat beading on the red-head's forehead the minute she walked into the cabin that persists.

Astrid is the first to speak to me. Carson looks like she has no intention of speaking to anyone and Bennet stares at his food like it's poison, which is disconcerting for everyone else at the table. Hayden munches away quickly, ignoring the awkward tension in the room.

'So, Horatio,' Astrid voices my name slowly, 'like from *Hamlet*?'

'That's the one,' I say.

'You know, despite what you heard us talking about earlier, you shouldn't worry, Horatio is the sole survivor at the end of the play.'

'Yes,' I say, 'well, I feel a lot more like Hamlet.'

Astrid smirks as the other three look like they have no idea what that implies.

'You have an evil uncle that you need to kill?' Bennet jokes with a shy laugh.

Somehow this feels like a bit of an alarming question and I try not to react defensively. No, I do not need to kill my uncle. *But is he evil?* I don't think so, anyway.

'Just an expert procrastinator,' I reply eventually.

The room is silent with nothing but the clattering of cutlery. Once we have eaten, Bennet and Carson disappear upstairs. Hayden and Astrid pick up the dishes and clear them to the side, with Hayden insisting he will get them later.

Astrid, still in her silk nightgown and animal print slippers, proceeds to the main room, turns on the TV and falls onto the couch. 'Horatio,' she calls me, 'your first classes are on Monday, but tomorrow is Saturday. Every new houseguest in the Nether Cabin has to go through the same...induction.'

'Induction?'

'Since it's been brought to my attention that Zebediah is your friend,' her tone sounds suddenly sorrowful, 'I thought that maybe we would make your induction that little bit more exciting, just to take your mind off of things while my father sorts it out.'

'Exciting?' I ask, starting to feel a little silly as I repeat the keywords of Astrid's statements.

'Well, we'd like to know that you're skilful and daring enough to be a member of our cabin.' Astrid turns her eyes from the television and stares directly into my soul. There is something slightly creepy about her heterochromia; her expressions are harder to read because the glint in her eye differs from the right side of her face to the left. 'Don't worry,' she assures, 'tomorrow night will be nothing crazy. Everyone had to do it, even Hayden.'

I wonder immediately why I need to be skilful and daring to be a member of the Nether Cabin, when presumably its only function is to house students at West Town University. I had imagined that this particular cabin was far larger and more contemporary than the others because it is home to the two most important young adults in Umbra society, but my uncle's suspicions that something far more sinister is going on among these people starts to weigh heavily on my mind.

There is something in Astrid's words that makes me feel heavy with anxiety. No one has mentioned the mark on Carson's neck since Gia left. She had gone home to her own accommodation on campus and had simply walked out the door without saying a word. The news that Randy Redding has the same mark on his neck as Carson had fallen dead on my ears. I had no insight into what this could mean. Carson remained reserved for the rest of the night and Astrid and Hayden pretended that nothing had been said, as if to tackle it another day.

Later that night, after my first shower in my ensuite, I pull on a pair of jogging bottoms and brush my teeth. I creep downstairs for a glass of water for the night, when I find Astrid still watching the television in the main room. Specifically, the news channel which speaks of the bombing of Centrum Tower. It seems to be the only thing on the news these days. Disturbed and confused by the abrupt way the topic had been dropped after Carson told us of the mark on Randy Redding's lifeless body, I take the opportunity to sit down next to Astrid in the hopes she will help me make sense of the situation.

As I sit down next to her, I observe that I'm only a little larger than her. She is tall and thin, although not incredibly so, with a presence so fierce, it is hard to imagine that such a creature sits on the couch and watches television. She does not look at me when I sit down beside her. I don't know if she has this ignorance about her to appear omnipotent and important, but it is clear that she is not looking at me on purpose.

'Zebediah didn't kill Randy Redding,' I say without realising that's how I wanted to start our conversation.

'We know that.' She finally looks at me.

It's hard for me to speak to Astrid at all. She is so beautiful and I am so intimidated by her that asking her where the bathroom is seems like a great enough endeavour. But there is something going on here, something to do with Carson Whitmoore. I feel it in my chest and the only way I can get to the bottom of it is by interrogating the people involved.

'You were all freaked out by Carson's mark and Randy having it too. Why did the revelation just get dropped? Tomorrow is my induction, but if I'm going to stay here I want to know what's going on. What were Carson and Bennet running from when they turned up on the doorstop and why was my best friend arrested on suspicion of murder?'

Astrid sighs, raising her eyebrows at the blunt volume of my questioning. 'When I'm not on campus, I live in the Urb with another model named Eydis Achebe. She's a little older than us. She's a Lux and has her religious practices, and I respect them. I don't wear shoes in her room, we light candles before bed and I hold her hand as she prays before mealtimes. She has her gods. She believes in an afterlife, but it's not heaven. Her gods would not allow hell.' I let Astrid speak, focusing carefully, waiting for anything that will help me understand. 'When Mayor Young gets up on his podium and speaks on the news,' she points to the television where I see my uncle doing exactly that, speaking of Centrum Tower quietly in the background, 'he speaks of god with a capital G. One god. Not Eydis's gods. Not the god of many Luxies. Everyone's beliefs differ, even slightly. We live in a society where you believe or you don't, but there is more conflict between Luxies than there is with us. Eydis is discriminated against for her differing interpretation of *next*.

'Mayor Young's god is followed by the book. They believe he created everything. *Everything* – trees, puppies, war, fucking cancer in children.' She's tearing up and her words are so powerful. I've never heard anyone speak about 'God' the way that Astrid is right now.

'If I did believe in God, Horatio, I wouldn't respect him. Mayor Young gets down on his knees for a god he believes created such a tragic and unmerciful world.'

I can't help but feel like Astrid is avoiding the topic of Carson and Randy and Zeb, but I'm so besotted by her that I almost forget. 'Why?' I half whisper.

'When I was younger and my birthday was approaching, my father would sit a little pink bear on the bookshelf that overlooked my bed. He told me that little Pinky would watch me and, if I misbehaved, I wouldn't get as many birthday presents. So, I tidied my bedroom every day after playing and I never talked back. I watched the pink bear as much as he watched me. I wanted his validation, I wanted to know that I was doing good. That's how you get a kid to do what you want them to do. You make them feel like they're being watched – it's how you train a guilty conscience.

How do you get societal control, Horatio? You tell people that there's an invisible man in the sky that will send them to burn in an eternal fire if they don't thank him every day for the good and the bad that he has created. I don't believe in God or an afterlife, but if I did, I wouldn't care for God's validation.'

Wow.

I blink rapidly trying to keep on top of the weight of Astrid's words. 'And Carson's neck?'

'I guess there are some people out there who find it impossible to live in a world where they don't know what will happen next. Maybe there are people who can't tolerate people like me, people who don't value their god. Or maybe there are people who can't tolerate the people who do believe in a god. Either way, it's fucked,' she breathes. 'I don't see why we can't just all respect each other's beliefs and leave it there. I'm not asking anyone to agree with me. Like I said, Eydis is one of my best friends.'

'What people?' I ask and Astrid shrugs.

'There are people in this world who are not content with not knowing and they will do dangerous, dangerous things to try and find out the truth so they can prove one of us wrong. Effectively, whichever one of us turns out to be right, the Shadows or the Lighties, will take over. They will take our spirituality, our religion, our choice to not have religion. They will show us the truth and they will send us into hysteria. But us human beings have a compulsive need to be right; to know the truth and to think that we are owed everything from nature. We think that this planet exists to serve us and not us to serve it.'

'What are you saying?'

'Silenda. You heard us talking about them?' I nod. 'Like I said, they're not my secret organisation to keep a secret, so you might as well know. They're taking people from the streets, particularly the Rowleys, and conducting experiments on them. They kill them and examine their brain waves to try to work out where our souls, or our energy, goes when we die. They are active, and thanks to Carson and Bennet's run in with an agent this afternoon, it's clear that they're onto us.'

'Onto us?'

'Carson was taken about a year ago, and so was Hayden's father. Carson still can't remember shit, but Jason remembers. We've been trying to find them, take them down, but now they know that we know about them. Chances are, that's why they've taken Zebediah down, as a sort of warning – a way to assert their power.'

'So, you think that Silenda framed Zeb?' My heart sinks.

Astrid takes a swig from her glass of wine. She looks pale in the television light. 'We suppose that Randy was taken by Silenda, killed and unable to be revived and it was made to look like suicide. Suicide rates are suspiciously high in the Rowleys, you know. Usually, the people that die there go straight into a hole in the ground and nobody gives a shit, but it turns out that Randy's parents are pretty important Luxies and despite their estranged relationship with their son, they want justice. And perhaps publicity.' This does not come as a surprise to me as I recall Randy's stiff upper-lipped father and his mother who always looked like she had a foul smell under her nose.

'Either way,' Astrid continues, 'it came to Silenda's attention that the suicide would soon be deemed a murder after Randy's post-mortem. I mean, the shape of the bruises on his neck would reveal whether he was killed by the rope or at the hands of someone else. Unfortunately, no toxicology report was carried out. At the end of the day, he is still a Rowleys corpse. There is only so much money they're willing to pump into him. Silenda have to clean up the mess they've made and while placing blame, they might as well take down one of us. It wouldn't be hard to get Zeb's DNA at the scene. He's always out. Follow him to the Panic Room, pick up his fingerprints from a glass of wine and you're winning.' Astrid dances her slim white fingers across the rim of her glass, as if imagining it being done.

'This is all just speculation, right?' I ask as I watch her lips connect to the glass.

She gulps and nods.

'Should you really be telling me all this?' I ask, worried about Astrid's apparent tendency to say too much. I think of the sort of trouble I could get her in if I so desired to. I could feed this straight back to my uncle. Whether I will or not, depends on what more I learn about these people.

'No point in not telling you,' she says. 'What will be, will be.'

'Why do you need me to be skilful for tomorrow's induction?' I recall what she wishes to see in me in the day that follows.

'When Carson disappeared, we decided that we needed to combine our skills to take down Silenda. Hayden is a whizz with a computer, Zebediah has his way with words, I have a platform that people will listen to and a dipsy blonde mask to avert attention. Bennet is caring and fuelled by passion. He doesn't think, but his recklessness makes him outrageously brave under pressure. What are you, Marino?'

I go to bed with Astrid's question floating in my mind.

What am I?

I decide tomorrow that I shall do my best to show Astrid Turrow who I am, and hopefully she'll like what she sees.

CHAPTER 14

STRAWBERRY JAM

Horatio

The winter sun pours sharply through the crack in the blinds. I wake only seconds before Bennet comes rushing into my room with the first smile I've seen on his face since we met. He's dressed in black except for his ultramarine Doc Martens.

I toss my hair back and run my fingers through it, almost forgetting that it's now short at the sides. I suppose that my impulsive haircut feels like a disguise if I am now Horatio Marino. I forget I'm not wearing a shirt when I emerge from under my new duvet, my white torso exposed in the grey light.

Bennet tosses me the jumper thrown over my desk chair. 'It's induction day.' He looks me firmly in the eye.

There is something troubling in his eyes. Something disjointed in his smile; something resembling fear. I can feel it burning my skin.

I'm relieved when he leaves.

The morning begins at a relatively normal pace. Carson looks swollen-eyed as she bites gingerly into an uncut slice of toast and Bennet does all he can with his inauthentic cheerfulness to try to make her smile. He nudges her and offers her a chocolate croissant but is met with a smile that is more of a grimace.

Hayden is up and dressed already: brown velvet trousers and a baggy cream sweater vest. He seems to have the grungy 'I stole my Grandad's clothes' look going on that I've observed many times in the Urb. I'm watching them all as I grab a jar of strawberry jam from the fridge and smother it thickly onto a burnt slice of toast that ejects from the toaster.

Strawberry jam is my least favourite kind of jam.

I prefer raspberry, blackberry or even cherry, but I always eat strawberry. Its rich red colour and the seeds of the strawberries give it a clotted-blood sort of look that used to really freak Zebediah out when we were younger. So I always eat it. Even when he's not around.

I'd spent the late hours of last night and the wee hours of the morning hunched over my notepad that I stashed under my bed, writing all the information about Silenda that Astrid had told me last night in as much frightening detail as I could manage.

I wrote about the dynamics of the group too. Hayden and Astrid are pretty assertive, if eccentric. Bennet and Carson are far more reserved and have more hiding in their bloodshot eyes. I drew a big red star on the corner of the page about Silenda and leave my entry about the Nether Cabin blank. The star is to remind me of what I should be wary about telling my uncle, and perhaps consider tearing out.

I decide it's harmless for him to know that Hayden has more of a mouth on him than Carson. This kind of thing shows my engagement with my mission but doesn't pass over any information that I'm currently unsure of the weight of.

Once I've dusted off my toast, I head upstairs to change. I try to look as much like an Umbra as I can, although this doesn't change much about what I would normally wear. I pull on a long black tank, jeans, some heavy boots, my favourite chains and my occasionally ill-received dangly earring. I decide that, with the fashion taste of the others, it may go unnoticed.

Bennet looks like an Umbra King, Hayden looks like he's never shopped anywhere but a thrift store, Carson looks like a homeless girl who won't stop pulling at the threads of her clothes and, well, Astrid is *Astrid Turrow*.

When I enter the main room, Hayden is sipping what he insists is water out of a paper cup, Carson looks slightly less pathetic than she did this morning in a long black hoodie and high-top Converse, and Bennet, looks – well, he looks way hotter than me.

Astrid is nowhere to be found but everyone looks ready to start the day. 'So what exactly does this induction day entail?' I lean on the kitchen counter, trying to look casual and not all like I'm slightly terrified and intimidated by everyone.

Hayden takes a sip from his cup. 'Astrid likes to lead induction, it's sort of her thing. I think we've to shut up about it.'

Bennet nods in agreement and Carson shrugs, 'In case you've not been updated, I don't have a fucking clue what's going on either.' Her voice is deeper than I expected when she's not crying and her profanity sort of makes me like her better. She's less of a downer than she looks. I feel myself smirk. There's a sudden shriek from the backdoor of the cabin that has us all up in arms until it evolves into a gleeful squeal. Astrid cries with excitement in a pitch that almost only dogs can hear. I don't think I'm the only one who assumes she is simply excited about the day ahead.

I fold my arms over my chest, only turning my head in response to the commotion. Hayden, however, pulls at his vest, cheeks flushed with colour as he walks through the room and down to Astrid.

My heart thumps in my chest and my head gets all dizzy when I see him strutting down the corridor. Clad in far too much denim and with a full white smile too broad for the circumstances, Zebediah enters the main room. 'He's out!' Astrid yells. 'Dad got him out!' She points at him as if we need a running commentary.

'Zeb!' I exclaim and embrace him before he has the time to realise it's me. He pulls back and looks at me, eyes scanning mine. 'Harry?' he exclaims before pulling me in for another hug. 'What are you doing here? Your uncle would—' before I let Zeb finish with what I'm assuming would be 'kill you for being here!', I pull him out of the room and back into the corridor, just out of earshot of the others. 'It's Horatio Marino now,' I say.

'Huh?'

'I ran away, Zeb. I changed my name and enrolled in a music tech course at West Town!'

'You're kidding!' he whispers, sharply. 'You wouldn't have the balls!'

'Yup! Turns out they just hadn't dropped yet.'

Zeb's expression turns from excitement to a somewhat disgusted amusement. 'Okay, enough with the balls analogy.' We laugh and it feels so good to see his yellow eyes crinkle with joy.

He smells like cigarette smoke and I really do hate cigarettes but for some reason, I love the way the smell clings to his denim. He smells like the city, like cold air and wet pavements. 'I can't believe you're here,' he says.

'Me neither.' And I can't. I really can't. 'But you can't tell the others about my uncle. I don't want them to know that I was ever a Lux. I just want a fresh start.'

'Oh, Harry, my friends really wouldn't care—'

'I just want a fresh start, Zeb. A fresh start.'

He says no more, asks no other questions. He places his hand on my shoulder and smiles at me, reassuringly. I know then that my secret, however much of a lie it may be, is safe with Zeb. Just as he's about to turn to the main room to greet the others, I grab his wrist to stop him. I lean into whisper. 'Astrid told me everything. I'm sorry, Zeb. You're home now.' He holds my gaze for a while, far too close. He smiles softly and I let him step away. I watch him walk and catch striking black eyes watching me, his jaw clenched tight. Hayden drops his gaze when our eyes meet.

Zeb sits on a stool by the kitchen island as we all gather round. He tells of his short time in prison like he was simply at summer camp. His tone is totally inappropriate – but that's Zeb. He's outrageously funny. He tells of some dude named Gerry in for carrying a knife who actually turned out to be an 'alright guy'. Zeb only peed once the whole time he was there because he'd 'rather die from dehydration than hover over that toilet seat again.'

Even Carson is almost crying with laughter. It's just the effect he has on people.

Eventually, his tone turns serious and the room falls quiet as he tells us of how Tyson Turrow cleared his name. It turns out that Randy's cause of death was ruled as asphyxiation, despite our doubts, but somehow forensics concluded that the person responsible for Randy's death was almost certainly right-handed, when Zeb is left-handed. With the mayor of the Umbras backing him, this evidence alone was enough to grant his freedom. Zeb reassures his friends that his prison time wasn't so bad and it's something to tick off his bucket list. We laugh again before he demands that we should all take this as a warning of how powerful Silenda can be.

Every smile in the room dissolves.

But he's right.

'So,' Astrid says, 'Horatio's induction is about to be even more exciting.'

'Wait!' Zeb turns to Astrid, 'we're recruiting Harry to the—' with her eyes still firmly on mine, she slaps a hand over Zeb's mouth, who pretends to nearly fall from his stool.

'What?' I ask.

'All in due course, Marino,' Astrid says. Her heeled boots stride through the room as she claps her hands, demandingly. 'Gia!' she yells. Gia materialises from the hallway and empties the contents of her rucksack onto the wooden floor. I peer over to see numerous colours of hair dye and latex gloves scattered across the carpet.

'Okay, Horatio. If you want to join the Nether Cabin, you have to be comfortable with a little ambiguity. Yes, we are technically an Umbra household, but we are open-minded and accepting. We do not hate the Luxies. In fact, some of us even envy their faith.' She looks at Bennet who looks down. 'In the Nether Cabin, you don't have to be one thing. You can believe in the dark and scream in colour. So... ' she picks up a bottle of aquamarine blue, 'we're all putting streaks of hair dye through our hair. A little splash of colour to start the day.' Excited, we all scramble to the bottles on the floor like a bunch of kids fighting over crayons. Zebediah selects a purple dye to enhance his already coloured hair. Bennet is the second to choose, confidently swiping a baby pink and a blood red which he hands to Cara who smiles, approvingly. Gia selects a hot pink and Hayden a sunset orange, which leaves me with electric blue.

We each sit on a kitchen stool and dye each other's hair. Astrid is desperate to do my hair. She bleaches my black locks unceremoniously and weaves in the vibrant blue. I dip-dye her already blonde hair an oceanic blue. Gia insists she doesn't trust anyone else with her hair and gives herself a vibrant dip-dye effect. Carson puts white-pink streaks of colour through Bennet's hair and then he does the same for her with the deep red.

Carson's hair arguably turns out the coolest. She takes scissors to her hair and chops in messy layers.

The arrangement leaves Zeb and Hayden to fend for themselves.

This isn't a problem for Zeb, but Hayden gets himself in a mess and eventually the orange hair dye is covering his hands. He gets frustrated, so Zeb sighs and goes over to help him. I try not to stare too much, but it seems like Hayden protests before finally sitting down and letting Zeb run his fingers through his hair.

Hayden doesn't look too mad after a while. I suppose he's had enough time-out from Zeb recently to let him close.

Astrid takes me upstairs to her bedroom to wash the dye from our hair. Astrid's bedroom has the most amazing view of the loch, and the university stands tall and Gothic in the distance. In her ensuite, which is slightly larger than my own, she detaches the shower head and insists I lean over the bathtub so she can rinse the blue from my hair. The warm water trickles down my neck and I try not to think about her thighs pressed against my back where I'm crouching.

We swap and Astrid bends over the tub, I try to move to the side of her, feeling weak and uncomfortable standing directly behind her. My cheeks burn, anyway. I try to make conversation, but I have no idea what to say. After last night's heavy topic, it seems strange to talk about anything mundane, but at the same time, enough has been said about Silenda. Too much in such a short time, probably. I know that I, for one, am overwhelmed and I don't want to draw attention to myself by asking any more questions.

She makes me anxious.

When the dye has washed from her hair and I relieve my proximity to her, she turns the hairdryer on us and insists we dry our hair at the same time, the top of our heads pressed together, which is odd but unexpectedly funny. Astrid says that the best way to make friends is to act like old friends who are stupid together, that way the ice is broken and there's no need for formalities. It sort of works, it makes her absolutely terrifying, but it sort of works.

She flips her hair back, screams at her stereo to play *Jealous* by Eyedress and opens the top drawer next to her bed to reveal a small, round plastic container. She brings it over and smears black eye makeup across my lids and hers. It's a weird sort of buttery texture that reminds me of face paint at children's parties.

'Are you ready for the best bit?' she exclaims with a wide smile. She uses her fingers to pull the makeup down my cheeks until I look like a member of Kiss or a sad mime. I stand and look in her vast mirror and the juxtaposition of my lanky white limbs are definitely more goth than rockstar. She does the same to her own eyes and she looks ready for the catwalk.

I stare at us both in the mirror. My blue eyes look almost opaque against the coal-coloured makeup. My hair is sporadic blue. I stare at her in the mirror as if she could not see me.

She makes me dance with her and, as we spin about her room, I see a quote written in thick black marker-pen along the backboard of her bed. It's a few spins with her chaotically laughing in my arms before I piece it all together:

There's a loch called insanity that most people swim in. It's your responsibility not to get in too deep.

General life advice or a note-to-self? Astrid Turrow seems moments away from getting caught in the current.

It's as though last night never happened. No Lux-Umbra tension, no crazy scientists trying to kill us and bring anyone back to life.

Astrid Turrow is crazy. Either that, or she's desperately sad and trying everything to distract herself from it. Umbras may be reckless and honest, but god, at least there was real glee behind Lucian's eyes. Astrid Turrow appears made of glass: transparent, reflective and one scream away from shattering. I decide I have to be careful with her. I bite my tongue to hold my words and I cup her head when she dips in my grasp, so she doesn't hit her head on the wooden bed.

•••

It's freezing in the Rowleys.

Carson wraps her oversized hoodie tighter around herself and Bennet stands close to her without touching. Hayden glares at Astrid who's about to speak and Zeb and I stand shoulder to shoulder against a red brick wall.

We look like a crazy group of protestors with our neon hair.

Or like a futuristic S Club 7. Luckily, the Rowleys is as good as deserted. There's a sinking feeling in my chest thinking that my Uncle Basil really did have his men 'clear' the Rowleys with their guns, but a couple of pedestrians wander past, unfazed by our presence and lacking commotion.

I assume my uncle had ushered through intimidation over anything else.

We circle Astrid as she rummages through the boot of her dad's black Jeep. Carson looks intrigued, but the others look bored. Zeb picks at his purple fingernails, Bennet folds his arms over his chest and observes a pigeon that wanders past and Hayden purses his lips and sighs dramatically until someone looks over at him so he can roll his eyes. Astrid pulls out a gun.

A proper firearm, like the ones that my uncle's men carry. Carson steps back. I try to and hit my head against the wall.

Astrid Turrow is not the sort of person you want to see with a gun.

'Okay!' she exclaims. 'Now that we all look the part, it's time to get Horatio's induction under way.'

'We're going to the shooting range?' Hayden asks, suddenly erect.

'Yes.' Bennet joins Astrid at the head of the car. Carson audibly winces. 'Things are getting serious now. We need to know if he can shoot.' He nods at me. 'But today isn't only about Marino. We all need to be a good shot if we're going to defend ourselves from Silenda. They're well and truly on our case. They nearly had me and Cara just yesterday. And it's not just that...'

Astrid turns as serious as I saw her last night. 'We need to work towards infiltration.'

Zeb steps away from the wall. 'Infiltration?'

'Hayden has been using Carson's diary and maps to locate the base. We've already checked all the marked spots, but if we can stalk an agent to their HQ, we have to be ready to go in. To really stop them.'

'You've been reading my diary?' Carson turns to Hayden.

'Fucking hell, Red, it's not like you can even remember what you wrote to be embarrassed about it!' Hayden says.

There's a tension that runs even higher when Bennet throws a khaki backpack over his shoulder and hands out the firearms. When he pushes one against my chest, I almost fall over. Zeb laughs. It feels a lot different from the time he laughed at me falling up the stairs at the cinema. This feels a lot different from anything, really.

We follow Bennet and Astrid into the building behind us like we're their personal army. They're both tall and present and hard to argue with, so nobody speaks. The shooting range is much how I imagined a shooting range would be, except for the graffiti on the walls and the damp smell. There's no headphones either, or goggles, which is great.

Zeb and I have our own booth, and Hayden and Carson take the one next to us. Astrid and Bennet wander between us, making sure we're totally focused on the red rubber men at the end of the stretch of tin-can metal walls.

'You gotta aim for their heads,' Astrid says. 'They have vests.'

'What if I don't want to kill anyone?' Carson says.

'They're killing us, Cara. They're the reason you can't remember shit.'

'But I'm an Umbra. I know I can't know, but I really do believe it's dark when we die. What if I don't want to take someone's life away forever?'

'They tried to take yours!'

'They brought me back. I don't think that killing us is the point—'

'They experimented on you, Carson!' Bennet shoves past Hayden so he can stare her down. 'They took you away. And they'd take all of us! They don't care if we die and that's as bad as killing us. Look,' he ducks to lock eyes with her, 'you're either with us or you're not.'

SILENDA

Carson falls silent and points her gun at red rubber. The bullet leaves steel with an inescapable thunder. She gets him in the neck. Red rubber shreds like blood.

Bennet backs away, satisfied.

I try to mirror Carson's new-found fire, but when I cock the gun and shoot, the steel rebounds against my chest so hard I almost fly backwards, the bullet exiting the gun at an angle that completely spares the rubber man. Hayden cackles and Zeb places his hand on my shoulder when Bennet sighs at me. He's about to walk over to aid me, but Astrid beats him to it, helping me raise my gun at the target once more. I'm thankful for her help as Bennet's teachings may have destroyed any masculine dignity my eye makeup and dangly earring allow me. When Astrid cradles my arms, I focus my eyes and my mind on the rubber man, trying to find some deep-rooted anger to motivate me. Carson shook with determination when Bennet's words had swayed her, reminding her of what Silenda had taken from her.

I feel numb.

That's my biggest problem. I don't think enough and I don't feel enough. I shoot and I shoot again, with Astrid's aid and without. The only time I scrape the rubber man is across the chest, but for the most part, I'm missing.

I try not to be too downhearted. The only person particularly frustrated with my lack of skill is Bennet, who looks on with a furrowed brow and an unmasked scowl.

Astrid promises to take me to the range every morning for practice and I agree. What choice do I have? To retrieve the information my uncle requires, I have to be at the centre of this party, Silenda, or otherwise.

Although the Nether Cabin seem to be especially concerned with the extermination of Silenda, their reasoning may be more than just the abduction of innocent lives. What if these Umbras are just afraid to be wrong? Afraid that Silenda should uncover

164

the existence of an afterlife, of a god?

I can only imagine the sudden weight of what was once guilt-free sin.

I'd thought a lot about it in bed last night and I'd scribbled my thoughts down in my notebook. I could hardly sleep for thinking, which is unlike me. I usually have very little floating around in my mind. But I thought of Zeb and all the Luxies I know who believe in sin: the really intense ones who condemn same sex relations, who condemn pre-marital sex, drugs, lies, envy, greed, pride.

Hayden is never sober. Zebediah never shuts up about his sexual escapades and often has a joint hanging from his mouth. And Astrid? She concerns herself with every pore of her own skin to make a living. And here I am, holding a gun next to Carson and Bennet, the epitome of wrath. I don't know if I believe in hell, but I believe in fire. I see it in people all the time. And it blisters and burns all the same.

• • •

The Urb is cool in the November wind.

Astrid drives her father's Jeep into the city. Zebediah had called shotgun, and the rest of us are squeezed tightly in the back seat. Astrid hasn't told us where we're going. We sit quietly, except for Hayden, who is slurping loudly on a chocolate milkshake where he is squeezed between Bennet and me in the backseat. The petite Carson is pressed against the opposite window, staring distractedly into the darkening evening sky.

Astrid comes to a halt at the city strip where the clubs are abundant and the neon lights tinge the sky purple. The buildings are packed tight in the strip, with Centrum Park acting like an opposing magnet, with rocky green and bodies of water that keep the buzz of the Urb at bay.

Astrid turns her key in the ignition and hops out of the car, expecting us to follow her. We scramble out like children off a bus on a school trip. 'What are we doing at the strip?' I ask.

Before Astrid can answer, there's a sudden grumble from the alley beside us and an older woman on a matte black motorbike comes flying around the corner. When she rises and removes her helmet, it feels like slow motion. Masses of thick black curls flow over her shoulders and she is dripping in vintage leather. It's a moment before I can tear my eyes away to see the bike. A Solar Glider. The world's fastest motorbike. There's only 50 worldwide, and I had assumed every one of them would be kept in pristine condition in Japan. But there is one right here, in the Urb.

'This is Eydis,' Astrid says to me. *The Lux*, I think. Somehow I feel warm towards Eydis on this knowledge alone. I may not be a Lux, but I'm comfortable in their presence. East Town, after all, had been home for two decades. But looking at her, it seems like Eydis is like no Lux I've ever met before. She dresses in all black. Like me.

She has a recklessness in her eyes.

Astrid gestures for me to step forward and hands me a helmet. I panic. 'I've never been on a motorbike before, I don't know how to drive—'

She stops me. 'I'm driving,' she says. 'Hop on the back and hold on.'

'What has this got to do with Silenda?' I ask.

'What? Nothing, just teaching you to live, Harry. This induction isn't training you to be a soldier. Just to be an Umbra, the special kind.' She winks at me. *Harry* sounds nice from her lips.

'Special kind?' I ask, but it falls on dead ears as she pulls a black helmet over her long blonde locks. I hop on the back of the bike and she encourages me to hold on to her. I reluctantly wrap my arms around her waist, feeling too close for comfort. Eydis tells the others to get back in the Jeep as she hops in the driver's seat. Astrid revs the engine.

I leave my breath behind. And my stomach.

My eyes see the flashing of lights. Pink, blue, purple. The sky is black. Blonde hair whips against my cheeks and I feel the vibration of laughter in my chest, but I can't tell if it's hers or mine.

My mind is back at the car.

Astrid guides the bike with her tall frame, caressing the curvature of the streets and shooting down the strip like a bullet. The wind blows up her lacy top and my hands are exposed to the warmth of her flesh. I feel her diaphragm expanding as her lungs fill with the freshest air I've ever breathed. The buildings tower above us. We are miniscule and we are fleeting.

The city is a blur. We are a blur. My heart pounds in my chest, if it's even still in my chest. The wind, the light, her skin, it feels like music. Beautiful fucking music. I want to kiss her neck. I want to jump in deep. I want to drink with Hayden and get angry with Carson and get high with Zeb and listen to him laugh about his past boyfriends while I try not to think about his mouth.

And I want Astrid.

I want her crazy. I hope it's contagious.

If this is sinning, *set me on fire*.

CHAPTER 15

AYIP

Carson

Hawk sits with his head in his hands on the end of my creaky wooden bed. The view from my room is hypnotic. Unlike Astrid's room, which has a large glass window that overlooks the loch, my room has a window which looks onto the deep greenery of the forest of cabins behind us.

I stare at Hawk in silence as he looks at the floor and I wonder how many times since our short encounter have I seen him look this way. Although, I suppose he isn't Hawk at all, and I am not Cara. We are Bennet Lee and Carson Whitmoore, post-Silenda, post-*us*. Whatever *us* may have been.

I don't say anything when I go to shower in my ensuite and he doesn't ask me where I'm going. The pressure of the water is unexpected after I am used to the pathetic old trickle from my boxy apartment in the Urb. I let the water soak my skin, glide through my hair and over my face as I think about nothing but breathing.

The water turns brown as it journeys to the shower drain, cleaning me of dirt and blood. The man in the woods never caught us. I can't say if he even saw us. But that didn't stop us from darting frantically between the trees.

Hawk had been practically dragging me behind him, not giving me the time to find my own footing which resulted in a lot of stumbling and grazed knees. I scrub the dried blood from my minor injuries.

When I emerge from the shower, I use a towel to wipe the condensation from the mirror and stare at my pale naked body. My knees are red and dry and my eyes are shadowed with dark circles that look like I'd need a lifetime of sleep to get rid of. My wet hair looks dark with the water and my face looks expressionless. I try to change it, but every smile or frown feels insincere, like there is nothing behind my eyes. And who knows, maybe there's not. I try to be comfortable with my body, but every look makes me wince.

My ribs show through, and I am far too slight, my knees kind of knobbly and my veins cobalt blue.

I almost forget to wrap my dignity in a towel when I exit the bathroom. Hawk has used the remote to lower the electric blind over the large window. He turns away as I dress.

We don't speak.

I pull on some grey jogging bottoms and an oversized Pink Floyd t-shirt that I found balled in a chest of drawers that feels cold and smells still faintly of washing powder. As I dress, I watch him. Our current existence is to observe each other. By now I have examined every inch of his skin, every mannerism, so much so that I'm sure I could beat him in a fight. I watch when his muscles move in his shoulders and the way he hunches over his knees, always on the edge of his seat. That's when he's most vulnerable.

I leave the room silently. I pad downstairs on the cold wooden floorboards and pour myself a cup of chamomile tea that I find in one of the kitchen cupboards with the name Hawk written on it. I wonder if he's had a cup since he changed his name. I decide to make him one. I choose an unconventional mug, bright pink with illustrations of unicorns and rainbows, hoping it'll somehow make him laugh.

As I head upstairs again, I notice that the dark living room is lit by the television, where Astrid and the new guy sit shoulder to shoulder, talking. She is speaking feverishly although I can't interpret her words and Horatio Marino, the Gothic-looking newbie, looks on in somewhat confused adoration. I walk by silently and they don't notice me.

When I return to my room, a thick blanket and a couple of pillows have materialised on the floor next to my bed. Hawk is absent and I hear water running in the bathroom. The door is ajar, revealing him shirtless and patting his face dry with a towel.

'Do you mind if I crash here for the night?' he asks as he catches my eyes in the mirror.

I nod more vigorously than I had intended to, tuning into the thunderous weather outside. 'It's far too wet out there for you to walk back to the uni.'

'It's not only that.' He edges closer and I ask myself weakly why on earth he should have to be shirtless when I'm feeling so cold and so lonely. I wonder whether he's doing it on purpose. He gets too close. I swallow thickly and I think he notices. He's close enough to touch me and I step back on impulse. His mouth forms and no words follow. Is he going to kiss me? *Hurt me?*

I don't like anyone being in such close proximity.

'What is it then?' I whisper, my face hot and my heart beating fast. I wish that I would spontaneously combust.

I read somewhere that can actually happen.

'Well, you know...' he says, dodging me, folding down his blanket and hopping underneath it, 'the guy in the woods, we don't know for sure he didn't follow us here. I'm not letting you sleep alone.'

An anxious weight lifts from my chest and suddenly I feel dizzy in his absence, like the tense energy between us had been holding me up and, as it evaporated, so did my coherence.

'Right,' I say, 'well maybe you should sleep with a bulletproof vest instead of half-naked,' I quip. He laughs and I'm glad my humour masks the fact that I'm completely embarrassed by the way he makes me feel. I feel stupid for thinking he was going to kiss me. I throw the duvet over my head, turn off the bedside lamp that lights the room and fall into sleep, forgetting about the tea.

The sun spills through the gap in the blinds and I roll over to find Hawk gone.

I assume he has returned home to dress and we have successfully made it through the night with Silenda off our scent. I glance at the cold cups of tea on the bedside table. My shoulders slump and my heart feels entirely deflated despite still carrying oxygen to my tissues.

I head downstairs for breakfast.

Hawk is dressed, cooking scrambled eggs over the stove. He offers me a selection of breakfast dishes, but I turn my nose up at everything he suggests. He is uncharacteristically perky this morning, and I fail to match his energy. The more I learn about Silenda and the more I feel some invisible wedge preventing me from getting close to Hawk, the more I feel like I am continuously running into the same brick wall. I'm starting to feel a little dizzy.

Hayden doesn't talk to us and Astrid runs around the main room trying to get organised for the day ahead. Supposedly, it's the new guy's induction. If it's anything like the initiation parties at the Urb college a block down from my old apartment with street long queues outside cheap tattoo parlours, boozy corner shops and young girls throwing up on the side of the road, it seems to be completely inappropriate timing. The new information we possess about Silenda's ability not only to abduct us and track us but to frame us for life-altering crimes we did not commit, simply to get us off their case, makes it difficult to think about anything else.

Horatio arrives for breakfast. The first thing I notice about the new boy is that he's unnaturally white. Even his eyes are lacking an opacity that seems to reveal the white behind them. His hair is jet black. He's tall and striking with high cheekbones, hooded eyes and a big white smile that doesn't match the rest of his face. He is also incredibly suspicious. None of the others seem to have supposed this about him, but it's an unusual time to enrol at the university. Hawk says term began a couple of months ago and that winter exams are edging close. I overheard Hayden explaining to Hawk that Horatio is an old friend of Zeb, which I suppose makes his transfer to West Town University a little more convincing.

I overhear most things that are said to Hawk. I'm starting to feel like his dog. Speaking of which, I wish he wouldn't leave Red at his apartment so often. Even if his sister dog sits.

Still, I hope to keep my eyes on the new boy. The others are reckless with the information they are willing to share with him.

When Zebediah returns to the cabin there is a flurry of conversation as everyone but Hayden and I scramble towards him. Hayden turns away, a small smile on his face that I know he would hate for anyone to see. As expected, Horatio and Astrid are competing for his attention as he reveals that Mayor Turrow successfully uncovered evidence to relieve him from his arrest. Hayden clings to a paper cup until the buzz dies down.

Hawk says I suit red.

He says it as he threads the colour through my hair. I don't mind so much that he chose the colour, not when he intends to redeem his candy-floss hair, even in part. It looks good on him. I feel closer to him. He screams in colour and so do I.

It seems, however, that Hawk screams in many other things too. Most conventionally, in anger. His brown eyes darken like coal when he holds a gun. I don't like the way he looks when he does. I don't like the way he paces in front of us. The eye contact he makes when he thrusts the weapons into our arms.

He's cold.

I'm watching his mouth when he talks about Silenda. Everything about them feels like a sort of fever dream. When I watch Hawk's lips, I don't really listen to what comes out of them. I just hear his aggressive pitch and see the alarmed expressions of the others around me. It's about time I tuned out, anyway. It's only when my name is called that I'm thrust back into conversation. 'You've been reading my diary?' I turn to Hayden.

'Fucking hell, Red, it's not like you can even remember what you wrote to be embarrassed about it!'

I'm caught off guard.

Hawk is throwing his backpack over his shoulder and marching into the building behind us, but I'm static against the brick wall, running my hands over its rough skin, my own flesh hot with blood as I think about what Hayden said. And it's not about the diary, not about whatever bullshit I scribbled on its pages.

It's the name he called me. So casually, so quickly, so *naturally*. Like it's the millionth time the name has crossed his lips.

Red.

I run my hands through my auburn hair and twirl a crimson strand between my fingers.

Red.

I think about the curly little dog that nearly took me out my first day at Hawk's apartment.

Hawk has replaced me with a dog.

Last night, when Hawk slept on the floor, he said my name in the wee hours of darkness. I rolled over to see him staring at the ceiling, thinking. 'This used to be our room,' he had said. I said nothing, looking on expectantly, breathing shallow in the black so he would know I was awake.

He continued, 'We shared it. There were two beds. You were by the window, and I was by the door.' He breathed deeply between his sentences. 'When you left, Astrid had a double bed put in so that I wouldn't have to stare at your empty bed every night. That *is* what I was doing. But I couldn't bear it, it felt like erasing you.

So, I moved to the uni. A top floor apartment with a view of the ground and echoing stone walls where I could practise my music without Zeb whining or Hayden yelling or hating myself every time I brushed past Astrid in the corridor.'

'And you adopted a poodle,' I said, smiling to myself.

'Yeah,' he scoffed, 'and I adopted a poodle.'

Right now, it's hard to see him as that same person. The vulnerable person who couldn't sleep for the words that he needed to vent, to me, or just to the room. There is nothing vulnerable about the way that he holds his gun, the way that he points and shoots the rubber man in the head every time. He's been practising.

He's not afraid to confront Horatio when he turns out to be the worst shot of us all. Despite Horatio having an inch or two on Hawk, Hawk is far broader and makes the new guy look small just by glaring at him. I don't like this side of him. The anger he has for Silenda is explosive – destructive if it's not kept in check. I feel bad for Horatio. I suppose he presumed that his induction would require him to chug a twelve-pack of beer, not shoot at the head of human-shaped rubber.

Astrid glances at Hawk. The pair interact very little but talk with their eyes more than I'd like to notice. They certainly have the same agenda as they talk my bullet into a rubber throat.

This is what I think about in the car. Pressed up against the window with my chin in my palm. The Jeep seats five. But I hardly count as a sixth person. I don't mind the squeeze. It's cold outside and our body heat keeps the car warm. The Urb dwindles past and I try not to grieve so much as we pass the rubble. I picture myself lying in it the night I fled from Astrid's apartment. I see the wreckage that once was the building that almost crushed me. I picture who I once thought as Bennet saving me from certain death.

In a matter of days, it feels as though a year has gone by. For the most part, the streets are empty of people. I imagine that fear hangs over the grieving city like a raincloud that threatens to burst. Fear that whoever took down Centrum Tower, may strike again. Not to mention the wedge that cuts the religious divide even deeper than before. Hawk had been right: the bomb did not make Umbras look good.

Hayden's obnoxiously loud milkshake slurping should really be enough to distract my mind, but all I can think about is *him*.

And not in the solely endearing way I had last night.

I think about the gun in his hand like a third arm. I think about Astrid having to step in to spare Horatio from Hawk's wrath before he turned the gun on himself out of pure humiliation. And something deep inside of me makes me feel like it's my fault. What happened to me did this to him. Constructed a side to him that is cold and ruthless, a side he seems able to turn on at the flick of a switch. He is not the man who was temptingly holding a croissant under my nose this morning.

As the sky darkens I realise how long we'd been shooting for. How many bullets I must have fired. How many people I could have killed had the rubber men been thread with veins. I feel nauseous, lower my head to my knees that I tuck up to my chest and focus on the silky sound of tyres on tar as I try not to slap Hayden's milkshake from his hand.

I'm jealous when the car halts and we watch Astrid and Horatio disappear into the distance on the back of the Solar Glider. I hope to convince one of the others to give me a ride, too frightened to take control of it alone. The only problem is, I'm not sure who I trust enough to take me.

Eydis doesn't tell us where we're going when she replaces Astrid in the driver's seat. Hayden throws his milkshake out of the car window which results in Zebediah screaming at him about littering.

The blonde looks around to see the reaction of the others when he catches my bewildered expression. He whispers in my ear, 'I've learned that it's more exciting if you don't ask.' He winks at me and his words settle in my chest, my shoulders dropping their weight as I decide to embrace the night.

The Jeep pulls up a dead-end street outside a building that scrapes the sky, graffiti crawling up its decaying walls like vines. Eydis silently exits the vehicle and the rest of us follow. I stand close to her, finding it comforting how she towers over me, smelling like leather and roses. I like how she talks to Hawk, brushing him off like an ant at her picnic. I wish so feverishly that he could be as insignificant to me.

We all stare up at the top of the building where bright coloured lights appear to emanate. An electric-synth beat drops. We look to Eydis.

'It's a party.' She gestures to the doorway at the front of the building which reveals a dark corridor and an escalating flight of stairs.

Hayden and I hesitate at the door. 'For the new guy's induction,' Eydis elaborates, pushing us all towards the door. 'It's a rooftop party; it doesn't matter what the ground floor looks like, get in here!'

'Isn't Astrid supposed to be a supermodel or something?' I ask, stepping gingerly into the run-down building.

'Aren't I supposed to be the mayor's nephew?' Hayden retorts, as we all somewhat miserably scale the never-ending flight of dark and dingy stairs.

Eydis scoffs, 'This kind of party wouldn't end well in the nice parts of the city.' She looks at Hawk and Zeb who keep their heads down.

'Then what kind of party is it?' I ask, breathlessly, but my question is answered as Hayden kicks open the door to the roof terrace.

At least a hundred people are gathered on the roof of the building. Everyone is dressed in black with beautiful tinges of colour through their hair, bright coloured nails, shoes, with some even donning bewitching neon masks. 'This,' Zebediah says, 'is an AYIP.'

'A what?' I ask, touching my freshly coloured hair.

'An admit your ignorance party,' Hawk says. 'Umbras and Luxies from all over the city come together to celebrate the fact that we're clueless.'

'That's worth celebrating?' Hayden rolls his eyes and Eydis giggles under her breath.

'We come together to admit to ourselves that we don't know the truth. Many people here believe in God, or some kind of god, and many people here don't believe in anything. But we are all willing to respect each other's beliefs and collectively agree that we just *don't know*. We don't force ideals on each other, we don't tell anyone that what they choose to have faith in is wrong. We exist in peace. Accepting our mundanity as artless humans, making the best of the lives we are living, in spite of what comes after,' Hawk says.

'That's beautiful,' I say, and I really do believe it.

'I guess it's nice,' Hayden says, but he has a soft smile on his face.

'So, let's get some drinks!' Eydis yells and I find myself following her eagerly to the fountain of vodka punch. I have a lot on my mind. I try to avoid Hawk, tired of following him around like a stray when he hardly communicates with me and cradles a gun like someone I don't know.

I don't know him.

By the time Astrid and Horatio walk through the door, Horatio looking simultaneously elated and dishevelled as he removes his helmet and looks around in awe, I'm already feeling the effects of alcohol. My head feels looser on my neck like I'm a bicycle that desperately needed oil on my chain.

Astrid turns heads as expected. Many crowd around her, trying to get her attention. Horatio looks disheartened as his 15 minutes alone with the supermodel has been rudely interrupted by a crowd of strangers calling her Triddy.

He walks straight to the punch. Wise man.

I approach him and he smiles at me before I reach him, which already makes me change my mind about him a little.

'Cool party,' he says, clinging to his cup with both hands as if looking for something to do with them.

'Yeah, I didn't know people like this existed.'

'I thought they'd end up in the Rowleys, but I guess they're low-key about it. Probably why we've ended up in this dump.' We laugh. Despite the corrosion, the fairy lights and fountains of punch brighten the place up in setting and in spirit.

'Beautiful view of the city,' I say, as we turn to the skyline and admire skyscraper windows dotted like stars across the horizon.

'That Hawk guy is a bit much, isn't he?'

I thought this might come up.

'Yeah,' I exhale, 'still trying to figure him out. He's okay when he's not waffling about Silenda.'

'Crazy isn't it?'

I nod, knowing exactly what he means.

'Sometimes I wonder if it would be so bad though, y'know?'

'What?'

'Knowing the truth,' I say. 'I get that they'd take away our choice to have faith, but if a god really does exist, I think I'd want to know about him.'

'Do you think you'd worship him if he did?' He stares into the distance as the wind blows his hair.

'You know, I don't think I would.'

'That's okay, I don't think I would either,' he says immediately. 'Bastard killed my hamster.'

I've lost count of how many drinks I've had, and Horatio and I are hysterically laughing and grabbing onto each other's arms to stay vertical. It turns out that the new boy is endearingly funny. As I hang on his arm, I find myself looking for Hawk, hoping that it will become apparent to him that I'm not as reliant on him as I once seemed. I can see Horatio looking for Astrid, too. Perhaps enjoying each other's company can be somewhat advantageous. That is, until I need to pee.

Horatio offers to walk me as I'm wobbly on my feet, but I assure him I'll be alright. A woman with hot pink hair points me in the direction of the bathroom, down the first flight of stairs on the landing. It's dark and the walls smell damp.

I run my hands along the graffiti as I walk. There's lots of writing about the woman who is 'made of glass'. I remember Astrid and Hayden supposing that it had been Jason referring to the fragility of our world. It seems that others have jumped on the idea.

There's a painting of her. The glass woman. An opaque human figure, revealing the neon graffiti behind her. She is like a ghost. I run my hand down her arm, placing my hand against hers. It's cold. My head is spinning and I realise I've walked too far. I'm a flight past the landing I was meant to reach, too distracted by the art to notice.

There's something else catching my eye that I simply can't pass by. Another painting. A man with fluffy black hair, pale white skin, his lips blue as the centre of the ocean, sharp teeth bearing at the pretty neck of a petite girl with two puncture wounds in her neck.

Like me. Like Jason. Like Randy Redding.

Under the graphic image, someone has written in cursive ink: *The Rowleys vampire.*

I'm running my hands down the wall, confused, drunk, scared.

There's a bang. A clanking of metal. A loud voice. I whip my head around to a dim room on the opposite side of the landing. The door is only three inches open. I step near, cautiously and stealthily peeking through the crack.

Hayden and Zebediah talk feverishly. A metal table has fallen on the floor between them. It appears like Hayden has pushed it and now it acts like a barrier preventing Zebediah from getting too close. 'I don't want to do this,' Hayden cries. *Do what?* I think as Zebediah edges into my view, moving the table that divides them.

'It just doesn't feel right.'

'It's not like it's a lifetime commitment, H. But we need your skill, no one knows a computer like you do. Think of the things you could do.'

Hayden is shaking his head vigorously.

'What proof does Tyson have?' Hayden pushes.

'He saw him. He saw Basilio Young. The day before I was arrested, Tyson saw Young and an army of men in the Rowleys. What else would they be doing there? He is the closest thing we have to a lead. He is Silenda. He wants to prove us wrong!'

Hayden is crying and I think he's drunk.

Zeb gets close, reaching for his hand. I wince, expecting Hayden to punch him in the jaw.

What's going on?

'It's so dangerous.'

'It's dangerous not to,' Zeb says, as Hayden's mop of blonde curls falls on his shoulder. Zeb runs his hand up his neck and through his hair as he allows him to cry.

I feel like I should look away, but I can't.

I can't when their lips meet either.

Zeb weaves his touch into Hayden's thick hair and Hayden kisses him back, feverishly, like the only oxygen remaining on the planet is inside of Zeb's mouth. His eyebrows furrow with a thirst that even the most immeasurable desert has never known. Zeb's whole body encases him. I think if he held him tight enough, Hayden would just wither away in his palms.

A saxophone sounds from the party.

I follow the music.

CHAPTER 16
HE WHO LISTENS

Horatio

We give power to that which we do not understand. That's what Alexandria supposes as she puffs smoke to the wind. 'Apes worship waterfalls,' she says, 'and the Egyptians worshipped cats. Then there was the sun and the stars. It's only as we evolved intellectually and became self-aware that we looked up at the sky and thought: 'there must be some kind of puppet master behind all of this.' And who knows,' she says, pink hair flowing, 'perhaps that was an intuitive and ground-breaking thought, or maybe it was an innate reaction to the idea that perhaps there is no reason at all for our being. No reason at all...' Her words drag off in a drag of her cigarette. 'Anyway, what do I know?'

What do I know? This question seems to be a last-ditch attempt at modesty at the AYIP. It seems to be ultimately acceptable to share our thoughts on next, but mandatory to omit any essence of factuality.

Asiqa and Petal are spiritual.

They don vibrant scarfs around their necks. 'The throat is a delicate thing,' Asiqa tells me, as he reaches for my palm and holds it. 'It holds the locutions of our passions, the egressions of our mind. It's a sweet spot. Sensitive, extraordinary. We ought to protect it. My God requires our modesty in such things.' His hands are soft and gentle. He captures me so wholeheartedly. 'What do you see when you look at me, Horatio?'

What do I see?

I see his eyes.

Black in the night sky. Kind, inviting, open. 'My eyes,' he answers for me. 'The windows to the soul. Mind not my mechanical body. My limbs, my bones, my blood, they are nothing but vehicular, my friend.' His hand moves from my palm to my neck.

Petal smiles. 'Your soul is in your throat, Horatio. Should there be a greater power, I know that he shall accept your spirit with open arms.'

He removes his hand from my neck and laughs. 'And should we be destined to be Shadows, where our corpses lay rotting in the ground, leave me drapes of flowering ivy, then I can be eternal in its evergreen and assured in its fidelity.'

Alexandria and Petal smile, shoulder to shoulder. I tell Asiqa that I admire his faith and the strength that he reserves for it.

Although I find it difficult to sew my heart wholly to his prophecies, I envy Asiqa. There is a deep fiery sadness behind Alexandria's eyes that is peacefully extinguished in Asiqa and Petal.

Perhaps if apes worship waterfalls, we were never supposed to make it this far. Perhaps we were never supposed to exceed a tribality, a spiritual purpose, a greater purpose. Maybe we've come too far, learned too much, exploited the mysteries of nature and the secrets of the sky, only to commit ourselves to a lifetime of furious sadness.

Our own personal hell.

Perhaps heaven and hell do in fact exist, here on earth. The Shadows resign to a hopelessness that bids their loved one's adieu into darkness and the Lighties send their lovers to the stars.

Zebediah says that Umbras are sad. That's why he smokes

so much. He puts a bullet between his teeth and threatens to swallow it with every wisp of cyanide and arsenic.

He has a silliness beyond his bleached white teeth, but not behind them, not in his throat.

Alexandria hangs on my arm when Carson leaves and, despite how much of a downer she becomes when Asiqa leaves and her alcohol consumption exceeds plentiful, I don't mind so much. Not when our proximity catches Astrid's eye. But she looks away, and she doesn't look back.

It's the early hours of the morning when we stumble out of Turrow's Jeep with a sober Eydis in the driver's seat. The cabin is cold and Bennet, who has been off my radar for most of the night, throws a newspaper flame to the log burner.

Carson is black-eyed and incoherent. It's hard to tell if the bags under her eyes are smudged eyeliner or profound exhaustion. She sticks closer to Hayden and Zeb than to Bennet, her usual overseer. But Zeb and Hayden seem to value the auburn divide between them, with the latter looking like he's seen a ghost.

It's an odd end to the night. The expected buzz of vibrant coloured hair and vodka punch is instead replaced with an exuberant silence that soon dissolves into unceremonious slumber, with everyone falling asleep in peculiar places. Hayden is staring cross-legged into the fire, until sleep has him fallen on his side. Zebediah coups in the armchair with Hayden like a dog at his feet. Astrid and Cara take the couch, and I take the rug. Bennet goes to the bathroom and passes out somewhere upstairs.

The fire flickers.

• • •

I place my hands over the stove.

The potatoes bubble when they boil and the heat, particularly when the water spits at me, is a comfort more than anything else.

SILENDA

My mother nudges me out of the way, shaking crystals of salt into the water and asking me if there's nothing better I could be doing other than getting in her way. It's Sunday dinner, and my first return home since I enrolled at West Town.

'Take off your beanie, Harry!' my mother yells, blonde bob swishing as she moves around the kitchen.

Well I can't, Matilda, I think, *because my hair is blue and you will kill me.*

My father and Angelo have yet to return from Angelo's football practice, so I'm instructed to set the table with Uncle Basil. Locks of his slick hair fall forward out of place. His usual suit jacket and tie are absent and his blue shirt is open at the collar. He looks a little dishevelled in contrast to his usual Sunday evening attire. He reminds me of his younger days, before he was mayor, when I was far fonder of him. It crosses my mind immediately as I fumble in my pocket for my small notebook, that Basil's appearance may be intended to appeal to me.

The notebook materialises in my hand. I ripped out the pages with the big red stars and left only information about the Nether Cabin and its hierarchy of authoritative figures. I tell him about Carson Whitmoore and that her dropping out of university as a result of a terrible accident that resulted in amnesia.

Nothing about Silenda.

And nothing about an Umbra uprising, for that information truly hasn't come to light, and likely won't in the wake of the AYIP. Despite such information immediately extinguishing my uncle's beliefs that Tyson and his associates are out to get him, Basil's own prejudice would immediately diffuse any further Lux-Umbra integration if he knew about the AYIP. And I don't want that.

I tuck a piece of hair up into my hat.

I hand my uncle the notebook and he pockets it swiftly, winking at me and reminding me of the thorough information he desires by the time the unity ball rolls around.

The table is set with a carving of succulent roast beef, buttery mashed potatoes and a mountain of stewed vegetables.

When Angelo and my father return home, I embrace them. We sit down at the feast.

'So, Horatio,' my father asks, biting into his puff pastry, 'how are you enjoying your course in music technology?'

I tell my family about the study of sound reinforcement theory and the technicalities of electronic music. I tell them about my 'friend' Bennet, whose studies centre solely on neo-soul and R&B, whereas I am edging more towards the sound composition of new wave synth.

As expected, my family gaze on cluelessly, which stops them from asking any more questions about my university experience and prevents me from panicking and caving.

Although my first week of classes following the AYIP had consisted of much of the same jargon, the vast majority of it was messing around on keyboards with Bennet, who seems to have warmed to me a little, especially since he clocked my Wednesday shooting range rendezvous with Astrid.

My uncle winks at me again and there is a severe pain in my chest. There's something sinister about being in alliance with him.

When the dishes are cleared, I head to my room, gathering forgotten things I'd like to take to the Nether Cabin: a couple of my favourite records that Caleb gifted me and a few guitar picks.

Angelo hovers in the doorway. 'I know what's going on,' he says, flicking his mop of brown hair out of his eyes.

'You do?' I say.

'You're an Umbra now, aren't you? Is Uncle Basil covering for you because he knows dad will kill you?'

I pause, unsure of what to say. Afraid of the truth, but afraid that Angelo's assumption is worse than the truth.

'It's not like that.' I rummage through my drawers, looking for anything else to pocket.

'Then what is it like?' He has his arms folded in the doorway and I pause in my tracks, accepting that perhaps telling my little brother the truth wouldn't be so catastrophic. Perhaps, if I leave out the minor detail of my insincerity in the task and our uncle's suspicions of a full-blown uprising, it would be alright.

I gesture for Angelo to enter and close the door behind him. 'I'm not an Umbra.'

'You're not?'

I shake my head. 'Uncle Basil just wants me to make sure that we, you know, have nothing to worry about.'

'Why should we worry?' he says.

'Well, we shouldn't. He just wants to be sure that Centrum Tower wasn't at the hands of—'

'The Umbras bombed the tower?' Angelo shrieks.

I clasp my hand over his mouth and sit him on my bed, hoping that standing over him will get him to listen. 'No, no, no, no!' I shush him. 'It was most likely a technical problem that started the fire!'

'Uncle Basil said on the news that it was a bomb—'

'You watch the news?' I ask, exasperated. 'Okay, well it could have been a dormant bomb from a war years and years ago or something. That stuff happens all the time!'

'It does?' Angelo flinches and wriggles as if there could be a bomb under my bed.

'Well, no, not all the time...' I'm fumbling, 'what I'm saying is that the bomb could have been a number of things, maybe just a homicidal maniac. A lot of the time those guys aren't particularly biased.' Angelo's eyes widen. I cough. 'The chances of it being a Lux-targeted attack by the Umbras is very slim.' I don't believe what I'm saying. I don't believe it at all. The Umbras I have met are very obviously inclusive. But I do believe in fear, prejudice and fire. 'Uncle Basil thinks that I can pass as an Umbra because of how I dress.'

Angelo nods, visibly calmer.

'So he just wants me to make sure that nothing fishy is going on. And so far, everything is okay. In return, he got me a place on the music course!' I sit down next to my little brother, making sure he's alright.

There's a pause.

'Do you believe in God, Harry?' he asks suddenly. I'm caught off guard.

I fumble again. 'Honestly?' Angelo nods. 'I don't know. Do you?'

He nods immediately. 'I have no doubt.'

I decide to quiz Angelo on his reasoning. 'So you suppose that *He* created everything?' I point to the stars.

'Yeah, I guess so.'

'Even disease?' I ask.

'Yeah. I think so.'

'Why would he do that?'

Angelo shrugs. 'I never said he was good. I just said I believe in him. I think he likes to challenge us.'

'Sounds a little sadistic to me.'

Angelo's eyes fill with fear as his fingers, like pincers, clasp my mouth shut. *What?* my eyes scream.

'He's listening.'

Maybe not all Luxies are happy, after all. There's a fire in Angelo's eyes too. But he didn't set it, he can't control it and it's burning him alive.

• • •

I mean to go straight back to the cabin when the train shoots through the Urb, but for some reason I can't pass the Grand Library.

It stands erect among the rubble from the block across the street. The grocery store is gone. No one would look up at me disapprovingly if I were to scale the immensity of the building. I think about it. About sneaking through the multi-storey car park and taking the stairs that lead to the roof.

SILENDA

Instead, I find myself edging through the large arched doors of the main entrance. The library is huge. The oak shelves scrape the ceilings, packed with thousands of thick dusty books in vintage leather bindings.

I'm not looking for anything, simply dancing my fingers across the shelves, breathing in the nostalgic smell of printed paper.

I try not to look at the woman across the aisle, who flicks through a book far larger than her hands. The aisles are tight. We are close, so I try desperately to avoid her eyes. I pretend to read a book that I snatched off the shelf in front of me and try to catch the title of the red-head's book. Her face is shielded by her hair, which is shielded again by the hood of a black hoodie. I see the title page: *The Rowleys Vampire.*

I don't usually talk to strangers, but I can't help myself. 'You like vampires?' I ask. She looks up, revealing her face for the first time. *Carson?*

'Harry?' she exclaims, quickly dropping her book to her side. She squints at the book I'm reading. She tilts her head. 'Fifty most adventurous sex positions?'

I laugh. 'I wasn't reading it. I was actually just trying to see what you were reading.'

'Well, that's for the best,' she says, 'you were holding it upside down. And that could be a bit of a hazard for your lady friend.'

We're laughing for a bit, a good chesty laugh. The most I've laughed in my week in West Town has been with Carson. She seems to have been distant from Bennet, so when I've not been in class with him or shooting with Astrid, I've been with her.

'I wonder why a sex manual is in the same section as a book about vampires?' I say. Carson's amusement dissolves and turns to dread.

'What?' I ask, suddenly concerned by her silence when I expected laughter. She looks up at me, scanning my eyes for a second as if deciding what to say next. I try to look gentle. The vampire book reappears at her chest. She takes a moment before she opens it again, flicking to the middle and coming close enough for me to read.

'There was an epidemic of murders, suicides and missing people in the Rowleys in the early 1900s,' she begins, tracing a petite finger across the page. 'Over the years, a rumour gathered momentum. It became a sort of urban myth.' She looks me directly in the eye. 'The Rowleys vampire. Corpses were turning up all over the place with two puncture wounds in the neck. Just like this,' Carson pulls her hair over her shoulder to reveal her mark. She points at the heavy book in her hands to show a black and white image of the same wound. 'At the time, the people of the Rowleys convinced themselves that the mark was that of a vampire bite. But we know now that it's the mark of...'

'Silenda,' I finish.

She nods, dejectedly.

'What does this mean?'

'It means that Silenda have been prevalent for a lot longer than we originally thought. With years of research and the progression of post-modern technology, they could be a lot closer to an answer than I'm comfortable with. Not only that, but their death toll ought to be extraordinarily larger than first thought.'

'Do you think that Bennet is right about infiltration? I ask.

'Hawk,' she corrects me, 'can get carried away by his own ego. I mean what are we going to do? Storm a hundred-year-old underground organisation with agents that have managed to go uncaught for all this time? They'll be armed to the tits, Harry. *To the tits!*'

'Let's hope they're only the height of you, then,' I say. I laugh as Carson's chest is only at elbow height for me. She's trying not to laugh too.

'I'm serious. Not only that, but we don't even have a clue where they are. They may not even have a base. They might function like a series of mad scientist pop-up-shops. How can we know?'

We stand silent for a minute, unsure of how to progress.

'I mean, can you imagine Astrid storming into their base in her Louboutins? Zeb in his dungarees and Hayden in his sweater vest? We'd look fucking ridiculous.' Carson is laughing but I think it's mostly to keep from crying or screaming.

We fall silent.

The hair on the back of my neck comes to attention. I run my hand over it, unaware of how much Carson's book had given me the chills. But that's not it. I follow Carson's gaze to the end of the aisle. A bald man in a blue shirt scans the shelf of books closest to his eye level. I wonder if she knows him. He looks completely mundane; somebody's father or teacher or accountant. He's middle-aged, holding his ear and speaking quietly into an earpiece. Carson's eyes snap to the other end of the aisle. Two more men scan the shelves. Both tall, both stocky.

The bald man looks over at us.

'Horatio,' Carson whispers, discreetly pulling at my sleeve, 'it's a busy aisle, don't you think?' I shrug. 'This is the 1900s history section, that's a specific genre.' I shrug again. She looks around and lowers her voice further. 'It's a Monday afternoon, Horatio and every other aisle is empty.'

That's when my heart begins to race.

She's right. And they're looking at us, too.

I grab her hand. She looks up at me. We walk as assertively down the aisle as we can muster without looking suspicious. Carson mutters something about trying to catch a train and we're in view of the helpdesk when we begin to feel safe again. But there's a tingling sensation on the back of my neck that just won't go away. A feeling of being watched. My phone beeps in the silence of the grand echoing walls and Carson hits me. I rub my arm. 'What was that for?'

'You gave me a fright!' I roll my eyes and open my phone.

A text from Zeb.

'What does it say?' Carson leans close to me. 'Need a couple of books for uni. Try 1950s fiction,' I read the text to Carson.

'How does he know where we are?'

The bald man reappears and my heart races again. Carson and I head towards the section of mid-1900s fiction. Anything in particular? I text back.

'I thought he studied law?' Carson says.

'He does.'

End of the aisle. Name of our home.

What? I think.

But that's when I see it. At the end of the aisle, right around the corner on the bottom shelf. Every book around it is thick and untouched with dust.

But not *The Nether Cabin* by AJ Berkley.

Take the stairs. Now.

What stairs?

Carson reaches for the book, flicks through it. 'The stairs? Is that a riddle or something?' I don't answer her.

My eyes dart around us, making sure none of the suspicious Monday afternoon library-goers have followed us around the corner. I look for clues. That's when my eyes drop to the floor. 'There's a cellar door!' I whisper urgently, pulling up a section of the floor by the bottom shelf and revealing a dark flight of stairs. We take them. When I reach the last step, I hear a voice. 'Close the door over!' it says. Carson climbs back up the stairs and pulls over the bulkhead door in the ceiling, leaving us in the black dark.

I reach for Carson.

'Where are we?' she says. 'Are we in the basement?'

'I have no idea.' My hands fly up to shield my eyes as a bright white light flashes in front of us. Zebediah stares at us, phone torch in hand.

'Guys! Guys!' A familiar voice yells in glee. Hayden sits at a desk in the corner with his feet up on a dusty old pile of books and a box of fries in his lap. He waves at us. Carson smiles awkwardly. I don't know if I smile.

The library basement is cold. It smells damp and is lit dimly by a couple of computer monitors next to Hayden

Zeb turns to look at us. Carson looks as confused as I feel.

Our eyes pose a question.

'You were being followed in the library.' Zeb walks to Hayden's humble setup and presses a button on the keyboard. The screen suddenly changes to CCTV footage of the library floor. From a bird's-eye-view, the men look even more suspicious, pacing the aisles looking for more than a book to read.

'Silenda?' I ask.

Zeb nods. 'Not agents like you ran into in the woods.' He looks at Carson. 'But they're definitely ears. Must have followed you. You shouldn't be going out on your own!' She looks at the floor. 'Luckily I trust the pair of you enough to have you here. Enough that I'm hoping that the basement can remain our little hiding place. You're lucky we were here and that Hayden's paranoid enough to have hacked the CCTV system.'

'So, what is it you do down here?' Carson asks, arms folded. 'Are you supposed to be Tyson's pathetic excuse for an army?' she jokes.

'Tyson has nothing to do with this. He knows about the AYIP and he knows we are trying to bust Silenda. But this,' Zeb looks around the shabby little room, 'this is just for us. We can't infiltrate Silenda without a plan, and we needed a more private space. What did you think we were going to do?'

Storm the base in Louboutins, I think.

I look around me. Asiqa, Alexandria and Petal emerge from the shadows.

The AYIP aren't just a group of inclusive socialites; they're trying to take down Silenda.

CHAPTER 17

BIRDS OF PREY

Carson

The damp room buzzes with anxiety.

The white light of the monitors gleams in the silence. Hayden types quietly and Zebediah watches him. My eyes dart between the pair, still stunned by what I saw at the AYIP.

Hayden stops what he's doing and offers me a bottle of juice and I accept it, desperate to wet my throat. Horatio and I stand static as familiar faces from the AYIP look on, scribbling in notebooks and flicking through old books. Zeb is talking but it's hard to concentrate on his words because Hawk is staring at me from the corner of the room. Except it's not Hawk at all, but a framed picture of him holding something I can't quite make out.

We haven't talked all week. He went back to the halls and my rejection of his proximity in the last days appears not to have fazed him. I suppose I felt threatened by the tension that bubbles under his skin. The way he stared me down at the shooting range, I don't think any version of me knows that person.

He hasn't made the effort to chase me, which is strange considering he risked his close relationship with the mayor to get me back. I was his prey for a while.

SILENDA

I move closer. Despite his striking deep-set eyes, there's something else about the photo that catches my attention. Hawk looks pissed. Not only that, but the photo appears to be a mugshot. He holds up a black place-card lazily in one hand, with his name, HAWK BENNET LEE, written in thick black letters.

Zeb sees me staring at the photo that hangs beside Hayden's desk. He pauses after telling us the true role of the AYIP as a collective organisation against Silenda. It's hard to listen when I'm so focused on the framed picture.

'I suppose no one told you about that, huh?'

I shake my head.

'Bennet was arrested?' Horatio asks.

'Tyson got Hawk a restraining order from Carson because he kept trying to track her down or follow her on her runs. He didn't want him to confuse her or hurt her in any way. Mostly, Hawk just rubs him the wrong way. He has that effect on people.' Zeb swallows, turning to Hayden's desk and back at us. 'Anyway, Hawk just wouldn't listen. He disobeyed the order, and Tyson had his men round him up and bring him home on numerous occasions. So, eventually he just called the police to teach him a lesson. He was held for a couple of days until Tyson got him out. Hayden just has it framed because he's a dickhead and it pisses Hawk off.'

'Have you seen him recently?' I ask.

'Hawk? No. It's mostly just Hayden and the others that work down here. Astrid storms in occasionally, but Hawk doesn't understand this shit. He just wants to storm something all-guns blazing, He doesn't realise we need to research Silenda's agenda and history before we can really do anything helpful.'

He gestures to the monitors where Hayden and Asiqa appear to be zooming in on street-view maps and roaming CCTV. 'Right now, the guys are trying to track the men from the library back to a base. It's easy to lose them along the way so it's tricky work. Hawk just sits around on his phone getting frustrated and impatient when Hayden tries to explain things to him. He never used to be like this, but since you left he's had a short fuse. I thought that it would change when he got you back, but I've hardly seen him around.'

'Me neither.'

• • •

Zeb takes us up some creaky old stairs when the library is deemed clear and somehow we end up in the alleyway outside. Horatio's talking but I don't hear him.

I have an inexplicably anxious feeling in the pit of my stomach.

My head feels heavy but my body feels so weightless that I might just float away. I have to get out of here. I take a big sip of the juice Hayden gave me and decide I need to run to burn the feeling. To clear my mind. I'm searching my pockets for my earphones, untangling them hurriedly and planting them in my ears. 'See you at home, Harry.'

The music blares as he waves awkwardly. A transcendent beat, eighties-style synth. I'm running in the blue-black rain. Not a jog, a sprint. The lights gleam down and I love my city. I love the rain and the sound.

The city is my arcade, I'll be its fucking Pacman. I'm running from everything. The beat is deafening. People always stare when I run because I run to the beat, I dodge them, I look through them. I have a destination, I just don't know where it is yet.

Everything is overwhelming, I feel my heart to know it's not failing me. I see a red car. Low, smooth, quiet. It takes me with it. We flood together. It heads for the bridge and I see him in my mind's eye. Bubble-gum pink. The driver looks at me through his rear-view mirror and scowls. If I chase you, could this be the start of something more? It was the last time I chased a red car like you.

He's driving fast and I let him go. I'm catching my breath and

SILENDA

I'm laughing because it's just so hysterical. The water is black. Blacker than the inside of my eyelids. The city bridge caresses the river, but it can't protect me from it. My throat burns for breath, my body hot and my cheeks cold. I'm close to the railing, climbing before I can stop.

Perched like a gargoyle, dear God, if you want me to fall, *push me.* I think about the Silenda agent that Eydis killed. His body yellow and swollen in the frozen abyss. *How's it going down there, buddy?*

You know what? I don't want to hear it. I think if I let go of the railing, I won't fall. Everything's slightly out of touch. Hawk's skin is hot, I bet. But I've never touched him. Not really. How do I know he's even real? How do I know any of this is even real?

Maybe I died on St. Vincent Street. Maybe we're all dead. Maybe this is hell. A neon city full of lights that never reach you, tears that don't leave your cheeks, glass windows that show you a great expanse only to remind you how incessantly small you'll always be.

I won't fall.

He's gotten under my skin, Hawk. There's something so magnetic about him and simultaneously repellent. I want him and he makes me feel so far away.

Talons under my flesh. He can carry me away all he likes. But I can fly away anytime I want. He may be a hawk, but I am an eagle. We fly too.

'Cara!' Okay, maybe we don't fall, but we do crash. He runs to me. Black sleeves. Black boots. Hair. Eyes. I feel faint. Hawk grabs me and ushers my grip from the railing. 'What the hell are you doing?'

'I'm flying.'

'*What?*'

'I don't know.'

'Are you high?'

I'm laughing hysterically because God, wherever you are, I wish

I was high. But now that he says it, I do feel funny, impulsive and silly and he looks so strange and the sky is as black as the water now.

I reach for the bottle of juice in my pocket that Hayden had given me back at the library and take a slug. Hawk grabs it with a thickly veined hand. I think I can see his veins moving. 'What is this?' He puts the rim to his nose and sniffs it. 'Fuck, did Hayden give you this?' I nod and he rolls his eyes.

He takes me to his car, ducking my red highlights into the low doors of his red car. I watch the city going by. My favourite feeling of all is being a passenger in the city. It feels like being the saxophone solo in the rhythm of the road.

The bass influences me. I am provocative. We pull up at his apartment in the halls. I don't think he's supposed to park on the grounds, but he does. I follow him upstairs. I place my hands on the cold stone of his walls and try to find my head.

'Sit down,' he says. He gets me a thick woollen throw, drapes it over my wet shoulders and gets me a glass of water. He throws a flame to the fire and sits down on the thatched chair opposite me, bottle of juice in hand.

'Did Hayden tell you what this was before he gave you it?' I shake my head. He sighs, exasperated. He weighs it in his hands. 'It's a memory serum. He's been working on it, like I told you. But he hasn't run it past Eydis. Or even tested it. He's of course, anti-animal testing. But he's not anti-human testing. And you just so happen to be his first test, despite being the intended subject.' Hawk shoots up and paces. 'God, he's an arsehole. Especially since it seems to be having *adverse effects*.'

'I'm better now.' And I am. I can't fly, so that's a start. 'It was just a momentary lapse. He's a dick for not telling me, yeah, but I'm willing to try anything, Hawk. It's not like you're helping me.'

'What do you mean by that?' He looks hurt.

'Well, you've hardly looked at me in a week. We were playing spies in the safehouse, running from the agent in the woods, and then you ignored me at the AYIP. You've pretty much ignored me all week, actually.'

'I've been busy.'

'Okay, well so has Hayden. Except he's actually been busy helping me!'

'He's putting you at risk.'

'I'm already at risk, Hawk. Of going mad! I don't know who the hell you are, or who I am!' I dig a finger into my chest and I feel it like a stab wound. His gaze spirals into an airborne knife. Any confessions could only ever egress as nausea. His eyes are wet like waterfalls are wet; completely, overwhelmingly and irreversibly.

My heart is imperishable like titanium metal. I feel it heavy in the soles of my feet. I wish he would hurt me. My wounds don't bleed, but the impact of his daggers could take me out. I'm resistant to the corrosion I want to feel. To feel alive. To feel like I ever existed at all; that I exist now. I want to bleed for something. Anything. I almost mention his arrest. His supposed infatuation with me may or may not have died with my mind. But I don't. I almost mention the Rowleys vampire and the early records of Silenda under the name. But I don't. I almost mention the base and the men in the library, but I assume that knowledge has already made his way back to him. So, I don't.

I say nothing.

When I stand, he's leaning over me. His mouth close. Breath hot. He's looking at my lips and his eyes are so black. So perpetually black. I look at his throat. I want to touch it, but I'm scared it'll be cold, that he'll be ice. We'll only melt together. He's going to kiss me. I know it this time. He gets closer. My mouth is opening, and I think I'm going to bite his neck.

But I gasp. 'I'll part the black sea for you,' I whisper.

'What?' He shoots up, stepping back. I gulp thickly, eyes daring to leave him. I feel a single tear stream that I didn't know was building. The stone room is dark, only slightly aglow in the firelight and the old-fashioned lampposts through the window. 'What did you say?'

'I don't know.' *I don't know.* I let the wool drop from my shoulders. 'I don't know, my head is a mess. I don't even know what that means.' My cheeks burn and I point a thumb at the door. 'I think Astrid said something about a party at the cabin tonight?' I'm backing out the door.

'Right, yeah. I think she has a thing for Horatio. It's an excuse to drink so she can talk to him. She's not as ballsy as she seems. Who has a party on a Monday night, right?' He attempts to laugh, but it comes out sad. He wipes a tear that he doesn't acknowledge and lets me go, shouting that he'll catch up later.

I get lost in the gardens on the way to the cabin. *I'll part the black sea for you.* I trace a white hand over the freckles on my wrist. Somehow my hands feel more mine than ever. I pick a rose. I admire its petals for a mere second before I tear away the head and use a thorn to prick my skin. I bleed.

• • •

Talons on my flesh. Grab me with hot hands, tear me apart piece by piece. Carry me away. I'm too sober when I see him again. Everyone parties. The cabin is dark, the music loud, the lights bright. Coal fire dances when I drink. Dark eyes strip my skin, I feel my throat in places I've never felt before.

I picked an apple in the university gardens before I made it to the cabin. I think a piece must be lodged in my throat.

I'll part the black sea for you.

I can't get it out of my head. The words. My head is dizzy with drink, my body is heavy with bubbling incoherence and I can't stop thinking these words.

I'll part the black sea for you.

SILENDA

I'm sitting. I couldn't stand if I tried. He's sitting, he couldn't stand if he dared. The others dance. Astrid clings to Horatio like she'll lose him if she neglects him of touch. Hayden's lips are swollen. I followed him to his bedroom when I got here. I was looking for my diary. My intoxicated mind supposed that a wild Monday night should be excellent timing to get to know myself. But there was a tall brunette in his room. A woman, a beautiful woman with lipstick bruises and lace that betrayed her chest.

I try to figure him out as he dances in his old-man sweater vest. He looks happy. Whisky does that to a person, before it makes you cry. Horatio and Astrid are crazy to watch. His translucent hands reach for her neck so naturally. I think he looks like a vampire. She cradles his touch shamelessly as they giggle with each boundary they cross.

I meet Hawk's eyes across the room, wondering if he'll ever jump. Hawk of the forest, do you only hunt in the day? If only you had been an owl.

When did this wall go up? It's like watching him through an iron cage. A mews chamber. Every time I try to squeeze through the gaps, I get stuck, caught in his grasp like a fluffy little dog. How ironic.

He never moves from his chair, clinging to a mug of tea and letting his eyes flutter across the room. He watches Astrid with Horatio and occasionally scowls at an intoxicated Hayden who tries to pull him onto the floor.

Neon blue disco lights graze his skin.

Astrid has built a makeshift stage from old wooden crates that formerly held bottles of beer. A pink plastic karaoke machine materialises from the storage cupboard. Astrid loves Kate Bush. Horatio horrifies with his rendition of *Taxi Taxi* by Cher. The whole room turns to Hawk, grabbing him from his chair and yelling things that smell like wine. Eventually, he caves. I don't recognise the song he sings but it's R&B synth. His voice is like butter.

Eventually, I stand. With a sip of rum and a moment of averting my eyes from him, I'm able to feel my legs again. The floorboards creak upstairs where the bass of the music below is quieter but the tension in the air is thicker. I'm somewhat incoherent and there is a sour taste in my mouth. My heart beats fast. God knows what is in Hayden's serum but it tastes like mangoes. For a moment I think it's giving the upstairs hallway an orange glow, until I realise the overhanging lights have been fitted with ambient disco bulbs.

I reach for the handle of the nearest bathroom door, finding myself too dizzy to make it to my room.

A muffled voice stops me. Careful whispers.

My heart races a little. In the latest chapter of my life, I am always fearing the worst. I poke my head over the wooden railing to watch the party downstairs. Hawk remains on his phone in a room full of other party-goers I've never met before.

Hayden is missing.

There's a sigh.

I begin to walk away at the sudden realisation that it's probably Hayden and the pretty brunette woman behind the bathroom door.

'Tell me you're obsessed with me,' I hear Hayden say. I stop, unable to help myself. At first I think he purrs, but when he says it again I realise he's crying. *'Tell me you're obsessed with me.'*

'There is not a centimetre of your skin that I am not obsessed with.' Zeb. 'But it kills me, Hayden. There's nothing healthy about it. You can't even look at me unless you're drunk!'

I walk on.

My head spins with the small snippets of conversation I hear at the party. Drunk people have no walls. No mews chamber. Everyone is so raw, so seemingly honest. It's impossible to tell whether alcohol makes a person *less* like themselves or *more* like themselves.

Maybe the self has no true form. Perhaps it is something that lives within us and is impossible to express. The everyday is far too scary and far too anxiety inducing for the self to show its true form.

Alcohol brings it out in extremes.

The self is a grey area in a black and white world.

It's not long before I leave. Straying along the cobbles of Bellumside village, leaving the thumping base of intoxication behind me. And him. In his silence. I end up in a cosy coffee shop, sheltering from the rain. It trickles down the glass windows in ambience with the gentle sound of jazz.

There's a live piano. The musician hides his face, intimate with his keys. The mahogany stools are aglow with warm hanging lights. The barista has climbed on his stool, etching onto the hanging blackboard behind the counter in dusty white chalk. I watch the back of his head as he writes. I don't order anything. I sit with my head in my hands, listening to the seductive sound of the stereo saxophone and the close vibration of the keys. I watch the rain flood the cobbles.

It's always raining in West Town.

The candles and the smell of coffee beans are a comfort. There's a woman with a steaming cup and an open book that she searches curiously. It's strange to imagine that she has a life. A life where the next most important thing she can be doing right now is running her finger across delicate black print. She furrows her brow. She's probably a student, studying.

I wonder if I enjoyed university, if I studied hard or was otherwise engaged. Astrid says I rarely turned up to my classes towards the end. It's not hard to imagine why, not when I was Jason's only believer. Supposedly I studied criminology. I had a brain for problem solving. It's hard to imagine that now when my brain is only just able to comprehend breathing.

The girl is quiet, in her own little world, in her own little three-dimensional, emotional existence. The jazz fades out as the pianist's fingers dance over the final keys, allowing the rain to fill the silence. A coal fire burns. I want to jump in it. I hear the pianist stand but I don't see him.

The wind chimes that hang on the glass door chorus gently when he enters, stumbling slightly where his leather boots scuff the wooden floor. Hayden flops down on the stool beside me. We stare at our reflections in the window. My eyes puffy with exhaustion, my hair tangled and my slight body drowning in black fabric. Hayden looks homeless.

'You followed me,' I state.

He ignores me, pointing a tipsy finger at my reflection. 'That's not really you, you know.'

'Huh?'

He turns to the innocent student whose eyes pour over her book. 'Hey lady!' he yells. 'There's no point in reading that. It's not real. It's all happening inside your head!' Hayden digs an aggressive finger into his temple. 'The author is a fucking ghost. A ghost when he wrote it and a ghost when you finish it, haunting your mind with his own righteous fucking opinions. That book isn't a comment on our world, lady, it *is* our world. *You* are our world and it'll change you. Be careful what you read!'

I push Hayden down onto his stool by his shoulder when he rises with his voice. 'I'm sorry,' I say to the girl who gathers her books and takes her coffee to go, an alarmed expression on her face. 'He's just had too much to drink...' But she's gone. 'What on earth are you on about, Hayden?'

His head wobbles where his eyes try to focus and he's pointing at our reflections again. My eyes go between focusing on us in the window and drifting to the drops of rain that grace the streets. 'That's not you,' he begins again, 'and that's not me. It's a comment on us. We're not like books, you see, Red. We're not haunting. But we do have agency, we can do something. And we can do it now.'

You drugged me, I want to say. But now doesn't feel like the time. 'It's scary what people read in books,' I say, instead.

'Right? It's letting a stranger inside your head. Some people believe anything as long as it's written down. Am I inside of your head?'

I don't answer. He doesn't speak for a while.

'I know you saw me,' he says. 'I know you saw *us*.'

'You and Zeb?' I'm too drunk to be tender.

He slaps his hand over my mouth and I flinch. His eyes are wide, he looks around and lifts a finger to his lips, 'Shhh! You can't tell anyone.'

'Why is it a secret? What happened to your agency, to *now*?'

'Sometimes it's easier to fight big problems than the really personal ones. You need to be careful what you read.' Suddenly the conversation begins to feel like a big fever dream, nothing he says makes any sense. My head is spinning and I can almost see Hayden's blonde mop about to roll off his shoulders.

'They have books,' he says.

'Who has books? Who?' I'm getting exasperated with Hayden's riddles.

He sighs. 'The Luxies. Some of them have books. The organised ones. Some of the shit in there is nice. I wouldn't mind living by it, living *on* it, I really wouldn't but...' he pauses. The pianist leaves, briefcase in hand and Hayden watches him. He's easily distracted. I poke him. His black eyes focus. 'When I was in high school, I was pretty, uh, promiscuous, you could say.'

'I've heard that.'

He rolls his eyes. 'Lots of women.' He winks at me. I grimace. 'Anyway, the only proper relationship I ever had was with a skater kid called Austin. A guy, Carson. I didn't care. I never even thought much about it. I like who I like when I like 'em. It was autumn, we went on a date in Centrum Park. The leaves were abundant and we held hands. It was sweet. I'm not a sweet guy, but it was sweet. I liked him so much. He had a tattoo on his forearm of a snake, and I just thought that was so fucking cool, you know?' His teeth protrude sadly over his vulnerable bottom lip at an attempt at a smile.

His eyes fill with tears. 'There's always preachers in the park, Carson. It's mixed there. People try to force their god on you, but we ignore it because some Shadows yell at them. They tell them their god isn't important, isn't real, and that's not okay either, man.'

I place my hand on his bare shoulder where his sweater vest has fallen.

'There was this lady and her son. Big guy. She had her book. She was screaming about her god, about how he loves us and shit. I tried not to be offended, because I hated him then. I was 16. I lived with my uncle because my mum was dead and Jason was drunk. Some god, huh?'

I close my eyes. Too distressed by his bloodshot eyes and unnaturally large pupils.

'We were just minding our own business, Carson. She ran at us when she saw us together. She pushed me against a tree, screaming with her book flailing in her grip. Her son got Austin and pushed him to the ground and beat him. She told us we were going to hell, that we'd burn and fry and melt and that God wouldn't save us. She didn't leave until she'd made me cry. And there was Austin on the concrete, bleeding as they walked away. His face was swelling already and one of his eyes was black. He wiped his bloody nose on his arm and got up and walked away, without saying a word. The last thing I saw of him was the blood dripping off the fucking snake on his arm. He never spoke to me again. And that's when I knew, if there is hell, we'll be damned.'

I stare at his reflection, too desperately sorry to look at him directly. 'But hey,' he says, 'if we are destined to burn, let's remember where we came from!'

He hands me a bottle and I drink.

CHAPTER 18

ARCADE ANARCHY

Horatio

I follow her long legs as she stumbles through the gardens laughing. It's safe to say the past week has been somewhat surreal. Astrid likes me. She wants to talk to me. And when she talks to me, we laugh. We have fun. She's like Zeb in a lot of ways: bold, unforgiving and hilariously impetuous.

'Where are we going?' I ask, laughing and gazing back at the cabin party behind us. I see Hayden and Carson hanging around outside.

'To Hawk's car! We're going into the Urb!'

'Do you think Hawk will be crazy about us stealing his car? Plus, you're drunk and so am I, we can't drive!' I say it with an air of a giggle but I'm serious.

She stops in her tracks as if she had forgotten that fact. But we've already reached his car: a red Ferrari, glowing under the Victorian lampposts like it's blessed with a mechanical halo.

'Wow.' I move towards the car slowly, snapping my sweaty palms away the second they graze the paint in awe. 'This is Hawk's car? Do you all come from money?'

'You don't?' Astrid asks, humoured.

I shake my head. 'Not money this big.' I'm staring so hard I'm worried my sharp eyes will burn through its vehicular skin. 'My parents are dentists.'

'Well, you do have nice teeth,' she says, winking at me as she tries the handle of the driver's door.

'Hey! What are you doing with my car?' Disappointment but an unmistakable tinge of relief washes over me as Hawk strides towards us, his knuckles rich with rings and his black hair falling over his eyes.

'C'mon, Birdboy! We were just going to take it for a spin!' Astrid whines and I laugh at her name for him, remembering Zeb telling me he had coined it.

Hawk rolls his eyes. He often does. But he unlocks the car with his keys, dodging Astrid out of the way to claim the front seat and ordering us to hop in the back. 'I'll take you into the city because I'm headed to the library base anyway. Plus, I've not been drinking. You're dumb as hell trying to drive like that, Triddy.'

She huffs. Somehow, a wave of jealousy washes through me. Hawk is a really attractive guy. And he calls her Triddy.

'What you going to the library for?' I ask.

He looks at me through the rear-view, obviously caught up on what I know. 'Asiqa and Alex are working late, tracing the guys from the library back to their base. I'm going to see if I can help, I'm too tired to party. It's Monday.' He sends daggers at Astrid.

I remember what Zeb said to Carson and me at the library about Hawk as good as getting in the way. I laugh to myself a little at the idea of Asiqa and Alexandria being nothing but irritated by his 'help'.

'Where are you guys wanting dropped?' he asks as the wheels flood the tar so flawlessly I almost cry.

'Arcade?' Astrid gleams.

I nod before Hawk reaches into his glove compartment and passes through two black semi-automatic pistols like the ones Astrid had been teaching me to shoot at the range.

'Hawk—' she says as he looks at us with the piercing stare that he has.

He stops her. 'You just don't know, Astrid. I wouldn't go anywhere without them. Not since Eydis had to throw a body in the Urb river.' My eyes catch Astrid for an explanation, but she simply nods, tucking her handgun into her black vinyl purse and handing one to me, eyes steady in search of my feelings about the situation.

Astrid sobers up for a second. She tells me about Eydis and the agent that snuck into their apartment. She looks terrified, that is, until the city lights and the plush arcade toys prisoned in cheap plastic cells and guarded by shitty metal claws send her spiralling into child-like excitement. It's unclear why a universally recognised supermodel should be so completely desperate for me to win her a googly eyed cupcake plush, but I hold the controllers like the pilot of precious cargo and try to focus my drunk mind on its beady little eyes.

It's also unclear why anyone with a Versace purse should choose to go to the shittiest arcade in the city. I thought Astrid would take me to some sort of elitist arcade-meets-casino, or at least Happy Island with the bright lights and the little train that crawls over the pinball machines and air hockey tables, where children laugh and teens eat at the burger van outside.

Astrid has taken me to Arty Arcade, where the fading font of the sign outside is printed on red plastic in big white circus font. Flyers for freakshows cover the lampposts. The dull ceiling lights flicker against the overwhelming grey of the walls. The black and white chequered floor is blessed with a 'wet floor' sign, but no one appears to work here at all. The lights on the pinball machine flicker tauntingly, and cigarette butts cover the ground outside. The arcade has no door and is open simply because the rusty metal shutters have not been pulled down.

An Elvis song whines quietly and tunelessly from one of the coin slot machines.

The arcade looks like it should be abandoned, and it almost is, except for us, a couple of scruffy looking kids in luminous socks and, of course, the business of the somewhat functioning lights and a depleted Elvis. The place spooks me. And I suppose I could blame my lack of concentration on this fact, and therefore the fact that I've spent at least 10 coins trying to take possession of a fucking anthropomorphic cupcake. I get exasperated. It makes no difference how much a guy can disassociate himself from the subsequent humiliation of toxic masculinity if he can't win a stuffed toy for the person he wants, it feels like shit.

'Hey mister!' a small voice squeaks. A couple of kids wander over in their neon trainers. The little girl removes a bobby pin from the folds of her braid and we watch as she uses the hair grip to manipulate the small screws in the corners of the plastic divide. She removes it, hands Astrid the cupcake and seals it shut again. 'There ya go, Triddy!' *Is everyone on nickname terms with this woman, but me?*

Astrid laughs. 'Harry, this is Leila.' The little girl waves. 'And this is Jude.' A smaller boy looks at the floor and scuffs his feet. 'They're Alexandria's little cousins,' she ruffles their hair, 'who shouldn't be out in the dark so late! Hang here, Horatio.' Astrid tosses me a couple of coins. 'I'm just going to walk the kids home, they're only a block away.'

'I'll come!' I say.

'No, just you wait here and look after Mr Sprinkles.' She hands me the wide-eyed cupcake and my drunk mind laughs. I nod, not wanting to insult her ability to look after herself.

I let her go.

After a couple of moments, perched in a plastic Ferrari, I realise only part of my proposal had been to protect Astrid.

It's terrifying here.

I think the gumball machine has something living in it. And it's so quiet. Except for the buzz of the bright white lights. I think I had a nightmare that looked like this once. The sinking feeling of bright grey walls. I don't know what it is about them and the misplacement of the vibrant colours that fill them. There's something mocking, sadistic about that contrast. I just can't put my finger on it. But I know there's a part of my subconscious, locked up and heart-clenching, that looks like this place. It's just so quiet.

So quiet, that I almost fall out of the shitty paint-chipped car when I hear the bang. I make eye contact with a metal clown. The paint is flaking around his eyes and his deteriorating smile epitomises this place.

It's the corrosion of joy.

The weathering of what once was a happy place.

I hate it. It roots itself inside me. Sometimes I have gut feelings so intense that I think I might stop working. My heart will just stop. My flesh will just rot away and I'll be nothing. It scares me how much I mean that.

There's another bang.

Footsteps.

I peer around the corner from the seat of the car simulation. There are more amusements. Little chairs for babies to circle the moon, a rollercoaster simulation, a ball pit, miniature bowling. The lights are darker and the carpeted floor is rust-brown. There's a grey door on the back wall. That's where the noise originates. I see a shadow cross the door.

Voices.

Astrid, where are you?

I put in my earphones. So loud. I close my eyes tight. If I can't hear it, it's not there. If I can't see it, it's not there.

But it is there. It is. My right eye disobeys me, and I see a hand on the metal door. I hear a struggle. There's a scream.

Shit.

I can't be static. I get up, edging towards the pillar that separates the grey flooring and the brown carpet that separates me from the commotion. I peer around the corner. There's a man dressed in black hanging in the door frame of the mysterious room. He's talking but I can only comprehend the bass of his voice. I edge to another metal clown. It hides me well enough but I'm afraid the men will sense me. Hear me breathe. Hear the fear that fills my chest when someone in the room screams again and even more at the silence that bluntly follows the final bang. The man that shadows the doorframe hurries out of the room and I duck.

When given the chance, I abandon the clown and make for a wall. My vision is compromised. It's only when the sound of scuffling boots dissolves, and another couple of minutes to be sure, that I deem it safe to emerge.

I'm thankful that Astrid hadn't materialised in the last 20 minutes, but then I begin to panic that something has happened to her on the dim streets outside.

A hand grabs me and pulls me to the floor. If the alcohol hadn't dulled my inhibitions, I may have screamed. Her hand smells like apples and the cold metal of her rings sting my cheeks. Her eyes are wide as she shushes and I wonder how long Astrid has been here, hiding in the faded arcade lights. A moment passes, with her pale hand against my equally pale mouth. Eventually, her hand drops to my throat where it hovers for a bit. Maybe she's heating it there.

She mouths something but no words come. She lowers her gaze and her words finally squeak out, 'I think it was them.' She knows what question my eyes pose without words needing to follow. 'Silenda,' she confirms.

'How do you know?'

'A feeling. The way they looked. It's what I imagined when both Cara and Eydis described them.'

I nod, in no position to argue.

'You heard the scream?'

She nods back. 'Do you think we should…'

I put my hand on top of hers. 'Go see?' I finish.

She nods again. I feel sorry for Astrid at how quickly her strength has wobbled.

'I'll go first.' I rise from where we crouch. I hold her hand as she follows me to her feet and we move towards the back of the arcade to the rusty grey storage door.

'What if they're still in there?' she whispers as we approach. The door is wedged open with a small plank of wood. Whatever has gone on behind this door, why would the perpetrators leave the crime scene out in the open?

'They're not.' I listen carefully for a voice.

'Did you see them leave?'

'I heard them.'

'But did you see them?' she presses.

I choose to ignore her. Because the truth isn't the answer she wants. Because the truth is that, either way, we need to find out what is behind the door.

If Hawk is at the base, Carson is scanning the library for clues and Eydis has infiltrated the Purgatorium Hospital and killed a Silenda agent, Astrid and I need to be brave enough to do this. She accepts my silence.

The distance between my torso and my hand that pushes open the grey door is as lengthy as I can manage, ready to run should there be anyone behind it. I have one hand on the door and the other on my gun. My shoulder is shielding Astrid where she peers over me, not as brazen as I've known her to be thus far.

The door creaks under my palm and I kick the remainder open with my foot. The door hits something sturdy behind it. Astrid winces at the sound. 'What is it?' she says. I want to answer but I'm scared to proceed.

I look at Astrid. She talks to me with her eyes. When her expression is sad, her brown eye looks sorrowful, but her blue eye looks vengeful. Strange how appearances can change so much.

I gulp and she watches my throat before her heavy lashes flicker north to my eyes. She says nothing and I know the next move is mine. She squeezes my shoulder as I press open the door again, sliding past the crack allowed by whatever is behind it. She follows me.

I fall back onto a metal filing cabinet, the drawers spilling out as I try to reclaim my weight. I try to step back but there's no way to lessen my proximity to him.

To the body.

Collapsed, pale, motionless. He lies slumped over an old plastic motorbike simulator, his arms dangling lifelessly by the handles. His mop of brown hair falls over his face and I'm glad of it, except I can't tell who he is. His t-shirt is ripped at the collar, exposing his chest, red and blue and pulsing with deflating veins.

I don't scream. I feel my eyes wide and my cheeks full with words that don't come out.

Astrid pushes past me, stumbling into the room, knocking me into the filing cabinets again and standing static behind the body. The colour drains from her face and she doesn't look at me. 'Who is that?' she asks.

'I don't know.' I hardly hear myself say the words. 'I can't see his face.'

'We should check.'

'What?' I exclaim. 'We can't touch him, he's—'

'You can't catch death, Harry, it's not contagious.'

'I think that, in a clearer mind, I could refute that.'

Astrid ignores me, creeping closer to the body.

'Are we sure he's even dead? His veins look inflamed.' Astrid touches his neck. I grimace.

'Didn't you hear the gunshot?' I say. 'He's very recently dead.' I step closer, my heart beating fast as my hand rises. I point to the wall behind the man's head, transfixed.

Blood spatter.

Astrid gulps as she cups the back of the man's head, twisting his neck to reveal the other side. It smells. The blood congeals around the entry wound. It pools on the floor, splattered on the wall, dripping from his shoulder. Concentrated in his skull, thick and viscous.

I'm never eating strawberry jam again.

'His flesh is burnt,' Astrid says as I wonder how she can stomach it. She is so close to the wound. 'Obviously with the size of the room he was shot at close range, so this must be the exit hole.' Her eyes find the other side of his head. 'And this,' she says, searching his hair with her bloody fingers like searching for head lice, 'is the entry wound.' I can't look. Astrid examines her fingers. 'Definitely dead. And definitely recent. His blood is fresh.'

'Thank you for the clarification,' I say, sarcastically. 'Should we call the city police?'

Astrid shakes her head as she gestures for me to come closer. She tilts the man's head again to reveal his neck.

The bite of the Rowleys vampire. The entry point for Silenda's needle.

'That explains the veins then. Cardiac arrest. I thought they needed their subjects alive? To account for what they saw?' I ask. 'What the hell are they doing in an arcade? This isn't science. They didn't assess his brain waves. They didn't ask him if he saw God!' I cry. 'They just killed him, Astrid!'

'I don't understand,' she says, 'they've always tried to keep their work on the low.' My eyes flick to her when I retreat against the filing cabinets again.

'I wouldn't exactly call it work,' I say.

Astrid sighs. 'They wiped Carson's memory. I mean, they saved her life. Why? And Jason? He just managed to get out. Why would they let that happen? Lots of people have turned up incoherent in the Rowleys. And dead.'

'Including Randy,' I say.

Astrid nods as she speaks. 'They couldn't revive Randy,' I can see the wheels turning in her mind, 'but when they realised he had high-ranking parents, you know, people that would miss him, they faked his suicide and put Zeb's DNA at the scene, so that if they ran a toxicology report or examined the bruises on his neck, they'd have someone to blame.'

'So why would they kill this guy if the injection didn't kill him? And dump him in a public place?'

'I have no idea.' Astrid looks dumbfounded.

'After all the effort they went to to keep things underground. Framing Zeb, breaking into your apartment, wiping Carson's memory. Why all of a sudden are they being so careless?' I ask.

Astrid is about to speak but she freezes. Footsteps sound behind the door. I look at her. She puts her finger to her mouth to quiet me. Astrid quickly pulls out her phone and snaps pictures of the anonymous corpse before grabbing my hand with a new sense of authority. We press our ears to the closed door.

'There's definitely someone out there,' she whispers.

We stand for a few minutes, hoping the scare will pass, but it only gets worse.

'We know you're in there, kids!' A man's voice, deep and hoarse.

Astrid grips my hand tight. She holds my eyes for half a second before mouthing a word I only process when the door is swinging open, 'Run!'

Astrid's blonde hair flows back into my face as she pulls me behind her in a sprint. There are at least four men clad in black. Their guns fire in pursuit of us. Astrid takes us onto the street, pausing under the purple sky to look both ways.

She pulls me down a flight of stairs into an underground basement across the street. I feel like I'm floating. I hardly feel a single stone step under my feet. All the days I dreamed of holding Astrid Turrow's pale hand, and not a second of it have I felt anything but fear.

SILENDA

The music thumps, a creepy electronic synth. Monotone robotic vocals, a base I feel in the sole of my feet, the pit of my stomach. My head is spinning. Astrid has run us into an underground club. Everything is dark except for the strobe of white and purple lights.

But this isn't just any club. It's an Umbra club. I see fleeting faces that I recognise from Caleb's record store. Everyone is dressed in black. I see a torrent of tattoos, lip piercings and heavy black eye makeup. I almost stop in wonder when I remember we're running. I wish that Astrid had better considered our destination.

It's dark. Loud. Everyone is dressed in black. The Silenda agents are impossible to see. Astrid stops and I nearly run into the back of her. She turns on her heel as her eyes scan the basement floor. I watch her mouth but I can't decipher a word that comes out of it. She stands on a floor a step above me, looking across the room. When I don't answer her, she looks down at me. She leans close to my ear and whispers. I get goosebumps. 'We should split up!'

I shake my head. 'That doesn't sound like a good idea, Astrid,' I say, firmly.

It's so loud that I have to focus every nerve in my body on her words. 'Look, Harry, I stick out like a sore thumb in here. I'm the tallest woman in the place. My hair is white-blonde and everyone is staring at me!' She's right and I only just notice it.

Everyone is staring at her.

Sometimes I forget that Astrid is a universal celebrity. She isn't just ethereal to me. 'You blend in well here. You know, with the other goth boys.' I scrunch up my nose. I have never thought of myself as a goth. She puts her slim hand on my shoulder and leans down again. 'One day we'll get you pierced somewhere else.' I laugh before I turn to protest against her wish to split. There's no way I'm letting Astrid sacrifice herself to save me.

But she's gone.

My heart races. *She's gone.*

I scour the dance floor looking for her, but Astrid Turrow is nowhere to be found. I push through the crowd, searching every inch of the club but I come across nothing but hot breath and the smell of beer. A woman with two drinks in hand and an eyebrow piercing tries to talk to me. She puts one of her drinks down and begins to rub my arm. I can't make out a word she says. In other circumstances I would feel rude, but I stare over her figure, searching for Astrid and for the men with guns.

That's when I remember the gun in my back pocket. I place my palm over it, keeping it secure on my person. My inexperienced touch trembles against the metal and I have a lump in my throat thinking about strawberry jam.

There's a firm hand on my shoulder. *Please be Astrid,* I think, before I turn. I have a feeling it may be the woman from before.

It's neither.

'Hawk?' I exclaim, partly because he's here and partly because he has a strip of duct tape across his mouth and his hands behind his back. Then I see the man in the black army vest, clinging onto Hawk like his prisoner.

I step back. Hawk moves his eyes to the door, gesturing for me to run. But I can't just leave him. They must have found him on his way to the base. It seems like it isn't just Carson who shouldn't go out on her own. I pull out my gun and hold it against the thigh of the man behind Hawk. I look him in the eyes. He's bald. Stocky. Unremarkable, except for the ruthlessness in his eyes. He has a black fabric mask covering the rest of his face.

He doesn't even flinch. 'If you know what's good for you, boy, you'll follow me outside.' I ignore his hoarse words. Surely he wouldn't fire a gun in here? I look around at the heavily made up faces of the drunks around me. Would they even hear it? No one bats an eyelid at the tape around Hawk's mouth.

Maybe they're into that here.

Hawk's eyes widen when I don't run and I can almost hear him cursing me. There's a moment of stillness. Hawk wriggles around a little but the agent behind him doesn't seem to notice. He's too busy staring me down.

That's when Hawk frees his hand from the ties and elbows the bald man in the jaw, he rips the tape from his mouth and yells, 'Run, Marino!'

And this time I do. When I look back it seems like Hawk has knocked him out and has disappeared into the crowd.

I run until I'm stumbling, catching every fall with the tips of my fingers, my legs flailing so quickly that my torso almost falls behind.

I'm stopped by the shaft of a gun.

Another agent. I should have known they would spread out. There is space between us. I couldn't grab the weapon out of his hand if I tried. His gun is pointed at my head. I'm so exhausted and out of ideas that I begin to accept my fate, until my view of him is compromised by locks of blonde hair.

Astrid has jumped in front of me, her arms out to shield me. I try to move her, to step in front. I grab her shoulder, I scream in her ear, but she kicks me in the shin. I peer over her shoulder, helplessly. The man holds his gun in place, between her beautiful eyes. His mask falls to reveal his expressionless face.

And then he disappears.

He drops his gun and ducks out of the club.

He spares Astrid.

Astrid drops her hands and turns to face me with her brow furrowed. Hawk materialises behind us with a swollen black eye, illuminated by pink and purple strobes of light.

'He didn't shoot,' Astrid says. 'He didn't shoot.'

CHAPTER 19

MAUDIFY

Carson

Hayden wears the thick plaid rug over his head like a fair maiden's shawl. He rolls about the floor laughing in the contagious way that he does. I really didn't like Hayden when I met him. I thought him arrogant and unpleasant; turns out only one of those things is true. I observe the ghost of a bruise that shadows his nose. A souvenir from his fist fight with Zeb. Little did I know the true nature of Hayden's resentment towards him.

Hayden hates that he loves him.

It's nice to see Hayden in such comical form following his café confessions. He has a wicked sense of humour. The sort that masks a deep wound. But, as he prances around wearing Hawk's fur throw like a pretty coat, his laughter is as genuine as breathing.

The party at the cabin had died down by the time we had returned from Bellumside village. Horatio and Astrid had vanished. So had Hawk. The brunette girl that Hayden had been entertaining for the night had also disappeared as the music died down. Zebediah decided to follow Hayden and I in our quest to Hawk's apartment and now he sits on the other side of me, giggling also at the sheer absurdity of Hayden's performance.

SILENDA

When we arrived at the turreted university halls, Hawk's red car was gone, but an intoxicated Hayden pushed past us and stormed up the stairs where he snatched a small silver key from an overhanging light above Hawk's apartment door. So now, we sit in the absent man's apartment, building pillow forts with his furniture and eating his Doritos.

I'm conscious of Zeb's eyes, the way they fall across Hayden's figure with an agonising longing. I try not to make it obvious that I know. Zebediah sits with his shoulder pressed to mine. He is toned and broad in contrast to Hayden's lanky white limbs. The latter's sweater vest falls from his shoulder when he dances. He's so slim he can hardly keep his clothes on his body.

Zebediah, I decide, has the best sort of laugh. Hayden's is manic and contagious, but Zeb's is husky and sweet – so toothy and white. It makes me want to pinch his cheeks. I've had a little more to drink than I can manage.

Hayden pulls Zeb and I up from the cushion-covered floor to dance with him, and we do, to the intoxicating beat of 90s disco. Hayden's loose blonde curls toss as he laughs, his grin brushing Zeb's bare shoulder. Zeb twirls me before pulling me in for a cuddle.

None of us speak. We just dance and laugh until our eyes are streaming. The invisible wall between the men falls for a brief moment of intoxication. Zeb twirls Hayden too and he falls around dizzily before being drawn close to the tank-top-covered chest of his secret lover. I step back. There's a slowing. A tension.

I've seen this flame before. That threatens to burst into a fire that burns as much as it warms.

It diffuses just in time.

Hawk's door slams open.

He stands in the stone doorway, only scowling momentarily at the chaos of his apartment floor. It seems like he has bigger problems. Hawk stares at us, his left eye a swollen violet. There's a stirring behind him as Horatio and Astrid come into view.

What has happened here?

We had supposed Hawk was at the base and the other two had been hooking up in a toilet or something.

The three of them enter. All tall and all exhausted looking. No one speaks for a moment. Hawk throws his hoodie over his velvet couch and falls onto it. Hayden and Zeb shoot apart from each other as Hayden awkwardly shouts at the radio to turn off the Spice Girls.

'What happened to you guys?' Zeb asks. Horatio looks exhausted. His black t-shirt appears stretched at the collar and his shoulder is bruised. Astrid's contrasting eyes are shadowed by smudged black liner.

The door closes.

'Silenda,' Hawk says lazily, his hand on his face as he lays back on a cushion.

'Wait, seriously?' Hayden asks, sobering. 'Where were you guys?'

'Arty Arcade,' Astrid says. 'And then Asylum.'

'Arty Arcade? Where Jason used to take us as kids? Isn't it shut down?'

'Sort of,' Horatio mumbles, walking over to Zebediah who ruffles his hair.

'They did that to you?' I ask Hawk, looking at his purple eyelid. I stand on the opposite side of the room, feeling safer there.

He looks at me. 'Yeah. There were agents chasing us around Asylum. It's a nightclub,' he clarifies for me. 'They got me on my way to the base. Jumped me from behind. There was an altercation,' he points at his eye, 'and then they took me to the others. Probably thought keeping me around would lure them.'

'There was a body in the arcade,' Astrid talks over Hawk.

Even Hawk shoots up now. 'A body?' he asks. 'You never told me that!'

Horatio nods along to Astrid's words. 'Harry and I found him in the storage room at the back of the building after we heard a gunshot and saw some agents. He had the bite of the Rowleys vampire. But he was shot in the head.'

'Why would they kill him?' Zeb steps forward. 'What happened to framing us to keep their crimes underground?' Astrid shrugs.

'I think they wanted us to find him,' Horatio says. 'It's like they knew we were there. They knew we would check out the gunshot. It seemed like they were waiting for us to come out. They tried to kill me.'

'And me.' Hawk's hand shoots up into the air where he lies on the couch again.

'But they spared Astrid,' Horatio continues. 'He held the gun right at her head when she jumped in front of me. But he ducked. I mean, he just *left*.'

Everyone looks on in deep confusion.

'You jumped in front of him?' Hayden yells at Astrid as he clings to his vest with a sobering disposition.

'Horatio got dragged into all of this. It has nothing to do with him,' she says.

Harry gulps with a guilty look on his face. He would never have forgiven himself if something had happened to Astrid, I can tell.

'Astrid, Tyson would never recover if he lost you!' Hayden yells, but I think it has more to do with his own feelings than he's letting on. 'Especially if he knew you died to save an effeminate emo-boy who cries to Foreigner in his bedroom!'

Astrid chuckles under a mask of tears as she reaches for Horatio's hand. 'It's like he was written by a woman.'

Hayden rolls his eyes. 'So, are we taking this to Tyson?'

Hawk removes his hand from his head. 'You think we have to?'

Zeb steps forward. 'I don't think we have much of a choice. If Silenda are upping their game, becoming more ruthless and careless, we have to tell him.'

• • •

Tyson calls a meeting. I debate going.

I sift through the Rowleys, leaving parts of me in my wake that I'll never get back. The old tattoo parlour, where I broke Hawk's heart under the neon blue lights. A boy I do not know, and may never know again.

I've pictured it a million times since he told me. His wet cheeks. My anger. The blue blue blue. The corrosion of a city backdrop. The factories far away. The rain falling from the heavens, sparking the faulty telephone wires like electric tears.

Sometimes I think I remember it. It's always hard to tell what you really recall and what you think you do because someone planted something in your mind that pulled on your heart strings. The tattoo parlour pulls on mine. A bitter-sweet melody.

Inharmonious. Screeching.

I think about Hawk. Bennet, now. He is Bennet, you see. A new version of himself that cannot be called the way he used to. The second I walked away, the moment his lips met Astrid's, the moment the neon blue switched frantically to black, Hawk was lost.

And so was I.

He said we would arrive at the meeting together. He wanted me to crash at his apartment when the others left. But I couldn't. I went back to the cabin, catching up with Zeb and Hayden. Afraid of what I would say if I stayed. Of what I would remember, looking into his eyes.

Maybe neon blue memories are better forgotten.

Drowned in the black sea.

I like the Rowleys. It's quiet. The Urb is in perfect view. Towering and tall in the distance. Sometimes I feel under pressure there. It feels like a simulation: a cybercity. No decisions I make there are really my own. The Rowleys is hidden in its materiality; a hidden code; layered; inaccessible.

I run my hand across the red brick wall that marks the entry to the Rowleys, the wall that divides it from the Urb. From West

Town. I trace the words that cover it. *We can show our own, but we will never know, she's made of glass but we never tiptoe.* I read it numerous times.

'Know what it means?' A voice. Jason. I shake my head as he joins me by the wall.

'It was you that wrote it, wasn't it?'

He nods. 'We express our faith in everything we do, Cara. All we do is think about *next*. Whether we believe in it or reject it. We spend our eternity forgetting about *now*,' he says. His eyes are brown. Not as dark as Hayden's. Or as angry.

'Who is the woman made of glass?' I ask.

'Our world. We don't look after her, each other, ourselves.'

I point to *Silenda*. 'Did you write that, too?'

'Only once,' he says. 'It's all over this place, but it wasn't me. I brought the knowledge of Silenda to the Rowleys. The other families here who have been impacted by their terror, they covered the wall with their name and vampiric symbols, to show them that we know. That they can't just take us.'

I nod.

'Are you going to Tyson's meeting?' he asks, hands in his pockets.

'I'm supposed to be heading there now.'

'What brought you here?'

'Memories. Well, at least I think that's what they are.' He doesn't ask.

'I'm surprised Hawk let you come here on your own.'

'Hawk,' I state, 'doesn't have a say in what I do.'

● ● ●

Jason walks me to Tyson's mansion. He leaves me at the door. I get the impression that he is not entirely fond of his brother, although he doesn't say this.

I feel nauseous when I enter.

The long table where Hawk and I had once feasted is set for seven.

Astrid and Horatio sit together. Hawk sits on the same side. Hayden and Zeb sit on the opposite side with a tense seat between them. I sit in it.

'Carson,' Tyson states as he sits proudly at the top of the long table. There's a large projector behind him. 'Nice of you to join us!'

Hawk makes eyes at me, as if to say, *where have you been?* Zeb pats my leg, reassuringly.

'Shall we make a start?' Tyson rises and points a small remote at the projector behind him. A birds-eye view of the Rowleys fills the screen. I look around me to see if the others know something I don't, but even Astrid looks confused and furrowed at the brow. We sit quietly, allowing the mayor to proceed.

'Following the revelations of the last few days, it is clear that Silenda are at large. Even more so than before. I have been working closely with Eydis Achebe, who you all know, to reach conclusions about the underground threat. It seems apparent that the AYIP has achieved very little.'

Astrid looks at her hands. Hayden has his arms folded defensively over his chest as he slouches in his chair, a sour expression on his face.

'Eydis and I have worked together to access security footage from the Rowleys. The cameras are old. As we all know, not many people care what goes on in that area. The footage was poor but Eydis has managed to restore it. And this is what we found from a couple of weeks ago.'

Tyson plays the clip. We lean in close to the screen, trying to make out what exactly we are seeing. A man in a navy suit comes into view. Then another shorter man, also in a suit. They stand outside a large metal building, talking to a row of a dozen men in black. The men have guns.

'Silenda agents?' Zeb asks.

'Seems like it,' the mayor goes on, 'it would be awfully coincidental with the suspicious death rate in the Rowleys that an army should be spotted and *not* be Silenda.'

'And who's that?' Hayden stands, pointing to the two suited men. Tyson zooms in and the pixels collectively create a clearer image.

'That,' he begins, 'is Basilio Young and his right-hand man, Lucian Fletcher.'

Horatio stands. Zeb shoots him a look.

'Let me get this straight, Dad,' Astrid stands with him, 'you're saying that the mayor of East Town is the head of Silenda?'

'Exactly,' he says.

'That can't be right!' Horatio exclaims. All eyes turn to him. 'I mean, that's impossible. It has to be, right?' He looks around himself but everyone is silent.

'It is right, new boy.' Tyson squints at him and Horatio sits back down from where he had risen.

Tyson presses another button and the screen switches to an image of the dead body in the arcade.

I look away, feeling a rising lump in my throat.

'This,' Tyson continues, 'is the handiwork of Basilio Young.'

'But why would he kill him?' Astrid interjects. 'Assuming that he is Silenda, why would he go to the extent of framing Zeb to cover up a murder when he's going to shoot people in the head in public places?'

'Excellent question, Astrid. Eydis!' Tyson calls, accompanied with the clicking of a finger. He doesn't turn his head. Eydis enters the room proudly with a briefcase that she sits on the table and unpacks. She takes out a glass container which she sits in the middle of the long table.

We all lean in.

'A dead rat?' Hawk deadpans, leaning back in his chair.

Eydis glares at him. 'I've been running a few tests,' she begins, taking out some papers. 'I have been attempting to mimic the methods of Silenda. At first, I had thought of using you as my test subject,' she winks at Hawk. He lets out a dimpled chuckle. I frown at their flirty banter. 'Instead, I used rats. I'm no condoner of animal testing, but I did what I had to do. I injected this rat with poison that sent it into cardiac arrest. It died.'

'Hooray!' Hayden supports his sarcasm with vigorous jazz hands that fall flat on Eydis.

The Nether Cabin are treating her like a substitute teacher they can't take seriously.

'However,' she pushes as she takes out another glass container with a rat that scurries around the perimeters of its spherical prison, 'I also injected this rat with a poison and sent it into cardiac arrest. But this time when I shocked it, it revived him.'

'What did you do differently?' Zeb asks.

'With this rat,' Eydis examines the glass jar, 'I chased it around for a while. I hit it with a newspaper a couple of times, just enough to graze it. I trapped him in a room where I had sprayed ammonia. It gives off the same scent as a predator's urine, but he couldn't get away from it.'

'Okay?' Hayden presses.

'The adrenaline saved him,' she says. 'The fear of the chase. The other rat was caught off guard, but this one had the time to fear his fate. The adrenaline coursing through him helped to revive him.' Everyone looks on in amazement. 'Now, it's not a sure thing, but the chances of reviving a frightened animal are greater.'

'How does this relate to the body in the arcade?' Astrid asks.

And that's when Eydis reveals the papers in her briefcase.

The Urb Daily. Front page. *Arcade Anarchy: Body Found in Arty Arcade.*

'Seems that you weren't the only people to find his body that night, or perhaps this was the work of Silenda. Either way, this death is now city-wide news. People are scared. Full of adrenaline. Susceptible to the work of Silenda.'

'So Silenda are instilling fear into the city to make the public more successful subjects?' Hawk asks.

'We're just a big circus of lab rats to them, aren't we?' Hayden adds.

'I'm afraid it seems like it. The worst part is that it's extremely clever. It's bound to work, even.'

'Great! Celebratory whisky?' Hayden pulls out a hip flask and offers it to Eydis. Tyson runs his hands over his face in exasperation. Hayden grins toothily and takes a swig when Eydis shakes her head.

'What now?' I ask.

'We expose Basilio,' Tyson states.

'How?' I continue. 'I mean, it's not like that video proves anything, despite how obviously suspicious it is.'

'Red's right,' Hawk says. *Red*. It's the first time Hawk has called me that. 'We need more.'

Tyson grabs his laptop and snaps it open like a book. He presses play on a piece of audio. It's Astrid talking. 'I never shut up!' her husky voice squeals through the screen. 'Gosh, why do I never shut up?'

Astrid looks confused. 'I never said that,' she says.

Hayden stands. 'I did.' He walks towards his uncle's laptop. 'Where did you get this audio, Tyson?'

'I saw you playing around with it. And then I heard you explaining it to Eydis, who was able to hack your laptop to access the program. We can use this, son.' Turrow places his hand on his nephew's tense shoulder.

Astrid frowns, seemingly satisfied, if unimpressed, with this explanation.

'It's Maudify, isn't it?' Horatio adds. Hayden looks at him. He doesn't have to nod or open his mouth to say yes.

'Maudify?' Hawk and I press, simultaneously. He looks at me, cheeks grazed with a scarlet shyness until he looks away.

'Courtesy of Hayden,' Turrow begins as the blonde winces.

'We are able to put any words in the mouth of any person if we have enough linguistic evidence of their language patterns. It's really impressive and very advanced technology.'

That's when it starts to sink in what the mayor is really getting at.

'You're going to put words in Mayor Young's mouth?' Zeb asks, nervously.

'Only because we know it to be true. I'm leaving it to you, Hayden.' The mayor ruffles his nephew's hair.

Hayden's frown and wide eyes soften in an attempt to appear enthusiastic. 'Okay,' he says. 'Okay.'

● ● ●

Back at the cabin, I follow Hayden to his bedroom.

He hadn't said a word the whole walk home. Most of us were silent, actually. Astrid squelched through the hills in her platform boots and Horatio and Zeb sauntered solemnly beside her. Hawk fell behind, scuffing his feet in the mud as I treaded ahead to avoid the complicated throbbing in my head when I look at him.

Hayden sits at his computer, staring blankly at the black monitor. I can't tell if he's looking at his reflection or looking past himself, his eyes glazing over as his mind focuses on looking inside itself instead. I don't know much about computers, short of nothing, actually. But I do know that the machine *brrs* and *whirrs* like how I imagine it sounds behind Hayden's eyes.

'You okay?' I eventually ask him. Whether or not he felt me sitting on the bed behind him is unclear, but his eyes flicker to meet my reflection in the black of the screen.

'Mmm,' he says. I'm not quite sure what that means. 'It feels wrong.'

'Using Maudify to expose Silenda?'

'No,' he says, 'that doesn't sound wrong at all, except we can't be sure that that is what we are doing. Can you imagine the mess we would make if Tyson turns out to be wrong?'

'You think he is?'

Hayden shrugs as my eyes follow the strands of ginger hair that weave through his blonde curls in place of what once was a vibrant orange. 'Do *you* think he is?' he retaliates.

We fall silent.

'It's a lot of responsibility, Red. And it's all on me.'

'Don't do it then,' I say, and his eyes widen at my words.

He scoffs. 'Like that's an option. Tyson would go through me. Like literally through me. Stake to the heart and everything.'

'He's your uncle, Hayden—'

'Not familiar with Shakespeare, are ya?'

Another silence washes over us and it seems that Hayden has made up his mind. He wiggles his mouse, illuminating the black. An hour passes of Hayden gathering as many public appearances of Basilio Young as he can and, in the process, as much linguistic evidence about his voice as possible. A carefully written exposition later, and he has it.

The voice of Mayor Young fills the creaky wooden walls.

'We keep it on the low, Lucian. Silenda thrives, and soon, Luxies will rule the Urb.'

'That's all you need?' I ask.

'That's all we need. Anything else would be too on the nose.' Hayden dances his fingers across an array of buttons, typing vigorously in a language I don't recognise.

Soon a small cassette ejects from a dusty old tape recorder. Hayden stares at it for a while before reluctantly labelling it: *Mayor Young: audio from the Rowleys CCTV.*

CHAPTER 20

BEHIND BARS

Horatio

The screen flashes on the dark walls of the cabin. I sit static on the couch, remote in hand, eyes glazing over at the white reflections of the television screen. All night, the news channels have played the same footage. Once the others had got their fill, they headed to bed; Hayden hid behind his blonde curls, and the others, most especially Astrid, harboured a troubled expression.

Something doesn't feel right.

The AYIP know it. I know they do.

It's hard to tell whether Astrid's unsettled features are a result of her uncertainty of the whole thing or if she feels the AYIP let Tyson down. Perhaps she just wanted her father's approval, to finally achieve something that wasn't handed to her in a designer bow. She wanted the AYIP to achieve something, to appear heroic.

There's a sombre feel over the Nether Cabin, not just over me. Not just me, as I sit frozen on the couch as the flashing cameras on the screen catch shots of my uncle in handcuffs. The Candidus Tower stands with tall planes of glass behind him, gaping faces at its windows as the city police usher Basilio Young into the back of the blue car. He never loses his grace, my uncle. He tucks his head steadily into the vehicle, a smirk never leaving his features.

They knew exactly where to find him when Hayden's tape was strategically and anonymously leaked to the police. My uncle chooses not to spend much time in his East Town home, and instead gathers his men in a penthouse office at the top of Candidus Tower. That is, of course, in the aftermath of Centrum Tower burning to the ground.

There is fear in the city.

Of course there is. It sits in the firmament with a colossally grey weight. I wander into the city the next morning. It's the only way I can get away from the uncaring smile on my uncle's face in the back of that blue car.

For a moment, I think Tyson could be right. That the footage of my uncle in the Rowleys is evidence enough to associate him with Silenda because there has been something eating at my mind, chewing on my heart and crawling up the hairs on the back of my neck since he recruited me. Something screaming not to trust him.

But he can't be Silenda. *He can't be.*

Most notably, because he was with me. That day in the Rowleys, Lucian in his pristine little suit, the men with guns. He was with me. At that very moment I must've been strapped to a metal chair in the tin building behind him, feeling like I was going to throw up on my satin shirt.

It's a miracle I went unseen. If the camera had been angled even a centimetre differently, I would have been caught, soon to be stumbling out of the building with Lucian beside me.

When Tyson clicked play on the projector, my lungs nearly swallowed my heart. How would they all have reacted? If I had stood there beside my uncle? Would Hayden have launched across the table? Would Hawk have punched me in the jaw? Would Astrid hold me down? Would the disappointment in Cara and Zeb's eyes have killed me first? Sometimes I think this is what will happen anyway if they find out why I'm here at all – heart in my task, or otherwise.

I walk along the strip. I usually feel calm here. The lights calm me. The tall buildings, the billboards, the cars – they remind me of how small I am. How insignificant. That might scare some people, but not me. It reminds me how unimportant the little things are, the mistakes I make, the things I say in anger, the fleeting things that keep me up at night. All tiny and stupid and a waste of precious thought.

I listen to music when I walk in the city. My mother hates it, she says that it distracts me, that I'll get hit by a bus. Sometimes I feel like, if that's how I'm supposed to go, then that's how I'll go. She's right though, music does distract me. It distracts me from my uncle. From my father's distress on the phone when he heard the news. From the look on Zebediah's face when he saw my uncle in the Rowleys, the pitying look of *did you know?*

I've avoided Zeb since. I've silenced my calls. I keep my head down when the electronic billboards switch to the city news.

I listen to the Cocteau Twins instead. *Pearly Dewdrops Drop.*

The unintelligible lyrics allow me to be in any place I want to be, to be anyone, to see anything. The lyrics say what I want them to say. I could be riding my bike through hilly woods in a time I didn't live, grasping a camera as a tourist in a trench coat. A model. A musician. Someone that can secretly play the harp. When I walk in the city, everyone who looks at me has no idea who I could be; the self has endless possibilities. I may be insignificant in this landscape, but I, as I understand myself, am boundless.

I am cosmic.

The Urb makes me that way, under an intoxicating purple sky.

When the purple fades, the sky goes grey. A washed out green-grey, exploding in neon lights. I shelter from the heavy rain under a rusty metal bridge on the border between the Rowleys and the Urb. There's hardly anyone around, except for tired looking women in short skirts and large men in white vests with skin fades and snake tattoos.

Why are those guys always in white vests?

Since my uncle's arrest, Silenda has become city-wide news. Who they are. What they want.

There's a panic that washes over the city streets. Suddenly a chain of unexplained murders are no longer unexplained. Randy's death and the bloody body in the arcade didn't help the drug rumours. Drug related murders don't scare the average citizen, because they're personal, someone else's problem, someone else's life. But Silenda? Nothing about them is personal. Death is not personal. Not to them.

Anyone could be next.

That is of course, unless they got the right guy. Unless my uncle's day behind bars has been warranted and fair and that these deaths and disappearances should not go on without his oversight.

But I don't believe that.

A young woman with violet hair blows smoke in my face as she walks by. She winks at me with a crooked grin. I duck into a building that once was a run-down burger joint to avoid the stares on this side of town. I stand in the shelter, leaning against the metal shutters. I watch the neon reflect on the wet pavements. I try to think, but little comes to mind.

The way that feelings are portrayed in movies is a lie. Most of the time when terrible things happen, I feel nothing at all. *Nothing*. I can't cry. I can't think. I go numb; static. And that's how I feel right now. My uncle is in jail, my family and my best friend have been trying to call me, and I've just disappeared. Ducked under the radar. Under a bridge. Away from facing anything.

Astrid Turrow has tried to call me five times today. *Astrid Turrow*.

I stare at my phone as it buzzes. I see her name pop up on the screen. I feel the vibration in my hand. The buzzing noise is mingled with the rushing sound of rain water in drains and the monotonous voice of the Urb announcements booming between the metal buildings. Her voice repeats, 'Stay inside. Stay calm. The city police are taking all precautions.'

Rain water. Police sirens. Car alarms and indicators. The intimidating cackle of night-shift workers. Astrid sending my phone into a frenzied vibration. My uncle's face on the cracked old television in the tattoo parlour across the street.

Is this real life?

Stay Inside. Stay Calm. The city police are taking all precautions.

I wave over the next beaten-down black taxi and hop into the back seat. 'Cava-Mastix Prison, please.'

•••

It turns out prisons have scheduled visiting hours, and that 10pm is a little late. But they make an exception for the big-shot mayor of East Town.

They always do.

Prison smells exactly how I imagined a prison would smell. Rusting metal and stale air. Everything is trying to cover up something. That's what prisons are, I suppose. A place where everyone thinks they're hiding, but really they're in plain sight. Drugs hidden under postage stamps, cigarette breath disguised by mint gum and sour bile disguised with pinecone detergent.

But a smile can't hide rotten teeth.

And my uncle's supposed innocence, by me, and many of his East Town followers, cannot hide the fact that something putrid bubbles under his skin pretending to be blood. The glass screen that divides us now may not have been enough to cut him, but something will be.

He doesn't look surprised to see me, despite my own surprise at seeing myself here, reflected in the glass. He supposes me his loyal nephew now, I regret. His Lux boy in a perfect disguise, plotting to take down Tyson at his side so that segregation can continue in the city.

I suppose I can play that role a moment longer.

'Harry,' he says softly, picking up the plastic handset as I pick up mine.

I speak through the transmitter as a large officer watches us through the green door. My uncle looks far more nervous than he had on the news. 'Pretty damning evidence they have against you, huh?'

'Most definitely,' he says, with an odd hint of a smile. 'Most interestingly, I don't recall saying a word of it. Or even hearing the word Silenda in my entire life.' He hums on this thought. He knows Tyson has got him. I can tell immediately.

'Peculiar,' is all I say as I hand him the notebook that I had tucked away in the inside pocket of my coat. I show him only my gatherings on Silenda and evidence that the students in the cabin are as much involved with them as he believes himself to be.

His eyes graze the pages. 'Curious,' he says. 'It seems rather alarming that such an organisation is only being brought to my attention now.'

'It seems they've been underground for a very long time,' I say, 'only they are taking things further. Seems like they may be closer than ever to getting the answer they desire. They're pulling out all of the stops now.'

He ignores me. 'Do you suppose that it was these Cylinder people that put words in my mouth?'

'Silenda,' I correct him.

'Right.'

'I don't know,' I say simply.

'Tyson?'

'I don't know,' I say again, although I worry I may have said it too quickly.

'It's pretty advanced technology,' he continues, 'far more

advanced than I've ever known. You'd think they'd almost got me, wouldn't you?'

I raise an eyebrow.

'Well,' he continues, 'my men know as well as I do, that those words broadcast across the city, are not mine. Whoever set this up may have their people, but I have mine. It won't be long before Mr Fletcher and I are comfy in our own beds again.'

A tense feeling washes over me and I'm not entirely sure why. I can smell something rotting. 'You really think so?' I ask.

He nods. 'Who do you think I am, Harry? I'm always prepared for this sort of thing.' I watch his eyes then, cold and bright. There's something missing in him. Something that used to be there before, when I was a child. When he soaked me with the garden hose, his long brown hair, tan skin and open shirt made him look like he'd been born in the sun and should always reside there. He was beautiful, bright; rain only meant a rainbow. Now he's bright like a cold grey sky and a frosty morning. He's pale now. His beliefs used to make him shine; now he has nothing but power in his heart.

There is no faith in this man. There is no love for any divinity. Only for himself and that which he can control.

'How is Lucian?' I hesitate to ask.

'Sleeping on the floor,' he says, flatly. I grimace.

'Is there anything I can do?' In all honesty, I don't want to help my uncle, though I can't help but feel somewhat responsible for his situation. He isn't who they think he is and I let my friends frame him anyway.

He leans in closer. 'Just keep an eye on Tyson.' He eyes my notebook once more through the screens. 'Your information on Silenda would have been helpful a week ago, Horatio. But I need more on Turrow. He put me in here. I just know he did.'

I can't argue. So, with my notebook tucked into my jacket pocket and a gentle expression masking my guilt, I bid my uncle adieu.

I sleep in an abandoned out-of-service bus that I come across on my way to the train. I'm too spent to make it any farther.

• • •

The next afternoon at the cabin, Zeb is waiting for me on the doorstep.

Rain pours heavily on the grounds and trickles off the small wooden patio roof and onto his black and purple hair. He clings to a cigarette like his lifeline, puffing smoke into the already grey air. He bounces his leg, his other knee tucked up to his chest, his arms bare in the winter sting.

'You prick, Horatio!' he yells when he sees me, stumbling into the squelching grass as I approach, soggy and sorrowful. 'Where the hell have you been?' He waves his cigarette in my face as he searches my eyes. I frown. Zeb crushes his cigarette under his foot and softens a little. 'I thought you'd died. Topped yourself or something!'

'Huh?'

He hushes his voice. 'Your uncle is in prison,' he reminds me, 'and you don't really think he...'

I shake my head.

'Either way, Harry. It's not easy news to take. I didn't know if you were okay. And how am I supposed to explain to the others why I'm so worried about you? Thus far, it's been slightly underwhelming. But as far as they're concerned, Silenda is dead and buried.'

'Well I'd get a refund for the coffin,' I say.

'Seriously?'

'It's not him.' We let the rain soak us as Zeb swallows thickly with fear. 'He says he has men who can debunk Hayden's tape.'

'What if they trace it back to him?' Zeb panics.

'I don't think they can do that,' I assure him, although I'm completely unsure. 'But they can supposedly break down the audio and prove that it's fake.'

'Shit.'

I walk past Zeb and into the cabin. He stands in the rain a moment longer. When I enter, the others are crowded around the television in the main room. The news. Footage of looters breaking into Lux shops, smashing the glass windows of Candidus Tower and setting East Town gardens on fire. Graffiti decorates the streets. *Basilio Young, rot in prison. Silenda. Silenda. Silenda.*

I stand still.

The Urb announcer voices again. We can hear her even from the cabin.

Stay inside. Stay calm. The city police are taking all precautions.

CHAPTER 21

FORSAKEN FLAMES

Carson

Horatio returns.

Unfortunately, the only positive thing about it is that Astrid and Zeb have finally shut up. Harry brings his sombreness with him.

Everyone stares at the television screen. The Urb has gone into riot. Hayden says that's what fear does to people. It makes them lash out. In a big way.

'Thank god Eydis is staying in the safehouse with Jason,' Astrid says, arms folded as she stares at the chaos unfolding on the street below her shared penthouse apartment. Her face turns sour. 'I left my poodle slippers in there.' Horatio puts his hand on her shoulder. Hawk stifles a laugh.

'I thought the tape would be a good thing,' Hayden whines, eyes covered in the heel of his hands. 'This is my doing.'

Zeb stops him, sitting on the couch beside him. 'It's not your fault, Hayden. It was Tyson's idea, he gave you no choice.'

'There's always a choice.'

'Well, what could you have done instead?'

Hayden thinks on Zeb's words before moving away from him on the couch. 'You're wet.'

Zeb sighs.

'He's right.' Hawk leans over the couch at the TV screen. 'These people are scared. Furious! Thousands have died in all of this, thousands of people have lost loved ones in Centrum Tower and now everyone is putting that down to Silenda too. It's like that whole "instilling fear" speech that Eydis gave us. What if that was the whole point of the bomb in the first place,' he says, 'to scare us all shitless?'

I give Hawk a look.

'Is this supposed to be helping?' Hayden turns his sad black eyes to Hawk.

'What I'm saying is,' I think I should cut him off but I don't, 'people are angry with Young, and maybe subsequently his Lux followers. There was always going to be outrage when the public found out about Silenda. But that's not your fault. If we got the right guy, you stopped him, Hayden!' *Better than I thought, but not great.*

'If?' he whines.

'None of us are entirely sure, are we?' Zeb says to the room. Everyone shakes their heads. Hayden buries his head in his hands, hidden in his curls. I think we'll be lucky if he ever emerges again.

Zeb moves closer. 'You're wet!' Hayden cries again into his palms.

'What do we do now?' Astrid asks.

'We wait for them to strike again,' Horatio says over the rumble of conversation. All heads turn to him. 'If Mayor Young isn't Silenda, they're bound to strike again, right? They wouldn't go to all this effort for their cause and then not see it through just because some guy is in prison. They've got to see it through now. Like Eydis said, they've gone to all this effort to instil fear and adrenaline into the city. It's at its peak now. This is the perfect time to strike.'

'He's right,' I say, emerging from the open-plan kitchen where I watch them all converse. Hawk looks at me like he had forgotten I was here. 'There'd be no sense in them disappearing now.' I take a swig from my bottle. Tropical punch mingled with Hayden and Eydis's memory serum. Hawk watches me drink.

'We should have a bonfire,' Astrid says, 'we always have a bonfire in December. We sit on logs and drink wine and dance!' She looks at Horatio when she speaks.

'I think this year is a little different, Triddy. It's probably not appropriate timing.' Hawk stares at a still hidden Hayden. Everyone hums in agreement.

'Not just for the fun of it!' Astrid retorts. 'If Silenda are still out there and we put ourselves on a silver plate, they might come to us. We'd be in the dark outskirts of the forest.' She looks over at Horatio and Hawk. 'I don't need to tell you two that we appear to be prime targets. I bet they know it was us that put Basilio behind bars. They seem to know everything, for a start. We're a threat to them. They're bound to try to take us out if we give them the chance!'

'But they didn't shoot you,' Horatio reminds her.

'Yeah,' Zeb says, 'what if they don't care about us as much as we think they do?'

'They do,' she says, 'but they couldn't shoot us in a public nightclub. One of the agents, his mask fell down. I saw his face.'

'I did too,' Horatio says. 'She's right, that might be why he didn't shoot. He knew that Astrid or I could go straight to the police with a valid description if he took the other of us out.' Everyone seems satisfied with this explanation.

'Okay, so we have our bonfire,' Hawk says, 'and what the fuck do we do if they do turn up with their guns, Astrid? Nothing will further the fear in the city like a celebrity death.'

'What was all our training for, honey?' Astrid pulls out a handgun from the back pocket of her vinyl trousers.

Astrid Turrow is not the sort of person you want to see holding a gun.

•••

When the crowd around Hayden dissolves and he sneaks away to his bedroom, I follow him. He's sitting on his bed with his knees tucked up to his chest when I enter. He doesn't even look at me before he speaks. Maybe it doesn't matter who he says it to. 'If you're here to convince me that I did the right thing, I don't want to hear it.'

'I'm not going to tell you that,' I say as he looks up from his knees. 'I just followed you to make sure you don't jump out your window or drink yourself to death.'

He smiles slightly. 'Two very appealing options.'

I sit beside him on the bed, resting my head on his shoulder. He lets me. I think we could both use a hug. He smiles when I meet his eyes. I trace the ghost of what once was a broken nose.

'I didn't like you when I met you.' I move his curls from his eyes.

He furrows his brow. 'Not many people do. But you did, actually.'

'Huh?'

'When you met me the first time, I mean. We were just kids. We went to school together. Your parents were away a lot so you used to stay with Jason and I before my mother died and I moved in with Tyson.'

'Really? Where were my parents?'

'They moved to Italy. You didn't want to leave your friends.'

'They didn't come back,' I state.

'Hawk has been writing to them the whole time. They know the situation. They came to see you when we found you in the city, but you were so distressed. We all just wanted to give you time and space. Hawk and I always planned to bring you home.'

There's a pause.

'I didn't like you the second time I met you,' I say.

'Really trying to rub it in, are you?'

'The first real thing I saw you do was fight with Zeb. What was that all about?'

'I'm bitter,' he says, 'and sort of stupid. I expected him to want me even though I was as good as pretending not to know him in front of the others.'

'I can see why that would upset him.'

'Hmm.'

My head falls into my hands like a bowling ball.

'Cara?' Suddenly Hayden's voice mingles with a million others. Dancing orange flames. A blue glow. A torch. Dark eyes illuminated in the white light. His laugh. The sound of crickets in the woods around us. The smell of lotion and Hayden's youthful, crooked grin. Horror stories and the smell of summer rain. His voice sounds. *'Carson.'* I think his voice is in a strange sort of font. Unfamiliar, familiar, distorted and totally clear.

'I remember!' I cry.

'Remember what?' He jumps from his bed. 'Silenda?' Hayden snatches the tropical punch from my hand.

'No!' I'm laughing uncontrollably. 'Us. I remember us! In a blue tent. There was a bonfire and we told ghost stories. You were just a kid.'

'Holy shit!' he exclaims, staring at the orange liquid. 'It's actually working! It's working!' He pulls me in for a long hug. 'We were 12,' he says, 'it was one of our first bonfires. Zeb and Astrid and Hawk used to play hide and seek in the Bellumside woods, but you and I told each other ghost stories in Jason's shitty old tent!'

'I remember!' For a moment all we can do is smile at each other.

Eventually I need to ask him. 'Hayden? Have you ever heard the words "I'd part the black sea for you?" Is it from a book or a movie or something?'

He pulls back from me. 'I've never heard it before,' he says. 'Why?'

'I don't know. It just came to me a few days ago. I just wondered if it meant anything to you.'

'No, it doesn't ring a bell. I'm sorry, Red.'

I sigh, despite being excited by what I can remember. Suddenly, Hayden really does feel like my friend.

•••

When the grey sky melts into black, the others head to Bellumside forest to start the bonfire. Zeb has spent the evening gathering firewood from around the estate of cabins and is now throwing it into the sparking fire that Hayden had spent an hour attempting to kindle. Hawk sits on a log, staring into the orange. Our interactions have been exceptionally mundane since I stopped his kiss with some drabble about a black sea. I'm lucky if he chooses me to pass the salt at dinner.

I watch him from across the flames. They dance in his eyes and glow on his cheeks. His black hair falls over his face in waves. It's a miracle he can see. Maybe it's safe for me to stare at him.

When the others materialise from the cabin and other guests cross the grass to us, the little log seats are filling up fast. Jason and Eydis hold hands as they cross the squelching green. Asiqa, Petal and Alex chat to Astrid as they pour some drinks. Gia ruffles her brother's hair before she joins Zeb by the fire.

Hawk remains sitting alone. I hover awkwardly by the flickering flames when I see Hayden making eyes at me, gesturing for me to sit beside Hawk. It's unclear what his intentions are, but I watch him pressed up next to Zeb on a log and I decide to listen to him.

I think I startle Hawk when I sit down.

He's listening to music. I hadn't noticed as his shaggy hair had been covering his wireless earphones. He doesn't remove them when he watches me beside him. He stares back into the fire. I can hear the beat of his music from where I'm sitting. It's loud; R&B synth I think. His expression is blank. I look at him. My eyes crystallise his fawn skin in my vision. I know he can feel me but he doesn't look back.

Hayden looks over at us. He frowns at me.

Hawk isn't trying anymore. Either that or he's furious with the lack of chasing I've been doing. Either way, the way he makes my chest swell isn't worth the way his warm eyes feel so cold. I'm so close to the fire, but too close to him to feel its heat.

I feel the anger vibrating in my throat as his music climaxes.

I approach Eydis and whisper for her to give me the safehouse key. She looks concerned but asks no questions, slipping the key into my hands.

I leave. Through the black woods, I find the wooden door.

The safehouse.

I have a memory for this sort of thing.

My eyes have been tearing and my chest hurting so much that I hadn't even considered the direction I was going in until I wound up on the doorstep. The door, of course, is closed and partially hidden by leaves as the cabin sits in a dip in the ground. I twist the key and push open the heavy door. I just need to be anywhere but the fire.

My boots hit the wooden floor. I run down the stairs to the main room where Hawk and I were shown Randy's post-mortem. It's there. Exactly what I had been looking for. I hadn't really processed it at the time, but the ground floor of the safehouse, decorated with Eydis's candles, is covered in photographs, letters, concert tickets: *memories.*

Maybe the photos can help render my broken memories.

Astrid hugging Hayden. Hayden pretending to cry.

Zeb and Hawk sitting at Hawk's keyboard with cheesy smiles.

Eydis and Astrid posing by the glass window of their city apartment.

A group photo. Eydis must have taken it. She's the only one missing. I stand with Hayden. Hawk rests his chin on Astrid's shoulder. His hands on her waist. I think my heart hurts. It feels separate from my chest. It feels so removable. Like I could just reach in and tear it out. I don't think I would feel much different if I did. I imagine his lips on her pale neck, the way his hair must have fallen over his face when he looked down at her. The couch in his Rowleys studio. Skin on leather. Bruised leather. Bruised lips. *Bruised forever.*

There are things that can't be undone.

Did Hawk break my heart? Is this what a broken heart feels like? When he held her close? When he turned his face to the fire and let my silhouette burn and my shadow deepen?

Or did I break my own heart when I left him crying in the blue neon?

Blue neon.

Red wine veins.

A heart muscle strains.

Stolen cigarettes.

I turn on Eydis's radio. The song Hawk was listening to by the fire. How poetic.

Part the black sea? Don't bother, just drown me in it.

I'm falling across the floorboards. Spilling like Ferrari tyres on a wet road. Neon reflections. Throat burning in the vino marine. I stare at myself in the photographs. Pale skin. Freckles. Olive sapphire. Hawk stands next to me. I look at him. Adoration. Laughter. A fire left to die.

I rip it from the wall.

I see myself in my wine glass. In the round mirror. My auburn hair weaving scarlet. No longer long and straight. Choppy layers. Messy. Chaotic. My eyes rimmed in black. Crimson ruby.

I look at my reflection in the rotund glass. Trapped aromas. *Trapped forever.*

The fire flickers in the window of the safehouse. An orange glow. So strong it lights the forest alive. Laughter echoes through the woods. Or perhaps it's in my mind. Swelling. Dormant. Edging to the forefront, swallowed by the present. It's hard to tell, since I started drinking Hayden's serum, what is really happening and what is crawling out of the shadows to taunt me, haunt me or make me smile.

The music plays loudly in the walls. *Trapped aromas*. Suddenly I wish I could be as chaotic as I look. That I could be the sort of woman who throws photos to the fire and dances around the room alone with a glass of wine in hand, intoxicated in her own feelings and escaping in catharsis. But I'm not that girl and I never will be.

All I can think about are the echoes in the forest, Hawk next to the fire and Hayden who sighed as he watched me leave.

I imagine him by the flickering fire, cold black metal pressed upon his temple. It's a risky game. Games played by a fire usually are. I pour my wine down the sink. I watch it run away like blood in the ocean. I search the drawers on the ground floor and press bullets into one of Jason's handguns.

I head back into the flames, a photo of Cara and Hawk folded against alloy steel in my back pocket.

Branches snap under foot. My hand is always gripping the denim-clothed metal. A shadow approaches. The darkest shadow I've known since the start of a new existence. His long black coat hangs off him like a cloak, his dark eyes hidden in the night. So sad, so hungry and so willing to make me suffer for it.

Predatory.

'Carson?' he says.

'Hawk.' A statement. 'What are you doing?'

'I was about to ask you the same thing.' He pauses and leaves a couple of metres between us. 'I followed you.'

'Why?'

'Because we're baiting Silenda and you're in the woods alone. Not the smartest idea.' He sounds pissed.

'What does it matter to you? You seemingly wanted me back so badly, but you hardly even talk to me.'

'That's not true.'

'It's not?' I retort.

He sighs. 'I didn't realise how difficult it would be. How hard it would be for you to look at me the way you do.'

'Oh? And how do I look at you?' I'm not looking at him at all, really. I'm watching the fire past his head, at the rim of the woods. I speak loudly, over the crackling flames and the indistinct chatter.

'Like you don't know who I am. What I am. What you feel when you look at me.'

I'm speechless. My eyes snap back to him, unable to leave him now. The cold wind blows in my hair and my feet are stuck in the squelching mud. He's right. I don't know him. I don't know him at all. Every memory, every story – none of it helps me know him. Maybe I've never known him at all.

'What were we like before?' I ask. 'What did we do?'

'You were my best friend.' Everything he says sounds like pleading, as though any of this is in my control. 'We watched movies. Laughed. Ran around town. Stupid shit that teenagers do. As we got older, things got a little complicated. We grew apart a bit as adults. Our dynamic wasn't what it used to be.'

'Why?'

He looks like he's about to tell me, but changes his mind. There's a ringing in my ears. It might be screaming. He breathes his words into the wind. 'You grew to be flighty. I couldn't keep track of you. I started disappearing in the nights to write music. There was tension, mistrusting. I'm not even sure I can explain why. We were still figuring that out when you...'

'Right.' Another silence. Another stretch of ground between us. The woods. The bridge. The kitchen. Never coming too close. But nothing changes that way. Nothing changes at all.

I step closer to him. It's impossible to look at him as I move across the earth. I feel like I've walked a mile by the time the toes of my boots meet his. I'm looking at our feet before I can bring myself to look up. My hair blows in the wind, catching my lips. I look at him, the top of my head only at his chin, his features glow in the black dark. His breath is warm on my face, his deep-set eyes narrowing as he looks at me. I look at his mouth, pink and full and painful to consider. I know I've looked at him this way before, I can feel it in my chest.

My heart has a memory. My muscles remember how to flex, my legs remember how to walk, and my heart remembers how to desire him.

He doesn't touch me. His arms at his sides. But he's leaning in, his eyes flickering, swallowing thickly. I can hear my heartbeat. So loud that I think it stops when a bullet sounds.

Hawk swears under his breath, pulls his gun from his coat and runs to the fire. I follow.

It all happens quickly.

It takes a moment to process the scene. Bodies standing around the fire look like dark shadowy figures. There seems to be a few too many broad shouldered guests. Astrid holds her gun in front of her, Asiqa and Alex at her side. She points it at a masked man, clad in black. Four or five men circle us in silence; a tense stand-off ensues. Astrid, Hawk and Zeb hold their guns, as do the five men, pointed at each other in a wordless altercation.

The agent that stands closest to Hawk falls suddenly to the floor, gripping his leg as a bullet echoes through the air. Hawk has shot him in his thigh. The sound acts like a signal for the war to begin.

Astrid falls across the grass, ducking bullets and taking the legs from beneath one of the agents. She straddles him, slams his head into the ground until he falls into unconsciousness. I watch in disbelief. Her eyes are smoky and dark; suddenly terrifying. But I don't have time to watch her.

One of the agents has a double-ended needle. The bite of a vampire, held at Horatio's neck as he struggles against the weight of a much larger man. I'm careless with my shot, unsure I was going to use my gun until a bullet pierces the air. I'm not a bad shot either. Horatio looks like he's going to throw up as he swings the man away from him, whose hand has been punctured and burst from the velocity of my bullet. Horatio grimaces at me, a sure attempt at a grateful smile.

There's a scream as Zeb's strength sees his struggle with a needle-bearing agent end in horror. The needle that brushes Zeb's thick neck motivates a clash that ends in the anonymous black figure being pushed into the fire. I can't watch. Zeb looks at his hands. Distressed and repulsed by his own strength. But he had no choice.

He had no choice.

Astrid has no shame as she claims her second victim. The man with the bloody hand is gone. The agent with the injured leg tries to crawl into the woods to safety but Eydis shoots him in the back of the head. I wince. I feel a lump in my throat. Gia throws up at the edge of the forest.

There is silence. The smell of burning flesh. The horror on the faces that surround the fire. A sternness in Astrid's eyes as she drops her gun. The confirmation that Silenda are alive and well. The presence of death.

It all happens in seconds. Jason picks Astrid from the ground where she kneels next to her gun, processing the ruthlessness of her actions. Hawk looks back at me. Horatio looks paler than usual when he returns to the fire, running to drag Zeb away from the flames that he stares into in shock. 'You had to,' I hear him say.

Hawk looks unfazed. But he didn't kill anyone. Eydis, however, already knows death. A body lies at the bottom of the Urb river. I feel like I'm going to throw up until I see Horatio, alive and well. Remembering what I was protecting makes my chest feel less tight. But my chest is always tight. Asiqa smiles sadly at me across the fire. Zeb holds his own arm, badly burnt in the fight.

SILENDA

Asiqa takes a look at it under the torch of his phone.

It's too late when we see the agent at the edge of the woods. It's too dark and too good to be true that we had made it through with everyone left standing.

One last bullet sounds.

CHAPTER 22

OLD FLAMES

Carson

It happens in cinematically slow motion. I'm running to him so immediately I could be shot in the midst of it all. But Zeb has already taken him out, with more bullets than he really needed to. The man at the edge of the forest collapses. Four bullet wounds to the chest.

Dead.

But it's too late. Hayden has already collapsed, bleeding heavily from his lower torso.

'Hayden!' I scream as I cross the others, shoving Hawk out of my way. Zeb is the first by his side. The others look on in a confused distress as they watch Zebediah break down in tears over the blonde's body, kissing his cheeks as his tears mingle with blood. Zeb presses down on the wound, trying desperately to stop the blood, but it pools in the dark. Zeb is covered in it, his tears falling into the red sea. He removes his shirt in the bitter cold, tearing it open and wrapping it tightly around Hayden's middle. Zeb's bloody hands reach for his face.

'You'll get blood on me, Diah.' Hayden chokes out a laugh, looking softly at him. There's a wash of relief at Hayden's humour.

But it doesn't dull the panic around him. 'We need to get him to a hospital!' Zeb yells. Jason runs to his son's side, pulling him up and carrying him through the woods. Hayden bleeds onto Zeb's shirt. Asiqa, as a student of medicine, advises Jason to hurry and to grip firmly to the wound as he carries him, despite how much Hayden protests. Astrid cries inconsolably as Horatio allows her to hold onto him for support when her legs give way.

Hawk holds my hand, but I feel too much like I'm floating to really notice or think much of it.

At the cabin, Gia and Eydis clear a space on the couch, throwing pillows to the floor as Jason rests Hayden on the couch. 'Don't call an ambulance, dad,' he chokes.

'Hayden, what are you talking about?' Jason kneels beside him. It's the first time I've heard Hayden call Jason dad.

'The city is in uproar. Silenda are winning. They know my face in the city. News will spread if I wind up in hospital, the hospitals are already full from the riots. It'll do more harm than good.'

'But you need medical attention, you fool!' Hawk is yelling at him.

'Look, Birdboy, I may not be able to scrap you right now, but if you raise your voice at me again, I swear to god I'll try.'

Zeb leans down beside him. 'Hayden, Hawk is right. You need to go to the hospital.' Zeb is trying to be gentle but his voice breaks when he speaks, still putting pressure on Hayden's cloth-covered wound.

Hayden ignores him. 'Eydis!' he yells, 'bring me some bandages, some boiling water and a pair of pliers.'

Astrid's eyes widen. 'Hayden, you can't be serious! Don't listen to him, Eydis!' But Eydis trusts Hayden and she is already obeying his commands.

Astrid tries to grab Eydis but Asiqa stops her. 'Look,' he says to the room, 'we can do this, but we need to work together. Hayden's a stubborn bastard and we're running out of time. Petal,' he says to his sister, 'get me and Eydis some gloves, a rubber band and the rest of you give us some space!' Asiqa spreads his arms to clear the area around him.

Hayden looks pained but satisfied with the arrangement. 'I want Zeb to stay.' His honesty makes me believe he's gone dizzy from blood loss.

We leave.

The others go to their bedrooms, but Astrid and I peek through to the main room from the hall door, too panicked to look away.

We watch the back of Asiqa's head, his blue-gloved hands working. Eydis talks to Hayden, passing Asiqa the pliers as he fishes out the bullet. Hayden winces, alternating between holding Zebediah's hand and snapping an elastic band around his wrist to distract himself from the pain. It won't do much. But it's something.

Jason couldn't bring himself to watch and Hayden didn't want him to. Tears stream silently from Hayden's eyes as Asiqa stitches him up. Eydis cleans around the wound with a homemade cleanser. Zeb had gathered calendula flowers from the garden and boiled the flowers in water; Eydis says the earth has healing properties, but this is used with a medicinal antiseptic too. Eydis dips a cotton cloth into the liquid and washes over Hayden's torso with it. Lastly, he's bandaged up tightly and forced to rest. He looks pale, but I think he's done it.

Eydis and Asiqa go upstairs to wash the blood from their hands. Astrid and I still peek around the door, unspeaking.

'You smell like sandalwood.' Hayden smiles wearily at Zeb.

'You smell like piss,' Zeb replies, 'although, I think it's the calendula.'

'Nah, I just pissed myself.' Zeb laughs.

I try to drag Astrid away from the door, feeling suddenly that we're intruding. 'Hey, come on,' I say, 'he's okay, we should give them some space.'

'But I hardly ever see them being lovey with each other, it's nice.' She pouts.

'Huh?'

'You think I don't know?' she says. 'I'm not as stupid as Hayden would like to think I am.'

'Do the others know?'

Astrid simply shrugs and leaves me guessing.

• • •

That night, I dream I'm on campus. A delicate glass lantern, a small flame. It's dark. The cloisters aglow with fairy lights. Abandoned in the December dark, a cold wind whips gently at the pages of his book, sometimes turning the paper at his convenience. He doesn't speak to me. After all, he doesn't see me. Another restless night of finding him gone. No crease in his sheets or glass of water by the sink. No trickle from the tap. No footprints on the floorboards.

The black night and the gold university brick insist upon candlelight. It would be disrespectful otherwise. He doesn't see me. I watch him read for a while, assured by his presence. Dressed in black, his dark locks graze the pages as he bends his neck. Like a raven in the night.

Reading.

The next night, I follow him again. Only this time, the midnight bell startles me. He whips his head around on his way to his usual reading spot. I suddenly wish I were invisible. I wish so hard in fact that I think I've achieved it because he doesn't say anything.

When I look up, he's walking towards me. A beautiful slow motion. An impending bass. A building tension in my chest.

He kisses me. Full on the mouth. Hands grabbing my face, forcing me up to him. He kisses me hotly. He's hot. He's warm.

I think there's a greater difference between hot and warm than is often accounted for.

Hawk is both.

The soft woollen throw flung over the couch. Soft on my bare back until I arch under him. Hot kisses on my neck. Skin. Flesh. The fire crackling. Rain on the window. *Hands*. Gripping for air. For breath. A clock strikes midnight in a place with no time. A single flame. Burning. Orange glow. Scarlett ruby emerges from an olive sapphire: impossible, eternal, true.

His lips leave my neck in a flash of blue neon.

I bolt upright, burst from my sheets and run to my mirror, examining my neck for any signs of him, but all I find is a vampire bite piercing the white.

A dream. So lucid and so rich in feeling I begin to imagine it as a memory.

But it can't be.

Hawk only fucks models on couches.

It's hard to look at him at breakfast without blushing or feeling like kicking him under the table. He only looks at me when he thinks I can't see him anyway.

But I always do.

'Carson,' Astrid calls me out of my own head as I'm about to bite into my croissant.

'Hmm?' I rise, still departing from my trance. Everyone turns their head to look at me. Hayden rests on the couch where he's been all night, turning his head in pain. Zeb and Harry butter some toast at the table. They can sense the tension. Is Hawk the only one who can't feel it?

Astrid frowns at me, gesturing for me to go upstairs with her. I walk silently up the creaky steps. She takes me to her bedroom where she throws open her large double-doored wardrobe. 'So, what are you wearing?' she asks.

'For what?' I ask, 'to sit around and watch the city burn on the news?'

'As sultry as that sounds, no. I mean the unity ball, Cara.'

SILENDA

There have been whispers about the unity ball since the month began. I had paid very little attention.

'That's still happening?' I ask. 'Even with all of the riots in the city?'

'I think it's needed more than ever.' She runs her hands through a rainbow of hanging fabrics. 'West Town students and East Town students are the future of academia. Surely we can turn our brains on and put aside our differences.'

'I'd like to hope so, Astrid, but I don't know if...'

She turns suddenly, eyes trained expertly on mine. 'It will be fine, Carson.'

Reassuring me or yourself, Astrid?

I decide to drop it.

'Right.' She removes an aqua blue gown from the hanger in her hands. It shimmers in the light. Astrid kicks off her heeled boots and slips out of her shirt-dress. I look away but she holds my chin and makes me watch her. 'You used to watch,' she says. 'We used to be best friends, remember? Nakedness never bothered you. Unless it was...'

'Unless it was what?'

She doesn't answer me. She just looks at the floor, guiltily. 'We used to kiss, you know.' Not a question. I don't say anything. 'You used to be chill about that sort of thing. You know, you would—'

'I don't want to know, Astrid.'

'Well surely you didn't think you were still a virgin!'

'Astrid!' I yell, but we're giggling now. So much that I need to sit down. She pulls her tights off her silky legs. And I don't feel anything. Not awkward or jealous, or anything at all. I've decided that the best friendships involve a lot of nothing.

Comfortable silences. Content nothingness.

Astrid slips on the dress. The sleeves hang from her shoulders, the trail gracing the ground. She really is ethereal, but sometimes her mouth doesn't match her face. She is so simply angelic. Whoever deemed lying as a sin that rejects purity had never

258

met Astrid Turrow. Astrid doesn't know how to lie, and there is nothing pure about her truths.

Honesty is the most impure thing of all.

'Gia's wearing pink,' she says, 'and I wanted you to wear this gold one.' She pulls out a petite gold ballgown, fraying slightly at the hem. I raise an eyebrow at her. 'I cut it in half myself!' *No kidding.* 'It's short and a little damaged, just like you.'

Astrid tries to keep a straight face but she can't. I try to yell at her but tears are streaming down my face with laughter. The Nether Cabin borders on hysterical.

'But really,' she says, 'I bought this one especially for you. Red is your colour. And I thought that it'd be nice if the girls wore the colour that's in their hair.'

'I like that idea,' I say.

She pulls out layers of scarlet red laced with intricately sewn silver diamonds. It's short but elegant with a pyramidic corset. It's beautiful.

'Well, try it on!'

I do. And I feel expensive. Radiant. Like a rainbow breaking through the clouds. Astrid dances with me across the rug-covered floor until we collapse on her queen-sized bed, laughing.

'I think you should ask Hawk to the ball,' she says suddenly, turning to me in a pool of blonde locks.

'What?' I know it sounds defensive.

'So it's nothing more than sleeping together for you guys then?'

'We don't sleep together,' I retort.

'You don't? Well maybe you should. The tension is so thick I don't think I could cut through it with a fucking axe!'

I laugh because I don't know what to say.

'You know, Cara, I heard that if you hold out on your soulmate for too long his dick will fall off.'

'That's not true.' I laugh and she returns a cheeky grin. 'You think we're soulmates?'

Astrid's eyes turn serious. 'I thought that you were just friends,' she says, 'but then when you disappeared and we were reading your diary to try and find out where you could've gone, some of the things you had written about him—'

'Did he see them?'

She shakes her head. 'I ripped out the pages. I thought that it might destroy him. He was as good as turned to stone when you left. That's when I knew. He loves you, Carson. He honestly does.'

There's silence. I don't want to talk about it anymore. 'So, have you had sex with Horatio yet?' I ask.

She lets out a breathy laugh. 'No.'

I sit up. 'Wait, really?'

She turns sad. 'I'm all talk really. I don't actually like sex very much.'

'Astrid...' It upsets me. It really does. Her casual approach about it all had made me feel safe until now.

'I've only had sex with two people. The prince, who was selfish and...' she breathes, 'and then once with...'

'It's okay,' I say. 'I know.'

'Oh, Carson, if I had known, I would never have...'

'I know,' I say again. And I believe her.

'It was a huge mistake. It never happened again. I guess I just wanted confirmation that not all men would treat me the way the prince had and I knew that Hawk—'

'It's okay. You don't have to explain yourself.'

'Why did you tell Hawk that you could never see him that way?'

'I can't remember, but I think that I must have been scared.'

She nods. 'I don't like to have sex on beds.'

I almost laugh. I can never get used to the impulsiveness of Astrid's statements. But she looks serious. 'When your face is on billboards and magazines, life is like a stage. Especially when you're advertised as a sex icon so much of the time. The bedroom just feels like another place where I'm expected to perform. The pressure gets too much. I think I won't be what they want me to be. If it's not on a bed it doesn't count, right?'

'Not if you don't want it to,' I whisper, feeling for her hand and squeezing it.

Silence falls over us as we hold hands in the grey light.

Astrid breaks the silence, as she often does. 'If you wanna know more about how you lost your V-card, you should go and ask Hayden —'

'Stop it,' I laugh, shoving her towards the edge of the bed.

'I wish I was kidding. You were one of his swollen-lipped conquests!'

'Oh god.' I bury my head in my hands, laughing in my embarrassment.

'Don't worry,' she says, 'he still talks about you being the best girl he's ever been with.'

I push Astrid off the bed.

•••

It's even harder to look at Hawk in the afternoon than it had been in the morning. Now that I know Astrid is watching how I look at him and that how I look at him is something to be questioned.

I stand at my bedroom window, the large square glass staring out over the loch. Hawk sits by the water, lounging on the wet grass with a book in hand. He doesn't seem to care at all about getting wet. He uses his arm like a headrest, his legs crossed at the ankles.

I just watch him.

Zeb walks over to him, handing him something to smoke, which he accepts with a puff, squinting up at him through the grey. They're talking now. Hawk handing back the joint and returning to his book.

Zeb sits with him for a moment, dipping his feet in the icy loch. Sometimes Zeb goes for a run in the cold mornings and this is how he cools down.

SILENDA

I listen to music as I sit on the windowsill. After a little while, Petal wheels out Hayden in a wheelchair to sit beside the boys at the water. Zeb smiles at him. Hawk stops Hayden from trying to roll himself into the water to drown.

I stifle a laugh.

No one talks about it.

About Hayden's gunshot wound or that Mayor Young may in fact be innocent. Nobody talks about it at all. Hayden wheels around in his chair like he's simply broken his leg. Asiqa says he should be walking again by next month. Miraculously, the bullet that tore through his flesh missed any internal organs. I heard Horatio telling Astrid he thinks this is suspicious, that men seemingly so expertly trained should be such a bad shot. *Or perhaps such a good shot.*

Harry enters my bedroom without knocking, the Rowleys vampire book that we stole from the library in his hands. He ignores my staring out the window. 'Carson, I've been thinking.' He sits on the windowsill beside me, skimming through pages and not yet looking at me. 'We know that an epidemic of murders and disappearances in the early 1900s were tied to the Rowleys vampire, right?'

'Right,' I say, still staring out the window, 'also known as Silenda.'

'Yes, but it says here...' he traces his fingers along a tea-stained page with minute text 'that the phrase 'the Rowleys vampire' has been found in texts from as early as the 1500s.'

I sit up straight.

'In a letter from Queen Meredith's secret lover from the 1600s, he describes a love bite as the "bite of the Rowleys vampire". Probably a way to cover up the implications of the letter. I mean, the queen was married, after all. But this could seriously mean that Silenda have existed for hundreds of years.'

'You don't suppose that Silenda are far more than just an organisation of scientists trying to prove a point, but they could be—'

'Some sort of cult,' Harry finishes my sentence with dread in his eyes.

'Should we tell the others?'

He follows my eyes to the others by the loch. 'They seem relatively calm, don't they?' I nod. 'Maybe we should keep this between us for a bit. Who knows, maybe they already know. Don't you feel kept at a distance?'

'I do. I think the AYIP have been dealing with this a lot longer than us. It's like they're numb to it now. They don't trust you because you're new. And they don't trust me because they don't even know who I am anymore.'

Horatio nods when I say this. Something I hadn't even realised I had felt until I said it.

Suddenly the Urb announcer's voice booms through the air.

Harry crosses the room and turns on the radio. The others by the loch stare up into the sky as if to hear it better from the speakers that are perched on the telephone wires.

Her robotic voice crackles: *'Recent damning evidence against Mayor Basilio Young has since been debunked. It has been revealed that leaked audio associating the mayor with criminal organisation, Silenda, has been faked. Investigators are on the case to track the tape back to its source. In the meantime, the mayor of East Town will be released from prison and cleared of all charges immediately.'*

CHAPTER 23

FAMILY FANGS

Horatio

Lucian tries to convince me that jail had looked good on him. 'Character building,' he calls it as he walks me to my uncle's new penthouse office in Candidus Tower. 'Coffee?' The small man gleams when we enter, pouring black steam into a tall mug without waiting for an answer. I nod anyway, despite Lucian already handing me the beverage.

'Where's my uncle?' I ask, cringing with a bitter sip.

'Basilio is across the hall in the studio room recording a message of *reassurance* for the people of the city. I shall take you to him if you'd like.' I nod as Lucian straightens his suit to take me across the hall.

The studio is set up with black walls, a large green screen and multiple cameras for varied angles of my uncle's confident exterior. The lights are harsh and all angled at his tanned face and white eyes.

He speaks from a scrolling monitor:

'The last few days have been unexpectedly devastating for the Urb and most distressingly, for my faithful East Town community. Following these adversities, I would like to formally speak out against the accusations made against me. Neither I, nor my men, have had, or know of, any associations with so-called Silenda. With a new knowledge of the organisation's criminal activities, I would like to assure you that I, mayor of East Town, not only have no relation to, but will continue to be appalled by, and work vigorously to protect our community from such a dangerous threat. The fabrication of evidence used against my men and me is of great concern and is currently under investigation.' He finishes his television appearance with a final grin. 'In the meantime, stay safe, stay calm and believe in me.'

His grin fades when the camera pans away.

'*Believe in me*' rings in my ears. There's an absurdity in his words and an absurdity in the green screen and the lights and the fluffy mics hanging overhead. Politics is nothing but performance. How frightening to put your life and stability in the hands of an actor. A rich white man with a Tom Cruise tan and teeth straighter than I'll ever be. Great panes of glass catch the city sun. Trees blossom by marble desks. Young women tour the halls with trolleys full of muffins and cakes and croissants.

I think of the young girl with the purple hair who blew her cigarette smoke in my face under the bridge at the Rowleys border. Her crooked yellow teeth. Her sallow skin. Ribs gracing ivory beneath an old, cropped shirt. When my uncle speaks to the camera, is he speaking to her? Is he speaking to kids like Randy Redding? Lost souls so desperately worth saving? Or is he talking to my father? My mother, who smells like aloe vera in a kitchen that smells of freshly baked scones? Is he talking instead to kids like Angelo, who will never need saving as long as they submit? As long as Angelo marries a lovely lady and has lovely kids with a lovely house and a healthy dentist's clientele, he'll be okay. The only thing that will taint him is the fear of God in him.

My uncle talks to those who *have* and wish for more.

Women with violet hair and shadowed cheeks flounder in empty promises.

SILENDA

He straightens his suit when he stands. It seems to be a thing that men like him do. I quickly check that I haven't tucked my t-shirt into my boxers when I went for a piss.

'Horatio!' he chirps as he glides towards me with open arms. He pats me on the back, roughly. Men have to gently slap each other when they hug, it's like the law or something. 'How wonderful to see you! Are you here to update me?' His voice lowers to a whisper at the latter and I nod.

He ushers me back through to his office, gesturing for me to sit on the leather chair across from him. A quiet young girl offers me a mini muffin which I decline.

'You might as well take a muffin, Harry. They'll just go to waste.'

I buy all of the muffins.

'I found some more information on Silenda.'

My uncle squints at me as I pass over my red notebook. 'Nothing on Tyson?'

I shake my head. 'I haven't seen much of him—'

'Aren't you sleeping with his daughter?'

'*What?* No!'

'That's what Lucian told me.'

Lucian laughs into his mug.

'What? How would he…' I drop it, exasperated. 'I've befriended Astrid and Hayden, yes, but they don't visit Tyson much. I've tried my best, but there's only so much I can do without arousing suspicion. But I have managed to get some dirt on Silenda. Maybe we can stop them together. You're a powerful man, uncle!'

He looks disappointed and scoffs. 'Seriously, Horatio? I put my trust in you and you don't have a single note on Tyson?'

I roll away from him slightly in my chair. 'Uncle,' I plead, 'I'd be putting myself in danger doing much more than I am. Silenda are killing people, surely that matters to you?'

'I know nothing about this Silenda nonsense, there's nothing I can do.'

'But, you said to the camera—'

'I said what I needed to say to end the riots in the city, Harry.'

'But if you just listen to what I have to say—'

He slams his hand aggressively on my notebook. My heart races. He leans over his desk, staring me directly in the eyes. 'There's nothing I can do. I have no time to take anything to do with it. It seems like a Rowleys problem, anyway.'

'They're still people, uncle. They're dying. Or turning up all confused and distressed. It's inhumane to allow it to continue.'

'My responsibility is to protect the people of East Town.'

'And the Urb,' I remind him. 'But either way, Silenda are spreading out. There will be deaths in East Town, sir. It's only a matter of time. Randy Redding was a Lux, sir.' The more I fear my uncle, the more I call him sir.

'Didn't your shadow friend go down for that?'

'Zebediah is innocent, uncle. His DNA was planted at the scene to make it look like he had strangled Randy. But his cause of death was revealed to be cardiac arrest as a result of a foreign drug in his system. He had two puncture wounds in his neck. The same wound that's been on all of the bodies that have been turning up. Zeb was relieved of any charges.'

'Randy Redding rejected the community of East Town a long time ago.'

'But, sir, he died! He was in my class at school. He was just a boy. We could have tried to save him—'

'Only God could have saved him, Harry. And obviously it wasn't in his plan.'

'How can you say that?' I snap.

'Are you raising your voice at me, Horatio?'

I cower. 'No, sir.'

'Why would your shadow friend's DNA be planted at the scene, anyway? Why him? Are you certain he isn't a murderer? He has that look about him.'

A rising anger bubbles in my chest.

'Before Silenda decided to go public with their careless attacks, they tried to cover their tracks. Either that or they were trying to protect their identity by getting Zeb and his friends off their case.'

'Friends? What are the names of these friends?'

'And how, indeed, did they know of Silenda before the rest of us?' Lucian interjects.

I'm nervous about saying much more.

My uncle speaks. 'Is this something to do with the young lady who moved out of the cabin. Amnesia, you said?'

I clear my throat. 'She was taken by Silenda,' I say. 'Not killed. But her memories were taken from her. The others found her wandering the city in great distress so they wiped her memory again, only this time wiping her of whatever was tormenting her. They found her an apartment in the city to start fresh. But she's come back.'

'So,' my uncle continues, 'if she couldn't remember anything, how could she tell the others about Silenda?'

'It wasn't Carson,' I say, 'it was Jason Turrow. He was the first known case in recent years since Silenda began to strike again. For some reason, he got away. He thinks the drugs didn't work on him or something. I guess some people are immune to things. When they thought he was unconscious, he managed to escape, taking everything he had seen and heard with him. Including the name and intent of the people who took him.'

My uncle thinks on this for a moment. 'Tyson Turrow's brother?' I nod. 'Quite peculiar, no? That the vast majority of the deaths are of the Umbra community?'

I shrug. 'I don't think they discriminate.'

My uncle is deep in thought, until he's not. He pushes himself away from the desk. 'That's all for now, Horatio. I have a business meeting in five. Please don't return until you have some information on Tyson, it's vitally important that we gather proof that he faked that audio. I want that proof the morning after the ball, no later. That's an order.'

I nod, tired and feeling my efforts futile.

I'm halfway down the building when I have to send the elevator back up to the top floor, realising I've forgotten my notebook. If I don't scribble down some shit about Tyson soon, I fear my uncle may threaten consequences.

I'm approaching the slightly ajar office door when I hear a hurried whisper. I hover at the gap. 'Who knows?' My uncle's hushed voice.

'Who knows, Lucian?' he says again. 'Who knows about Centrum Tower?'

My heart begins to sink.

'No one, sir,' Lucian whispers back. 'We shall begin to frame Tyson after the unity ball. It'll give us one last opportunity to prove ourselves open to integration. Once Tyson goes down for the bombing, mixing with the shadows will be the last thing on anyone's mind when they believe that Tyson killed all of those people.'

'How fortunate we were!' my uncle cries in an act of distress. 'How fortunate we were that we had just popped out for a spot of lunch when tragedy struck!'

'Almost 3,000 people – dead!' Lucian laughs. 'The horror!'

Hysterical laughter.

I'm in the elevator with no recollection of how I got there. A basket of mini muffins. The reception lights are so bright that I can hardly see.

I stare out the window of the rocket train.

Numb.

• • •

A violin screeches in chorus with the bass of a cello. Perhaps any other day I could conjure a serenity in the sound, but all I can hear is the fast-paced beat of my heart and the orchestra that taunts it. I can't bring myself to eat anything. Not even a single mini muffin from the basket at my feet.

'Where did you get all these muffins, anyway?' Astrid asks, her mouth full of the chocolate kind. Hawk snatches the basket from the ballroom floor.

'Hmm?' I hum. I heard her, of course, but I stall for time, trying to make something up. Trying to avoid uttering 'oh, these muffins? I just bought them at my uncle's office – you know my uncle, the mayor of East Town, who has just been released from prison for being the suspected leader of an underground terrorist organisation. But that doesn't matter anyway, because he's still a terrorist who bombed the largest building in the city so he could place the blame on your dad. Fancy another one? There's blueberry.'

'Uh, the bakery in the village was giving them out for free,' I say instead.

Astrid raises an eyebrow.

'For free?' Hayden says excitedly like he isn't one of the richest socialites known to the Urb. He wheels himself over in his chair to steal the basket from Hawk.

'How long do we have to stay here?' I ask.

'Just until the caterer arrives so I can approve his menu for the ball.' Astrid spits the crumbs of her second muffin when she speaks.

The ballroom in the university's main hall is sublime. Large arched cloisters are decorated with gold lights. The ceiling is encrusted with gold art, arching over the marble floor. Rows of balconies gaze upon the room and solid gold dragons perch over the stone divides. The ballroom is lit only by a series of coal fires and hanging candle light. The orchestra that Astrid has hired for the ball plays gently in the corner.

I could admire the ballroom for a million years. If I didn't feel like I was going to throw up.

I listen to the crackling fire that the six of us sit around. Alex and Gia practice dancing across the floor. They fall about laughing.

Zeb leans against Hayden's chair, his back to his legs. Astrid and I sit face to face in a couple of chairs stolen from the round dining tables. We sit by one of the coal fires, warming our hands from the bitterly cold winter. Cara and Hawk appear to be ignoring each other. Asiqa had asked Carson to the ball, and she had said yes. Hawk had already decided he wasn't going, which provoked Astrid to throw an orange at his head.

We managed to calm her down.

I haven't asked Astrid to the ball. I know it would do no good. Some socialite guy has probably already beat me to it. Or another prince. Not that it should be on my current list of priorities, anyway.

The caterer arrives. Astrid disappears for a moment to talk through the menu. After everything has been approved and then reapproved by the others, Astrid allows us to leave. Zeb helps Hayden back to the cabin. Zeb hasn't looked me in the eye since he pushed that agent into the fire. But it's okay, because now I can't look at him either. Not now that I'm suppressing a secret so overwhelmingly dark I think I may spontaneously combust in a matter of seconds.

Carson follows Zeb. Hawk joins his sister. Astrid and I are the last to leave. I follow her across the floor. She wears knee-high boots with a short pink flowing dress. It's the first time I've seen Astrid in pink. She's so pale. So impossibly ivory. When she turns to face me it's almost in slow motion, her long blonde hair falling over her shoulder. Such a pretty neck. Astrid Turrow is blue opal.

'Aren't you going to ask me?' she says.

'Ask you what?'

'To the ball, of course.'

'I didn't know you wanted me to ask you.'

'Then you should have asked if I wanted you to ask me.'

'But I didn't know you wanted me to ask you if you wanted me to ask you.'

'Horatio?' she suddenly huffs, moving too close to me.

'Hmm?'

And she kisses me.

Astrid Turrow kisses me. Not even a peck on the cheek or a graze of her mouth. She really kisses me. Her hands in my hair. I don't know where to put my hands, but soon they end up on her cheeks, cupping her face, trying to feel her skin, to feel that this is really, honestly, happening.

I feel cold when she walks away, her back to me. 'So I'll see you at the ball then?' She doesn't turn back when she says it, not until she blows me a kiss from the door as I stay floundering in a pool of white marble.

Her kiss pierces like a stake to the heart. I decide I'd rather die than feel this way about anyone.

The intensity of it all might kill me.

CHAPTER 24

WHEN WE BREAK

Horatio

When we break, remember that I am nothing.

I am not gospel.

She kisses my chest.

Remember that I am a fool.

Pretty hands on my torso.

I'm going through the motions. But never with you. Never with you, Astrid.

We are the motion.

Today, I called Astrid 'Triddy' for the first time. The way that Hawk does. There's something in me that suspects he has been where I am right now. I wonder if she likes to hear her name from his lips; I wonder if she prefers to hear it when she is under him instead.

Triddy. It felt wrong from my lips. *Why did it feel so wrong?* There's a wall between us. She can't break it down with her mouth.

Astrid calls me Horatio. Sometimes I paddle in the loch. Sometimes her pretty voice calls 'Marino!'

Sometimes I don't turn around.

There's a wall up.

SILENDA

Being with her is like being drunk. We wandered through the forest, forgetting about the dangers in our town. Forgetting anything but each other. She giggled into my mouth as we closed the safehouse door behind us.

Astrid likes to pull my hair. She has a firm touch. The sort of touch you want to be on your side. The sort of touch that could knock the air out of you if you cross her.

She is terrifying.

I like to kiss her neck. So white and so warm. She whimpers when I do it, writhing under me, the cold silver of my piercings tickling her cheek when I come up for air.

'*Aren't you sleeping with his daughter?*' It sounded vindictive when my uncle said it. Deceitful, evil. Does it make it any better that I care so much about her? That I would take the barrel of my uncle's gun to save her?

I bite her neck.

There's a wall up. The walls crumbled so fast from Centrum Tower. Fire tends to do that. But not with us. We're burning alive and yet we can't get any closer – not when she doesn't even know my real name. She doesn't even know who I am.

Her bare chest is hot against mine. She pants for air and I catch her breath on my tongue, keeping my eyes on her when I'm truly as close to her as I can physically be. I catch my heavy breaths in the crook of her neck. The hidden cabin is dark, lit only by a few candles. I think we could survive here forever; as long as forever may decide to be. If we were the only two people on earth and the four wooden walls were our world, I think I could be okay with that.

Maybe I'll leave myself behind here. Maybe everything I feel right now is so intense that it will just dislocate itself from my conscience. This desire cannot exist in the same place as my mundane thoughts. I think I will leave my soul behind. Safe in the safehouse; safe with *her*.

I pull the blanket across our bodies on the floor so we have our dignity if anyone barges in. Astrid likes to have sex on the floor. At first I thought she was joking, and then I thought it was a kink. Until I realised that Astrid is just like Zeb; using any mechanisms she can to keep herself from losing. From losing to the world; from the raw adversities it throws at her.

'You don't have to perform for me,' I whisper in her ear.

We go slow, my mouth never leaving her, even when I speak to her. I catch everything she has to say. If she whispers in my mouth, my heart will hear it.

Oh, Astrid, I think, *when we break, tell me you'll want to fix it.*

We will break, you see.

The wall has to go down eventually, and there will be nothing left when it does.

But for now, I'm careful with her. Astrid is tough, she's independent, a firecracker. But it makes her fragile, sensitive, easy to break even if she can put herself back together. I don't want to hurt her. So, we go slow.

'I wanted you from the moment I saw you,' she whispers. 'You've been in my dreams.' She pushes my hair from my face. 'Maybe I knew you in a past life, but I was meant to be with you. I recognised you when I saw you, and yet we've never met.'

I caress her cheek when she speaks, moving against her. Astrid feels so much. Somehow, we have fallen into each other so quickly, so naturally. *So contagiously.*

Her hands move down me, gracing my white ribs. Candlelight flickers, blown out by a gust of wind under the door. She digs her nails into my back.

Deep intimacy. We are complicit.

A fire burns bright in a world with no heat. A wave crests in the desert. A vampire shudders. I collapse on top of Astrid's milky skin, she presses me down onto her and begs me to stay close.

She catches her breath, and this time I let her.

SILENDA

•••

I rest my head on her chest, her long hair tickling my cheek. She fiddles with my nose ring.

We sit in silence for a moment. I'm content. She strokes my hair as I nuzzle under her arm. It's been a lifetime since I've felt this safe; this *natural*. Maybe it's been a few lifetimes, who knows when our souls have crossed paths?

I'm not sure I believe this. I don't think Astrid does either. But there is no other way to explain the way I feel when I look at her; how seen I feel when I look into her eyes.

She crosses the room and pours a glass of wine. She passes it and I take a sip. Astrid drinks red. She watches my arm as she sits back down on the rug beside me. I try not to stare at her and pull the blanket across my torso.

'Your tattoo,' she says. 'Zeb picked it for you?'

'Yeah,' I say. 'Do you like it?'

She nods. 'What does it mean?' I get goosebumps when she traces her blue nails over it.

'Zeb knows I've always been uncertain about my beliefs. He says that if I ever do go to the sky, that I'll be lightning. That I'll light up the whole sky.' I blush a little at my explanation.

'Zeb thinks a lot of you, Harry,' she says, looking at me quizzically. 'Did anything ever happen between you two?'

'Like in a...' She nods before I can finish. I clear my throat. 'I guess so,' I begin. 'I mean, I kissed him when we were 16.'

'That was you?' Astrid asks, giggling. 'I remember Zeb getting all confused because his friend kissed him.'

'Yeah, it was a mistake,' I assure her. 'I like women.'

'You sound like Hayden.' I'm about to ask what she means but she continues. 'You don't have to be one thing, Harry. You know that, right?'

'I guess I've never really thought about it.'

'I think you should.' Astrid puts her hand on my shoulder. 'But you don't need to define everything you are, Horatio. In any aspect of your life.'

I'm scared to ask, but I do anyway. 'What about you and Hawk?'

She laughs awkwardly. 'What about us?'

'There's a tension between you two. Haven't you ever...'

'Well, we have.' My heart sinks a little. 'But any tension between us now is purely an awkward one. A guilty one. I really like *you*, Horatio. Only you.'

It hurts when she says it, because Astrid Turrow should not like me. She shouldn't want me. She shouldn't have slept with me.

Because I am not me. Not right now. Even under 'Marino', under the Umbra music tech student, I still wouldn't be me. Not when I know what I know about my uncle. I am working on the side of the devil. I am evil by association.

I have to do something.

When Astrid showers, I sit naked under the woollen blanket, staring at the telephone. I could call the police. I could turn my uncle in, my own flesh and blood. I could tell Astrid the truth here and now and treat her the way she deserves before we get in too deep, before we really fall and my betrayal drives her crazy. Astrid Turrow cannot be Ophelia; she cannot be a casualty in this mess with my uncle.

I stare at the phone. I wrap the blanket around my torso and walk to it. The rain hits off the roof, and the tree branches scrape the windows. I stare at the phone. I hold it in my hand. My fingers grace the buttons.

I can't do it.

I see my uncle in my mind's eye, throwing Angelo around the garden like superman. I trace my arm. I remember the giant milkshakes he made us when we watched the fireworks from his office. The lightning storm. His unnaturally white smile made Angelo and I glow with excitement.

My father's brother. My Uncle Basil.

I can't do it.

I throw the phone on the couch when the cabin door swings open. *Hawk*. 'Uh, hi?' he says, looking me up and down.

'Hey.' I cling tightly to the blanket that covers me. 'I was just, um...'

Hawk looks around the room. My messy hair. The candles. The dishevelled rug on the floor. The shower running. 'Okay, I'm gonna go—'

'No!' I cry as he turns to walk away. I'm not sure why I do it.

He gives me a weird look. 'Look, Marino, I'm guessing it's Astrid in that shower right now and it's kind of uncomfortable if I don't dip.' He points an awkward thumb over his shoulder. 'And if it's not Astrid, it's even more imperative that I leave now—'

'No, please!' I say again. 'Please sit down. I could use someone to talk to right now.'

Hawk sits down nervously on the leather couch across from me. 'If this is a sex thing, I don't really wanna—'

'No!' I say quickly. 'God, no. I just wanted to talk about tomorrow.'

'The ball?'

'Yeah,' I say. 'Aren't you worried about Silenda? In case they show up? It's just that you're not going and—'

'I don't know, Harry,' he says. 'Since Hayden was shot it feels pointless to worry about the ball. They could take me and you out right here, right now. But what are we supposed to do? Spend every second worrying about it? It won't do us any good.'

For a moment, I want to tell Hawk everything.

I want to tell him that I'm Mayor Young's nephew and that he sent me here because he thinks Turrow is trying to take him down. I want to tell him that my uncle bombed the tower so he could frame Turrow and take over himself. I want to tell him that my uncle lied to me, that he's the evil one and now I'm in a mess that I can't get out of. I want to tell him that I'm scared because he's my friend, the others in the cabin are my friends, and that I'm falling in love with Astrid.

Instead, we sit in silence with the telephone off the hook and Hawk gives out a sigh that sounds like giving up.

CHAPTER 25

THE BLACK SEA

Carson

I'd part the black sea for you.

The grass is dry. At least there's that.

It doesn't smell as good when it's dry. But at least my gown isn't getting wet. I stare down at my thighs, hidden in layers of scarlet netting and scarlet cloth. My feet are bare. My toenails are painted red to match the streaks in my hair. I dip my feet in the loch, tilting my head up into the grey, praying for rain. Praying for rain to wash the black makeup from my eyes. To wash me of all the uncertainty. To wipe away all of my returning memories.

I don't want them back, you see.

Not since they started coming back like dreams. Some like nightmares.

Last night, my dream was black. Until it was wet. Until it was water. Until I was drowning in it.

I don't think I can swim. At least I can't in my dreams.

I look through the cabin window. The orange glow that warms it in the darkening sky. It's easy to see the bustle behind the large windows. Hayden and Zeb sit in the main room, talking. They move closer when the others leave the room.

Astrid fixes Horatio's tie. He wears an entirely black suit with a velvet jacket and a safety-pin earring. I see Hawk cross the top floor in his hoodie. Hayden had said that Hawk had been hoping to help Jason and Eydis stock up at Jason's pub in the village.

At least he won't be sitting in the cabin alone.

In all honesty, I don't want to go to the ball either. Not while Silenda are still around. Not when uniting with the Luxies after the city riots feels so dangerous.

Not when my memories are returning to me so hastily. So overwhelmingly.

Silenda killed me. And brought me back to life, sure. But they killed me. I've known that for a while, and I'm terrified that soon I'll remember what it feels like to die. That I'll remember the feeling of the drugs, too thick for my veins. Swelling and pulsing and bursting.

I let my legs dry in the cold wind. It stings but there's something pleasant about the sharpness. The pain lets me remember I'm alive, and then I go numb. I think that's the process with all kinds of pain. There's only so much a person can take before their body just starts to reject it.

The body is its own hero: it adapts and strategises. We learn defence mechanisms, how to put up a wall. The small hairs on my arms contract in an attempt to insulate my body. When Zebediah calls for me from the cabin window, my feeling of hollowness is hidden by a smile. My body knows how to get by.

But it can't protect me from him.

There are some feelings too intense to disguise, and there are some gusts of wind too icy to remain outside.

I wander back to the cabin.

Hawk diffuses a jasmine tea bag into a mug of boiling water. The steam of the kettle wets the air, the sack of herbs pulsing in and out of ceramic. His eyes are glazed over, his body going through the motions.

All the lights are on in the cabin. Hawk ignores the bustle of the others as they get ready for the ball. Astrid storms up and down the stairs, encouraging everyone to 'get a move on'. Zeb supports Hayden as he attempts to walk around the cabin. In the kitchen, I can hear his careful, rhythmless footsteps above us.

I close every door behind me. It's the creaking of wood that alerts him to my presence. Hawk turns around. 'Cara.' He takes in my appearance. 'You look great.'

'Thank you.' I use my fingers to pull a gap between my corset and my ribcage. 'It's not the most comfortable, so at least it looks alright.'

Hawk smiles. He turns back to his tea, taking a small spoon to stir the rich green liquid. His hood is up. I think if Hawk could choose to disappear right now, he would.

'Why aren't you going to the ball?' He has answered this question many times from everyone in the cabin, but never has his reply felt like an answer.

He sighs. 'Jason and Eydis and some people from the Rowleys are meeting in the village tonight to hatch a plan. We're going into the city. See if we can find a pattern to Silenda's victims.'

'Oh,' I say. 'Don't you think the ball will be vulnerable to an attack?'

'We're not leaving until late, anyway. But you won't need me when the others are around.'

'Couldn't you just come for a little while?'

'I just don't want to go, Carson.' *Carson.* My full name sounds harsh from his lips. 'You and Asiqa go have fun.' He grabs his mug with both sweater-covered hands and begins to walk away.

'That's not fair.' My words get away from me and chase him across the room. I have to continue. 'It's not fair for you to be so possessive of me when you look at me like I'm broken.'

'I don't look at you like you're broken.' He doesn't turn around when he speaks. 'I look at the world like it's broken, because it is broken. I am broken. Nothing is whole when you're looking at it through a broken lens.'

Hawk walks away and he doesn't look back.

My heart cries. I try to hide it. I try to numb it with the cold water in the loch. I try to numb it with champagne in the Jeep. Surprisingly, Astrid hasn't hired a fancy car to whisk us off to the ball. She takes Tyson's car, which suits me better.

'You look beautiful, Cara,' Asiqa whispers as we sit in the backseat. It's quite a strange feeling. I don't feel flattered when I blush; I feel embarrassed. I really like Asiqa. He is lovely, intelligent and pretty. But he's not – *stop*, I think, before he enters my mind.

Hayden, who has refused to take his wheelchair despite being a long way from recovery, sits in the very backseat of the eight-seater car with Zeb at his side.

The ball is lit with golden candlelight that illuminates the encrusted pillars. I feel out of my depth when the violins sound and waiters in black tailcoats carry silver trays of champagne and nibbles that I would not usually recognise as edible.

The ceremony to welcome the Luxies from East Town University will commence in 10 minutes. In the meantime, Umbras dressed in black, deep blue, blood red and other muted colours, buzz uncomfortably in anticipation.

The AYIP scrub up pretty good. Gia wears a vibrant pink and Alex a deep mauve. Petal looks ethereal in tangerine. Asiqa wears a scarlet cloth around his neck with his black suit, and Zeb wears black denim overalls with intricate detailing and a loose violet tie to match his hair. Hayden doesn't wear a jacket. His white shirt hangs open with his tie untied as he leans on Horatio for support. Not even Astrid bothers to scold him.

'Shit,' Astrid says. We all look at her as we huddle in an awkward circle in the middle of the floor. 'It's scarier than I thought it would be. Waiting for Basil, I mean.'

'It'll be okay,' Zeb whispers. 'He's not Silenda. It's all over now. We have nothing to worry about.'

SILENDA

'He may not be Silenda,' Hayden says, 'but what if whoever is gets in. I mean, it's not like the ball is top-secret or anything.'

'Don't worry,' Asiqa adds. 'Look at all the security. They'll never get in. Even the waiters look ready to rumble.'

We laugh. Asiqa's right. Large men dressed in fancy black suits surround the entrances. The waiters who carry the trays are also quietly intimidating.

'Now that you mention it, why are all the waiters so... broad?' I ask.

'They're my father's men,' Astrid says. 'Some are his bodyguards, but those guys are mostly at the doors. Some of the waiters are his friends and associates, here to help protect us if anything should go wrong. Asiqa's right, we should be okay.'

The tension dissolves around us and Asiqa asks me to dance. He holds my waist in one hand and cups my hand in the other. He moves me across the floor among the crowd of other dancers. He tries to meet my eyes and I try to look anywhere else. He lets go of me when the music stops.

Tyson stands behind a marble podium. 'Thank you, my dear Umbras, for joining us this fine winter evening at the unity ball. You all look terrific. Now, it is time to welcome our very special guests.' Tyson appears to be retrieving information on their arrival through an earpiece. 'Please welcome Mayor Basilio Young and the lovely students of East Town University!'

Mayor Young enters the ballroom. He is a tall man with unsettlingly pale eyes. A flood of young people pool behind him in ballgowns of pale pink, dusty lavender and other gentle shades. The men wear pale grey suits with various coloured ties. Initially, there is a stark divide in the room, until the colour bleeds into black. Asiqa greets old friends and we follow him. Astrid finds it easy to talk to the Lux girls, they smile and laugh at her stories and Horatio has a talent for rendering them. He gleams beside her.

I spin around the room looking for someone to talk to. My head is thumping.

'Red or white?' a waiter asks me, holding a silver tray.

I choose red.

My head feels like it's going to explode. I want to yell at the orchestra to pack it in. I want to tell Mayor Young to go home because he makes me uneasy. I want to tell Asiqa to stop trying to hold my hand. I stare into my wine glass. It's almost black. Only red at the edges where it reflects on the glass. I swirl it like a little pool. It makes me nervous. I don't know why. A whirlpool. A black whirlpool. The waiter who handed me the glass is watching me play with the liquid. I down it.

'Another, madame?' I nod. He seems too young to be calling me 'madame'. He looks 20 at most. He has ditched his tailcoat which doesn't help. His sleeves are rolled up to his elbow and his ashy hair is a little scruffy. He hands me another glass of red when I nod. As he passes me the wine, I see a large tattoo on his opposite forearm through the transparent red.

A snake.

I freeze. *Why do I know this tattoo?*

I stare into the back-crimson again. My heart cries.

I'll part the black sea for you.

The black sea. That's what the wine resembles as I swish it around in the glass. The black sea. I imagine myself on the bridge, the wind in my hair. I spread my wings like an eagle as I dangerously climb the railings.

He spreads his wings like a hawk.

Hawk.

I'll part the black sea for you.

Ignoring the waiter and his serpent tattoo, I shove my half-empty glass back into his grasp. 'I need to go.' That's all I say, and I'm still realising why when I'm already running.

A pristinely dressed man flings open the gold encrusted doors. The black wind throws my hair back, falling from the pretty bun Astrid had tied up for me.

SILENDA

I don't care.

I'm running.

Running in the dark like I always have. As long as always has been always. I feel the chill of the air on my bare arms.

I don't care.

I'm running. I was born to run. The black sky was made to shelter everything I am. The roads are ready to take me wherever I need to go. Whenever. I'm running so fast. Faster than I have ever moved. I've always been running from something, never have I ever been so desperately running towards something.

He is everything.

Somehow, the heels of my shoes don't sink into the grass. They scrape the pavements. I stop, throwing off my red heels and sprinting barefoot on the wet cobbles.

I would part the black sea for you.

There he is.

Unpacking crates of beer and large bottles of spirits from the back of Jason's van. He passes them to Eydis who walks into the pub. I know she sees me from the corner of her eye. Maybe that's why she doesn't come back out.

He wears the very same outfit he had worn the first night we met on the bridge. *The second time we met for the first time.* Long legs in tight black jeans. Broad shoulders in grey cotton. Thick lace up boots. He has his earphones in and his back to me.

I yell his name.

He removes one earbud.

'If I was still me, and you were still you, there's so much that I would say!' He stares blankly at me as I yell through the wind and the impending rain. 'There's so much I would say to you. If you were still Hawk and I was still Cara. If blue neon didn't feel like my kryptonite. If seeing you cry didn't make me feel like I'm on fire!'

He doesn't say anything, his eyes warming under street lamps.

I continue. 'If somehow, the black abyss would just swallow

me up, I would say so much to you. I would tell you the truth. If I didn't have to see your face afterwards. I look for you every day, Hawk. I search my mind. I know that when you found me, you were disappointed.'

'Cara, you could never disappoint me.'

'But I was empty when you found me. I don't know what once lived in me. But it knew you. And the person you found didn't. That's why you distance yourself from me, isn't it?'

'I can't make you feel anything you don't feel.'

I would part the black sea for you.

He says again, 'I'm just trying to hang on.'

My head hurts. The rain bounces off the cobbles. My hair sticks to my forehead. I try to breathe.

I remember.

'The blue neon,' I yell, 'I made you cry because I was trying to protect you. I knew Silenda were going to take me. I wanted them to. I thought I could save us. That's why I told you I could never feel that way about you. Because I didn't know if I would ever come back.' I shout louder through the pouring rain. I can't bring myself to get any closer.

I'd part the black sea for you.

The bass in my heart builds.

'That wasn't the only conversation we had on the day I left, was it?'

Hawk shakes his head, rain pouring down his cheeks in the gold street lights.

'We were on the bridge. We spread our arms as we looked over the water. The river always made me nervous. Sometimes I dreamed I was drowning in it!'

'You called it the impenetrable black sea,' he says.

'I'd part the black sea for you. That's what you said to me, wasn't it? You told me that you loved me!'

'You never said it back. Next time I saw you was outside the old tattoo parlour where you told me you couldn't feel the same.'

'Hawk, I—'

'It's okay, Cara. Really. I'm okay.'

'I'm covered in scars, Hawk. Not just here.' I trace my neck with blood red nails. 'Every day I am healing. They took so much from me. But no wound cuts deeper than you. You could destroy me with a word. You could bring me to life with a single look. A four letter word – nothing cuts deeper. Because I do. I do!'

His eyes pose the question, but I'm already running to him. I jump into him when he's ready to catch me. I feel dizzy. The streets flood with everything I've ever been and will ever be with him.

His lips are hot when I kiss him. We are engulfed, his hands in my hair, my legs wrapped around his torso. He clings to me like I might dissolve if his touch is too light. My hands grip tight to everything we ever were. He's so warm. I reach for the hood of his grey hoodie and pull it down so I can touch his hair.

Spinning worlds. Tongues of fire.

He is everything.

'I love you,' I say, pressing my nose to his cheek. 'I always have. Not a single cell of me could forget it.'

'The black sea got me,' he says. 'I've been dead in the water all this time.'

We are drenched.

My heart races at the ghost of his mouth on mine. We have no time to calm it.

There's a rumble in the distance. Screams.

Hawk and I turn immediately towards the university. The ball I had run from. Jason and Eydis emerge from the pub to look over at all of the commotion. Jason drops a bottle of beer with a shatter on the cobbles. 'Dear god!' Eydis shrieks into the wind.

West Town University is on fire.

Burning with billowing smoke, untainted by the floods of rain.

'Is that lightning?' Jason asks as we watch bright white sparks light the sky above the crumbling stone.

'There's no thunder,' Hawk observes. 'Do you think the lightning struck the turrets?' His eyes are glazed over until he realises. 'Red! Red is in my apartment!'

Hawk runs as fast as I feel under a black sky. I run beside him, barefoot. Jason and Eydis follow suit. Over the hills of grass, the rim of the loch.

Cobbles. Wet pavements.

'Don't get close to the flames!' an unknown voice yells as Hawk runs up the stairs of the east wing of the building. The west wing of the ballroom is alight with flames and the east wing is slowly going down with it. I stare helplessly at the fire, crying silently, knowing hysterics will do me no good. I try to stare through the small windows that are still intact, praying to the sky that Hawk will make it out okay. A black figure emerges from the smoke. But it's not Hawk. It's the man with the snake tattoo on his forearm. *Who are you?* I think again.

A tall figure sprints out from the rubble. He is nearly crushed by a falling turret. *It's Hawk.* I almost collapse with relief. He is choking. Red curls in his arms, crying. Her fur is blackened in places and her big brown eyes are frightened.

'Gia!' Hawk yells, handing the little dog to his sister. 'Take Red away from the smoke. Get out of here!' He yells firmly so his younger sister is too afraid to argue. Gia and Alex cross the grass to the cabins. Red peers over Gia's shoulder, little claws clinging to her arm, crying for her dad.

Horatio and Astrid stare up at the burning building. Harry looks distraught. Zebediah holds Hayden up, who's dark eyes narrow at his uncle. Hayden leaves Zeb, who is too horrified by the fire to notice. He hobbles closer to the building, his right leg struggling to keep up with the rest of his body. He stands in front of Tyson and when Horatio sees him and rushes over to stop him, it's too late. Hayden punches Tyson in the face. So hard that he falls to the ground and Hayden stumbles back at the impact.

SILENDA

I look on, utterly bewildered. Hawk is running in and out of the fire, making sure no one is left behind. Astrid doesn't help her father. She is crying. She says nothing.

What is going on?

CHAPTER 26

SUPERMODEL SAVAGE

Horatio

I kiss her neck.

She is so pale that I expect her to be cold. But she is warm to the touch. She giggles when I pull her close to dance with me in an empty stone corridor. The castle walls are tall and echo when I tease her. She makes me laugh. She clings to a full glass of champagne that she puts on the floor to hold me instead. We wander under grand chandeliers. We hide behind marble pillars, pulling each other close.

There's only so much time I can spend in crowds before I start to feel like I'm shutting down.

We had been dancing in the great ballroom for what felt like a very long time. Time slows with Astrid. I'm too busy being completely mesmerised by every colour in her eyes. I had been anxious that someone from East Town University would recognise me, but no one has. I suppose that's one of the privileges of not having had any friends from home.

'Did you really cut your gold ball gown in half at the prince's ball?' I ask Astrid as she dances between the pillars.

'You know, Horatio, it doesn't surprise me at all that you read those tabloids.'

'Seriously though, did you?'

'Yes, I did. I cut my dress in half and I shoved some cake in the dickhead's face, threw back on my Docs and left.'

'Awesome. Did you really replace all the champagne flutes with bottles of beer and replace the orchestra with a Blondie record?'

She laughs at this. 'You shouldn't believe everything you read in the press. Does that disappoint you?'

'Not at all. I think you totally could if you wanted to, though.'

'I think I had already pushed my luck at the prince's ball. And my father would kill me if I pulled anything like that tonight. And for your information, I really like champagne, and violins help me clear my mind. But I do play the electric guitar.'

'You do? Why did you never tell me when I was practising in the Nether Cabin?'

'You never asked.' Astrid Turrow is an enigma. She leans in to kiss me and then ducks away. She thinks this is hilarious.

'My little brother threw my first guitar out of my bedroom window because I wouldn't take him to see a movie.'

'I didn't know you had a brother,' she says. 'Why didn't you take him to see the movie?' I remember suddenly that I can't be completely myself around Astrid, no matter how badly I'd like to be. How easy it would be. *Am I the villain of this story?*

It's regrettable, really. Especially when emotions are running so high tonight. All I want to do is tell Astrid about my uncle because I haven't been able to look at him all night. I shoved my notebook in his suit pocket when I pretended to greet him for the first time. I haven't written anything new but as long as he has my book, he has no reason to come anywhere near me for the rest of the night. Astrid had curtseyed and shook his hand. Something about that interaction made me sick. I think my uncle would kill her if it would benefit him. That he would gesture one of his men to pull out a gun and watch her beautiful eyes as they shot her between them.

I hate him.

Basilio has no faith. There is no god in him. He is not drunk on his lust for heaven. He is drunk on power. Basilio Young is his own god, and I will never worship him. I would rather burn.

I had tried to focus on anything else but him as Astrid and I had spun around the dance floor earlier in the night. One thing that had distracted me, just for a moment, had been Hayden and Zebediah. I hadn't meant to watch them. But I couldn't stop myself. Zeb danced with him. He let Hayden stand on his feet and he spun him round the floor as they laughed. But it wasn't the laughing that stayed with me. It wasn't the fact that they were so openly getting along. It's what I had heard Hayden whisper to him.

'I don't care if I burn,' he had said. 'I don't care if the ground swallows me up. I don't care if a million flames spit at me for a million eternities.' And then he had said it: 'Because I have already found heaven in you.'

I think Hayden is wise that way. Maybe heaven is something we should be looking for every day. Not something we sit around waiting for. But something we should actively pursue. *Maybe this is my heaven,* I think, as Astrid twirls me around, giggling. Maybe I could be happy if I never left this hallway ever again.

'Hey,' Astrid says, 'these little cucumber sandwiches are so good. They are far too small, though.' Astrid had filled her purse with nibbles, accepting every silver tray offered to her. 'We could sneak into the kitchen, you know? I mean, no one would be too angry. Not that we're going to get caught, anyway.'

Astrid drags me down the hall on a quest for more cucumber sandwiches. The kitchen has a small door at the end of an empty corridor. Astrid calls it the secret door, explaining that on busier nights, waiters would use it as a shortcut to get to the opposite end of the ballroom. She opens it gingerly and we sneak into the bright white kitchen.

We duck behind a silver unit that is abundant with plates of nibbles. Astrid empties a plate of mini sausage rolls into her bag. She covers her mouth to stop from laughing.

But then she freezes. Her face drops so suddenly that I begin to panic when I realise she isn't kidding.

'Astrid, what's wrong?'

She slaps her hand over my mouth and ducks down further. I copy her, peeking slightly around the corner of the table to look for what has frightened her.

Then I see it. One of the waiters tucks a handgun into the waistband of his trousers, hiding it with the tail of his coat. But that isn't where Astrid looks. She looks at the larger waiter who looks silly in his tailcoat. He has a round face and a shiny bald head. At first I don't recognise him but, as I look back at Astrid, the realisation begins to sink in.

'It's the Silenda agent from the arcade,' she whispers, completely emotionless. 'The one who's mask fell down in Asylum.'

'Fuck. What are they doing here?'

'Where better to stage another attack, to instil fear in us, than at the unity ball?' she whispers. 'I knew this would happen.'

'You did?'

She nods, pulling out a pistol from the secret pocket of her aqua dress. My eyes widen. Before I can question her, Astrid shoots a bullet into the air. The young waiter makes a run for it, but the bald man stands static. 'Hands in the air,' Astrid orders, rising from behind the table. I follow her. 'On your knees!' Astrid's voice turns deep and scary when she screams at him. He drops to his knees, putting his gun slowly on the ground beside him.

'Miss Turrow,' he says, 'don't be so hasty, please. I beg you. I've known you since you were just a baby.'

Astrid's gun falls a little, for just a moment as she narrows her teary eyes at him.

'What are you talking about?' she says. She looks like she is trying to recognise him, and I think she does. She lowers her gun, but still keeps it held in both hands, ready to erect it again. 'You are one of my father's men,' she says, stumbling back slightly at the realisation. 'How...' she breathes so heavily that I hold onto her in case she falls. 'How could you do this to him? How could you betray my father like this? After all these years?'

The man looks pitiful. 'Oh, Miss Turrow—'

'Don't!' she says. 'You tried to kill me in the club.'

'No, I didn't,' he says. 'I didn't shoot you and I never intended to.'

She's shaking her head vigorously. 'I don't understand.'

'We needed to scare your friends into leaving us alone. To protect our identity. You were getting too close. What Silenda are doing is vitally important.'

'You're killing people!' I cry. 'Innocent people! The Rowleys are nearly wiped out. How fucking dare you!'

He drops his head in shame. 'If we can find out the truth about what happens when we die, the division in the city could end. We could live in the shelter of right and wrong. There would be no divide.'

'You are robbing people of choice! What if we don't want to fucking know? What if the truth is so unbearably terrifying? How could you?' Astrid says again. 'Who else is involved in this? Who is in charge? Is it you?' Astrid yells. 'Answer me! Are you their leader?'

'The other waiter had a gun,' I say. 'I saw him put it in his pocket.'

'Miss Turrow—'

'Who is your leader?' Astrid cries painfully, raising her gun again. I know she is starting to realise what I am too.

'Astrid—' he says.

She moves close to him, placing the barrel of her gun at his temple. 'I'll ask you one more time. Who is your leader?'

Tears stream.

'Your father.'

SILENDA

· · ·

A cold wind fills the castle. A cold taunting whistle. His body lies in the kitchen, bleeding onto the white walls, a bullet wound between his eyes, bursting the flesh of his face.

Astrid drops her gun. Red tears streaming. An acoustic guitar plays in the distance. She crouches down beside his dead body, his disfigured head. 'A life for a life, huh?' Astrid is covered in the ricochet of blood spatter. 'Fuck that.' She tosses his gun to me. 'I hope it's dark wherever you are now.' Astrid kicks his body over, wiping blood from her eyes with the back of her hand.

She walks away. A supermodel walk. One heel in front of the other. Tall. *Fucking badass.* She twirls the handle of her pistol around in her hand. Astrid takes the news badly. I think she might kill her own father. She has a crazed look in her eyes.

She enters the ballroom, gun pointed out, switching from waiter to waiter. The young man from the kitchen. He has a snake tattoo. She shoots him in the shoulder from across the room. The ballroom is in hysteria, but it hadn't been Astrid's crazy eyes that caused the uproar.

The ballroom is on fire.

The injured waiter runs in the opposite direction of the exit. Hayden and Zeb run for the door. Cara is nowhere to be seen. Gia and Alex are running too. My uncle is missing. Tyson stands in the middle of the room, staring at his weapon yielding daughter. She drops her gun to her side, staring at him, eyes welling, she lets the fire build behind her.

Eventually, I'm forced to take Astrid's hand and drag her out with me. She's reluctant. I think for a moment that she might prefer to burn, but there's no time.

Outside, the hysteria doesn't calm. Hayden runs towards Astrid.

'Why the fuck did you shoot Austin?' His eyes are panicked. Zeb holds his arm.

Astrid is numb. She doesn't look at him. 'Who's Austin?'

'My ex-boyfriend from school, you remember him!'

'Right, yeah,' is all she says.

'Astrid, what the fuck is going on?' Hayden jumps around her blank eyes trying to catch her attention. But Astrid is long gone. I squeeze her hand but it's limp in my touch. She stands staring at the fire. 'Astrid!' he yells again. Hayden is crying now. He knows something is very wrong.

'It's daddy,' she says. '*He* is Silenda.'

'What are you talking about? Astrid?' Zeb says. 'What is she talking about, Harry?' Zeb is breathing heavily. Hayden is frozen.

'It's true,' I say. 'One of the waiters was the agent from the arcade. He told us.'

'Maybe he was lying.'

'He wasn't'

'Where is he now?'

'Dead,' Astrid voices. 'I killed him.'

Zeb drags Hayden away from the fire. Astrid insists on watching the building burn a little longer and I am in no position to argue until the top floor starts to fall. Lightning strikes over the building. I hear my uncle's voice behind us, talking to a small crowd of West Town students. 'Now you get out of here, young ones! What a terrible tragedy,' he says, staring into the flames. 'It must have been the lightning, you see. Must have struck one of the turrets. How awfully unfortunate. A tragedy, an utter tragedy. You get out of here, young ones,' he says again.

A fire engine sounds in the distance. Police sirens, too.

I turn around to look at my uncle. I let go of Astrid's hand. She continues to stare up at the fire. Hawk runs out of the building with his little dog. He drags Astrid away too.

The fire sparks in my uncle's white eyes. I march over to him, grabbing him by the scruff of his neck. *What a tragedy!* 'This was you!' I yell at him.

'Horatio!' he says. 'What on earth are you talking about?'

'There's no thunder, uncle!' I push him. 'Where's the thunder, huh? Where's the thunder?' The rain doesn't cool my fury. 'The lightning, uncle? Really? *What a tragedy!* That's what you said about Centrum Tower too, wasn't it?' I'm yelling. Everyone who remains on the grounds stares at us. The garden begins to burn too.

'Look, young man, I have no idea who you are, or *what* you are talking about,' he says for the benefit of the nearby audience.

I push him to the ground and watch the rain drench him.

I walk away.

I have no proof. *He's the mayor*, I think. For now, there is not much else I can do.

I return to Astrid who stares at her father across the green. He is with Hayden. I run to him, knowing what is about to happen. But it's too late. Tyson lays on the ground with a bloody nose. A dozen guns are pointed at Hayden, emerging from a crowd of tailcoats. The boy with the snake tattoo points his gun at his face. 'You're a coward, Austin,' Hayden shouts. 'A fucking coward! This is what fear does to you, huh? You think you're better than their fucking book? You're a murderer!' Austin doesn't drop his gun.

Tyson rises with his own gun pointed at Hayden's already injured torso. They are face to face. 'Do it then,' Hayden says. 'You never liked me anyway, uncle. On you go! Do it! Maybe I'll tell my mother you said hi! Or maybe I'll beg the darkness to swallow you too.' The fire hisses with his words. 'Come on then, Tyson! Shoot me!'

The circle of suited agents look at each other, nervously. And they should be nervous. Because Astrid isn't next to me. And Eydis has arrived. Distracted by Tyson's confrontation, Astrid and Eydis begin to take them out, one by one. Shooting them in the legs, the head. Zebediah disarms Austin and flings his gun into the flames. Zeb has his hands around his neck spitting inaudible words at him. Zebediah has no gun, so he tackles

Austin by the fire until he pushes him, screaming into the flames. His snake tattoo melts in the orange. Zeb stands back to watch him burn.

Some of the agents dart into the woods, but Astrid, Eydis and a weaponless Cara have conjured a heap of dead bodies.

A gunshot sounds. Tyson has shot Hayden in the shoulder.

'You're a stupid fucking kid, Hayden! You always have been.' Hayden falls at his feet, cradling his arm. Astrid points her gun at her father's head when Tyson points his gun at Hayden's. She isn't going to shoot. She can't. 'You don't know you've been fucking born! I gave you everything when your mother died and my idiot brother turned to drink. You would be nothing without me! And this is how you repay me?'

'You're a murderer!' Hayden grimaces in pain. 'Why? How could you?"

'Why?' Tyson mocks. '*Why*? Our entire system is a mess. Evil men like Basilio Young use their books and their words to control crowds and crowds of vulnerable people. They tell people like you who you can and can't love. They scare people into doing what they're told. It's fear-mongering and it's not faith. There's nothing pure about that man – he's a power hungry maniac!'

'Not all Luxies are like him,' Hayden argues bravely. 'Some people are afraid of the dark. They find solace in the light. They believe that everything will be okay. That the people they love don't perish forever. Everyone is entitled to that. You want power. You want to use the things we fear against us. It's what you've been doing this whole time.'

Tyson ignores him. 'If I could prove that the Luxies are wrong, the city could be free. Hayden, you could be free!'

Hayden does not cower under steel. The barrel pressed to his forehead does not extinguish the fire in his eyes. He wells with tears, not daring to look over to Zeb who stands strong behind him, willing to dive for him if Tyson is crazy enough to cock his weapon.

SILENDA

Hayden finds his words. 'And then what will we have? A society just waiting to die? Saying goodbye to loved ones knowing we'll never see them again and that they'll never see *anything* again? That they as good as never existed? You believe what you want, Tyson. But you will *not* decide for me.'

'Or me.' Zeb steps forward, his strong shoulders glowing in the light of the flames.

'Or me,' I say, my hand on Zeb's shoulder.

'Or me.' Carson stands steady.

Astrid steps forward, dropping her gun. Tears streaming. 'Or me.'

'Oh, but I can decide something.' Tyson put his finger on the trigger, pressing the tip of the weapon deep into Hayden's head again. No one can shoot him. Not me, not Zeb or Eydis – *not for Astrid.*

Thudding footsteps sound. Hawk appears from nowhere, jumping out in front of Hayden and tackling Tyson Turrow to the ground. His gun flies from his hand and Eydis grabs it. Hawk straddles Tyson, leaning down until they are face to face. 'Or me.'

Hawk pins the mayor further into the ground and punches him violently. Blood splatters from his nose, but Tyson does not lose his crooked smile.

'Hawk!' Zeb cries, cradling Hayden on the grass. 'You're going to kill him.'

Hawk stands up, staring at his already bruising fists. Hayden bleeds on the grass, cheeks stained red.

Jason ushers over the police when they arrive, clicking Tyson's wrists into metal handcuffs and dragging him away, 'Idiot brother, huh?' he shouts after him as his brother's head is tucked into the police vehicle.

A team of firefighters tackle the fire as the beautiful building suffers in the flames.

We sit on the grass, staring into the fire.

'All my things are in there,' Hawk says as Carson rests her head on his shoulder.

'I don't know where we go from here,' Astrid says. No one answers her. I put my arm around her, and Hayden smiles at her softly.

It's all we can do.

The ambulance Zeb had called for Hayden arrives and he clings onto the purple tie wrapped around his wound.

When the ash settles, Cara and Hawk walk hand in hand to the cabin.

'Harry?' Astrid says to me as we remain sitting. 'Can I have a moment to myself? I need to think for a bit.' Her tears are flowing more slowly. I nod, getting up from where we sit and breathing deeply.

Everything is still red and hot.

I wander through the gardens. Surprisingly, the greenery hasn't been completely destroyed. I walk across the edges where the green is still green and the apples are still red.

There is a small flash in a distant bush. Like a spark of electricity.

I approach the greenery cautiously, crouching down to the source of light and then backing away a little to get a better look.

A small metal box is tucked under the bush. I kneel down beside it again, pull it out from the shrubbery and examine it. When I turn it around, it has a clear disc and lots of buttons that I don't understand the purpose of. For a moment, I worry it's a bomb and begin to back away.

But it flashes again, glitching until lightning bursts full in the sky.

Holographic lightning.

I jump back. It cracks as white bursts in the black. *Oh no.* I so desperately want to be wrong. So desperately.

Lucian's holographic lightning.

My uncle started the fire. There is proof of it now. The lightning that struck the turret had been nothing but a performance, another attempt to take down Tyson, to destroy his university, his culture, the future of hundreds of young

SILENDA

Umbra's in a terrible 'accident'. Not that Tyson needed any help in destroying his image, he managed that all on his own.

There's only one thing I can do now. I have no choice.

I take out my phone from the pocket of my suit jacket. My heart beats heavy with the beeps of the impending call. When the phone voices, I take a deep breath. 'I have reason to believe that Mayor Young started the fire at West Town University this evening.'

The operator sounds sceptical. 'And what makes you suppose this?'

'Because I'm his nephew.'

A breath catches behind me. Astrid watches me, sadly.

I yell after her, but it's too late.

She's already gone.

CHAPTER 27

C FOR COMPLICIT

Carson
5 months later

Astrid locked herself in her room for months.

I leave plates of food at her door but they're rarely touched by the end of the night. Hayden is back in his wheelchair, staring at the television without really watching it. His shoulder is on the mend and his torso almost completely healed, but he sits in his wheelchair anyway.

I drink Hayden's serum every morning.

My memories return to me in dizzy bursts. It can be confusing sometimes, distressing, even, but Hawk's arms are always there to soothe me.

I know now how I felt about him in the past. I've always loved him. I've always watched him eat at the kitchen counter and dip his feet in the loch in the afternoons. I've watched him play on his keyboard and read with his headphones on and the concentration on his face when he does the things he loves.

I remember aching when he left in the nights. Now he writes his songs with me.

Hawk has moved back into the cabin. The cabin is as good

as ours now. We are the only souls that occupy it. Astrid never leaves her room no matter how many times I scream at her door. Zebediah disappears into the city for days at a time, posting pictures on social media of his clubbing and getting high and drunk under purple lights. Hayden doesn't talk. He stares at Zebediah's socials and sips whisky from a paper cup. Hawk tries to take it from him, but he becomes aggressive, perfectly capable of fighting back despite his wheelchair.

Hawk picks me yellow tulips from the university gardens that still thrive on the side of the east wing. We picnic at the fountain by Tyson's mansion. The fresh air keeps us sane, being Hawk and Cara again keeps us sane. He kisses my forehead and tells me he loves me, but it doesn't stop my eyes wandering to the big house at the top of the hill.

Every day I think about visiting Tyson in prison, about taking a pocket knife to his cell and slitting his throat for taking my life away from me. For hurting my friends; for betraying his own family. For mocking the AYIP.

I walk through the hills in my bare feet, it squelches under a grey sky. I watch the castle ruins across the water and think of nothing but revenge. Sometimes Hawk creeps up on me, snaking his hands around my waist and perching his chin on my head. He wants to keep me exactly where I am. He wants to spend winter break walking through the forest and drinking cocoa by the fire. He wants a happy ending. He wants to kiss me in the rain and remember the first time our lips met. But Hayden stares at the TV screen in the evenings and doesn't bat an eyelid when the channel changes. The only time we see Astrid is on the screen and on billboards when Hawk and I spend the day in the Urb.

One afternoon, I saw Horatio crossing the street. Hawk had been waiting in a long queue for an iced tea. I waited outside on the corner to watch the world go by, and there he was. Crossing the road in a silk zebra-print shirt, Versace leather jeans and designer sunglasses. He pushed his black locks from his face, a new tattoo on his neck. He crossed the street like a supermodel. I guess he's a rich boy now. Probably inherited his uncle's fortune when he went down for Centrum Tower.

The next night, I saw him again, picking up some Thai food and heading to his new big-shot apartment, so I followed him.

'What the fuck, Carson?' he had said when I stopped his front door with my foot and followed him inside. My first impression of Harry and his new-found wealth was that he appeared to be floundering in it. His right eyebrow was red and freshly pierced and, when he turned away from me, I examined the new black ink on the back of his neck. A pair of eyes, beautifully shadowed with thick voluminous lashes. Despite the black ink, one iris appeared to be unmistakably brighter than the other one. 'Oh god,' I'd said, 'this looks like a breakdown.'

'What do you mean?' – too defensive – 'I'm fine!'

He has a fancy marble kitchen and a bin full of pot noodles and old takeout boxes. I looked at the mess and then back at him. 'What the hell are you doing, Harry?'

'Trying to get on with my life.'

'I know you didn't know about the tower. You need to fix things with the others—'

'Cara, they all hate me. I lied to all of you.'

'Astrid hasn't left her room since the night of the ball.'

He looks pained. 'And what am I supposed to do, Red? I'm just as bad as her father.'

'Don't, Harry. You know that's not true. You can make it up to her!'

'How?' he said. 'All I have is money! She has enough of that on her own.'

'You care about her, Harry. You have that. And right now she has no one. The men in her life have been ridiculously shit. Don't be just another guy that lets her down.'

He sank his head, rubbing his hand across his face.

And that's when I saw it, on the coffee table behind him. The book. *The Rowleys Vampire.*

I ran over to it. 'You still have this?' I said.

'I don't think it's over.'

'You *what*?'

'You remember what we said the day before the unity ball. Silenda are like a cult, Carson. They date back to the 1500s. Catching their current leader doesn't mean we've caught *them*.'

'But there haven't been any more deaths, Harry. I've heard nothing of the sort in the Rowleys.'

'Obviously they're going to give it some time.'

'Are you sure you aren't just hanging onto this because it's the only thing still tying you to the Nether Cabin?'

'Okay, Carson, whatever. Take the book then. Read it and get back to me if I can't make you believe me now.'

So I did.

I took the book and I left. Now, I carry it under my arm, squelching through the grey and trying to get Hawk off my case so I can take it to the Cava-Mastix Prison.

So I can take it to Tyson Turrow.

Hawk, understandably, rejects any desire I have to leave the cabin on my own. When I read on the grass, he sits beside me on his phone. When I sit in the coffee shop in Bellumside, he winces with every sip of his own bitter cup. When I call his name in the cabin, he materialises in seconds. This is why I had to sneak out when he was sleeping. Slumped on the couch with an empty mug in his hand, Hawk sits opposite Hayden in the main room, who stares blankly again at the television screen.

I hold the book in my hands and breathe. I know what I have to do.

I rush to the front door of the cabin and pull on my black leather boots and run to the West Town train station. The rocket train strips through the atmosphere and I know now that there is no turning back; when Hawk wakes up to me gone, I will never have another chance like this. The sky is a cool blue in the Urb when I wave over a taxi. 'Cava-Mastix Prison, please.'

The driver squints at me through his rear-view mirror.

'What business has a young thing like you got at the prison?'

'Just visiting a friend,' I lie, tucking the head of my pocket knife back into my sock when it pokes out. The driver looks disturbed as he puffs out his cheeks and caresses the wheel.

The building is huge, daunting. The grey walls decay under grey clouds and the whole complex is surrounded by towering barbed wire. Men in orange jumpsuits play basketball behind it. An old man with crazy eyes throws himself against the fence like a rabid dog, bearing his teeth and spitting through the diamonds as I approach the visitors door.

I stop at the glass entrance for a second and think.

Both mayors reside here now. Turrow and Young. Equally as violent and equally as malicious as each other. My heart races when the guard at the door gestures for me to raise my arms as she scans the metal detector across my frame, never quite reaching my boots. I sigh, relieved, when the door swings open to let me enter the security complex.

'Carson Whitmoore?' A man in uniform approaches me with an outstretched hand. 'I saw your face on the news, you...'

I clear my throat, 'Yes.' I shake his hand.

'I'm Alexander Clark, I'm a prison guard at the Cava-Mastix. What business could you possibly have here?'

'I'm here to speak with Tyson Turrow.'

He looks alarmed, looking from me to the book and back again. 'Are you quite sure, miss?' I nod as he walks me down a long corridor. He uses his earpiece to alert the guards to release Tyson from his cell and take him to the visitor's room.

When we approach the glass divide and the headset phone, I protest. 'Is there any way that I could be in the same room as

SILENDA

him?' Mr Clark, once again, has saucers for eyes. 'It's just that I'd like to show him something.' I look down at my book. He gulps thickly and nods, asking no other questions, pity in his eyes.

After half an hour of waiting in a musty blue corridor, Mr Clark reappears and gestures for me to follow him into a small black room. Through the two-way mirror, Turrow sits in a ripped orange jumpsuit, his hands handcuffed behind his back. Blood gushes from his mouth. I retreat slightly from the mirror.

'What the hell is wrong with him?' I say.

'Poor bastard has lost his mind,' Clark says. 'God knows if he ever had one. We have to keep him tied up otherwise he tries to knock himself out by running at the walls. He's chewed right through his bottom lip, not much we can do about that.' Clark pauses. 'Are you very sure, Miss Whitmoore?' I nod my head. It's worse than I had expected.

When I enter, the silence is unbearable. I hear nothing but my footsteps and the dripping of blood on metal. He doesn't look up until I sit down, and when he does, the glint of evil in his eyes is so overwhelming that I want to throw up.

'Miss Whitmoore,' Turrow croaks, spraying blood on the table, 'to what do I owe the pleasure?'

I don't answer him, I simply place the thick dusty book in front of him. He laughs manically, chaotically. 'Our legacy,' he says between laughs, choking on his own tongue.

'What is it?' I press. 'Silenda, what the fuck is it?'

He laughs again. 'Oh, dear Carson. I think you know fine well what you're dealing with.'

'You're a cult,' I say. 'Aren't you?'

Tyson raises one thick eyebrow and he doesn't need to answer me for me to know I'm right. 'It's a noble quest,' he says, 'the truth.'

'A noble quest? You're killing people!'

'Less frequently than you might imagine, Red.' My stomach turns at the name. 'We kill to promote life. We kill, we instil chaos and fear. We trigger cortisol. Our subjects live.'

'Don't try to convince me that you care about their lives. You only care about your research.'

'Aren't there worse things to care about?'

I sigh, infuriated and intimidated by the chaos in his eyes. 'How could you do this to your kids? You raised Hayden like your son. Surely you knew how this would end?'

'I did this *for* my kids. Their quality of life would be improved without the segregation and the prejudice. Hayden won't even step foot in Centrum Park because of those malicious Luxies.'

'What happened to Hayden is disgusting and unforgivable. But those people weren't evil Luxies. They were evil people. People made evil by fear, by the fear of the dark. You know they would fear it more if they knew it to be true. You would strip them of a right to hope.'

Tyson's eyes dart around the room. He wriggles in his chair, trying to break free, spitting on the table and glaring directly into the mirror. It's difficult to tell whether he is staring at his own decay in his reflection or trying to communicate with the officers behind the glass. 'You say this is how it ends?' he begins before chuckling under his breath, 'this is only the beginning.' He looks through me. 'We are closer than ever to the truth. I risked everything for it. I am only a catalyst in a major reaction. A minor catalyst.'

'Are you saying you have never been their leader?'

He begins to laugh so violently, so bloodily, that he nearly tips out of his chair. 'Oh, Carson! I am nothing but a simple mayor in a little town. I may have been overseer of what little I had control of, but I am afraid I am not the be all, nor the end all, of any of this. What sort of pool of subjects did I have to work with? My daughter's idiot friends and the brainless scum in the Rowleys? That's not to mention my failure of a brother who was mistaken as a disposable homeless man by one of my agents.

We had to make him believe that he had escaped so he could go home and spread terror in our name.'

'You prayed on the weak and the vulnerable. You are evil all the same.' I stop and think for a moment, knowing my next efforts will be futile. 'Tell me where they are!' I'm standing, leaning over him in his bonds. 'Tell me where their base is! If you're not their leader then tell me who is!' I'm screaming at him now but all he does is laugh. The anger bubbles in me so furiously that I want to take the pocket knife from my sock and slit his throat with it.

I think about the grieving families in the Rowleys, their lost loved ones branded as 'brainless scum' by the one who took their lives. I think about Astrid in her room and Hayden in his wheelchair with a fully healed torso. I look in Tyson's eyes and all I see is evil. All I feel is furious resentment.

Tears stream. Fiery fucking icicles. Icy fucking flames.

Lost his mind, they say?

I crawl under the table, holding a hand up to the mirror to show that I have simply dropped my cabin key. I slip my pocket knife into Tyson's shoe. He gives me a wicked smile.

I walk away and don't look back.

• • •

On my way home, I find Zebediah sprawled out on the concrete outside the Panic Room, laughing in the purple rain. He fishes out a bag of white powder from his wallet and I grab it from his hands, leaning over him.

His smiles fades. 'Oh, fuck.'

Zebediah is a big guy to carry home; huge, actually. He leans on my shoulder the way I suppose he would lean on a desk. His biceps are like bags of boulders.

Somehow he loses his shirt on the way home. It was dangling off him when I found him on the street and now it's gone completely.

Zebediah has a tattoo on his back of a wolf howling at the sun.

'Why the sun?' I ask.

'It burns. And the moon didn't do anything.'

'Oh.'

'And it's ironical,' he mumbles.

'Ironic?'

'Hmm.'

'And androgynous.'

'*Ambiguous?*'

'Hmm,' he hums again in agreement.

'I saw Harry a few days ago.'

'Potter?'

'No.'

'Styles?'

'No. Harry Young.'

'Ew, that's like the worst one.' He sways onto the late train.

'He was the one that turned Mayor Basilio in, you know. It can't have been easy.'

Zeb shrugs. 'It seemed to be easy when he was lying to us. Singing karaoke in the cabin and hooking up with Astrid. He's totally ruined Cher for me.'

'And what did Hayden do?'

There's a silence. 'He won't talk to me.'

'You haven't tried.'

'I'm scared that it's different now. That he'll reject me. He switches on me sometimes. It puts me in a bad...place.'

'And you're not in a bad place now? You tried to push me off the bridge when I threw your coke in the river.'

'It's expensive.'

'You'll survive.'

And he will.

Zebediah has moved back into the cabin. He stumbles into the living room in time for the ten o'clock news.

SILENDA

'Tyson Turrow, West Town's disgraced ex-mayor has been found dead in his cell at Cava-Mastix Prison with the letter C carved into his cheek.'

EPILOGUE

THE ROWLEYS VAMPIRE

Horatio

I used to believe in the light like a vampire believes in the dark.

I suppose it became about survival. That was when I was a Lux – when my faith lay beyond black leather and dangly earrings. Before my earphones and a saxophone solo became my only refuge when the world got too loud.

I used to believe. *In next.*

In a better place – a place beyond the dirt and the grime and the sickness. Beyond Randy Redding's sallow grey skin and yellowed fingers. A place where I wouldn't have to feel *everything*.

I thought that the dark would scare me, and it does.

But nothing scares me more than eternity. An eternity of feeling like this.

Lost, empty, lonely.

If Randy resides in darkness now, he's still in a better place. All that awaited Randy's Friday was Thursday. For some people, yesterday is all that tomorrow brings with it.

I stare at the posters on my bedroom walls. Zeb had mailed them back to me from my room in the Nether Cabin. He'd written insults all across the back of them. Sometimes I hang them up the wrong way round, just so I can remind myself of what a 'dickhead' I am.

He isn't speaking to me. None of them are. Not since Astrid ran away after the fire and the truth came out about the real nature of my time in the cabin. They know I turned my uncle in and they know I didn't tell him as much as I could have. But I still lied to them. I still led Astrid on knowing that I wasn't being truthful.

On reflection, I think lying to someone about your name is one of the worst things you can do. We are on this earth for such a short time and that little noise a person makes when they include you, talk to you, acknowledge you – flatter and confirm your *existence* – it's the label to your soul. To other people, it's *what you are*. To lie about it just feels so corrupt. If I lied about my first name, I wouldn't forgive me either.

There is one person who still speaks to me when I'm in the Rowleys. Sure, she ducks under the table when she sees anyone looking at us together and she hides her face when I make her laugh, but Carson has more forgiveness in her.

So do the people of the Rowleys. You see, I'm sort of like their king now. Well, if kings handed out soup and blankets in cold weather.

My father came into a lot of money when Uncle Basilio and his men went to prison *again*. I suppose my uncle knew I was about to take him down so he left a hefty amount of cash to his brother beforehand. No one visits him in jail. My father shared some of the cash with Angelo and me. Angelo has already bought himself a car. I started a food bank in the Rowleys to care for the impoverished families of the fallen. Carson works there on the weekends.

I still work in Caleb's record store, too. He still ruffles my hair, but Zeb doesn't come by anymore.

I finally came out to my parents, too. You know, as a Lumbra. That's what I'm calling it. Middle-aged people need labels, don't they? At first my mother thought I was trying to tell her I'd gotten a job as a lumberjack.

Oh, Harry, you're not strong enough to chop down trees.

We talked through it for a while. A long while. I've moved out of my family home with a great deal of my uncle's cash. I live in the Urb now. The top floor of a flight of glass windows. It's right in the centre of the city and I can see for miles across the river. I can see Astrid's penthouse apartment, too.

I think about her all the time, no matter how desperately hard I try not to.

It's Saturday. I stare out of the Urb window, my hoodie hiding my face. My earphones are pulsing loudly in my ears. Music helps me forget. It helps me forget all the evil I have seen. The bodies. And the friends who don't want anything to do with me anymore.

When I'm walking into the Rowleys, I watch her red hair swishing around with a big white smile as she talks with the customers at the food bank, wrapped up in new woollen coats. They smile, too. They love Cara.

The brick wall at the entrance of the Rowleys has been scrubbed of all the graffiti. No trace of the word Silenda remains. Instead, there is a mural. For me.

A large painting of me covers the wall. White skin, shaggy black hair and my black hoodie. Underneath, it reads 'the Rowleys vampire'. Jason says it's like a reclamation. The people of the Rowleys are redefining it. They think I look like a vampire, and they appreciate what I've done to help the community. And well, they just really love to paint. The wall surrounding my face is covered in the names of those who lost their lives to Silenda.

I wrote Randy Redding's name myself. Cara and I had spent all night once carefully writing each name in the favourite colour of the one who lost their life.

As I get closer to Carson, who is handing out mugs of hot tea, I notice a tall man behind her. When I realise it's Hawk, I think about turning away.

'Hey, Marino!' he shouts over to me and then clears his throat.

SILENDA

'That's not actually your name, is it?'

I shake my head. 'You can still call me that if you'd like.'

He laughs uncomfortably. 'Harry works too.' Cara nudges him. Hawk clears his throat again. 'Look, Horatio, I—'

'You don't have to be my friend because you feel sorry for me.'

'We just needed some time, Horatio. A lot has happened. Without the mayor, it's been—'

'It's been tough,' Carson finishes. 'Especially for Astrid and Hayden.'

'I haven't heard from Zeb in five months.'

'He talks about you a lot,' Hawk says. 'Yeah, he's pissed. But he misses you. I think he was mostly hurt that you didn't at least tell him the truth if you thought it too dangerous to tell the rest of us.'

A small bark sounds from the soup tent behind them. Gia emerges with Red cradled in her arms. 'Hey, Harry,' she says shyly. Alex is behind her. And Asiqa and Petal too.

'We came to help out at the foodbank,' Asiqa says. 'We think it's really cool what you've done here.'

Carson leaves the tent with a teapot, asking around for refills. I follow her, holding her arm to get her attention and keep my voice down. 'Cara, this is starting to feel like a bit of a pity party. Did you beg all those guys to come down here so I don't off myself soon?'

'No.' She's still smiling as she fills steaming cups. 'They wanted to come. Plus, the pity party is later.'

'What are you talking about?'

She finally turns to me. 'Look, Harry, you shouldn't have lied to us. But at the end of the day, you're one of us.' She traces her fingers across the faded blue in my hair. 'Astrid is hosting a party tonight.' I go to walk away. 'Horatio!' she calls, 'she doesn't know you're coming. I think it would be a great opportunity for you to talk things out with her. She's calling it the reunite ball. It's only at her apartment!'

316

I huff but she knows she's got me when I turn back around. 'And by the way, if you think we're all here because we pity you, then there's some more pity waiting by the wall.'

I walk back to the mural where he stands, painting the name Austin Timentes in red paint. 'Silenda killed him, too,' Hayden says without looking at me. 'My uncle prayed on the vulnerable. Austin was scared. He probably thought he was saving himself.' I nod, worried to come too close. 'You know Carson has been worried that she'll remember what it feels like to die,' Hayden continues. 'I don't think she will. When Tyson sent her away, he watched her almost every night, you know? It gave the rest of us reassurance because we thought he was protecting her. But do you know what he was doing, Harry? Do you know what he said to me when I saw him in prison before he died?'

'What?'

'He was spying on her to make sure that she wouldn't remember it was him. That he personally picked her up in the Rowleys. That he himself stuck the needle in her neck.'

I don't know what to say. 'You visited your uncle in prison?'

'You don't visit yours?' I put my head down. Hayden laughs. 'He didn't last very long, did he? Tyson? I brought him marmalade twice a week for the five months he was there.'

'Huh?'

'I brought him marmalade when I visited him. Every Monday and Thursday Hawk would wheel me there when Carson was in class. I'd sit it in front of him. I said nothing. And then I left.'

'Why?' I ask.

'He fucking hated marmalade. He just fucking hated it.'

Hayden finally looks at me. 'Do you still hate me?' I ask.

He comes closer, paintbrush still in hand. 'I never hated you, Horatio. It sort of pissed me off that for a moment you were looking like a bigger dickhead than me. That's the only claim to fame I have.'

I laugh. 'Thanks, Hayden.'

'For what?' he says. 'Surely you don't mean thanks for this?'

Hayden paints a big red streak across my face.

• • •

I don't go to the party. I watch it though. The light that emanates from Astrid's window across the water mimics a star.

I can't stay at home. I can't sit at my kitchen island eating a pot noodle and listening to Fleetwood Mac. Not for the fourth night in a row. So, I walk. I've been walking a lot actually. Sometimes I get so far in the nights that I have to call a taxi home. It's funny that I used to grudge money for a taxi and sit on the run-down city buses. Now I have more money than I know what to do with. I thought maybe my riches would make my palate change but I still can't get my head around hummus.

I'm on autopilot. That's why I walk so far. I have a theory that when there are too many things to think about, my brain just stops. The floodgates go up and I stop feeling anything. I used to smell the pavements and feel the rain and think about the sky in relation to myself. Now everything passes me by.

Blue blurs.

I don't go to the party. I edge closer to it though. I stand on the bridge and watch Astrid's light fade to black. I let the wind blow in my hair and my skin chill and buzz and bump in the cold.

I'm climbing up the precarious metal stairs at the side of the Grand Library on a moment of impulse, knowing that, when the sky fades to violet, I'll find him there.

And I'm right.

Standing on the edge of the golden wall in his fishnet-stitched denim and his indigo Doc Martens, is Zeb. He has a joint in his hand, and he blows smoke to the wind with a firm stance that defies the elements that challenge him.

'Don't jump,' I say gently so as to not startle him. 'A mere mortal such as yourself will simply plunge to his death.' He doesn't turn around. He doesn't look at me. He simply steps down from the wall and wanders around the perimeters of the roof with bloodshot eyes that I try to catch.

He takes a drag. 'Look who it is,' he finally says. 'Horatio Young has finally decided to show his face. How's your uncle?'

'I don't know.' He comes close to me and I take the joint from his hand and smoke it until it burns my throat.

'You don't know?'

'I don't visit him,' I say.

Zeb has a harsh glint in his eyes. Five months is a long time to let a person simmer. 'Why ever not?' he scoffs. 'Supposedly you two were very close in the winter.'

'He lied to me, Zebediah. He told me that Tyson was out to get him. He is my family, I had no reason not to believe him. In the end, the only person I really hurt was him.'

'Do I not count? And Astrid? You think you haven't hurt us?' he says, eyebrows furrowed. 'It's been five months, Horatio.' I wish he would call me Harry. I wish he would hold me, but he snatches back his joint and hops back up onto the golden ledge.

'That's not what I meant. He was the only person I intended to hurt. I never wanted to betray you. I never wanted to hurt Astrid. I'm just ridiculous, Zeb. I'm static. I have no agency. I watch things crumble around me and my feet are cemented to the ground. I just watch things as they break. I don't know why. It's something I'm trying to change.' I stand on the ledge beside him.

Zebediah sighs. He says nothing for a while, glowing a beautiful shade of moonstone under the purple sky, the wind blowing through the holes in his jacket. He fishes into his pocket for his phone, taking his time to untangle his earphones and plug one into his left ear. I'm comfortable in his silence, somehow reassured by it. 'Phil Collins or Hall and Oates?' he asks suddenly, handing me the other earphone. He gives me a small smile and it feels like forgiveness.

'Hall and Oates,' I say. 'Always.'

I plug the earphone into my ear and we sit on the edge of the roof, watching the traffic beneath us and the city lights brightening as the sky darkens. The rubble of the street below is surrounded by tape where Centrum Tower once stood tall. The street is quiet. Only a few people cross at the traffic lights and hang out the windows of the remaining buildings. I try to look past the broken parts, far into the city where the towers are still tall and the pavements have no cracks. I try to look past the hurt in Zeb's eyes and instead to the many memories where his orbs have been yellow and happy and bright.

It's the only way I can stop being so still. It's the only way I can move forward.

I can't keep looking back. But sometimes I have to.

Because there she is on the side of the road, clinging to a bottle of red wine. She is at least 20 stories below me and yet it is the closest we have been all year.

Astrid Turrow stands tall, clinging to her bottle and her vintage leather purse. But her head is down, curtained by her tresses of blonde hair. When the rain falls, she pulls her black hood over her head and waits for the green light to say GO.

I watch her, knowing for once that I should move.

So I do.

Zeb doesn't say anything when I spring up from the ledge and remove my earphone. I think he knows.

I sprint across the concrete landing and down the creaky red stairs. I don't think I've ever moved so quickly. The rain is pelting now. It drips from my hair and into my eyes and my mouth. I deserve the adversities that the sky pours on me as I slide down a couple of metal stairs and onto my back. When I'm halfway down, I run into the unkempt rooftop garden on the tenth floor of the library and pick a lavender rose that is prisoned by a rusting copper gate.

I continue my cascade down the metal stairs until I'm standing on the opposite side of the road, cars splitting the concrete between us. I hold the flower in my hand. She raises her head, her hair soaked. Her eyes make my heart race at a dangerous pace. I think I might pass out. I'm either very unfit or very infatuated with Astrid Turrow.

Indubitably, I am both.

When the green man glows in the cyber-grape sky, the city stops. The road clears. Nothing stands between us.

She walks towards me slowly, surprised to see me and perhaps a little sad.

When Astrid Turrow is less than a metre from me, I hold my hand out to her, gripping the thorns of a lavender rose. I say nothing, blinking through the wet and waiting.

She stares at me, watching the rose as it wilts away in my grip, sodden in the rain and sorrowed by her white hand that did not reach for it. I think I stop breathing, her ambiguous eyes piercing me like a thousand needles until I need to look down.

When I look up again, Astrid is no longer in my vision. Instead, she kneels at my feet, cradling lavender petals like drowning butterflies and putting them in her hair.

I realise then, that I will never be the feared thing.

I will always be the thing that fears everything.

Because I am also the thing that *feels* everything. And right now, as Astrid stands in front of me with wilted petals in her hair like thistle teardrops, I have a feeling in my chest that an infinite number of stars have witnessed an infinite number of times in the hearts of an infinite number of people.

I am the thing that feels.

And I will live forever.

THE END